Also,

By Barbara Williams Brown

My Invisible Lover

Love Like a Lady

When Age Becomes Just a Number

Barbara Williams Brown

This book is a work of fiction. Certain events did take place, but names, characters, places, and incidents are either products of the author's imagination or are used fictitiously. Any resemblance to actual events or locales or person, living or dead is entirely coincidental.

DBEM Publishing
133 Annacy Park Drive
Columbia, SC 29223
dbempub@gmail.con
843-372-8274

Love Like a Lady

Cover art by Deryl Brown

ISBN: 9781735806129

Printed in the United States

First Edition

Dedication

This book is dedicated to the memory of my mother, Emmie Singletary Williams Dozier, who has always been my greatest inspiration, and has supported me in all my endeavors. Even from beyond, her legacy of power, strength, and knowledge are still embedded within my being. This book is also dedicated to those that have experienced, or have been touched by any form of abuse and or domestic violence; and especially to those of you that have taken the time to read my written words.

Acknowledgements

I would like to thank my almighty God for giving me the ability to have a creative imagination and being able to put them in the form of books. I thank my amazing son Deryl, for his loyalty and dedication in helping me develop my book cover and design, and for keeping me up to date with the latest computers and other technologies. I thank my beautiful daughter Tiffany, for allowing me to use yet another one of her portraits to grace the cover of my book.

Chapter One

Tina's birthday was approaching, and she was feeling somewhat lonely because even though she had chosen to spend it alone, deep down she really did not want to be alone on this special day. She had previously told her children not to come home since her birthday was on a Monday and they lived a distance away, but she was rethinking her decision. As she sat staring at the television, she thought of birthdays past when her family and friends would all get together and help her celebrate. Those were happier times for Tina, but even then, she felt a certain level of emptiness. It had been years since she was in a romantic relationship and had convinced herself that she was good with being single. When she turned forty, she had the party of a lifetime. Her friends hired a professional artist to perform at her birthday celebration and the ambience was out of this world; she didn't think that a party could ever top that, so why bother trying to plan anything.

Tina spent a great deal of her life caring for others in one capacity or another, and always neglected herself and her needs. At a very early age in her life, as far back as she could remember, she'd developed this nurturing personality, or maybe she was born with it; whatever way she received it, she was driven to serve and protect everyone she came in close contact with. Even in her personal relationships, she would find herself behaving like a mother figure.

Just like any other teenager, Tina had dreams of how she wanted her life to flow. Her goals were to become a journalist, and an interior designer. She wanted to marry and have six children with the husband of her dreams. Tina was always extremely ambitious, and was often criticized, because of it. She was constantly bullied in elementary school, and it continued throughout high school. Because of the bullying and other factors that occurred in her life, she developed many hang-ups which contributed to her developing into the insecure person she finally became. When Tina was around the age of eight, she was sexually molested by a family member, and even though she did not understand the ramifications of it all, she knew that she did not like the way it made her feel, so she tried blocking it from her mind.

When she was the age of nine, she went to visit one of her girlfriends, Shanell, at her home and was told by her friend's brother, Neil, that she was in her room. When Tina got to Shanell's room which was at the far end of the house, she began calling out to her, and when she got no response, she realized that her friend was not there. Inside the room was dark, due to the dark draperies covering the windows. When she turned around to leave, she saw the figure of someone standing in the dark. She hastily began walking towards the door to leave, but the person stepped in front of her, barricading the door with his body to keep her from leaving. "What are you doing? she asked, move out of my way." Instead of moving so that she could pass, he grabbed her and dragged her across the room and threw her on the bed. This was so unexpected because she had visited this home and family more times than she was able to count, and no one had ever tried to harm her or cause her to believe that they would.

Tina could not remember if she'd screamed as she was fighting him and trying to push him away from her. The only thing she could recall was his sweaty smell and the musky smell of the room. After he threw her across the bed, he began tugging at the closure of her pants. She fought and kicked but he overpowered her. He pulled her pants down below her knees and pulled her legs apart. Tina felt the room spinning around her and was frightened beyond any child's imagination. She clawed and pawed but nothing stopped him from climbing on top of her.

Fortunately, he did not penetrate her, but she remembered feeling his penis between her thighs. After he had finished molesting her, he stood up and stuffed his penis back into his pants as if he had not just violated her. Tina eyes had adjusted to the darkness, and she could see his face clearly, it was Neil, her best friend's eighteen-year-old brother. He had lied to her and followed her to Shanell's room. When he released her, she felt the way her mother's hens looked after the roosters had chased and violated them. She was merely an innocent child wanting to play with her friend, and now her entire world had turned upside down within seconds.

When she was free to walk out of the room and into the other area of the house that led to the porch, she could see her friend Shanell from across the yard standing at her mom's fruit tree picking fruits. When Shanell looked up and saw Tina, she came running towards the house to greet her, but Tina did not stop on the porch or in the yard, she felt dirty and ashamed. She walked down the steps and kept walking without saying a word to her friend. How was she ever going to be able to explain to her best friend that her brother had just basically raped her? Would she even believe her, or did she already suspect? So just like a robot, she kept walking until she reached the street and headed for home.

"Hey Tina," shouted an excited Shanell. There was no response; Shanell called even louder the second time; "Tina, where are you going, why are you being this way? Come back, didn't you come to see me, don't you want to play with me?" Shanell could not understand why Tina was behaving the way that she was, and she did not see the fear in her face or the tears that were pouring from her eyes. Tina felt ashamed and alone, as if she had no one to confide in. So, she kept on walking until she reached her home and put on her happy face as if all was well within her world. Tina decided that she would not tell her mom, or anyone else what had happened to her; she didn't believe that anyone would believe her, and even if they did, they would blame her. So, like the good girl she was striving to portray, she tucked it all inside her little heart and carried it like the burden it was.

After many years had passed since Tina's childhood molestation, she graduated high school, and decided to apply for a summer job before going off to college. Her mom had to work but told her to ask the neighbor if he would drive her to fill out some job applications. When she arrived at the neighbor's home, his wife had gone to work, and he was there alone. While she was waiting for him to drive her, he came out and propositioned her. Although he did not physically touch her, he got right in her face and asked her, "has anyone ever asked you a personal question?" The memory of all the pain she thought she had so carefully tucked away came rushing back to the surface. This time she decided that she would not be defeated, and she was not going to allow herself to be victimized yet again. She verbally attacked him with everything she had in her and threatened to tell her mother what he had done. He became apologetic and begged her not to tell her mom about him. She knew in her heart that she was not going to tell her mom, not to protect him, but to protect herself from the humiliation and shame of her mother not believing her. The irony of it all, was, she had to get in a car with this man and ride with him to preserve her secret, because if her mother was to ever find out that she didn't go with him, she would demand to know the reason why.

Several days later, Tina's mom told her to ask that same neighbor to take her to the doctor so that she could get a physical for her new job. When Tina refused to ask him, just as she imagined, her mother wanted to know why. "No reason mom I just don't want him to take me." "That is not a good enough reason for me Tina, unless you have someone to take you, you're going to have to come up with something better than that." "No, I don't, I am a grown woman and if I say that I am not going with him then I am not going with him." Tina's mom looked at her as if she had just gone and lost her mind. "What did you say to me young lady? grown; well then maybe you need to find your own house." With tears in her eyes, Tina apologized to her mom and told her that she really did not want the neighbor to take her anywhere ever again, but she still refused to tell her the reason why she was so against it.

Although Tina never explained to her mother why she was so against the neighbor driving her anywhere, she never questioned Tina about it again. Mrs. Elena was a wise and smart woman and figured it all out, or at least she thought she had. After some time had passed, Tina felt comfortable enough to tell her mom in detail what the old man had said to her. However, she never told her about the molestation that happened to her at the age of eight, or the rape at the age of nine. She was still too ashamed and felt that somehow, she would be blamed for what happened. Personally, she never felt that she was to blame for what happened to her even on her darkest days. She wished that she could have told someone, maybe then she wouldn't feel so weighted down all the time. When she told her mom about the old man, Mrs. Elena just looked at her with saddened eyes; "why didn't you tell me before?" "I didn't think that you would believe me, and even if you had, I was too ashamed." "Ashamed, why, did you do or say anything to cause him to make such remarks to you?" "No, I did not, and that is the reason I didn't tell you then, and the reason I hope I hadn't told you now." "What do you mean Tina, what are you talking about?" "Nothing ma, nothing, I am talking about absolutely nothing, so let's just drop it and change the subject." "Fine by me, it seems like nothing happened anyway, just a few unpleasant words." "I said let's drop it mom, please, can we just not talk about this ever again." "Okay, sure, whatever you say, I am done with it."

All and all, Tina was a go getter; she allowed very little to stand in the way of her achievements. Whilst others were thinking of things to do, Tina was on it. Because of her wide abilities, there were times when she was referred to as "jack of all trades." She would often identify herself as knowing a little about a lot, but not a lot about much. She prided herself on what she knew, and never pretended to know what she didn't.

Chapter Two

As a young lady, Tina's mom was somewhat restrictive but that didn't bother her much. She was kind of a homebody, and often a wall flower at events. Not only was she shy, but she was also bashful. The strange thing though, she could deliver a speech in front of thousands of people, but found it difficult to relate in one-on-one conversations, or in smaller gatherings. Tina always preferred to be either alone, or with one or two friends at a time. That was also confusing because she grew up in a large family. She had six sisters and five brothers, and she fell right in the middle of them all. As a child, she was often referred to as being spoiled, because she would cry, and no one understood her reasons. They would just assume it was because she could not have her way, but no one ever bothered to ask. Even when she was laughing on the outside, her heart was in constant pain, and she was always crying on the inside. Wherever Tina went, laughter followed, she provided the comedy for her friends and family. No one ever suspected that she was covering up her pain. Some of her friends and relatives often referred to her as the life of the party. Tina never drank alcohol, but she always seemed to be on a natural high. If only they could see inside of her heart and mind, they would be shocked. Shocked at the idea that she was an unhappy child and grew into an unhappy adult. Some of her siblings saw her as being strong, while others saw her as being overly sensitive, but none of them were able to see inside of the real Tina; the Tina that often wished she was dead and, on several occasions, had foolishly attempted to make her wish come true.

Tina lost her father at an early age which devastated her even more, because she was always a daddy's girl. When he died, a part of her died with him and the part that was left behind, spent most of her life searching for someone to substitute for him. In every relationship she encountered, she scanned his characteristics to see if she could find her father. Little did she understand that she was angry with her father for leaving her but would not allow herself to think that way for fear of betraying his memory, so there was yet another pain she buried in the repertoire of her life. She remembered, returning to school after having been out for days after her father's death, and how the children laughed at her when she boarded the bus, or at least she thought that they were laughing at her. She wondered why it was necessary for her father to leave while all her friends still had their dads. Somehow it just didn't seem fair to her, but no matter what, she was going to be there for her mother and make sure that she was always taken care of.

Although Tina was not as close to her mother as she was to her father, she quickly turned her affections to her mom after her father passed away and became her protector. If anyone did or said anything negative against her mom, like a tiger, she was ready to pounce. Over the years she never felt as if she was her mother's favorite child, but she was certainly her favorite mom. After her father was no longer there, Tina became her mom's right hand. She learned to clean and cook at an early age and helped with her younger siblings. Tina didn't know if she was born with a nurturing spirit or developed it through the years, but what she did know was that she mothered everyone she encountered, old or young. When she loved, she loved hard, which often caused her pain, because those feelings were often not always reciprocated.

At the end of Tina's summer job, she decided to further her education. She had enrolled at an in-state college and was accepted and began her pursuit for a degree in education. Things were going well, because she had managed to save up enough money to purchase herself a new car and was able to drive to and from classes. One night as she was preparing for class, her mom asked if she could drop her off at a friend's house, and then pick her up once she got out of class. Tina was glad to have her mom's company and told her that she would be glad to take her to her friend's house and pick her up.

After she dropped her mom off at her friend's house, she decided to stop by a local service station for gas before going on to class because they may be closed when she got out of class later that night. She pulled up at the station and a handsome older man came out to fuel her car. When he had finished, he told her that her tire was going flat and asked if she wanted him to fix it. Tina knew that if she got the tire fixed before going to class that she would be late, however, she did not want to become stranded on the dark roads with a flat tire either, so she agreed to have Israel the owner of the station fix her tire. After a few minutes, he told her that he needed to pick up a part and asked if she would drive him to get it. Tina didn't know him very well but knew that he owned his business and was a reputable businessman, or at least that is what she believed. She asked him where his vehicle was and why it was necessary for her to drive him. He told her that his attendant had taken it out to run an errand for him, but if she felt uncomfortable taking him, they could wait for him to return. Tina wanted to know how long it would be before his attendant returned, because she needed to get to class. When he replied that he wasn't sure how long it would be, she agreed to take him where he needed to go. Israel asked Tina if she mind him driving, since it was dark, and he knew exactly where he needed to go. Tina slid over on to the passenger side as Israel got behind the wheels. He drove about three miles out of town to a house, got out and went into a garage. When he returned, he had some mechanical looking thing and put it into the trunk of her car. He returned to the driver's seat and headed back towards town. Tina was thinking, "that didn't take long, maybe I won't miss too much time from my class after all."

When they got into town, Israel did not stop at his station but kept going through town until he had reached the other side. "Where are you going now?" Tina wanted to know but there was no response from Israel. Tina began to feel uneasy and asked him to please take her back because she needed to get to class. It never occurred to her that she was riding on the very tire that was supposedly going flat, in her young mind, it did not register.

When they had reached the other side of town, Israel kept driving in silence until he finally, turned off the main road down a steep hill into a wooded area. By now, Tina was beside herself with fear. But the strangest thing, she never thought that he would hurt her, she just thought that he would try and make out with her, she would say no, and he would take her back. Tina had prided herself on keeping her distance from boys in the past. She was saving herself for marriage and certainly wasn't going to let some old man that she barely knew touch her. She was the only one in her circle of friends that had not given in to the temptation of lust, and she had every intention of keeping it that way. Even though she was often teased by her friends for still being a virgin at nineteen.

"Why did you bring me down in these woods sir?" Tina asked. Still no reply. When Israel brought the car to a stop, he got out, walked around to the passenger side and without saying a word, attempted to push Tina down in the seat. She began to fight with everything in her, but she was no match for him. Tina was a petite young lady weighing one hundred and five pounds. Israel was over six feet tall and appeared to have weighed over two hundred pounds. By now she had come to the realization that this man was planning to hurt her. She attempted to open the driver's door so that she could escape, but he grabbed her and pushed her head underneath the steering wheel. In the process, Tina's arms were trapped beneath her body, and she was unable to pull them out. She began to cry and begged Israel to stop and to please let her go. It was as if he had suddenly gone deaf, he just kept tugging at her jeans trying to get them down. The fact that Tina was terribly uncomfortable did not have any impact on his intention. Tina cried and prayed but to no avail. There was no way anyone could hear her screams that far down in the woods. She felt that she would die. Just when she thought things couldn't get any worse, he had gotten her pants off, and she felt his body plopped down on top of hers, and he began to rape her. Tina could not move in any direction. She had screamed until she was hoarse, and though she opened her mouth, nothing came out.

When he'd finished raping her, he got up from off her, pulled up his pants, went around to the driver side of the car, pushed her over, sat down, and started the engine. He began driving, with a hysterical Tina bent over on the other side. She was in such physical and emotional pain that she felt she would lose her sanity. Israel drove her car back to his station, stopped the car, got out and after taking out whatever it was, he'd placed in her car trunk, walked into the building leaving her without a glance in her direction. Tina sat there in shock, not able to process what had just happened to her.

Little did she know the long-term effects that night would have on her life, for the rest of her life.

Somehow, Tina was able to shift herself from the passenger side of the car and into the driver's seat without getting out. Israel had left the engine running so she pulled the gear into drive and drove off. Aside from being over an hour late, she knew that she would not be able to sit in a classroom after what had just happened to her. "How am I going to explain to my mom why I am back so soon? I will never be able to tell her what happened to me. She will blame me for not going straight to class and allowing this guy to drive me anywhere. She may think that I am not telling the truth, and that I wanted this to happen to me; I cannot tell anyone because I am so ashamed. I should never have gone with him; how could I have been so stupid?" All these thoughts were playing in Tina's head as if they were on a cassette. Her heart was broken into pieces, and her spirit for life had died. In her mind, she was thinking, "how could someone do this to another person?" She was young and naive. Tina's parents were extremely restrictive, which did not allow her to have any worldly or street knowledge or experiences, so trust was something that came naturally for her.

Chapter Three

When Tina arrived at her mom's friends' home, she decided not to get out of the car; she didn't want to have to explain her early return, and she did not have enough energy left to make up an excuse. So, she sat there in a catatonic state trying to make sense of what had just happened to her. It felt like a bad nightmare. She prided herself on her ability to hang on to her innocence until marriage, and for it to have been taken from her in such a cruel and vicious manner, and from someone she barely knew seemed unbearable. Tina began crying hysterically, but there was no one to comfort her, and no one she felt comfortable with sharing what had happened to her. She knew that she would somehow have to pull herself together before facing her mom.

After sitting in her car for what seemed to Tina an eternity, she managed to get out and stood beside her car. She looked down at her clothing and there were blood spots, reminding her of what had just been taken from her. "Can I do this, she thought, can I pretend that I am fine, and that nothing has happened to me?" She knew that she had to decide whether to tell her mother, or once again store the pain of being violated into her secret volt, called her heart. She decided that re-living it by telling anyone what happened to her was more than she could bear. "Besides, she thought, what if she blames me? That would just kill me." So, Tina wiped the tears from her streaked face, walked up to the door and rang the bell. When her mother's friend opened the door to let her in, she told her that she would not be coming in, but please tell her mom that she would be waiting outside. "Also, please tell her to take her time and visit as long as she likes, I am in no rush."

Tina returned to her car, opened the door, and sat. She felt like a mechanical being as she waited for her mom to come out. After she had been sitting for about fifteen minutes, her mom came out laughing and in a cheerful mood. Tina had to match her mother's enthusiasm and began smiling too. "What has you in such a good mood?" she asked. Her mom returned the smile and began telling her about the wonderful time she'd had with her friend. At that moment, Tina wanted to fall into her mother's arms and confess all her pains, but something held her back. Instead, she said, "that's great, I'm glad that you had such a wonderful time, you deserve it." Tina's mom, Elena Watson, was a wise woman and noticed that something seemed off with Tina. "What's wrong, she asked, you don't seem yourself." Tina first thought was to lie, but in her fragile state, she could not think of a single lie to tell, so she said nothing. Mrs. Watson turned and looked at Tina; are you ok?" "Why are you asking, does it seem like something is wrong?" Stalling bought her some time to think of a lie to tell. "Yes, it does, as I said, you don't seem yourself." "I'm sorry mom, I just had a long day. I went straight to class from work and did poorly on my exam, I am just feeling a little down about that." "Well don't let one bad test deter you, you are such a bright young lady, I'm sure you'll make it up." Tina was glad for the kind words and support from her mom, but she felt terrible having to lie to her; she didn't know what else she could have done. Sadly, she thought to herself; "this secret belongs in my life's storage with all my other secrets."

Tina drove her mom home in total silence; Mrs. Watson did all the talking, telling Tina about her evening and her plans for the next day. She was glad for the distraction and that her mom was so chatty, she didn't have to think for a few minutes. That didn't last long though because in ten minutes they had reached her mother's home. Since she was still living in the home with her mom, she had no choice but to walk in with her. Once inside, she went straight to her room. This was a lot for a nineteen-year-old to handle alone, but she planned on trying. She headed for the bathroom to try and wash the residue of Israel from her body. She found a bar of lye soap that her mother used for cleaning purposes and began scrubbing her body with it. She rubbed her skin so mercilessly that she bruised it. She had made the water hotter than normal, before sinking down into it. Tina swished and rubbed her body for what seemed like hours before lifting herself from the tub and climbing into the shower. Once again, she set the water temperature to steamy hot. With all the washing and scrubbing, she still felt dirty. "Will I ever get clean again?" she thought.

The next morning when it was time for Tina to get up for work, she just could not master the energy to do it; she laid stiffly on her bed until her mom came in to wake her up. "Wake up girl, you're going to be late for work." "I have the day off," Tina lied. "Okay sleep as long as you like, I am going to work in my garden." "Thank God, Tina thought, I won't have to keep telling lies to cover up my truth." She turned over in bed and began to cry; "my life is over; it will never be the same." After a few minutes of crying, Tina stopped, rolled over to the edge of the bed, and crawled out. "I am going to tuck this hold thing away and never think of it again; and so, she thought that she had carefully tucked it away so that it would never be revealed.

Chapter Four

Several years had passed and Tina continued with her life as if everything was normal. She spoke normally, laughed normally, and participated in life's events as a normal human being, but deep inside, she never felt normal at all. She was tired; tired of pretending that she was good but continued with her daily tasks of living as a clown, in a show. She began to have men call on her for dates, but she never felt comfortable with any of them and never knew if she did too much or too little within her relationships.

Tina would meet good men, but the relationships would all end the same way; with her being hurt and feeling abandoned. She would ask herself if there was something wrong with her, why wasn't she capable of holding on to a relationship for more than a few months. Each time a relationship ended, she felt as if she had lost a part of herself. It seemed that she was looking for a father, and not a mate, to somehow take away all the pain, frustrations, disappointments, confusion, and uncertainties that life had thrown at her over the years.

One valentine's day about three years after Tina had been violated, she met a young man by the name of Derrick, who was completely opposite from her father. He seemed kind and was admired by all the ladies. She was pleased that of all the other women that were chasing after him, he was interested in her without a chase. She believed that he would be a good fit for her because he was ten years older than she was; he could provide that father image that she was so desperately lacking. He was somewhat shy like herself and was the total opposite of what she physically liked in a man. Because of her low self-esteem and her fear of intimacy, she decided to give him a shot. After about two months of dating, he asked her to marry him. She had no idea that he was serious because of the cavalier way in which he asked her.

They were on their way back from visiting one of their married friends, when Tina noticed the time. It was near two in the morning, and they still had a distance to travel. Tina became restless because she knew that her mom would be waiting for her in a not so pleasant mood. When she expressed her concerns to Derrick, he just laughed and said, "we could always get married." Tina chose to ignore his comment, but he refused to let her off the hook, so he asked, "what do you say?" "What do I say about what Derrick?" "About us getting married?" Tina wanted to shut his mouth, so she said sarcastically, "Yeah; yeah; sure, we'll get married." Little did she know that he was being serious and thought that she was also. He had taken her response as a yes.

When Derrick pulled into Tina's mom's yard, what seemed like hours later, just as she suspected, Mrs. Watson was waiting on the porch. "Where have you been Tina, do you realize what time it is; how am I supposed to go to bed and sleep with you out all hours of the night and my not knowing where you are and if you're okay?" "I am sorry mom, but Derrick and I just lost track of time, I didn't mean to worry you." Just as Mrs. Watson was about to chastise Tina for making her worry, Derrick spoke up. "Go on inside he said to Tina, I would like to speak with your mom." Tina humbly walked around her mom and into the house. Just as she was closing the door behind her, she heard Derrick apologizing to her mom again. "I am sorry he said, but as Tina said, we just sort of lost track of time. However, I would like to ask you a question." "Ask me a question" repeated Mrs. Watson, what type of question?" "I would like to ask for permission to marry your daughter." Tina's mouth flung open so wide that she could barely close them again. "Permission to marry me, what the hell is he talking about?" She continued to listen as her mom responded to Derrick; "Marriage, are you sure that you are ready for that?" "Yes man, I love your daughter and would very much like to marry her if that's ok with you." "That is fine by me, you have my permission. It is late, or shall I say early, so good night, I'm going to bed." After having said that, Mrs. Watson shook Derrick's hand and headed for her bedroom.

Tina didn't have the energy to confront Derrick at that moment but decided to wait until she saw him again. In the meantime, Mrs. Watson returned to the kitchen where Tina was getting a glass of water and asked; "married; isn't that kind of fast? You just met that boy a few weeks ago, are you pregnant?" Tina was offended, because in her heart she was still a virgin. That is what she told herself and that was what she had told Derrick. She made it clear to him that she planned to save herself for marriage. Derrick had respected her wishes and agreed not to pressure her into doing anything she didn't feel comfortable doing, which was probably the main factor in him proposing so soon after they met.

"No mom, I am not pregnant, how could you think such a thing?" "Well, what's the rush?" "I really don't know mom he totally caught me off guard." "Are you saying that you had no idea that he was going to ask for your hand in marriage?" "That is exactly what I'm saying, I am as shocked as you." "Well, do you love him?" "I don't know, I guess so." "It's no time for guessing, either you do, or you don't, I am exhausted we will finish this conversation in the daylight, after I've had a few hours of sleep." "Okay ma, good night."

Tina went to bed, but she could not fall asleep; she kept thinking about Derrick's boldness in asking her mom if he could marry her. "How dare he, she thought, why would he do something like that without discussing it with me first?" She was furious but a little excited at the same time; no one had ever proposed to her before. It didn't matter to her how Derrick proposed, she was simply happy that he had. Derick was not very romantic, but that didn't bother her because she really was not in love with him. She cared for him and was in love with the idea of him, but she had just come out of a heartbroken relationship when she met him and was still healing from the sting of it. Also, she was not so quick to give her heart again only to have it broken into pieces.

Tina decided that she would wait until after she married Derrick to fall in love with him just in case things didn't work out. She'd be dammed if she was going to lose any more tears over a sorry ass man. "Come on Tina, you're thinking too much, a handsome man just proposed to you so get a grip." Tina decided that she would have a long engagement which would give her more time to get to know Derrick, and to plan their wedding. She crawled into bed and began fantasizing about her wedding plans. After a few minutes of daydreaming, she gave a huge yarn and drifted into a deep peaceful sleep.

When Tina awoke, the sun was shining bright through her windowpane. She rolled over and tried to fall back to sleep, but unfortunately that wasn't going to happen. The sound of footsteps on the hardwood floor reminded her that it was Sunday morning, and her mom was not going to have her oversleep and cause her to be late for church. "Wake up girl, you were woman enough to stay out half the night so get up now and get ready for church." Mrs. Watson didn't bother to knock; she just walked in and began pulling the cover of Tina. "Mom please, you could have given me five more minutes." "Five minutes won't make a bit of difference, so go ahead and get up, besides, I made breakfast and it's getting cold." Tina reluctantly rolled on to the edge of her bed and sat upright. "Why are you just sitting there? asked Mrs. Watson, you need to get up and get yourself together." "I am together thought Tina, I'm getting married;" she would not dare say it out loud, so she just smiled to herself and headed for the bathroom. Once inside the bathroom, reality hit her like a ton of bricks; "oh hell, she thought, this is no dream, I am engaged for real, how the hell did I get myself into this?" Tina didn't know if she wanted to be happy or afraid. "Suppose I get stood up at the alter she thought, that would just finish me off." She decided right then and there that she did not want a big wedding so that if he didn't show up, there wouldn't be many people there to witness it. "I will just have a private ceremony she thought, and a large reception later if all goes well."

Later that Sunday evening, Derrick returned to call on Tina. She pretended to be upset with him for the way things had gone the night before. "Why did you ask my mom if you could marry me before we had a chance to discuss it, and to be honest, you still haven't properly proposed." Derrick just stood there grinning from ear to ear; he knew that the only way he was going to get Tina in bed was to marry her, so he was willing and ready. "Have you set a date?" he asked. "Hell no, boy, you just asked five minutes ago." "Well, I was thinking about next week, what do you say?" "I say are you out of your dammed mind? We just met a few weeks ago and to be honest, we know very little about each other." "I know that I love you and that's enough for me," said Derrick. "Don't you love me?" "Sure, Tina lied, why would you ask me such a question?" "Because I have never heard you say the words." "Well perhaps you have never given me the chance." "So, what do you say, a week?" "If you are that eager to get married in a week, we will not be able to have a big wedding." "Will that bother you" Derrick asked? "Sure, it will, Tina lied, every girl wants to have a big wedding." Tina agreed to have a short-term engagement instead of the long one she had previously thought off. "Okay Derrick, we can get married soon but I need at least two weeks to plan and prepare." "Okay, I'll go along, if you need two weeks, then you shall have two weeks but not a day over," said Derrick.

Chapter Five

Tina did exactly as she said she would; Two weeks after their engagement she married Derrick with only five people invited, one of them being the minister. The following weekend she had a large reception just as she wanted. She was over the moon that things had gone off without a hitch, which was unusual for her; bad karma seemed to always follow her. Tina invited all her family and friends and everyone from the neighborhood to the reception. She had a blast. The reception lasted from early evening throughout the late night. When it was finally over, Derrick took his bride to their new home. That is where the honeymoon would begin.

Tina was so afraid that she could hardly contain herself. All her past experiences came rushing back to her. The rape was at the forefront of her mind. "What if he is able to tell that I am not a virgin" she thought. Derrick believed that he would be her first, and in her mind he would be. She never consented to the rape, and she had convinced herself over the years that she was still a virgin, and as far as she was concerned, she was. "There is no way he can know she thought because I have never told another living soul about what happened to me and that was years ago." She was not about to allow the cruel act of some random man to ruin her wedding night. When Tina and Derrick finally reached their home in what seemed to her like half the night, she was feeling all sorts of emotions. Caught between fear, excitement, and anticipation, she could hardly wait to go inside. Although someone had stolen her virginity, she had not allowed any man since then to touch her. She was adamant about preserving herself for her special night. When Tina entered the home that she and Derrick would be sharing, she put her belongings down on a nearby chair and headed for the bathroom to prepare for her big honeymoon night. She walked into the bathroom, turned on the lights and began running water in the bathtub. She was so happy that she was singing a little tune in her head. "I am a grown woman now she thought, no one will be able to tell me what to do, or what not to do, nor when to do it, anymore."

When Tina stripped off her clothes, she found a big surprise. Because of all the excitement planning and preparing for her wedding, and the nervous tensions of not knowing if her new husband would be able to tell that she was not really a virgin, her menstrual cycle appeared early. "Dang! How am I going to explain this? Of all the things that could go wrong, this is what happens."

Tina was disappointed but also relieved. This would give her more time to mentally prepare herself and adjust to having a husband.

After she'd finished taking a lengthy bath, she walked back into the room where Derick was waiting for her. She was not wearing a sexy negligee, but rather a satin pajama set. As she was entering the bedroom, Derrick just stared at her. She walked over to where he was sitting on the bed and sat on his knees. "Guess what" she said. "What?" asked Derrick. "You will never guest what happened." "I probably won't, so why don't you tell me." "When I went into the bathroom, I discovered that I have a visitor." "Oh, hell no! You had better not ever tell anyone about this or I will be the laughingstock of the town." "Of course, I won't tell anyone," Tina promised, pretending to be overcome with sadness.

When it was time for Tina to get into bed, she was somewhat reluctant. She had never slept with a man before under normal conditions, and now to be sleeping with the same man that was her husband, with her cycle, she had no idea how either of them would handle it. She slowly crawled into bed beside Derrick and turned her back towards him. "Come here baby, let me hold you; I have waited all this time, a few more days won't kill me." Tina turned over to face Derrick, and he took her in his arms and held her close. She laid her head on his shoulder and buried her face underneath his neck. "This feels great," she thought to herself, not at all what I expected, then she closed her eyes and slowly drifted into a deep and peaceful sleep, wrapped softly in her husband's arms. It took Derrick much longer to fall asleep; he was more in love with Tina than she was with him, but he had no idea. He just kept thinking how great it felt to have such a beautiful young girl like that as his wife. Not only was she beautiful, but she was innocent. He just held her close and kissed her head until finally he drifted off to sleep. As he slept, he began dreaming that he was making passionate love to his beautiful bride. His body began to respond to the dream, and he threw his leg across Tina's. The movement woke her, and she pushed Derrick and asked; "what are you doing, did not I told you what is going on with me?" I am sorry baby, I just got caught up in my dream; maybe it's not a bad idea for you to turn your back on me." Tina did as he suggested; when she wheeled over and turned her back to Derrick, he got close behind her and placed one arm across her waist and placed his leg over hers. "That feels really good," she said. "Yeah, it does feel good; if I find myself getting carried away, I can just feast on what's back here." "You had better not, you better control yourself; I promise that it will be worth the wait." "I plan to hold you to that." "You can."

Chapter Six

Three years into Tina and Derrick's marriage, things became strained. Tina wanted to have a baby but was having difficulty getting pregnant. She was beginning to wonder if it was Derrick since he was ten years older. After she had gone to the doctor and had everything checked out, it was confirmed that everything was good with her. After several failed attempts to have Derrick see a doctor and get checked out, she finally gave up. One evening she was sitting on the chair beside Derrick just enjoying the moment when the phone began to ring. She got up in haste, and as suddenly as she stood, she fell to the floor. Derrick ran over and helped her to her feet. "What happened?" he asked. "I don't know, said a shaky Tina; I guess I must have jumped up too fast, I got really dizzy." "Do you need to lie down?" "No, aside from feeling a little woozy, I am ok; I didn't hurt anything when I fell.

As the day progressed Tina began to feel somewhat rotten. "I don't feel too well Derrick, maybe I should go see the doctor and get checked out just to be on the safe side, there has to be a reason for the lightheadedness." "Yea, I think that you should, it certainly won't hurt anything." "Will you go with me?" "I wish that I could, but I have already committed to something else." "Well, what could be more important than your wife's well-being?" "Tina don't start with me now; I am really not in the mood for an argument today, my not going with you is not going to be the end of the world, so please, why don't you stop picking, and just take your mother with you."

Tina left for the doctor with a long face, she was upset that Derrick had not taken the time to drive her to the doctor. After she had driven a few miles down the road, she decided that she would swing by and ask her mom to go with her. "I sure hope that she is not too busy to go, I am feeling sort of poorly and I don't want to be alone." When she arrived at her mom's, Mrs. Watson was sitting in her recliner watching a game show on TV. When she saw Tina coming in, she turned the TV off and began smiling, she was excited to see her daughter coming in; it had been several weeks since she had seen her.

"Hey, come in; are you ok, you look sort of pale." I am feeling a little under the weather, do you think that you will be able to go with me to see the doctor?" "Are you going now?" "Yes, I am going as a walk-in, I don't have an appointment." "Okay, well give me a few minutes to freshen up and I'll go with you." Tina was glad that she asked her mom to go along; she and her mom had grown very close, and she had missed seeing her every day. "Okay, I am going to wait for you on the porch so I can get some fresh air." "Well, I won't be long, before your fanny touches the chair, I'll be back." "Ok, well go on then speedy McCready." They both burst into laughter at their corny humor.

By the time Tina had reached the doctor's office she was really feeling awful. After she registered, the nurse called her right back. When Tina told the doctor her symptoms, he ordered her to have a pregnancy test. After a few minutes had passed, he returned with the verdict. "Congratulations Mrs. Felton, you are four weeks pregnant." "Pregnant?" "Yes, are you surprise?" "I am, after trying for two years without anything happening, I gave up." Tina thanked her doctor for delivering such good news and walked back into the waiting room where her mother was waiting for her. "Well, what did the doctor say, is everything alright?" "Everything's find mom; I am just a little pregnant.' "A little pregnant, how did that happen?" They both burst into laughter as they walked from the doctor's office. They got into the car and headed for home.

When Tina took her mom home, she did not leave right away; she wanted to spend some more time with her because it would be a while before she saw her again. They sat for hours, talking about everything and nothing. Finally, Mrs. Watson asked Tina, "when are you going home to tell Derrick the good news?" "Are you trying to get rid of me Ma?" "No, I could sit here and talk with you for the rest of the day, but I know that you are anxious to get home and share your news with your husband." "You are right mom, I am, but I will be back real soon to spend some more quality time with you; I really had fun hanging out with you today, you know you're my ride or die, don't you?" "Yes, I do, and you're mine. I always enjoyed hanging out with you too baby."

After Tina left her mother's house, she put the pedal to the medal, she was excited and could hardly wait to tell Derrick the good news. Derrick was lying across the bed, but when he heard Tina turning the lock on the front door, he got up to greet her. "Hey, how did things go with the doctor?" "Everything went well." "So, what did he say, what caused you to get dizzy and fall?" "Nothing much." "Nothing much, that seems like something to me; he didn't say what may have caused it?" "Yes, he did." "Well, what did he say Tina?" "He said that you are going to be a daddy." Derrick stood looking at Tina, the impact of what she said had not registered. Tina looked right back at him; then it hit him; "What did you say?" "You heard me; you are going to be a daddy." Derrick was so excited that he jumped up what seemed like ten feet into the air, then he picked Tina up and swung her around. "A daddy; me; I am going to be a daddy."

For the duration of Tina's pregnancy, Derrick treated her like a queen. He pampered her and catered to her every whelm. He was right by her side when she gave birth and helped her with both the baby and her personal needs. He was the most attentive husband a girl could ask for, and she had fallen deeply in love with him. All the old baggage had been carefully tucked away and she was happy for once.

Two years after giving birth to their son, Tina was pregnant again with their daughter, and history repeated itself. Derrick spoiled her even more the second time if that was possible. Tina wanted to return to work after her daughter was a few months old, but Derrick insisted that she stayed home until the children started school; he didn't get any argument from her; that is exactly what she did; things were going well with their marriage. The little strain that their marriage suffered before the children were born seemed to have been forgotten. She never thought that after all she had been through in her life, she would end up happy and contented in a relationship, but here she was, happier than she'd ever been before.

On her daughter's first birthday, Tina planned a small party to celebrate. The event was to take place at four o'clock in the evening and last for a couple of hours. On the day of the event, Tina sent Derrick to the bakery to pick up the birthday cake. After picking up the cake, he was supposed to return and help her finish putting everything together. It was eleven A.M. when he left, and he should have been back by eleven thirty A.M. Tina was busy and didn't realize how long Derrick had been gone. When she finally stopped long enough to feed the babies, she realized that it was twelve thirty and Derrick had not returned. She became worried and wondered if something might have happened to him.

Tina finished feeding the children and walked outside just in time to see Derrick pulling up in the yard. "Where have you been all this time Derrick? It is one o'clock; I had to finish all the decorations and preparations myself as well as feed the children." "Don't ask me where the hell I've been, I'm a grown man I don't have to answer to anyone. Tina didn't want to get into a fight with Derrick, not today of all days. "Why are you in such a foul mood, and where is the cake?" "Cake, what cake? I don't know anything about no dam cake." That was it, birthday of not, no one was going to speak to her that way, not today nor ever, and sure as hell not in front of her babies, she would never let anyone harm her children. Tina could smell alcohol on Derrick's breath and asked him if he'd been drinking. "What if I was, it's my liquor and my money, what the hell you got to do with it?" That added the finishing touches, he had gone entirely too far. "Derrick where is the baby's birthday cake?" Derrick did not answer, instead he went into the room and fell on the bed. Tina was hurt and disappointed, how could he do this to her and the kids? She walked outside to his car to see if the cake was left inside. There it was, sitting on the seat melting in the hot car. She didn't even bother to take it out. She looked at the clock and it was now almost two o'clock. She pulled out her baking utensils and began baking her baby a birthday cake. By the time the party began, the cake was finished and decorated, and the children were dressed and waiting for their guests to arrive. Derrick was still passed out on the bed; Tina looked at him lying there as if he was dead and decided that she would deal with him later. She just walked out of the room and closed the door as if he wasn't there. Tina continued entertaining her guests as if nothing had happened. Several people asked where Derrick was, but she just shrugged and said, "you know how men can be sometimes." Deep down in her heart she was hurting because this was the first time since she had given birth to her two children that Derrick had behaved this way. Missing his own baby's birthday party was a big deal for her, one that she would not likely forget or accept, unless he told her that he was dying. So, Tina continued keeping a happy face with her guests until the last one waved goodbye.

Chapter Seven

After all of the guests had cleared out from celebrating little Tiana's birthday party, Tina took the children into the bathroom and gave them a lingering bath in lavender bath wash to calm them down. When she took them from the tub, she rubbed them down with lotion and put them in their pajamas, then gently laid them in bed and said a prayer over them. When she had finished praying, she kissed their sleepy little heads and said good night. She turned out the lights and walked out of the nursery into the living room where she began cleaning the mess from the party. Just as she was putting away the last pieces of evidence, Derrick came walking in. "What's going on with you" he asked? "Tina kept silent for fear of saying the wrong things. "Tina, do you not hear me talking to you?" "I heard you Derrick but quite frankly I wish that I hadn't." "What the hell is that supposed to mean?" "It means that I am tired and don't feel like being bothered right now." "So, is that what I'm doing, bothering you?" "Yes Derrick, you are bothering the hell out of me, so if you have something else to do, I suggest that you do it." She went into the bathroom and closed the door behind her. Once inside, she took a long steamy shower. After her shower ended, she took her time getting dressed and coming out of the bathroom. When she finally did come out and walked into her bedroom, Derrick was sitting on the side of the bed waiting for her.

"What time is the party starting" he asked? Tina wanted to curse, but instead she laughed; in fact, she kept laughing until she began to cry. Derrick looked confused as he tried to soothe her. "What is it baby, what has you so upset? I know that I ran out on you and left you with all the work, but I am here now, can't you just explain to me what you want me to do." When Tina was finally able to compose herself, she looked at Derrick and walked out of her bedroom to check on her babies. Derrick followed behind her still confused; "Tina, I am only going to ask you once more what is going on with you and then I'm out." Tina carefully pulled the blanket up on the baby, looked at Derrick with a long daring look, then walked out of the nursery with an even more confused Derrick following closely behind her. Tina knew that if she attempted to speak with Derrick, she would become emotional and she did not want to give him the satisfaction of seeing her in an emotional state. Intoxicated or not, no one should ever speak to their spouse the way in which he had spoken to her earlier. It was as if he was an entirely different person. "What is happening to us, she thought? Seems like there's some type of wedge between us lately."

Tina had not taken the time before to think of it but now that she had, she realized that things had been off for a minute, Derrick had been going out more often and returning late. She was so busy with taking care of the children, working a full-time job after she'd decided to return early, and taking care of the home, that it left her little time to be inquisitive about his goings and comings. Just as she sat on the recliner to catch a breath, here came Derrick again. "So, Tina, did you decide to cancel the birthday party at the last minute?" To get him off her back she said yes; yes, I cancelled the party." "Why?" "Because I wasn't feeling up to it Derrick." "You should've let me know, I am all tuned up, when is it going to be?" "Next year when she turns two." Derrick didn't catch the sarcasm in Tina's voice, nor did he sense the pain in her heart; he bent down and attempted to kiss her. "That does it, if you don't leave me alone, I am going to throw a fit all over you, I have had it with you for this day, just leave me alone!" That was music to Derrick's ears, he was looking for an excuse to leave again and now he had the perfect opportunity just thrown at him. "Ok, dog-gone-it, if that's the way you are going to be, I will get out of your way, maybe when I return you will appreciate me."

When Derrick walked out of the room and closed the door behind him, Tina broke down and began to weep. At that very moment, she realized that her marriage was over, and they would never be the same. When she was finally able to drag herself up, she took one more glance at the children before getting into bed. She climbed into bed, but she knew that she wouldn't be able to sleep after all that had just occurred with Derrick. After an hour had passed, she was still unable to fall asleep, trying to reconcile with the entire evening. She realized that this evening was just one in many of late. Derrick had become mean and self-serving. The children were so precious to her that they often filled the void in her life. "I be dammed if I am going to lose anymore tears or sleep over someone who obviously doesn't care a hill of beans about me." Just when she turned the lights out and laid her head down on her pillow, the door to her and Derrick's bedroom flung open.

"Who the hell put a cake in my car and messed up my upholstery Tina?" Tina just laid there and kept silent; "Tina, I know that you hear me, why did you mess up my car, what are you trying to prove?" "Derrick, I did not put a cake in your car, I have not been in your vehicle, you need to rethink your steps." At that moment Tina saw a side of Derrick that she had never seen; he picked up a glass vase and raised it up to hit her. Tina screamed out saying "you had better not hit me with that." Just then the baby cried out and Derrick dropped the vase to the floor smashing it. When Tina returned from calming the baby, she found glass all over the floor and no sign of Derrick. The door was left wide open and when she looked outside, his vehicle was gone.

Tina decided to get to the bottom of what was going on with Derrick. I refuse to live in fear she thought, either he will end up hurting me, or I him, but something has got to give. She slowly closed the front door, wondering what Derrick was thinking, leaving her and the children in such danger. She walked back to her bedroom but this time she did not get into bed. She was waiting; waiting for whatever came next. Just as she thought, Derrick burst back into the bedroom frothing at the mouth. "I am going to leave you Tina, and I'm taking my children with me, and if you try to stop me, I will blast you." Tina knew that the only way Derrick would take her children in his drunken state was over her dead body, and she told him so. "That can be arranged," said Derrick. Tina knew that she should be afraid, but she wasn't, her whole intent was to protect her children, so she shouted at Derrick to get the hell out if he knew what was good for him.

Derrick was shocked at the aggressiveness in which Tina told him to leave. He was about to open his mouth to retaliate when Tina screamed, "Get out! Get out now!" Derrick turned and walked out of the bedroom mumbling, with an irate Tina following behind. When he reached the front door, he turned and looked at Tina, but instead of saying anything, he walked out slamming the door behind him. Tina went over and latched the chain so that he would not be able to return unless she let him in. "Oh my God, she thought, this is a mess." Tina said a prayer, crawled into bed and fell asleep, it had been a long, dramatic, and tiresome day.

When Tina awoke the next morning, she decided to make some decisions about her life and her future. "I am not going to keep doing this she said, it is not fair to me or to my children." Tina raised herself from her bed and went to check on her children; they were still asleep and doing well. She headed for the kitchen to prepare breakfast. When the children finally got out of bed, she fed and bathed them and got them ready for church. No matter what happened in Tina's life, the one place she found comfort was in church. She did not join the choir even though he had a beautiful voice, because of her shyness.

When church service had ended for the day, Tina took her two children and headed for her mother's house who lived twenty-five miles away from the church. When she arrived, her mom was happy to see them. "Come on inside, I wasn't expecting to see you guys today, but I am glad you came. What's going on, and don't tell me nothing because I can see it all over your face." Tina decided to tell her mom from start to finish about the events of the previous evening. She shared all that Derrick had done and said to her. Mrs. Watson was furious; you are not going back there today, that man must be wild. I didn't like it when he asked if he could marry you, I thought I smelled alcohol on his breath then." "That was a long time ago mom and things were great, or at least I thought they were until recently." What do you think happened?" "I'm not sure, but I have my suspicions, he has been going out often and staying out late at night, some nights he stays out all night." "Do you think he's doing something shady?" "I don't know, but I do know that I will not speculate, I will get facts and then I will have my answers.

Tina did just that; she confronted Derrick and found out that he had been cheating on her with another woman and had gotten her pregnant. Tina kept her cool, or at least that's the way it appeared to Derrick. She decided to tell Derrick about the birthday party that he had missed, and how the cake ended up in his car. She also told him about the threats he had made to blast her and take the children away from her. Derrick denied everything and told her she was making it all up. Tina did not care if he believed her, she just wanted him to know. "If I did all of those things, why don't I remember, and why are you so calm about it?" Tina just smiled and walked out of the room. The next day she headed straight to her attorney's office and filed for divorce. In the meantime, she had gone and rented an apartment for her and the children, she did not want to move back in with her mom.

Chapter Eight

When Derrick returned home from work on that evening, Tina and the children were nowhere to be found. He went over to his mother's house to inquire whether they were visiting her. She informed him that she had not seen them in a few days. Derrick did not take the time to notice that Tina and the children's clothes were all gone. Although the drive to Tina's mom was an hour, Derrick found himself headed in that direction. Bits and pieces of the things he had done were flashing in his memory, and he was beginning to believe the things Tina told him that he had done.

When he arrived at Mrs. Watson's home, she was sitting on the porch. "Good evening, said Derrick, how are you doing?" "I am doing well, said Mrs. Watson in a curious voice, how are you?" Little did Derrick know that Tina had told her mom the entire story of his recent behaviors. "I am looking for Tina and the children, are they here?" "Why do you want to see her, so that you can blast her? Well, let me tell you something son, lay a finger on my daughter and I will make you sorry that those words ever uttered out of your mouth." "What words?" Derrick asked looking confused. "So why are you looking for Tina, did she not tell you where she was going?" "No, she hasn't." "Haven't she always told you in the past where she was going, what changed, what did you do to her?" "What make you think that I've done something to her?" "Well, I haven't seen or heard from her today and when I do, she had better be alright," said Mrs. Watson. At that moment, Derrick realized that Tina had told Mrs. Watson what she told him. When he attempted to get back into his car, Mrs. Watson called him out; "Derick, what have you done to my child, is she alright?" "I haven't done anything to her, and as far as me knowing if she's alright, that is the reason I am trying to locate her, to make sure that she is." Mrs. Watson was furious with Derrick and wasted no time telling him so.

"Derrick, you know that I have always treated you like a son, but I don't like some of the things I've been hearing lately. Do you love my daughter? Because if you do, you would not have treated her the way that you have. It is not my desire to interfere in your relationship, but as a mother I cannot keep silent when someone threatens my child." "I have no recollection of threatening Tina, I apologize for missing the baby's birthday party because I had a little too much to drink, but beyond that I am not guilty of any wrong doings." "Your overindulging in alcohol is no excuse for some of the things you've said and done, what type of example are you setting for your children? Again, if you don't want my daughter, let her go, I'm sure she will find someone else that does." "Where is all this coming from Mrs. Watson, I never said that I don't want her, do you think that I would be wasting my time looking for her if I didn't care about her?" "Just get back in that car of yours and leave before I say or do something that I will regret. Don't say another word to me, just go!"

Derrick did as Mrs. Watson asked and got back into his car. As he was pulling out of her driveway, he stuck his head out of the window and yelled, "mind your own business." Mrs. Watson became angrier but chose not to respond. As Derrick was leaving, Tina and the children arrived. He wanted to turn around but thought better of it given that he had just insulted her mother. "What's wrong mom, what did Derrick want?" "He was looking for you and the children, where were you?" "The children and I have moved out of our home and into an apartment. I thought it was time to make some necessary changes." "Do you think that you may have acted too hasty, I mean, it was just one incident." "Mom, have you forgotten the extent of the incident?" "I guess you're right, I don't want you staying in a situation that maybe dangerous for you and the children."

What Tina didn't tell her mom is that she found out that Derrick had been cheating on her and was having a baby with his mistress. She also didn't tell her that one night when he came home from drinking, he wanted to have sex with her, and when she refused, he raped her and left her crying. When he realized what he had done and the emotional pain it brought to her, he tried to justify his behavior by trying to convince her that because they were married it was not rape. Just like all the other times, she kept this secret buried in her heart and soul. Tina was tired and did not feel the need to justify or explain her decision, not even to her mother. Tina got out of her car and said to her mom, "the children and I came to spend some time with you but if you are going to spend the whole time talking about Derrick, I am leaving." "I have no desire whatsoever to talk about Derrick unless there's more you want to tell me." "No mom, there's no more that I have to say, so let's go inside, it's sort of chili out here." "Mrs. Watson caught the hint and went inside the house with Tina and the children.

When the sun slowly bowed its head behind the trees, Tina told her mother that she was leaving to go home. "Why so soon?" She asked; I was just about to make dinner; why don't you stay just a little while longer." Dinner sounded like music to Tina's ears, she had not eaten all day and was famished. "Okay mom, you twisted my arm, the children and I will stay for dinner." Mrs. Watson was pleased and went into the kitchen humming a tune.

While Mrs. Watson was preparing dinner, Tina went into her old bedroom and began looking around. Everything was exactly the way she left them. She looked at a photo of her that was taken on her nineteenth birthday and grimaced. "That was not my year she thought, that was not my year." As she stared at the picture, she was unaware of the tears falling from her eyes. "What's wrong mommy?" Her three-year-old son asked with head tilted waiting for an answer. "Nothing is wrong, Tina lied. Everything is fine." "Then why are you crying, are those happy tears?" Tina had cried so much in the last few weeks that she was often discovered by her son, DJ, and he always asked her what was wrong; she would tell him that those were happy tears, and he would ask, "what are you happy about?" Tina would respond by saying, "I am so happy that I have you and your sister Tiana." This time was no different, he wanted to know what she was crying about this time. "I am happy to be here with Grandma Elena for dinner." "Are you happy because you don't have to cook?" "Exactly, that is the reason why I am so happy, I don't have to cook tonight, now go back and play with your sister, and I will be out in just a few minutes, ok?"

After DJ left the room, Tina sat on the bed bench at the foot of the bed; she tried her best to shake her sad feelings, but they would not bulge. "Why now, she thought, of all the times I come to my mom's house, why today?" As close as Tina and her mom had become, she wondered why it was so difficult to tell her about the things that happened to her throughout her life. "I still can't tell her, she thought, what if she doesn't believe me, that would just finish me off, and I need to be strong for my children.

Tina was so deep in thought that she didn't hear Elena tapping on her door. "Tina, she called out, what is it, for God's sake tell me what's bothering you, I may not be able to fix it, but I can listen and maybe give some advice." "Nothing ma, nothing, Tina lied; I am just reminiscing about the times I spent in this house and this room, I feel so blessed to have been here, and I miss it terribly." "You know that you can always move back, there's plenty of room now that practically everyone has moved out, and on their own." I know that I'm welcomed, and thank your mom, but I need to build a life for my children and me."

"Well come on to the kitchen, the food is going to get cold, plus, I'm ready to eat." No one had to twist Tina's arm this time, she was right on her mother's heels, heading for the kitchen. "Where are the children Tina?" asked Mrs. Watson. "Oh, they are in the playroom with Elaine." Elaine was Tina's youngest sister, and she lived in the home with her mother. Well go and get them and tell your sister to come as well. Tina did as her mother asked and got the rest of the crew to the kitchen. No one suspected that she was in pain, no one knew that she felt that she had died inside; "if only they could see into my heart, they would not be able to eat their delicious dinners," Tina thought. She went to the table with a brave attitude, and a wide smile. "You seem so happy Tina," said Mrs. Watson, "despite your current situation," attempting to speak over the children's head. "Mommy is happy, stated DJ, that's why she was crying, because she is happy to be here with you grandma, and she's happy to have me and Tiana, but she is not happy to have dada." Everyone began laughing, which brought the gloom and doom of the day to an end.

Chapter Nine

Several weeks after Derrick's encounter with Mrs. Watson, he was served divorce papers on his job. He became so enraged that he threatened to declare Tina an unfit mother and file for full custody of their two children. He even threatened to pay someone to testify to those threats. Tina reported all the threats and accusations to her attorney, and on the date of the hearing the attorney presented all of Derrick's threats to the court, and as a result, the judge granted full custody to Tina, as well as child support, and alimony. Derrick was granted supervised visitation at Tina's discretion away from her home. Because the children loved their dad, Tina would never keep Derrick from seeing his children whenever he wanted, but as for her, she was done with him.

For months after the divorce, Derrick kept trying to convince Tina to come back to him. He told her how much he still loved her, and how he missed her. Not once did he apologize for cheating on her and getting another woman pregnant during their marriage. Tina had reached a point where she could not stand to look at Derrick, she just wanted him to leave her alone. On one occasion when he came over to visit with the children, he attempted to kiss her, when she said no, he grabbed her and pulled her into him. At that moment, every rape, and every form of molestation came rushing back to her mind, and before she knew it, she had grabbed a butcher's knife from the kitchen drawer. "If you come anywhere near me ever again, I will slit your dam throat! Do you hear me, Derrick?"

A startled Derrick got the message loud and clear. "Okay, I am going but just remember, I own you, I paid the minister for you, and don't you ever forget it." When DJ heard the loud commotions, he came rushing into the room and ran to his mom; Are you alright mommy, are those happy tears cause dada is here?" "No honey, they are happy tears cause dada is leaving." Derrick took one last quick glance in Tina's direction before saying good-bye to DJ and walked out. Little did he know; it would be a long time before he ever graced her floors again with his feet. Tina reached down and picked up DJ; she held him ever so close and whispered, "little man, from now on, you're the king of this castle."

It took some adjusting and getting used to, but Tina finally settled into her apartment and began to feel at home. Taking care of her two children on her own was no problem since she mostly did it alone anyway during her marriage. She had an excellent job as an executive assistant at a large media marketing company, and the support of her mom.

After living in an apartment for a year, Tina decided that the children needed more space to play, so she bought a beautiful home with a huge backyard. Because of her high salaried job, she was able to hire a nanny and part-time housekeeper to help her with the children. Though it appeared that all was well with Tina, she felt lonely most of the time. Her children were comforting, but they did not fill the void of a loving romantic relationship. She longed to meet someone that would love and cherish her.

Having been through so much in her life, Tina felt much older than her twenty-seven years of life. She had gotten married at the young age of twenty-one. Although she was still somewhat childlike when she got married, she soon learned that she needed to grow up fast; and she did. Tina grew into a strong mature lady that carried herself well. Everything she did, every conversation she had, every move she made, she did with eloquence. She was both hated and admired by women in her circle. Even though her parents were very authoritative, they never failed to teach her how to be a lady and how to carry herself as such.

Tina walked like a goddess, and when she entered any room, she turned heads without even trying. She was not a narcissist but was genuinely charismatic; her problem was insecurity and low self-esteem when it came to her personal life, she had no idea of her feminine powers. She preferred one-on-one conversations and often shied away from social group interactions. Tina always knew that she was gifted, but she was never conceited or boasted about it. In fact, she was the type of person everyone wanted to have as a friend. Despite her congeniality, Tina had a limited number of friends, because she found out early on that people had the tendency to mistake her kindness for weakness, and she had an extremely low tolerance for hypocrisy.

Three years after Tina's divorce from Derrick was finalized, she decided to go out with a couple of her girlfriends, Shanell, and Marley, to a dance. Shanell was sister to the man that raped her as a kid. She had never told Shanell what her brother had done to her because of her own embarrassment, and that she didn't know how her friend would react to her accusing her brother of such behavior. Like a good little wound-up doll, she continued to hold on to her ugly past and put on her fake faces.

It was a warm night, but not hot; she and the girls were excited because they were going to a dance where there were live performances. "I wonder if we will be able to get close to the performers?" asked Shanell. "I don't see why not, stated Tina, they are a pretty down to earth group, so I wouldn't be surprised if you are able to talk with them, at least some of them." "The good thing about tonight stated Marley is that we have no curfew, we are grown now." All three girls laughed out so loud that their ribs ached. "You are so right Marley, said Tina, when she was finally able to catch her breath; No having to be home by mid-night."

Chapter Ten

It had been such a long time since Tina enjoyed anything accept her children; so much so, that she wondered how the night would go for her. She had only agreed to go dancing with her friends because the children's babysitter was willing to spend the entire night with them. She did not feel comfortable leaving her children at home to go partying, so most weekends, she did things that involved them.

When Tina and her friends entered the club, they noticed the large crowd, but she did not notice the guys watching them as they sought to find an available table. Tina looked around and noticed that there were several vacant tables to choose from. "Let's go over here girls, there's a table not too far from the band." "Are you sure you want to sit so close to the band, I mean the music is sort-of loud, said Marley as she wiggled to the beat. "That shouldn't be a problem especially since you guys want to socialize with the performers" Tina said in response. "I don't know about socializing said Shanell, I just want to say hello." "You can do that from across the room laughed Marley, just lift your hand in the air and wave, hello there!"

"I suppose that was meant to be funny," said a somewhat annoyed Shanell. "Just breaking the ice Shanell, no need to get your panties all in a bunch." Shanell chose to ignore Marley's last comment and said to Tina, "lead the way honey, I am right behind you."

Tina began walking towards the side of the room where there was an available table not far away from where the band was performing. As she glided her way through the crowded room, she felt someone touching her on her arm. She turned around swiftly to smack it as if something had bitten her. "Woe girl, came from an unfamiliar voice, hello, you must have fallen from the moon because stars are all around your head." Tina wanted to say something to the guy, but instead she burst out laughing. "What's funny" he asked. "You are Tina replied, you are." The gentleman looked confused as Tina continued walking towards her soon to be table.

"Well, you will never meet anyone behaving like that," Shanell said after watching how Tina blew off the stranger. "Just what make you think that I am looking to meet someone tonight?" "You said tonight, does that mean that you will be looking in the future?" "That means my dear, that I will not be looking tonight, tomorrow, or anytime, but I will be available if someone wants to find me." "What the hell is that supposed to mean?" asked Marley. Simply put, it means that I am in no rush to meet a man, but should one come my way, I may consider." "Humm," Marley groaned under her breath. "What was that Marley?" "Nothing, not a thing." Tina, being the gracious person that she was, ignored Marley's comment, and proceeded to sit down.

When she had comfortably positioned herself in her chair, she looked up and directly into the eyes of the stranger who had touched her arm. He had followed her to her table and was waiting for the opportunity to introduce himself. "Hello, my name is Delvin, and who is this lovely goddess?" "Not interested." "There seems to be a lot of ladies in here tonight with the same name, what do you say, you change yours." "No offense Delvin, but I came to enjoy the performance, not to hook up with some random guy, so if you don't mind, buzz off." Delvin was highly offended and walked away whispering, "your lost."

Tina was glad that Delvin left so easily, she could now focus her full attention on the band without him hanging around. Just as she was about to exhale, she felt a tap on her left shoulder. "What now?" Tina asked while furiously spinning around to face the intruder. When she had completely turned in her chair, she came face-to-face with the most gorgeous man she had ever laid her eyes on. "Hello, he said, would you do me the owner of dancing with me?" Tina opened her mouth, but the only sound that came out was a little squeak that sounded like a trapped mouse. He reached his hand out towards her, and she gently placed hers within his.

For the next few minutes Tina had forgotten all about Shanell and Marley; heck, she had forgotten about everyone else that was crammed up inside the building. The band was playing a love song, and the artist was singing ever so sweetly. As she moved to the beat of the music, she felt as if she had finally found a soft place to lay her head. She looked up into the intruder's eyes and asked, "what is your name?" Because of the loudness of the music, he could not hear her, so he gently pulled her closer to him and laid his chin on the top of her head. She wanted to pull away, but her will to do so failed; it was as if this man had taken every ounce of strength she had so carefully stored over the years.

Finally, the song ended, and the gentleman walked her back to her table. "What did you say your name was," she asked. "I didn't say," came the reply as he slowly walked away. Tina just sat there with her jaw in her hands, looking as if someone had just told her she'd won the lottery, and then snatched it away and ran. She tried to see where he had disappeared too in the crowd, but no luck. When she was finally able to come down from the high of the dance with the stranger, she ordered a Pepsi and began sipping on it.

"Who was that guy," Shanell wanted to know. "What guy are you referring too?" "Girl, don't be tripping with me, that guy that has you all hot and bothered." "I don't know his name, he never told me." "I know you're not telling me that you let a hulk like that just walk away without a name or number?" "That is what I'm telling you." "Well, I be dang, you have certainly lost your edge. "To be honest with you Shanell, I've never had an edge." "Yes, you have, you're just not aware of it." Tina was so intrigue by the man that had just serenaded her to care what Shanell thought of her at that moment, so instead of responding, she just turned her head in the direction he had gone in.

Marley and Shanell got their wishes; they were having the time of their lives laughing and talking with the band members during intermission. Tina did not care one way or the other about chatting with the band members or the artists. Her previous plan was to listen to and enjoy the music; she had no plans to dance, and the only beverage she was interested in drinking was a cold Pepsi. After about an hour of sitting, listening, and singing along when she heard a song that she loved, she was ready to call it a night. She realized that her prince charming had probably moved on to the next available lady and had forgotten all about her.

"Well ladies, I don't want to be a party pooper, but I am really ready to leave." "No problem, Shanell replied, it has been quite a long day and we are no longer spring chickens." "Speak for yourself, laughed Marley, I am still hot, and I ain't too proud to show it." "Well come on hot momma, let's go," said Tina teasingly. The other two girls laughed at Tina's comment as they followed her out of the club. "That wasn't so bad for a night out" said Shanell, yawning. "What did you say, asked Marley, I did not understand a word you said." Tina quickly responded before Marley got a chance to repeat herself; "She said that the night wasn't bad, and I agree, it felt really good getting out for a change." Marley agreed with the other two girls in her mind but did not verbalize her thoughts. "So, do you disagree Marley, asked Shanell, you don't think that the night went well?" "The night was fine Shanell, just fine, so let it rest, will you?" "Come on ladies, don't start tonight, I was beginning to believe that this night would end without the two of you going after each other, I'm getting too old for this." Both girls apologized before exiting the club.

Chapter Eleven

Tina was glad to be back at home; when she entered the house, she felt a sense of relief. Going out was not something she did often and each time she did, she felt that she did it mostly to please her friends; she was just as contented staying home on weekends and playing with her children. When she got inside, the babysitter was fast asleep. Tina tipped around her and went to the nursery to peep in on the children. They looked so peaceful as they laid on their bellies sound asleep; the way Tina wished she could feel. "If I could just have one day of internal peace she thought, I would cherish it for the rest of my life."

Tina wondered if she would ever be normal; as hard as she had tried, she just could not feel complete. She felt like there was a hole in the center of her heart, and she had no idea how to fill it or what she needed to fill it with. As much as she loved her children and the rest of her family, they were not able to fill that emptiness that taunted her, her entire life. How she longed just to be able to sit and talk with her family about all the abuse she had endured in her life, but just as before, she was ashamed, and felt they would not understand, and would make her feel worse. How she longed to just fit in somewhere.

Tina finally made her way to her bedroom where she plopped herself down on her bench. She just sat there for a few minutes allowing the aftermath of the night to roll through her thoughts. A light tap on her bedroom door brought Tina back into the moment. "Yes," she called out. It was Judy, the children's babysitter. "Ms. Tina, I am so sorry I fell asleep, but after feeding, bathing, and putting the children to bed, I found myself more exhausted than I realized. I closed my eyes for just a few seconds, but I fell asleep and did not hear when you came in." "That's okay Judy, you have been going overtime with the children, you deserve a break, besides, I checked on them when I came in and they are fine. It is good that you are spending the night, so you won't have to drive so late tonight, besides, it's foggy outside." "Thanks Ms. Tina, I appreciate you letting me stay the night, you are the best." "As long as you know it," laughed Tina.

After Tina had finished speaking with Judy, she took a long cold shower, oiled her skin with baby oil and crawled into bed. For some unknown reason, she slept better than she had in years, and woke up the next morning with a song in her heart. She began humming, "Hope for tomorrow, forget your sorrow, last night has escape, today you're awake." Because she had taken a shower just a few hours before, Tina went into the bathroom, brushed her teeth, washed her face, and headed to the children's room in her pajamas. When she entered the room, the children were not there; Tina called out, and as she turned towards the kitchen, she could hear their cheerful little voices.

"Well good morning nuggets, you guys certainly are bright eyed this morning." Both children ran to their mom and jumped up on her knees. When they wrapped those little arms around her neck, she remembered how blessed she was despite all her unhappiness. "One would think this would be enough Tina thought, and under normal circumstances it would be, but how do I find normalcy, where do I start looking?" Of all the abuse, molestations, insults, and rapes, there was one dark place Tina refused to allow her mind to travel. She convinced herself that it didn't matter, because it was different from the others, so she held on tight and promised herself that she would never tell a sole about that time in her life.

After the children had finished their breakfast, Tina sent the babysitter home, and got the children bath, and dressed herself.

When she had fully clothed them, she took them to their room and put them inside the play pen so that she could dress herself. When she had completed the task of dressing herself and the children, she loaded them in their car seats and headed for church. When service was over, Tina did what she did every Sunday after church; she went straight to her mother's house.

When she arrived at her mother's house, she took the children from their seats and went inside. "Where's mom," she asked her older brother who had arrived just ahead of her. "She should be here shortly, she left church to go visit Mrs. Flora and take her some tonic she made for her cold." Just as Tina opened her mouth to comment, Mrs. Elena walked through the doorway. "Hey yawl, if you're looking for something to eat, too bad, because I did not cook a thing." "Mom, how dear you," laughed Tina as she took in the aroma of fried chicken coming from the kitchen. Mrs. Elena chuckled as she embraced both her children. The two little ones lifted their arms in an attempt for grandma to pick them up, which she did. "It's so great to see you guys, said Elena, it's been a while." "Mom, I saw you a few days ago, what do you mean it's been a while?" "Well seems like awhile to me, anyway, let's go into the kitchen and feed these little ones." That sounded like music to Tina's ear since the big one was hungry as well. "What about me," asked Westley, Tina's younger brother. "What about you" Elena asked laughingly. "Aren't you planning to feed your old boy too?" "Sure Westley, come on in the kitchen, and don't try and eat all from everyone else." "Would I do that?" "Of course, you would" replied Tina before Mrs. Elena could respond. Just looking at her from the outside, one would think that Tina was a happy well-adjusted young lady, but in retrospect, she felt as if she was drowning a slow death.

Tina's mom and brothers were going on and on about the children and how smart they were. "Must have taken after me," Westley said. "Who must have taken after you?" asked Tina. "Who do you think, where your mind at girl?" "I wish I could tell you." "That sounds intriguing, do tell." Tina just smiled and said to her brother, "if my telling you would make things better, I would talk to you all day." "Talk to me sis, tell me what's bothering you, is it some guy, because if it is, I will smack his behind." Despite herself, Tina had to laugh; "I bet you would, I just bet you would."

After spending most of the evening with her mother and brothers, Tina took the kids, and headed for home. On her way, she decided to take a detour and visit her friend Nancy. She had not seen Nancy in church and that was odd. When she arrived at her friend's house, there were several vehicles in the yard. Tina became concerned and a little hesitant about going inside. "I don't know if I am prepared to hear any bad news today," she thought. Tina felt it would be selfish of her not to go inside and find out what was going on, so she took the children from the car and slowly made her way across the yard and up the steps. When she reached the door, she lifted her hand to ring the bell, but the door opened, and a teary-eyed Nancy stepped out onto the porch.

"What happened, why are you crying, did something happen to you?" Without a word, Nancy fell into Tina's arms and began sobbing. "My sister was all Nancy was able to get out, before she broke down again. "What about your sister Nancy, what about her?" Tina asked, on the verge of breaking into tears herself. Nancy was finally able to compose herself long enough to tell Tina that her sister Lena had died without warning early that morning. "What happened, Tina wanted to know, was she killed?" "No, she died in her sleep, she just did not wake up this morning." Tina was sorry to see her friend having to go through this, but she needed to get the children home. After spending a little time with Nancy and comforting her as best she could, Tina apologized for having to leave, but explained that it was getting close to the children's bedtime. Nancy thanked Tina for coming, and said she understood. Tina promised to return the next day after the babysitter came to be with the kids.

After Tina left Nancy's, she went home and got the children ready for bed. When they were finally asleep, she sat on the bench at the foot of her bed and reminisced on the happenings of the day; she started with early breakfast with the kids, church, then her evening with her mother and brothers; finally, she let her mind trailed to the time she spent with Nancy. Of all the events of the day, the time spent with Nancy hit hardest. Not because of the obvious, but because it stirred some strange emotion in her that she had never allowed herself to feel before.

Ever since Tina's failed marriage, she'd disconnected from her emotions, but somehow, all her defenses had fallen. Tina was confused because, for the most part, she did not like Nancy's sister, mainly because they were so different. She was always looking down her nose at people and finding unnecessary faults in them. Although Tina wasn't that fond of Lena, she was still Nancy's sister and Nancy was one of her oldest friends. Just the same, "Why am I feeling so emotional" she thought. As she attempted to work out the details of her revived emotions, she suddenly became very sleepy.

After getting a good night's sleep, Tina was in a much better frame of mind in the morning, than she was the night before. "Something has got to give, she thought, I just don't want to go on this way, there has got to be a better life for me out there somewhere." At that moment, Tina had and epiphany; she understood exactly why Lena's death had such a profound emotional effect on her. "Life is short and can be taken away from you at any moment. "I need to get over myself, and live life for me and my children while I have a chance."

At that very moment, Tina declared that she would not allow herself to continue living as a victim. She decided then and there that she was over every negative thing that had ever happened to her, or so she thought. She went into the children's room to check on them and found that the nanny had let herself in and was with the children. Tina backed out of the room quickly before the children could see her, she did not feel up to dealing with them at that moment, not when she was on a roll. She hurried back into her room and began brainstorming as to how she would spend the rest of her life. "Today is the first day of the rest of my life, I will make the best of every moment, and I will not look back."

Chapter Twelve

The next morning, Tina decided to call out from work so that she could spend some time with her friend Nancy. When she arrived at Nancy's home, she found her alone and much calmer than the day before. Nancy was previously married but had divorced her husband after he cheated on her several times with several different women. At the age of twenty-eight, she had four children and was raising them alone. Although her husband was ordered by the court to pay child support and alimony, he had rather sit in jail than to work and pay them. Tina admired Nancy's spunk, and often wished she had just an ounce of it. Tina was always oblivious when it came to her own strength and self-worth.

Tina spent the entire day with Nancy. They took the two oldest children to school then went to Nancy's mom house to pay her a visit. Nancy's mom insisted that she leave the other two children with her, while she and Tina met with the mortician to make funeral arrangements for Lena. Tina stuck close by her friend's side helping in whatever ways she was needed. When they had gotten everything in place, Tina took Nancy to get some lunch before picking up the kids from school.

"This has got to be the hardest thing I've ever had to do" stated Nancy with a squeaking voice. "It is hard watching you go through this; I know how it feels. Tina had lost her dad suddenly when he had a heart attack and remembered the pain all so well. "I know you do, said a teary-eyed Nancy; I know you do." Tina and Nancy went to a little Bistro down from the funeral home for lunch, but Nancy was unable to eat a bite. "Maybe I'll just take it with me and eat it later, I'm sorry, but I can't eat a thing right now, you understand, don't you?" "Of course, I do, but you really need to force yourself to eat at least part of it so that you don't get weakened." "You're right, I'll try."

Nancy was able to eat most of her chili cheese steak sandwich before they left to pick up the kids. Once they had gathered up all the children, they returned to Nancy's home and settled them in. Tina was feeling the stress of the day and wanted to go home and play with her own children. "Nancy, are you going to be ok, I really need to get home." "Sure, having to feed these four children and get them ready for bed will erase all the sadness from my mind for a while, I'll be alright." "Thank God for little ones, call if you need me, you hear?" "I hear."

Tina went home still in her uplifted mood from the day before. Despite all the sadness she felt coming from Nancy, she did not allow it to enter into her spirit. She was determined to move forward. While she fully sympathized with her friend for losing her sister, she was not going to allow it to bring her down from wherever it was that she thought she had gone. She was in a fool's paradise. Little did she know that you cannot run or hide from your past, you must face and deal with it and then if you are lucky, you will be able to cope with the outcome. But in Tina's mind, she had self-healed.

Mrs. Elena taught all her girls to always present themselves as ladies, so no matter where Tina went, or how she was feeling, she was the epitome of what she termed a lady. It could have been her darkest moment, but when she entered the room, she turned heads. Not that she tried, but her charisma was powerful. Most of the time, if not all the time, she was not aware that she had that ability. She often downplayed her looks and did not understand her own power when it came to interacting with people of all races, gender, nationality, or age. It was just something special about her. Not knowing made it even more special. When she smiled, she lit up a room, and when she spoke, which was rare, everyone paid attention.

Tina decided that she wanted to begin dating again, she was still young; some guy might consider himself lucky to be in a relationship with her. Just because Tina decided that she would start dating again, didn't mean it would be easy. First, she had to make herself available to men to attract them. Tina had never done much dating. She met her husband and married him within three months, and prior to him, there was not much dating. "How do I start? It has been so long, and I cannot just bring anyone around my children. How do I date without getting my children involved, or letting him know where I live?" Now that was a difficult one. Not only did she not want him to meet her children, but she did not want him knowing her place of residency.

Tina remembered when she first separated from her husband, men seemed to migrate from everywhere. It appeared to Tina that they believed she was desperate. Quite the contrary, she was sick of men; anything with a penis got on her nerves, especially those so-called friends of her ex-husband. Every time she turned around, someone wanted to take her out. "I guess I was too hard on men after my husband treated me so terrible, thought Tina, but I felt justified then and I still do, I guess I'll figure it out."

With determination in her heart, Tina decided that it was time to get back in the dating race. She did not want to spend the remainder of her life as a single mom. She resolved that the past was the past, and as far as she was concerned, her future looked bright. "If only I could just bury all of the awful things that happened in my past, and they would stay buried and stop popping up at uninvited times, I might be able to secure a happy future for myself." With those thoughts, like everything else in her life, Tina began to organize a plan of action.

Tina was good at organizing her finances, her household, and especially her job. Everything was always in order; people often told her that she was obsessively compulsive, but she knew that she wasn't. She was just well organized. Her organizational skills were the cause of her getting such a prestigious job, and frequent promotions. But how would she organize her dating situation? That would be her greatest challenge; mainly because she had such little experience in the dating arena. Nevertheless, she was determined to make things work in her favor.

"Just wait, I'll show them, Shanell and Marley won't see it coming; when they know anything, I will have found me a good man." Tina could not help but smile at the thought of her idea, something she did very little off, and when she did, it was often fake. "Am I really doing this, she thought, am I really putting myself out there again?" Tina allowed her mind to go back to her relationship with her ex-husband Derrick, and she thought of all the ways in which he'd hurt her. She tried to imagine positive times with him, but there were few. She did think of her pregnancies and how he would cater to her cravings and desires. She remembered the day she told him that she was pregnant with their first child and how happy and excited he was. She also remembered telling him about the second pregnancy and his nonchalant response. She had no regrets of marrying him because from it came her two beautiful children. "I would do it all over again, she thought, if it meant being blessed with these two beautiful little souls, some things are just worth the sacrifice." Tina quickly snapped back to reality, pulling her thoughts with her. She began to devise a plan for the rest of her life. She sat quietly in her room writing and rewriting what she considered to be her perfect dating plan. When she had completed it, she felt accomplished. She placed the pages on her writing table, looked down at it and declared that it would come to pass.

Chapter Thirteen

Two weeks had gone by since Tina made her list of life altering goals, and she had not done one thing towards achieving them. Things had become more demanding at her job, and her babysitter had contracted the flu. Aside from having to put in extra time at work, she also had to do everything for the children including getting them to and from school and daycare. "I wonder, how do single parents do this every day without any outside help; I can barely manage for a week." Although she was hard on herself, Tina deserved a pat on the back, not only was she killing it at work, but she was a heck of a mom and was doing an excellent job with her children without the help of anyone. She did not even solicit the help of her mom, mainly because she didn't want to burden her with extra work. Mrs. Elena would have gladly assisted had she known the dilemma Tina was facing.

After a week of recovering from the flu, Judy was able to return to work. Although Tina was getting along fine without her, she was thrilled to have her back on the job. "Welcome back Judy, I hope you are feeling much better." "Thanks Ms. Tina, I have totally recovered now, but I had a few rough days." Well, I am glad that you've recovered so quickly, the children missed you and so did I." Tina did not want Judy to know just how desperate she was to have her back. Even though she managed to keep everything well organized and under control, it took quite a toll on her. She was tired and felt overwhelmed.

Once Judy had settled in, Tina took off for work. It felt great not having to drop the children off at the daycare. When she arrived at her office, her boss was sitting on top of her desk waiting for her. "Oh, good morning Mr. Douglas, is everything alright?" "Yes, I just wanted to see the look on your face when I gave you the good news." "What good news sir?" "Do you remember the meetings we had with Dye-graphics to determine if they would be a good fit for our growing company?" "Yeah, I remember, that was several weeks ago, did something happen with them?" "Yes, indeed it did, after much debating and considerations on both our parts, we decided that a merger would be beneficial for both companies." "Oh great! Congratulation sir, but why did you need to tell me personally, will these changes uproot me?" "Uproot would not be the term I would use to describe these changes, more like increase responsibilities."

"More responsibilities, hell my plate is already filled" Tina thought to herself; but with a big fake smile on her face, she said, "gee, that sounds interesting." "Wait until you hear all of the details, said Douglas, it will blow your mind." "Now you have me curious, like I don't know if I can wait for the details." "You don't have to Tina, girl, I am going to give you the whole enchilada right now." "Please have a seat Mr. Douglas and do tell." "What have I told you about being so formal with me, I told you to call me Phil." "Okay Phil, what is it, aside from the merger itself, what is it that have you on such an emotional high?"

"Sit-down, sit-down girl, let me fill you in," said an excited Phil. Tina did as she was told; she went behind her desk, and gently sat herself down all the while looking directly into Phil's eyes. "Ok, I'm sitting." "Ok Tina, let me put it this way; the merger has caused a shift in management, and requires a few new positions to be filled. One of those positions is Chief Operating Officer." Tina was looking at Phil as if he were speaking a foreign language; "why is he telling me this, why doesn't he just get to the part where I will be having more responsibilities." "I see, Tina said politely, and just who will be filling this position?" "That is what I have been trying to tell you since I came in; you will." "I will what? Oh my God! Are you saying that I am being promoted to C.O.O.?" "Yes Tina, that is exactly what I am saying if you will accept the position. I realize that you were just promoted a few months ago and are still learning your roles in that position, but I feel that with your talent and experience, you will adapt to the changes faster than most. What do you say, do I have a C.O.O.?" "Yes sir! You most certainly do have a C.O.O."

When Tina left work that evening, she was on a natural high, one that would last her for quite a while. "Chief Operating Officer, me, hot dam!" Tina could not erase the huge smile that covered her face, and she carried it with her inside the house. "My goodness, what has you so happy Ms. Tina?" Before she could tell Judy her reason for her fixed smile, the children came rushing to her for hugs and kisses. For a few minutes, Tina forgot all about work and her big promotion. The only things that were on her mind now were DJ and Tiana, her two little angels. When they had gotten enough attention for the moment, they both returned to the playroom and resumed what they were doing before Tina arrived.

"Okay Ms. Tina, now you can tell me what has you in such an intoxicating mood." Tina told Judy all about her new position and how happy and honored she felt. "If anyone deserves it Ms. Tina it's you." "You do know what this means don't you," asked Tina. "I'm not sure, what does it mean?" It means my dear, that should I get a big raise, and I am thinking I will, you will be able to go from part time to full-time, with benefits." Judy began dancing around in the floor as she gave thanks to God. "My prayers have been answered, she said, this is the best news I've heard in a long time." "So, I take it you will be good with the extra hours and responsibilities." "I will be more than good, I will be great with it, thanks Ms. Tina."

It felt good telling her babysitter/housekeeper about her big promotion, but she wanted to tell someone else. She wanted to tell her friends, Shanell, and Marley; they shared practically everything. After she had settled in for the night, Tina curled up on her bed in her freshly washed bathrobe and called her friends. She purposely did not call Nancy; Nancy was more of a pessimist, and she did not want to be brought down from the high she was experiencing.

"Hello girls, how's tricks?" Marley responded first, hey Tina, who's tricks?" Both Tina and Shanell burst into laughter at the same time. Marley was always the last person to catch a hint or get a joke. Shanell decided to milk the situation. "Girl, you haven't heard, Tricks is Tina's new boyfriend." "OMG Tina, you never told me that you had a boyfriend; is it the guy you met at the club the other night?" Shanell continued to play the devil's advocate and jumped in before Tina could respond. "Yeah girl, that's him the one from the club." Tina was so overcome by laughter that she could no longer contain herself. She didn't want to embarrass Marley by telling her that tricks were just a metaphor, so she lied and said, "he's not really my boyfriend Marley, just someone I know." "So then why would you ask us how he's doing; I don't even know him." "Dam Marley, just drop it, said a now frustrated Shanell, it doesn't matter, I don't know him either, she was just making conversation, okay?"

Marley was more than a little upset with Shanell for speaking to her that way even though she should have been used to it. "So, Tina;" "yes Marley;" "What is the reason for this call, you seldom call us on two-way unless you have something exciting to tell us." "Yeah Tina, said Shanell, do tell." "Well ok then, if the two of you think you can shut up long enough to hear." "We are all ears, what is it?" "Guess who just got promoted as C.O.O of Phillip's Innovations?" "No, shouted an excited Shanell, you're kidding me, oh girl, congrats." "What is a COO Tina? I've heard that term before, but I never knew what it meant and didn't much care until now." "C.O.O stands for Chief Operating Officer." So is that better than what you're doing now because you practically run that company now." "Much better, I will have a larger staff working directly under me, and I will be reporting directly to Mr. Douglas. Not only that, but I am now second in command. Next up, CEO." So, tell me Tina, does this mean you will be getting a big fat raise?" "Yep, it certainly does." "Well look at us, we have a rich friend; they all laughed with excitement.

After Tina had ended her call with the girls, she hopped down from her bed and headed for the children's room. They were both sleeping soundly and looked like little angels. Tina could not hold back the tears. She was so thankful for all her blessings. She never in a million years believed that she would have such a wonderful life after everything she had gone through. But here she was, a beautiful home, a great job, and most of all, two wonderful children. She was also grateful that she could afford to hire someone to help her and at the same time, make their life a little better. She bent down and kissed the children on their little cheeks as tears fell from her eyes and dropped on their precious little faces. She didn't want to wake them so she eased her way out of their room, and gently closed the door behind her leaving a small crack so she could hear if they called out during the night. "This is great she thought, everything seems to be in place, but there's still one aspect of my life that needs some attention."

Chapter Fourteen

When Tina left the children's room, she felt like having a little snack, so she made her way to the kitchen. She looked in the refrigerator for something light and decided that she would take the strawberry yogurt that was staring back at her. When she attempted to pull it out, something more appealing in the freezer was calling her name. She opened the freezer and there it was, a tub of butter pecan ice cream. "Now that is what I'm talking about; with a smile on her face, she apologized to the yogurt and placed it back into the refrigerator. Next time dear, but tonight, it is ice cream all the way." Tina scooped up a sizable portion of ice cream and placed it in a bowl; "Forgive me calories, but I will burn you off tomorrow."

Tina finished her ice cream and went back to her bedroom with the intension of going to bed. However, the ice cream had taken all her sleep away, so she decided to watch a little TV instead. The only thing she found interesting was a romance movie, so she turned the volume up and focused her attention on it. As the movie unfolded, Tina felt a little lonely. "I bet I am the only person in the world who's single at my age, I am tired being alone." She realized that she was having a pity party and that was just not like her.

As she sat on the edge of the bed, her mind drifted away from the movie she was watching and wandered back to the night at the club when she danced with a nameless stranger. She wondered who he was and if she would ever see him again. The thought of him holding her so close made her shiver. "What a great feeling, having a man hold me after all this time, and dam he smelled good. Come on now Tina, do you really want to go down that road again, are you willing to put your heart out there like that?"

Since her divorce from Derrick, Tina was skeptical about putting her trust in another man. She was afraid that it would only lead to more heartbreak, and she was not sure if she wanted to take that risk. "I know that they say all men are not alike, and somewhere in my subconscious I may believe that, but I have yet to find the one that's different. Most of the pain that I have experienced in my lifetime, were caused by men." Tina's mind drifted back to some of her unpleasant experiences with the opposite sex and she cringed.

"No Tina, hell no, you cannot allow yourself to go back to those dark places, let it die, you're on a quest for a new beginning, a better life experience." Although she tried convincing herself that her past did not matter and had no bearing on her future, she was not completely sure that she was being realistic. "Can I really put my past behind me and leave it there? Can I have a happy future despite my hang-ups? I have got to believe that I can, and I have got to give it a shot, I am so ready for a change in my life."

After much reminiscing, Tina finally crawled into bed and pulled the sheet over her head. She had underestimated how sleepy she'd become and fell asleep as soon as she turned over. As she slept, she began to dream. She dreamt that she was on top of a roof, and that she had wings. She could see across the entire world. As she looked, she saw herself in the middle of a crowded street. Everyone was rushing to get somewhere, but she was just standing there. Finally, she spread her wings, and flew down from the roof to where she was standing; she picked herself up and began flying higher and higher into the clouds. The higher she climbed, the better she felt, as if she was floating on one of those clouds she saw as she passed them. When she'd reached the top of where she was going, she gently let herself down and flew away. Tina stood there gazing at herself as she descended into the clouds; she lifted her hand and waved goodbye.

Slowly Tina began to open her eyes; for a split second she thought that she was in Heaven. As she became fully awake, she realized that it was only a dream. "What a dream, I wonder what it means? It must have some significance to my life, but what?" Tina felt a sense of restlessness, like she should be doing something. "Oh well she thought, whatever it is I will figure it out in the morning because right now, I need some sleep.

The next morning, Tina devised a plan she believed would help her keep her pass life buried once and for all. She would become more involved with the church, helping others who had issues. "That is what I am going to do she thought, maybe that's what my dream was all about; maybe I am supposed to be doing more to help others and less dwelling on my past." So, on Sunday mornings when the church doors opened, Tina and her children were front and centered. She listened to the morning messages which seemed not to have anything to do with her, or her life, but there she was, nodding and agreeing anyway.

After service was over, Tina met with all the auxiliary heads and began joining everything that had a vacancy. She joined the choir, the youth ministry, the usher board, the planning committee, and the trustee board. She was so caught up in religion, that she forgot her spirituality. She went through the motion of being a dedicated Christian. Although she was not a bad person, she was going about it in the wrong manner and for the wrong reasons. She found no peace nor long-term satisfaction from any of those church extra curriculums. As soon as she returned home from church, she would find herself in the same old predicament; seeing a therapist never entered her thoughts.

When her involvement in the church did not reveal any changes in her life, Tina decided to take a break from attending at all. "I think that, maybe I am just a little too close to the mirror. I am going to stop procrastinating and devise a plan for me and my children's future. The first thing I am going to do is return to that club where I danced with the stranger. Who knows, maybe I'll get lucky, and he will be there again and ask me to dance, and if he doesn't ask, I will just have to ask him. Either way, I will not let him get away without finding something out about him.

Tina picked up her phone and dialed Shanell. If it was one person she could count on, it was her childhood friend Shanell. She and Shanell had covered much ground together as children and in their teenage lives. They both had gotten married at early ages, and both marriages had failed. They were both in their late twenties and looked like teenagers. When Shanell called, Tina answered, and vice versa. No matter how close she felt to Shanell though, she had never told her about her past, she was just too embarrassed. Even if she had gotten the courage to tell her, she did not think that Shanell would understand, heck, she didn't even understand.

"Hey girl, came an excited voice on the other end of the phone, what's up?" "Hey Shanell, I was just thinking, it's about time I put myself back on the dating market, it has been a while since my divorce now and I don't want to spend my life alone." "So, what are you thinking of doing?" "I was thinking that maybe we could go back to the Irish Club, what do you think?" "Hey, you know me, always ready for a good time, but can we leave Marley at home, I really don't feel up to her lame ass right now." "Shanell, what a thing to say about our friend, but you are right, I would just get exhausted trying to break everything down for her, and quite frankly, I am not in that frame of mind these days." "Okay then, let's do it."

Tina and Shanell headed for the club without Marley and had no intension of telling her that they had gone. Although Marley did not catch on to things quickly and sometimes never unless it was broken down, and even then, she would often miss the point, they loved her dearly and would not want to hurt her in any way. "Girl I am excited about tonight; I just have a good feel." "Just what is it that you're feeling Shanell?" "I don't know, just a sense of expectation." "Well, I hope that you're not setting yourself up for disappointment." "No matter what happens or not happen I will be fine, just getting out of the house is good enough for me." "I agree with that; it is such a great feeling to be going out knowing that your kids are in good hands." "By the way Shanell, where are your kid's tonight?" "With your Momma." "My Momma, girl for real?" "Yep, when you called, I had no idea what I was going to do with them, I didn't want to disappoint you so I agreed, hoping that your mom would say yes to keeping the children." "And of course, she did, that's my mom, always willing to help out for a cause, so what cause did you give her?" "I told her that I wanted to go out with you tonight, hopefully to meet some fellows." "Shanell! Tina said laughing, you are such a mess, and she agreed based on that story?" "Yep, said it was high time we got back in the saddle, then she asked if we were taking Marley." "Why would she ask about Marley?" "To put it in her words, "if yawl wanna catch a man, I suggest you leave Marley at home tonight." "Yeah, and I bet you didn't have any problem agreeing with her, did you?" "Nope; agreed one hundred percent." "But really Shanell, I'm not looking for any man tonight, just want to get out and mangle a bit." "Stop lying girl, you know that you are hoping to see Mr. Anonymous." "Ah haw girl, you ain't never lied, I hope he's around tonight."

When Tina and Shanell arrived at the club, they were surprised by the small number of vehicles in the parking lot. "I wonder what's going on, I thought for sure that we would have to fight for seats tonight." "Remember Tina, we are somewhat early, the shing dig doesn't start until around midnight, it's only nine thirty pm." "Yes, you are right, well that gives us an advantage, we can sit wherever we choose." "Well let's hope so." "What do you mean, why couldn't we sit wherever we want to?" "Reservations, have you ever heard of them?" "Girl your ass, let's go find a seat."

Just like Tina predicted, the seating availability was unlimited; she had so many options that she had a tough time deciding where she wanted to park her derriere. Finally, she found seats not too close to the stage because the loud noise bothered her eardrums, but close enough to be involved in whatever was taking place on stage. When she was comfortable, she turned her whole body around to get a better view of the surroundings. "What, or shall I say who are you looking for?" "Whom" "Whom what?" "Okay Shanell, don't be pulling no Marley on me." Both girls laughed until tears ran from their eyes.

"This seems like a good night for laughing so if you tell me what you girls find so funny, maybe I too can have a laugh." Tina and Shanell were caught off guard by the voice of an unknown gentleman. "Hello ladies, my name is Gerard, may I have the pleasure of knowing yours." Shanell spoke first, hi, Shanell, my name is Shanell, please to meet you." "The pleasure is all mine, and who might this pretty lady be?" Tina wanted to say, "this pretty lady be minding her own business, but instead, she said hello, my name is Delores." "Nice to meet you Delores, is this your first time coming here?" "Yes, it is," she lied, though she didn't know why. Shanell looked at Tina with laughter in her eyes but didn't say a word. "Well, it was nice meeting you ladies, I hope you enjoy your stay; if there's anything I can do to assist you, just knock on my office door." "Thanks, I shall," Tina said feeling a little foolish, there was absolutely no reason for her to tell that elaborate lie.

"Well, that was a shocker." "What was Shanell?" "The owner of the club actually came over and introduced himself to us and extended an invitation." "How do you know that he is the owner?" "Tina, that's common knowledge." "It's not common knowledge to me." "Why do you keep looking around Tina, are you looking for someone?" "Yes Shanell, if you must know, I am looking for the guy that I danced with last time I was here." "I thought this was your first time being here, Delores." Tina could only laugh; "how do you propose to correct that statement?" "I don't, Delores is my middle name;" "say what! I never knew that." "That's because I don't like it and I've kept it well hidden." "So why bring it out tonight of all times?" "It just kind of slipped out."

"Ok, can we please change the subject now, I want to focus on something else." "You mean someone else." "No, something else, look, they are preparing for open mic, why don't you sing one of those songs you wrote." "Oh no, I could never stand up before a crowded room and perform impromptus like that." Tina didn't say a word, she waited until everything was set up and people were going up performing before she brought the subject up again. "Really Shanell, you have a beautiful voice, this may be your opportunity to shine, and maybe get discovered." "So, why don't you do it; you sing as well, and you write poetry, why don't you recite one of your poems?" Tina thought about reciting one of her poems for just a second before dismissing the idea. "So, what do you say, are you going to read one of your poems?" "No Shanell, I will not be reciting any poetry tonight, but you feel free to go up there and sing your heart out." "You know what Tina, I am, I am going up there and blow these folk minds." "Well alright then, that's what I like hearing."

When the opportunity presented itself, Shanell made her way to the stage and began singing. The audience were cheering her on, which gave her the confidence she needed to blow their minds as she promised. Tina was so proud of her friend as she sang and strutted across the stage. She knew that Shanell had a great voice, but she had never seen her in action like this. When she brought her song to an end the crowd was still applauding and shouting, encore! Shanell just stood on the stage smiling and thanking the audience. Tina wondered why Shanell hadn't left the stage after she'd finished singing. Then she got the shock of her life.

When the audience calmed down, Shanell began to speak. "Think you guys for your kindness; I have a friend sitting in the audience that is just as talented as I am. Not only is she a great singer, but a poet as well. I tried to convince her to come up and share those talents with you but she's a little shy, maybe if you guys help me encourage her, she will come up." Tina was annoyed with her friend; if looks could kill, she would have been a dead friend.

She sat shaking her head trying to escape the request of the audience. When she thought that she was in the clear, Gerard walked on stage beside Shanell and began calling her out. "Come on up Delores we want to hear what you got, don't we" as he beckoned the audience help. Once again, the audience chanted, go on up, go on up. "Oh, what- the -heck, what have I got to lose, I will just go on up there and make a big fool of myself. Maybe that will make Shanell happy." Tina got up from her seat and slowly made her way to the stage while the audience applauded. When she'd reached the stage, she looked the audience over and gave a huge smile, then she looked over at her friend Shanell and pointed her finger as if to say, "I will deal with you later." "Good evening, everyone; it's true, I can do a little singing, but for tonight, I will share one of my poems. It's titled, Fantasies of the Heart." Tina picked up the mic, wet her lips with her tongue and began reciting her poem.

Chapter Fifteen

FANTASIES OF THE HEART

"I can feel your arms around me.

Your lips pressing against mine,

kissing me and whispering words of love into my ear.

As you mumble my name, expressing how much you love me.

Tears begin to flow from your eyes.

You tell me that you have never felt this way about anyone,

or anything in your whole life.

I respond by pressing my body closer against yours

and feels the hardness of your manhood.

I encircle your neck with my arms,

as my breast presses gently against your chest.

I can feel my heart beating against yours

as my tears mix with yours into a salty sweet passion

that I cannot begin to explain.

The room begins to spin as if we are on a merry-go-round,

while everything else around us disappears from our sights.

The only sound I hear is that of your heavy breathing and cries of
ecstasy.

I pull your lips softly between my teeth and nibbles on them,

just enough to make you cry out even louder.

We are lost; lost in each other's emotions.

And just like magic, we surrender to the power that has driven

us to this point.

Neither of us understands the strong emotions we describe as love

But the height that it has taken us is incredible.

In my mind, I know that it is only a fantasy,

but in my heart, it is as real as love can get.

If only you knew what you were missing by not knowing me.

If only I could find you outside of my fantasies.

If only you could see into my heart,

there would be no distance between us.

There would be no need for fantasizing.

No need for melancholic thoughts of you.

How do I make that happen?

Where are you, how do I find you,

And when I do, what do I say to you? "Fantasy, of my heart.

When Tina had finished reciting her poem, she headed back to her seat. The audience was still cheering her as she slowly made her way through the crowd to find her table. She was so incredibly proud of herself and annoyed at her friend Shanell at the same time. When she'd reached the table where she found Shanell sitting, she sat and placed her hand on Shanell's shoulder. "Don't you ever do that to me again." "What do you mean, the audience loves you." "That is beside the point Shanell, I was not prepared to do that and the poem I chose to recite may not have been appropriate." "Well, the audience seemed to think that it was appropriate, look at how they reacted." "Well, it was quite an experience, I always did want to be a celebrity." "That's my girl." Both girls laughed as they found forgiveness for putting Tina on the spot.

After Tina came down from her celebratory moment, she was extremely thirsty. "I have got to get something to drink before I pass out from dehydration." "You probably won't become dehydrated that fast, but you did just forgive me for putting you on the spot, a good spot mind you, but the spot just the same, so drinks are on me, what's your pleasure?" "My pleasure would be a Pepsi with loads of ice." "A Pepsi, is that the best you can do?" "Ok Shanell, make it a virgin strawberry daiquiri." "Now that sounds better, whipped cream and cherry?" "Yes please."

Shanell signaled for the waiter and asked if she could have two large virgin strawberry daiquiris. "Be sure and add whipped cream and cherries on both." "The waiter smiled and nodded as he exited to get their drinks. "Thanks Shanell, you are such a great friend, even when you're not." "What the hell is that supposed to mean, even when I'm not; when have I ever not been a great friend to you?" "Just messing with your girl, you're the best, always have been." "Your batcha, and always will be."

When Tina's drink arrived, she could hardly wait until the waiter placed it on her table. She picked up her glass and downed half of it before the waiter could sit Shanell's glass on the table. "Well dang Tina! Were you that doggone thirsty?" Tina chose not to respond to Shanell because she had already expressed to her that she was unusually thirsty, instead, she began looking around the room as if she was looking for someone. "Are you expecting someone?" "And just who would I be expecting Shanell?" "Don't know, why don't you tell me."

Tina was looking so fiercely that she did not hear Shanell's response, nor did she see the gentleman that had walked up on the other side of their table. The band had resumed playing and the music was loud. "Hello there" came from a voice over speaking the loud music. Tina jumped, as she turned around to see who was speaking to her. "Sorry, I didn't mean to startle you, but I wanted to compliment you on your performance tonight, it was very touching. Are all your poetries as intimate as the one you recited?" "Yes, they are, not all are romantic, but they are all passionate." "Well would you like to dance with me and perhaps whisper one of them into my ear?" "No thank you, I'll pass." "Okay dear, your lost." As the gentleman walked away, Tina could not help but laugh. "My lost, just what is it he thinks that I am losing? I would rather whisper into the ears of a chimpanzee."

"Tina, wasn't that the same guy you danced with the last time we were here?" "Oh, hell no!" "Why did you say it like that?" "I would know him anywhere; his smell alone is distinctive." "His smell, did he smell?" "No silly, not that way, maybe I should have said his aroma." "Ok, so now he's a candle." "Girl, your ass, his cologne; the aroma coming from his cologne." "I'm just messing with you again, but I could have sworn that was the same guy." He was certainly not the same person as before." As Tina was trying to convince Shanell that the man that made the negative comments to her was not her dream man from before, she caught a glimpse of a tall slender figure walking towards her. She stopped talking and just stared in the direction of the man. "What's wrong Tina?" "Don't look, but he's coming over here." "Who is coming over here?" "Shush." Shanell turned and looked despite her warning not too, and there he was, the real mystery man.

"Hello Tina, may I have this dance please?" Tina did not say a word, she was afraid that if she tried to speak, she would fail, nothing would come out, so, she stretched her hand out towards him as he gently took it into his. They headed towards the dance floor with a mesmerized Shanell looking on. "How does she do that? She always attracts the cutest guys, and I get left with the one that's dancing alone." Shanell found herself feeling somewhat jealous of Tina. Although she was an incredibly beautiful woman, she did not have that Je ne Sais quoi that Tina possessed, without even trying. "Oh well, let me look around and see if my guy is dancing tonight."

As Mr. Mystery serenaded Tina around the dance floor, she became intoxicated; intoxicated with feeling of emotions that she had stored in her subconscious for what seemed like an eternity.

With each move, she gazed into the eyes of what she considered, the most gorgeous man in the world. The gaze wasn't going unnoticed, in fact, they were reciprocated. He had the most beautiful smile that ever graced a pair of lips, and his teeth were as perfect as pure pearls. The song ended, but Tina hadn't noticed; she kept dancing until Mr. Mystery slowly closed the gap between them and pulled her into his arms. She realized that the fast song had ended and a slower one had begun. As a baby falling onto their mother's shoulder for nap time, she laid her head ever so softly on his broad shoulders and closed her eyes. Not for a nap, but to bash in the moment. It had been a while since Tina felt comfort in the arms of a man.

When the song ended, Mr. Mystery walked Tina back to her table, pulled out the chair for her to sit, then slowly bowed as he backed away, turned, and left. "So, what's his name?" "I don't know." "Girl, stop playing around and tell me his name, you can trust me, I won't go after him." "I'm not playing Shanell, I really don't know his name, he didn't give it." "Well did you not ask for it?" Tina didn't answer Shanell, she did not want to spoil the feeling she was experiencing. "If he truly desires me as much as I him, she thought, he will return and let me know his name, but until then, he will remain my mystery man.

Tina, you know what you're doing right." "What are you referring to Shanell?" "You know what you're doing, you are playing hard to get." "If that wasn't so ludicrous it would be funny, hard to get, really Shanell?" "Then what do you call it, why didn't you ask him his name?" "Has it occurred to you that perhaps I don't want to know his name, that I am satisfied with the way things are?" "No Tina, it hasn't occurred to me because it makes absolutely no sense, we came here tonight with you hoping to see him and find out who he is and now you're telling me that you are fine not knowing. Something is wrong with your girl, want to share?"

Chapter Sixteen

Shanell's questions struck a nerve with Tina; it caused her to flashback to the day her brother raped her when she was nine years old. "Maybe I should tell her what her brother did to me, maybe then she will get of my case and leave me the hell alone." "Tina, why are you so quiet, what's wrong?" "Everything is wrong Shanell; I was just fine until you started grilling me about a name. I am not at all concerned about that man's name, for all I know he could be married." "You mean you never asked?" "No Shanell, I never asked, he asked me to dance, not to fly away into the sunset with him, I was just trying to have a little fun, but you are trying to marry me off to the highest bidder." "Come on Tina, wait a minute now, you were the one that wanted to come here tonight, and you were the one that wanted to see your mystery guy again, and you were the one that said you wanted to know his name, now I'm the villain?"

I'm sorry Shanell you're right; come on let's go home." "Oh, hell no, I am not going anywhere until I dance with the lonely man." "What lonely man?" "Just wait, you'll see him in a minute, oops, there he is, dancing alone in the middle of the floor." Despite Tina's feeling of outrage with herself, she had to laugh. "Girl you are one sick puppy." Shanell's joke seemed to have calmed Tina down a bit, but she was still not quite herself. "Tina, laying all jokes aside, you seem pretty tense, is everything ok, did that guy say something inappropriate to you, what has you in such a funky mood all of a sudden?" "I said I'm sorry, beyond that, there's nothing to report. Mr. Mystery was a perfect gentleman; he did, nor said anything inappropriate; I am just contented without knowing his name; that may change in the future if I should ever see him again, but as for now I'm fine.

Shanell was not satisfied with Tina's explanation and told her so. "I'm sorry if you don't believe me, but there are things from my past that you don't know about." "Girl, I know all of the important stuff; we have been joined at the hips since we were toddlers." "Yes, we were, but we did not spend every wakened moment together." "No, but we told each other everything." "Did we, did we really; are you saying that you told me every significant thing that happened in your lifetime?" "Yes, that is what I'm saying, didn't you?" "I would be lying if I said that I have, and if you maintain that you told me everything, you're lying too. Everyone have secrets, some are darker than others, and lord knows I have my share."

So, what does having skeletons in your closet to do with you not wanting to get some guy's name?" "Don't go there Shanell, let's just forget it; maybe it's one of those skeletons that I don't want to dig up, so, could we please drop it." "Ok, I will drop it for now, but if this happens again you have some splaining to do." "Okay, Shanell, she said laughingly, if it ever becomes necessary for you to know, I will splain it to you." "Now can we please go home, it's been quite a night," "Sure pooper we can go home." "Call me whatever you like, I don't give a dam, let's go." "Well ok then, I guess you told me."

When Tina and Shanell left the night club, instead of going straight home they made a detour to the all-night breakfast café. "I am starving Tina, and I don't have a thing at home to eat." "I know you're lying, but I will go with you anyway because I am still thirsty." When the girls arrived at the cafe the place looked deserted. "Where is everyone" asked Tina. "I don't know, but as long as the cook is here, I don't care." You are one greedy heifer." Shanell was about to respond to Tina calling her a heifer when the waitress came over to take their orders. "Save by the apron," Shanell said laughing.

Shanell ordered a double burger with a side of fries and an apple pie. "Oh, and a large coke too please." Tina just sat there looking at Shanell; are you really going to eat all that this time of night?" Shanell laughed and said, "I most certainly am, why, do you want some of it?" "No Shanell, I don't want any." "What can I get for you mam," the waitress asked, looking at Tina. "I'll have an omelet with toast and a large Pepsi, thank you." Well, I am not the only one hungry, I guess you worked up an appetite on the dance floor." "And I guess you worked up a bigger appetite minding my business." To anyone else, it would seem as if Tina and Shanell were fighting, but this was how they've always gotten along; to them, it's just friendship's love.

Tina and Shanell spent the next two hours just sitting and chatting long after they had finished eating their meals. "Tina, may I ask you something?" "That depends, Shanell." "Depends on what?" "Depends on what you want to ask." "Okay, that's fair; so, I will ask and if it's too personal for you to answer, I will not be offended." "If you think that it is a possibility that I may become offended, why ask?" "It's just that; well, the thing is, I mean;" oh come on out with-it Shanell, it's not like I can stop you." "Do you remember a long time ago when we were just kids, you came over to my house and" "no Shanell! No! Do not go there, believe me you do not want to know anything about that day and frankly, I don't want to relive it." "But Tina, as nice as you are and have been over the years, you became somewhat different that day." "Different how?" Tina knew exactly what Shanell was referring to, but just like all those years ago, she still had no intentions of sharing her secrets with her. "Just different, like closed off and secretive, we used to share everything, but you started keeping things from me. It made me wonder if it was something I did or said." "Shanell, sometimes in life we must do whatever it takes to survive, but you were never at fault for any negativity in my life; I love you as a sister and that will never change, but I beg of you, please don't ever asked me about that day again, just know it had nothing to do with you.

Tina did not want to spoil the relationship that Shanell had with her brother. He had become an alcoholic so that was punishment enough for him. Every time she saw him, she wondered if he remembered what he had done to her, and if he was sorry for what he did. Each time she saw him or heard his name called she struggled to keep her emotions hidden. "There's no need to put my friend through that, I love her too much." Also, once Shanell found out, what her brother that she idolized had done to her best friend our relationship would probably never be as great as it is now." As difficult as it was to drop the conversation, Shanell conformed. She did not want to do anything that would bring grief to her friend, yet she could clearly see that there was a story.

After the gruesome conversation with Shanell, Tina felt drained. "What a night she thought, this was supposed to have been a fun stress-free night, but now I am beginning to have regrets of ever going out tonight." What started out as a pleasant evening ended with Tina feeling down and depressed. "Shanell just had to bring up ancient history." What most people don't understand is that being abused in any form is a lifelong battle; you want to let go and hold on at the same time, and each time you believe that you have let go, something reminds you that you are still holding on. That's the position Tina was now battling in; it was as if all the work she had done to cover her past and her pain had resurfaced. Not just the incident with Shanell's brother, but her whole history. A history that included abuse, molestation, rape, bullying, and domestic violence.

When Tina arrived home after her bittersweet night, she did not go right in to see the children right away. She knew that Judy was there and that they were in good hands, so she went straight to her bedroom. Once inside, she sat on a side chair by the window, and stared into the darkness. There was nothing to see except blackness and that was what she was feeling. She felt dirty and alone as if she had not a friend in the world. Psychologically she didn't, because she had pushed everyone away from getting close to her and closed the door behind them. She always felt alone, even when she was in a crowd, but she'd convinced herself that everyone feels that way. After staring through the windowpanes for what seemed like hours, a teary-eyed Tina went into the bathroom to freshen up before checking on the children. She did not want Judy or the children to see her in such a funky mood.

After freshening up and drying the tears from her eyes, Tina put on her happy face and walked into the children's room. One would think that she had just won the lottery by the size of her smile. The kids were asleep as Tina figured they would be. She bent down and kissed each one on their little heads. Despite her efforts, a big tear the size of a raindrop fell on Tiana's little face; she wiggled and turned over causing Tina to broaden her smile. Judy was asleep in the next room and when she heard Tina's footsteps through the monitor, she immediately entered the room. "It's just me Judy." "I figured as much, but I needed to be sure." Tina gave Judy an affectionate hug to remind her of how special she was to her. "Good night honey, and thanks for being such a great nanny." "Good night, Tina, or shall I say good morning?" "Touché."

Tina returned to her room feeling a lot better than when she left. Seeing the children and talking with Judy had temporarily taken her mind off the memories she'd been having of her past. She walked over to her dressing table and looked in the mirror. She had an urge to talk to herself, so she began. Looking straight into her eyes, she began asking herself some serious questions. "Why are you so upset over something that happened to you all those years ago? Why can't you just turn it loose? Why have you not told anyone about what you experienced as a child and as a young lady? When will it end for you? What do you want to do about it, Tina? What are you going to do about it?"

With tears running down her face, Tina began to answer her own questions. "Hell, I have a right to be upset, I was just a child, an innocent child; I never asked for any of it, I just wanted to be a child, a happy child, but that was taken away from me, so yes, I am angry, angry as hell, and it doesn't matter how long ago it was there's no deadline for the pain I'm feeling. It may seem like a long time ago, but for me it was yesterday; turn it loose? I thought that I had, I thought that I had buried all those feelings and emotions and that they would stay buried, but someone or something keeps digging them up again. What good would it have done to tell anyone. No one would have believed me, and even if they had, just think of the shame and humiliation I would feel. Not to mention the questions I would have to answer. So, for me, keeping it hidden is my solution. The tragedy of what happened will never go away, but the effects of it should phase out at some point. I've thought about counseling, but that is not for me. I cannot see myself bearing my soul to some stranger and I refuse to tell it to anyone I know, so that's out. So, Tina, since you refuse to seek counseling, just how are you going to rise above this? I am going to stuff it way, deep down this time so no one will be able to dig it up again. As for Shanell, I don't think she will ask me about that day ever again and no one else knows or suspects anything." After her own private counseling session with the mirror, Tina walked back into her bedroom with dry eyes and strong convictions. She was more determined than ever to get through this without the aid of a therapist or anyone else. She crawled into bed, said her prayers, and fell asleep.

Chapter Seventeen

The next morning Tina was back to her old self. The self that had a great career and loving children as well as a loving and supportive mother. She sat on her bed and reminisced about some of the positive things in her life. She thought about her children and the joy they brought to her. She thought of how blessed she was to have a job that she loves, and a boss that appreciates her and recognizes her value as an employee. Most of the people she knew were dissatisfied with their jobs and some of them were even unhappy in their personal lives. "Well, I'm not on top of the moon in my personal life, but my family and professional lives are on target; I am going to do a little work on this personal thing." Tina smiled at the idea of having a personal life. It had been a while since she felt like dating and falling in love was out of the question. She was in a state of distrust when it came to romance. "Just look at that stupid guy at the club implying that I would lose by not dancing with his simple ass, hell, he's the freaking loser."

"Okay Tina, get your mind out of the gutter and go check on your children." Tina laughed as she responded to her thoughts; yep, that is exactly what I need to do, I am over thinking." Tina draped herself in her bathrobe and headed barefooted towards the kitchen where Judy was giving the children their breakfast. "Good morning, Judy" she said with a cheerful voice. "Good morning, Tina, you are very chipper this morning, is there something you want to tell me?" "Yes, there certainly is, you are the greatest nanny ever and I love you to pieces." "I love you too, but that was not what I was expecting." "What were you expecting me to say, that I met someone last night?" "Yes, that is exactly what I was hoping for, so did you?" "Not exactly." "What do you mean not exactly. Did you meet someone or not?" "I didn't actually meet him, but I did dance with him." "So, does him have a name?" "I'm sure he does, but I don't know what it is." "Okay." "Well, is that all you have to say, aren't you going to interrogate me too?" "No, I'm not, when you get ready to tell me, you will, until then I will patiently wait." "See that is one of the reasons I love you so much, you never push." "Well thanks, it's not that I don't care, I understand that sometimes people need their time and space to sort out and make decisions without distractions or inquiries." "Well, you're one in a million, most people would be curious." "Oh, I'm curious, believe me, I'm definitely curious." Tina laughed at how comical her friend was and asked, do you mind getting me a cup of coffee?" "Okay, changing the subject is good, one coffee coming up. Would you like some breakfast to go with that coffee?" "No, I think I'll skip breakfast this morning." "That's not good Tina, breakfast is your most important meal." Tina burst into laughter; "girl you sound just like my momma; it shows who raised you." Judy's parents had given her to her maternal grandparents when she was only two weeks old because they were young and immature and still in high school when she was born and had no means of caring for her. By the time they graduated, they had gone their separate ways. Her mother had gone off to college and her dad joined the Marines. "Yes, and they did a great job, that's why I know the importance of a good breakfast." "I certainly am glad that you know, I don't have to worry about my children's nutritional intakes." "No, you don't, I give them hot breakfasts every morning." "You're better than I am because it would be, cereal and milk, and maybe some fruit." "No, you wouldn't Tina, said Judy laughing, I've seen you in action, you are just as conscious as I am when it comes to eating healthy." "I guess you're right."

"Tina, are you and the children going to church this morning?" "No, we won't be going this morning, I'll take over here so that you can go home and get dressed." "Ok, I am not going to ask why." "Good, because I really don't feel up to explaining it, besides, you probably wouldn't understand." Tina was appreciative of Judy's ability to mind her own business. She did not feel the need to explain her decisions to anyone, especially her children's nanny. So, instead of going to church she got the children dressed and headed for her mom's house. She knew that her mother would be at church, but she would just sit and wait until she came home.

When Tina arrived at her mother's home, she unloaded the children and went inside using the key that her mom entrusted her with. Usually on Sundays Mrs. Watson gets up at the break of dawn and prepares her Sunday meal, but today, there was not a single thing on the stove cooked or cooking. "This is strange, I wonder what's going on; from the look of things, I may be the one that gets surprise." No matter what the situation, her children needed to be fed, so Tina went and checked out the fridge. "Dang if I'm in any mood for cooking, maybe I'll just take the kids out to eat, but I wonder what's going on with mom?" She didn't waste much time debating; she took off her shoes and put on a pair of her mother's slippers, and one of her aprons, and headed for the stove. "I am going to do this; I will shock the pants, or shall I say the choir robe right of her." Although Mrs. Watson taught all her girls to cook, having a nanny caused Tina to find herself in the kitchen less and less except for when it was time to eat. Her mom had not seen her cook in years.

Tina dragged out the pots and pans and began humming a little tune as she prepared to make a surprise dinner for her mom. She didn't have a lot of time because her mom is usually the first to leave church every Sunday. Tina wondered what the quickest thing would be to prepare. She took out some chicken and placed them in warm water to thaw. Then she pulled out a gourmet ham that her mom left in the fridge. "I am going to make a feast fit for a queen." When she was well into her meal, her brother Willis came in. "Oh, my goodness, girl, what are you doing? I thought momma was in here, but it's you?" "Yes, Willis it's me, why, you don't think I remember how to cook?" "Oh, I don't doubt your cooking abilities at all, you were always my favorite cook, but you didn't hear that from me. The thing is, I haven't seen you cook in a while." "And I didn't plan on it today either, by the way, do you know where momma is?" "What do you mean, do I know where she is? She's where she always is on Sundays, at church." "But why didn't she cook before she left the way she usually does?" "Oh, she was up late on last night, didn't get in bed until after midnight." "But why, that doesn't sound like her, she usually goes to bed as soon as the sun sets behind the trees. She isn't sick or anything, is she?" "No, mom's not sick, but Mrs. Lena came over crying about something they wouldn't let me in on, and they were up late in their secret room." "Good, as long as she's alright." "You're not curious about what they were talking about?" "Hell no, I've learned to mind my own business and stay out of everyone else's, I just hope everyone else would learn that lesson." "Dang sis, when did you become so hard core?" "Since I was burnt by life, which is most of my life, can we change the subject? How's tricks?"

Tina was almost finished cooking when her mom came in humming a song. When she walked into the front of the house, the aroma of the food cooking in the kitchen was shocking. Mrs. Watson had spotted both Tina and Willis's vehicles in the yard, and when she smelled the aroma of food, she assumed that Willis was heating himself a frozen dinner, but when she entered the kitchen and saw Tina standing over the stove with one of her aprons on, she gasped.

"What's wrong momma dear, cats gotcha tongue?" Mrs. Watson walked over to Tina and gave her an affectionate hug. "I was going to ask why you weren't in church today, but now all I can say is praise the Lord." Tina began laughing so loud that Willis joined in; Mrs. Watson just walked over to the stove and began peeking into the pots, ignoring their mockeries of her. "So, Tina what made you decide to cook a meal? Maybe I should miss cooking every Sunday." "You try it then, and see if you don't go hungry, this is a once in a lifetime deal." "Whatever the reason, I am grateful, thanks honey."

Tina had gone all out, she tried to cook everything she saw in her mom's refrigerator. She had roasted chicken with dressing, baked ham glazed with honey, wild rice, honey biscuits, snapped garden peas, candied yams, macaroni and cheese, and a green salad to die for. For dessert she had apple pie and peach cobbler both with whipped toppings. When Tina cooked, she cooked very differently than her mother, who cooked more traditional southern meals. Mrs. Watson found no complaints; she was just happy that for once in a long while she didn't have to do it.

"My complement to the chef," said a stuffed Willis. "Well thank you brother, and thanks for the complement earlier." "What complements Tina?" asked Mrs. Watson. "Willis said that I am his favorite sister." "I bet he did, the others are not here cooking for him." "Girl, you know that is not what I said, but for the sake of argument, I am going to leave it at that." Mrs. Watson was confused, but Tina did not feel compelled to explain any further.

"That was some dinner Tina, thanks so much." "You're welcomed ma, I'm glad that I could help." "Now do you want to tell me what's going on with you?" "What do you mean?" "Usually when you're not able to attend Church you bring the children to go with me, what happen today?" "Nothing happened, I just decided not to go, and I didn't feel up to dressing the children for church and bringing them here early this morning." "Well, you must have gotten here pretty early to have made such an elaborate dinner." "Yea, well can we drop it, I really just want to relax and enjoy the cool of the evening out on the porch." "Okay Tina, I taught you children to mind your own businesses, so I suppose I need to take a page from my own book. They all laughed and went out on the porch to enjoy what was left of a beautiful Sunday evening.

Chapter Eighteen

Three years had gone by since the night Tina danced with the nameless man at the club. She never found out his name and often wondered over the years who he was and why he never identified himself. Though she wondered, she never lost any sleep over it. Shanell seemed to have forgotten all about him, as she was caught up in her own world. She and her ex had reunited and were getting along poorly. Tina was more determined than ever to make it on her own. Both Shanell and Marley were struggling in their marriages, and she did not want that for herself nor for her children. She had met a couple of prospects that turned out to be just that, but nothing serious. It seemed that each time Tina met someone she would find some type of fault with them; he was either too short, too tall, too fat, too loud, too fast, too slow, talked too much, talked too little, or too something. So, she'd decided to take another break from dating, and for two years, she had not even gone out to dinner with a man.

Marley and Shanell were so busy trying to please those husbands of theirs to keep them off their behinds that they never went anywhere anymore except church. She had a couple of other friends, but their lifestyles were so different from hers. She was never much of a party girl, but they were, so that often caused conflict. Tina's mom had taught all her children well. She taught her daughters to be ladies, and her sons to be gentlemen always, and in every situation. Tina took her mother's teaching to heart and was always conscious of her behaviors. She was the tallest of her mother's six girls and had the body of a well-built statue. She was innocently beautiful. Others always saw that breathtaking beauty she possessed, but with everything she had endured, she refused to see what was in front of her eyes; she only saw herself as common looking. Whenever anyone commented or complimented her on her beauty, she felt insulted.

Tina's job was thriving, and she had climbed the corporate ladder. She was next in line for the position of chief executive officer of her company after her boss's retirement in a few years. The children were doing well in school, she had great relationships with her family members, and the center was doing what it was designed to do. "So, why do I feel so melancholy? I should be on top of the world; after all these years, I am still so terribly unhappy, even when I try not to be. I am still fooling everyone; I have gotten so good at it until I often fool myself." Tina was not all pensive, she had her moments of happiness with her children and family, but there was always that sense of something missing.

"Should I try again, should I put myself out there and run the risk of being violated and hurt?" This was a huge struggle for Tina. On the one hand she wanted to love, and be loved, but on the other hand, she was so afraid of being used and tossed aside, or even worse, being abused again. Tina thought, "life is about taking chances, so maybe now is the time for me to do that." Some of the ladies at her Church had told Tina that if she met a man in Church, he would be a good man, and would be good to her and to her children. "That is a bunch of bull-crap, most of my friends that are getting their asses kicked by their husbands attend church every Sunday with their no-good husbands sitting right next to them. I'll be doggone if I want one of those, I'd rather stay single for the rest of my life; besides, there aren't any single men in my church except for a couple old dried-up deacons. If I am going to do this, I am going to do it my way."

Once again, Tina believed that she was ready to get on with her life and find true love. She even found herself flirting a little with some of the single guys at work, there was one in particular, by the name of Hanson. During Tina's marriage to Derrick, Hanson, one of her coworkers, was also married so she never gave him a second glance. Three years after Tina's divorce from Derrick, Hanson lost his wife in an automobile accident. Many of the women on the job were after him before the ashes cool from his wife's cremated body. Tina remembered giving him a sympathy card, but she never once thought of him in any other capacity other than a coworker. She felt sorry for him when he first lost his wife because he had a sadness on his face that she knew all too well, for different reasons, but sad just the same. Once when she saw him crying when he thought no one was looking, she had gone over to him and suggested he take some time off from work to allow himself time to heal. Hanson was grateful and decided to take her up on her generous offer. Little did she know he would take several weeks, but she did not question his absence. When he returned to work, he seemed stronger, and as before, the ladies were all over him; this time though he didn't seem to mind so much.

Hanson was an information technologist and was exceptionally good at his job. In fact, he was being considered by the executive board for the position of senior vice president. Tina was on that board and felt that Hanson was a great choice. She was asked to interview him as a formality, then offer him the position. During the interview, Tina looked at Hanson for the very first time. All before, she saw him as an employee and colleague, but not as a man. But now this handsome gentleman was sitting across from her with a smog smile on his face causing her to feel a little flush. She found herself out of her safety zone, she was always in control even when she wasn't, but this, wow, this was so new.

"So, Ms. or is it Mrs. Tina?" "Tina will be fine thanks." "Great, so Tina, what is the possibility of me being offered the position?" "Your chances are as good as any, better than most." "When will I know the outcome?" "Either by the end of the day, or first thing in the morning, I still have a few more interviews to conduct," Tina lied. "Oh, I see, will it be ok if I called you at home later this evening? I won't be able to sleep wondering if I was chosen." "Will you be able to sleep if I tell you that you were not chosen?" "Good point, but I think I would sleep better if I knew, regardless of which way the ball rolls." "Sure, why not, give me a call after seven and before eight." "Precise, I like that, so am I free to leave now?" Yes Mr. McGrady, you are free to leave." "Now who's formal, would it be disrespectful if I asked you to call me Hanson?" "Of course not, Hanson, enjoy the rest of your day."

When Hanson left the boardroom Tina could finally exhale. She had been trying her best not to flirt, but her eyes and sexy voice tone gave her away. "Woo! That Hanson is one sexy fellow, if he wasn't a co-worker, I don't know what might happen." Tina had made a point over the years of not mixing business with pleasure, and although she had not implemented any rules to that effect, she highly believed that romance and work just don't work well together. With new emotions that were stirring up inside of her, she was rethinking her position. "I see why these women are all over him, he's quite the catch." Tina was even more impressed that Hanson didn't fall into the prey of those women's schemes. He stood his ground, and as far as she knew, he was not dating anyone.

When Tina got home from work around five thirty, she had forgotten about Hanson's call. After checking in on the children, she took a long bath. As she was coming from the bathroom with only a towel wrapped around her body, her phone began to ring. "Who could that be?" Tina's first thought was to not answer and call back whomever it was later when she'd settle in, but instead she rushed over and picked up her phone. Because she had never spoken to Hanson from her personal phone, his name did not appear in the caller ID. "Hello," she said in a cavalier voice. "Hello Tina, is this a bad time?" "Oh, hello, no, it's fine, I mean your timing is fine." "You promised to put me out of my misery and tell me if I am being offered the position." "Yes, I did, didn't I." "Well, that doesn't sound too promising." "Mr. McGrady, the board has decided to offer you the position of Senior Vice President if you are agreeable to the terms." "Oh, hell yea, I'm agreeable, thank you so very much." "Mr. McGrady, you have not heard the terms of the agreement, will you have some time first thing in the morning to come by my office for the details?" "Yes, I will be there, but first I need to correct something." "What is it?" Tina thought that she may have said something inappropriate or offensive. "We promised not to be so formal with each other, and you called me Mr. McGrady." "I always address my constitutes professionally when conducting business, even my closest friends." "So, am I one of them?" "One of them who?" "Your closest friends?" "Let's just say we may be getting there." "I'll accept that, as long as it doesn't take too long before I'm added to that special list." "We shall see Mr. McGrady, we shall see." "Hanson." "Okay Hanson, we shall see, in the meantime, have a pleasant night." "Good night, Tina, same to you, and thanks for everything."

After Tina said goodnight to Hanson, she hung up the phone with an inquisitive look on her face. "Huh, that was interesting; I wonder if his not being able to wait until tomorrow just an excuse to call me, either way, it was nice chatting with him." Tina's mind drifted off to the land of Tina and Hanson; in that dream they were engaging in deep conversation with him gazing deeply into her eyes, while she drank every moment of it. "Come on Tina, don't get ahead of yourself, he may not even be interested in you, there's a lot of women on the job that looks far better than you do, so why would he choose you over them?" Oh, if only she could see herself the way others did. After all these years, she had no idea of the magnitude of her femininity. To her she was just a brainy nerd with no beauty and no sex appeal.

The next morning, Tina was more excited than usual to get to work. She always loved her job, but today was going to be special. Today is the day she got to meet with Hanson again and look into those big brown sexy eyes. Today may be the beginning of a new life for her. After spending time with the children as she did every morning before they left for school, Tina picked up her purse and laptop and headed towards the door. "Whoa Tina! Why the rush, are you running late for a meeting?" "No, but I do need to get in to work a little earlier than usual, there's something I need to prepare for before the others arrive." Judy learned early in her and Tina's relationship to mind her own business when it came to Tina, so she asked no further questions. "Be safe Tina and have a wonderful day." "Thanks Judy, you do the same and I will see you later this evening."

Tina arrived at her office thirty minutes earlier than she normally would. She wanted to make sure that she was calm and composed when Hanson arrived. When she drove into the parking lot, just as she expected, it was empty. "Good, she thought, now I don't have to answer any questions as to why I'm here so early." Once inside the building, she walked across the hall that separated her office from her boss's, opened the door, and walked in. She looked around as if she had never seen the inside of her office before today; then, walked over to her desk and planted herself in her cushioned leather chair. "Aw, this is what I'm talking about, all I need now is a steamy cup of coffee."

Five minutes after she'd entered her office and made herself comfortable, there was a knock on her door. "Yes, come in." Tina was wondering who had the same idea as she did, coming in early. "Could it be Hanson, is he in such a mood that he couldn't wait until office hours to come in?" She didn't have to wonder for long, because the door was pushed open and in came Mr. Douglas, her boss. "Good morning, sir, what has you coming in so early this morning?" Mr. Douglas was a punctual man, but he didn't do early. "I could ask you the same thing, but I won't, I know you like to keep your privacy." Tina laughed and said, that's generally my rule but not for you Mr. Douglas, not for you." "I guess you're wondering why I'm here." "Yes sir, it has crossed my mind." "Well, I wanted to be here when you break the news to McGrady about his promotion; you know he's very special to me, and ever since his wife's death, I have taken it upon myself to keep a close eye on him; wouldn't want him falling into the wrong hands, if you know what I mean." Tina was about to tell Mr. Douglas that she had already given Hanson the news when a second tap on the door interrupted her.

Instead of Tina calling out for the tapper to come in, she walked over to the door and opened it. "Good morning, Tina, I mean Ms. Bradshaw, am I too early?" After the divorce from Derrick, Tina held on to her married name so that she and her children would identify with the same last names. "Good morning Mr. McGrady, and yes, Ms. Bradshaw will do just fine." Mr. Douglas was listening to the exchange of greetings between Tina and Hanson. His eyebrows raised at the cool way they addressed each other and the ease with which they did it. He cleared his throat to remind Tina that he was still in the room. "Oh, come on in Hanson, Mr. Douglas has been waiting for you to arrive." Hanson walked around Tina and extended his hand towards Mr. Douglas; "good morning, sir, it's good to see you." Mr. Douglas responded by placing his hand into Hanson's and returning the greeting with a handshake and a smirky grin.

"Mr. Douglas, I was just about to explain to you that Mr. McGrady already knows about the outcome of the interview, when he knocked on the door." "He does, when did that happened, I thought that I got here before he did." "You did sir, said Hanson, but I was so anxious about the outcome that I bothered Ms. Bradshaw to tell me the results last night." "Oh, is that so?" "I'm sorry Mr. Douglas, I thought that it was ok to give him the results since I was the one that interviewed him, and ultimately made the decision to choose him over the other two candidates." "You're right, which is why I am so early, I wanted to get ahead of him and get in on the action; I wanted to see the look on his face when you told him." "Well sir, my face looked like this," as Hanson made a happy facial expression. The three of them exploded into laughter at the silly face he made. "Tina, what do you say the three of us have dinner to celebrate unless you have other plans." "I don't have any other plans responded Tina, what about you Hanson, is tonight good for you?" "Sure, I'm free tonight, a celebratory dinner sounds like just the thing I need." "So tonight, it is, seven good for the both of you?" Both Tina and Hanson agreed that seven would be fine. Mr. Douglas began walking towards the door, then stopped, slowly turned around, and said as he winked his eye, "see you guys tonight." "Hanson turned and looked at Tina, "what was that?" "Who knows, just Mr. Douglas being Mr. Douglas, so shall we get this meeting started?" "We shall mam, but first, I want to thank you again for choosing me, I promise to make you proud." "I know you will Hanson, I know you will."

The meeting with Hanson went as Tina had hoped; they were able to cover a large amount of material in a brief period. Hanson was a fast learner, which made it easier on Tina. When they had finished going over the highpoints of his new position, Tina handed Hanson a stack of papers to take to the human resource office. "Once all of these are completed and recorded you will be all set. Your new position will officially start at the beginning of workday on Monday, are you ready?" "As ready as can be, looking forward to it." "So now Mr. McGrady, all that is left for me to do is show you to your new office, shall we." "After you, my lady." When Tina and Hanson arrived at his new office, Tina stepped aside and gestured towards the door for Hanson to open it. He humbly did as he was directed. When he pushed the door open, Mr. Douglas was standing inside with a chilled bottle of champagne and three glasses. "Congratulation McGrady, I couldn't let Ms. Bradshaw have all the fun, I figured I would up one on her." "So that's what the wink and the smirky grin was about." "What wink, what smirky grin?" Thy all burst into laughter at Mr. Douglas's humor.

After congratulating Hanson again on his appointment, and giving a touching toast, Mr. Douglas left the office leaving Hanson and Tina alone. Hanson stared into Tina's eyes as he walked closer towards her. "I have a question for you." "What is it?" "Would it be considered sexual harassment if I hugged you?" "Why of course not, I think that a hug would be appropriate for this occasion." Hanson walked over to where Tina stood, and slowly and gently pulled her into his arms. "This is not how this is supposed to go, he's supposed to give me a grateful embrace and let me go." As he held her, Tina did not have the strength to pull away, so she encircled his waist with her arms and gave him a strong but gentle hug. When she finally found the strength to pull away from him, he slowly let her go just enough that he could look into her eyes again. "So, if I kiss these beautiful lips, would that be sexual harassment?" Tina opened her mouth, but nothing came out. Hanson lowered his head so that his lips could reach hers and placed them gently on hers; as she responded, the gentle kiss became a passionate romantic kiss that Tina did not see coming. They were both caught up in the excitement of the moment and neither wanted to be the first to let go. They stayed in a locked position for several minutes before Tina got the energy to push him away. "You had better get those papers down to HR and I had better get to my office and get some work done." Tina slowly dragged herself away from Hanson, while he just stood still and watched her as she walked away.

When Tina returned to her office, she was flushed to say the lease. She sat at her desk and relived everything that had just taken place. She was so caught up in her thoughts that she didn't hear the knock at her door, nor did she hear when someone entered. "Good morning, Tina. Good morning, Tina! Startled, Tina jumped to her feet to see who had entered her office without knocking. "You scared the hell out of me Diane, why didn't you knock, suppose I was doing something important." "I did knock but you didn't answer so I came on in. I saw when you left out of McGrady's new office, so I followed you to see how things went." "Things went as they should have, what's the interest?" "What's the interest? I know you've notice that he's available, every gal around this building is after him." "And are you one of those gals?" "I certainly am, and I don't plan to let him slip through my fingers." "How do you plan to catch him, has he shown any interest?" "Sure, we've gone out several times, as a matter of fact I am making him dinner tonight." "Does he know?" "Does he know what?" "That you are making dinner for him tonight?" "Of course, he knows, we planned this night two days ago." "Ok, have fun, in the meantime I need to get back to work, was there something you needed?" "Not really, just wanted to see how things went with Hanson, but I guess I will just go and see for myself." "Great, you do that; see you later."

Tina could hardly wait for Diane to leave her office; she was steaming, but mostly with herself. "Did I underestimate his character, I thought that he was a standup man, is he really that lose?" Tina started to cry; "why did I make such a fool of myself; I can't compete with Diane, she's everything that I'm not. She's young, beautiful, and outspoken, I could never win over her;

besides, I don't have the energy to fight for any man, I've done enough sharing for a lifetime, and I don't plan to go down that road again. Hold on Tina girl, the man only gave you a kiss, he didn't ask you to marry him, for God's sake get a grip." Tina took some tissue from her desk and dried the tears from her eyes, when she'd calmed down, she decided to put the whole thing out of her mind. She was doing a pretty good job of not thinking about Hanson when she heard someone knocking on her door. "What now, I just don't feel up to another visitor today asking about McGrady's appointment. Yes, who is it?" "It's me McGrady may I come in?" "I am sorry Mr. McGrady, but I am really behind on my work and need to catch up, I don't have time right now, but you may schedule an appointment with my assistant." Hanson was confused; "Oh hell, I think I did too much too soon; is everything alright Tina?" "Why do you ask, why wouldn't everything be alright?" I don't know, you seem upset about something, I'm sorry if I crossed the line, if it's upsetting you, I promise that it will never happen again." "No, it won't, just forget it, I have, and by the way, you need to tell Mr. Douglas that you have other plans for tonight and won't be able to have dinner with him." "Why would I do that?" "You wouldn't want to disappoint Diane, after all, she has gone through a great deal of trouble making dinner for you tonight." "Where would you get an idea like that?" "From the horse's mouth?" "Are you telling me that Diane told you that she is making dinner for me tonight?" "Yes Hanson, that's what I'm saying, so you need to call Mr. Douglas and cancel, I am not going to do it for you." "In The first place, Diane can barely boil water, and in the second place, I do not have a dinner date with her or anyone tonight except you and Mr. Douglas, and that is where I plan to be." "So how do you know that Diane can't cook?" "That is a story for another time, but right now my concern is about you, I never meant to upset you. I find you very attractive, and my actions reflected those feelings. I thought you felt the same way, but if I'm mistaken, I apologize, and will refrain from ever touching you again." "Thanks, that would be greatly appreciated." Hanson mumble under his breath, "women, boy you sure can't figure them out, as he walked out of Tina's office and closed the door behind him.

Chapter Nineteen

When Hanson returned to his office, he was thinking about what had just happened. He thought how wonderful it felt kissing and holding Tina in his arms. It had been several months since he was that close to a woman, and he would treasure it forever. He wondered why Diane would tell Tina such a blatant lie. His head was in a totally different place from Tina's, he thought that she was just angry with him because she believed there was something going on between him and Diane, and as soon as he explained to her that there wasn't, things would be ok between them. On the other hand, Tina was thinking just the opposite. She was feeling like a fool because she was so weak. "How could I have allowed myself to give in to the temptation of a loose man?" Tina swore that she would never have anything else to do with Hanson, and there was nothing he could say or do to convince her otherwise. Hanson's plan was to give Tina enough time to settle down while he confronted Diane about her accusations. "When I see her tonight, she will have gotten over it, and we can pick up where we left off." Little did he know how guarded Tina was, and that once she made up her mind about a person or situation, it took the jaws of life to get her to see it differently.

Tina was reluctant to keep the dinner appointment with Hanson and Mr. Douglas, but how would she explain it to Mr. Douglas without either lying or telling him what happened. So, she decided that she would go despite her feelings, just to save face with Mr. Douglas. When she arrived at the restaurant, both Hanson and Mr. Douglas were already there and seated. When they saw her coming towards the table, both men stood. Hanson went over and pulled the chair for Tina as she slowly lowered herself into a sitting position. "Thank you, Hanson." "Sure." Mr. Douglas picked up on the tension between the two and asked, "is everything alright between you two?" Tina and Hanson answered at the same time; "oh yes sir, everything's great." "Good, because I was beginning to think that this may not have been such a good idea." "Why do you say that?" "I'm not sure Hanson, am I picking up on some tension between the two of you?" Tina jumped in and answered before Hanson could; "It's my fault sir, I accepted this invitation on a whim without realizing that tonight is my children's babysitter's night off. I had somewhat of a struggle getting them to a sitter and then getting here, that's the reason I was a little late; otherwise, things are fine." Mr.

Douglas exhaled as he said to the two; well that certainly is a relief; I'm sorry you had such a rough evening, but I am glad it has nothing to do with riff between you two, I have great plans for the both of you." Hanson was intrigued; "Oh really, and what might that be?" "Just you wait and see my boy, just you wait and see." Hanson stretched his eyes and looked at Tina but decided not to respond any further.

Dinner was a strain for Tina, but she managed to get through it with her dignity intact. Hanson on the other hand was miserable, he was wondering what was on Tina's mind and had a difficult time restraining himself from getting personal with her. Every now and then, he would throw a quick glance in her direction; Tina missed each glance, but Douglas never missed one. "Something is definitely going on with these two so I think I will make myself scarce, maybe they will be able to work it out." When Mr. Douglas had finished his dinner, he yarned and said to Tina and Hanson; "It's past my bedtime, I think I'm going to leave you too kids to finish off desert. Congratulations again Hanson, Tina could not have made a better choice, good night." Tina opened her mouth to object, but Mr. Douglas was off. "That was strange." "What, that he left before desert?" "That he left period, dinner was his idea." "I think that he picked up on the tension between us and wanted to give us some time alone." "Are there tension between us, I hadn't notice." "Come on Tina, you know that this evening is filled with tension, I certainly didn't mean to put you in an uncomfortable position, I think we need to talk." "Yes Hanson, let's talk." "Would you like desert?" "No, I do not want desert, I want to talk per your suggestion."

"Listen Tina, I am sorry that Diane lied to you and made it seem as if we have something going on, we do not now, nor have we ever, been in a relationship, and we never will. You asked me earlier how I knew that she couldn't cook, well I am around those ladies all the time and I heard them talking. She said herself that she can barely boil water, I just repeated what she said." "It's ok Hanson, I got carried away earlier in your office; the excitement from the day along with the fact that I haven't kissed a man in a very long-time sort of caught up with me. Please forgive my behavior, my mother taught me better than that." "So, you are not angry with me?" "No, I'm not angry with you." "Dam! I almost wish you were." "Why is that?" "Then we would get to make up, but the way you are talking, I don't see anything happening for a long time if ever." "You're right, I had time to think this through. I have made it a point during my entire career not to get involve with anyone working at the same organization as I, that way there would be no awkwardness when things don't work out." "So, what are you saying Tina, am I just supposed to forget about what happened between us?" "Yes Hanson, you are to just forget it; it was only a kiss, nothing more." "Suppose I can't forget it, then what?" "You will, you have enough ladies or shall I say women around to keep you occupied." "That's cold Tina, could we at least be friends?" "Yes, I would like that, but anything beyond that is out of the question." "May I have a hug to say goodbye to our romance?" "Sure, this is not goodbye, it's hello to our friendship." Tina and Hanson walked over and held each other close, but this time she was in control. She looked up at Hanson, and he noticed something different than before; she was confident in her stand, not timid and submissive as before. He realized at that moment that if he was ever to have an intimate relationship with this one, he had his work cut out for him.

Chapter Twenty

Life for Tina was consistent; she had stuck by her decision not to become romantically involved with a co-worker. It was more difficult for Hanson in the beginning, so he kept trying. After several firm rejections, he finally gave up and accepted that there would never be anything more between him and Tina than friendship. He had moved on with someone outside of the office and had become engaged. Tina was a little jealous at first and wondered if she had made a big mistake by allowing him to get away. When she saw how happy he was, she knew that she had made the right decision. "I would never have been able to make him that happy, she thought. He's been through so much in his lifetime and I need a man that can help hold me up, not one that I am responsible for holding up." Tina and Hanson had become such good friends that they were often referred to as being joined at the hips, even his fiancée joked about it. Whenever she needed advice concerning important decisions, Hanson was the first one she would call. No matter what he was doing, he always stopped and made time for her.

Although Tina continued to see her friends, Shanell, and Marley from time to time, she felt a disconnect between them. They had chosen to remain in dysfunctional relationships for some unknown reasons, and she refused to subject herself to that environment. She left her husband because of cheating and abusive behaviors, so she be dammed if she was going to sit and watch them get abused. Late one evening, Shanell called Tina crying and complaining about something her husband Nash had done. "What are you planning to do about it, Shanell?" "I don't know, I am tired of him beating on me and accusing me of things I never did, and to top it off, I found naked pictures of him and his mistress." "Are you really questioning what you need to do?" "Yes, I am, I love him and don't want to lose him." "Well, from where I stand, it sounds as if you have already lost him, that is, if you've ever had him in the first place." "Tina, please tell me, what do you think I should do?" "I think you should ask yourself that question then answer yourself, but I am not going to be the one to tell you what you should do. I will tell you this though; for anything else you need you can call on me, but if you continue in that relationship the way it is now, don't call me in the middle of the night to complain. All I have to say is, leave him, or stay with him and shut the hell up, if I wanted to deal with that type of drama, I would be dealing with my own. I didn't leave my ex-husband, so that I could battle the same situation with you. So, now that I've said my piece, I hope you find the answers you're looking for; good night, Shanell."

"Shanell was stunned by Tina's assertiveness, her friend had never spoken to her that way, she was always able to dump all her troubles right into Tina's lap. "Well good riddance to her, who needs her anyway?" Shanell was angry that Tina had stood up for herself, but deep down she knew that her friend was right. She would wait until both cool off and apologize to Tina for calling her so late at night and being such a nuisance. But for now, she had to figure out what she was going to do with the rest of her life.

Marley was also dealing with a lying, cheating, abusive husband but she chose to handle hers in a different way. She felt that no matter what she did or said she would be accused of wrongdoings, so she decided to make it a reality. "At least when I get my behind whipped, I would have deserved it," she said. Marley was not one to share her private life easily, but one evening when she and Tina had gone shopping, she decided to share her story with Tina. "Girl, you know that's wrong; two wrongs just don't make a right; don't you believe that you deserve better than that, what will you say if your children found out what you're doing?" "To be honest with you Tina, I have gotten to a place where I don't care about much of anything, I feel trapped." "I wish I could tell you what to do Marley, but I refuse to get in the middle of anyone else's relationship, what I will say is that the game you're playing is a dangerous one; be careful." "I know what I'm doing is wrong, my parents didn't raise me that way, but it feels so great to have someone love me and appreciate me; if I wasn't so afraid of Jamal, I would leave him and be with the other guy, who's name I won't mention." "What are you afraid of?" "Jamal has threatened that if I should ever leave him, he will kill me and the children." "That is serious Marley, I don't think that you should try to handle it alone, you need some type of intervention." "I have reported him so many times and he's gotten out after a few days, or after paying a fine, and goes right back to the same old things. I just don't know what else I can do." "Have you thought of going to a women's shelter?" "No, I haven't but he would just find me, I've got to figure this out, and sooner or later I will. Thanks, Tina, for taking time to listen to my problems, I didn't mean to burden you with them." "You didn't bother me at all, I just hope that you find a solution soon." Tina was much gentler with Marley than with Shanell because Marley was somewhat naïve and extremely sensitive." Her main concern for her was that Jamal didn't hurt her or the children, and that she gave thought to what she was doing behind his back. "Oh, well, she thought, I am only one person, I cannot solve all the world's problems."

With all the drama going on in her friends' lives, Tina was almost contented with her boring life, only thing, she wasn't one hundred percent contented. Over the years she had done some casual dating, and even got somewhat close to a couple of guys. Each time she'd allowed herself to meet a gentleman, she would put up the wall or close the door just when things began to get serious. She was still living in her past, without realizing or acknowledging that she was. One of the men she dated was really into her but told her that he could no longer see her because she was comparing him to other men in her life. She denied that it was true and told him to get lost. After he left, she cried for days because she had really begun to feel him and had hopes that something permanent could develop between them. "How can I expect someone to love me when I have such a hard time loving myself?"

The toll of everything that happened in Tina's life had really left her taunted towards herself. Even on her best days she questioned the validity of her sanity. She wondered if she was normal and most of the people she knew, were abnormal. Most of the time, Tina coped well with her issues and never gave them much thought, but when someone went to the trouble of telling her that she was frayed, she would revisit her past, and had to start all over. So, to defend herself and her emotions, she developed a kick ass attitude. No one was ever going to mess with her again in any capacity and if they tried, they would receive a dose of her venom.

Despite herself. Tina had to laugh. Everyone thought that she was mean and tuff, and she was at times, but mainly she just wanted to be loved. Her sense of love was different from most people, but she didn't know it. For Tina, love meant being underfoot twenty-four seven; not getting out of her eyesight without giving an account. It also meant she was always in control of what took place in the relationship; she called the shots and expected everyone else to conform. She did not believe in fifty-fifty, forty-sixty, thirty-seventy, or ninety-ten, she believed it was her way or the highway, and all sacrifices should be made by other people, not her. She could not see that she needed help. In her opinion, she overcame her atrocious life each time someone or something reminded her of them, and she was able to push it back into her subconscious. To her that meant victory.

Chapter Twenty-One

After many years of trials-and-errors, Tina decided to give up, she was no longer interested in pursuing a relationship. Both of her children had graduated high school and gone off to college, her oldest DJ, had graduated college and was working at his dream job as an electric engineer. Her daughter Tiana was a senior in college and would be graduating in a few weeks. Life seemed good to Tina, she had managed with the help of her mother and her nanny to raise two marvelous children. Several years back, her boss Mr. Douglas retired and left her as his predecessor. She was now Chief Executive Officer of the company, and Hanson had moved up to President. Because of her job and her ability to invest and save, neither of her children needed to borrow money for their college tuitions. She felt blessed, because when she graduated from college, she started life in debt with student loans the size of her annual salary. When she was promoted to C.O.O, her salary increased enough that she was able to get a traditional fixed loan and paid off her remaining student loan in full. So, although she had to face debt as a young woman starting out, she was still blessed more so than some others that were not fortunate enough to get rid of their student loans so quickly.

Each milestone Tina overcame, she gave thanks. When she turned thirty, when she turned forty, when her children graduated high school and college, and now that she was approaching fifty, she was extremely grateful. After a short sabbatical from Church, she returned with a different perspective; she no longer felt the need to join all the committees in the church, but she did like singing so she joined and remained a member of the choir. She was a normal Christian not trying to prove anything to anyone, but she was sincere about her commitments. She also took it upon herself to organize an advocacy program for battered women. She felt that this would be a way to help women who were not as fortunate as herself. When she first started the program, she only had five members, but in less than a year, she had over one hundred women that were either being abused or had been the victim of abuse at some point and time. With so much going on, Tina had forgotten about her own troubled past. When one of the women would ask what made her decide to open a women's shelter and start such a program, she would just smile and say, "because it's my destiny, my calling."

When Tina made the decision to remain single, she knew that she would have some lonely nights, but that would be better than some of her past relationships. "How did I allow myself to get caught up in some of those situations?" Tina was never physically abused by any of the men she dated after Derrick, but they just didn't seem to add up. They were either too demanding, boring, cheaters, or had drinking problems.

One of those men was Ernie Capers. Tina met Ernie on a cruise ship. He was tall and handsome with a perfect body. During the cruise she noticed that Ernie was mainly alone. She wanted to know if he was single, but she didn't want to just go up and ask him, so she solicited the help of one of her friends to find out for her. "What do you want me to do Tina, just go up and ask him point blank?" "I don't know Janice, just do what you do, you are good at stuff like that." "Sure, I am, you're just saying that because you need me to do something for you." "Oh, go ahead girl, you know you got this," with a sly grin on her face. Janice did pride herself at getting information out of people, so she was up for the challenge. After walking around and snooping around, she finally got the answer she was seeking.

"So, what is the verdict, is he single or not?" "Jackpot! Not only is he single, but he has never been married." "Well, is he straight or gay?" "Straight as an arrow." "So why is he still single?" "Maybe he's been waiting for you." "I doubt that, but maybe he's been waiting for some of the same things I have." "And what's that Tina?" "Darn if I know, but I'll recognize it when I see it." "Thanks Janice, you did a great job and so fast." "That's me, fast mama." Both ladies laughed as Tina inched her way towards the corner of the dance floor where Ernie was standing alone. "Hello there, she said in her sexiest voice; I'm Tina." "Hello Tina, I'm Ernie." "Does Ernie have a last name?" "Yes, Capers, Ernie Capers he said a little hesitantly; and do you have a last name Ms. Or is it Mrs. Tina?" "Yes, I do, Bradshaw, and it's Ms. Bradshaw." "Very nice meeting you Ms. Bradshaw, are you alone or just getting some space?" "I'm with a couple of my female friends, but other than that, yes, I am alone; what about you?" "Same here, a buddy and I decided to go on this cruise together to celebrate his freedom." "Freedom from where, was he in prison?" "Yep, the prison call marriage, he recently divorced his wife after years of being abused by her."

Tina was amazed; she knew that men were victims of domestic violence, but to hear him say it was simply astonishing. The first thought that came to her mind was that he must have provoked her somehow for her to retaliate. "Come on Tina, you know darn well that there is no excuse for anyone putting their hands on anyone else, male or female, so get a grip." Instead of responding to the comment that Ernie made, she just nodded her head and said, "well Ernie, it was a pleasure meeting and talking with you, but my friends will be sending out a search party if I don't show up soon;" then she walked away without waiting for his response.

Tina was intrigued by Ernie, but she did not want him to know it, at least not for a while. She located her friends at the bar and went over and joined them. The band was playing a slow song and she was waving her body to the beat of the music when someone tapped her on the shoulder and asked if she wanted to dance with him. She was about to say no thanks, when she turned and saw Ernie standing there with his hand stretched out towards her. Without saying a word, she jumped down from the stool where she was sitting and placed her hand in his. "Of course, you may," she said.

Tina and Ernie hit the dance floor and danced to every song the band played. They even entered the ship's dance contest and won. By the end of the cruise, Tina was in love. She found out that Ernie lived in the same city as she did, and only a forty-five-minute drive away. She was thrilled at the idea of dating him when she returned home. The children were all grown up and she didn't have to worry about how they would feel or react to her dating. She was on a natural high and looked forward to getting home and starting a new life with more hope for her future. It had been a long time since she was that enthusiastic or even optimistic about a future other than the one, she'd been living.

When the cruise came to an end, and Tina walked back on land, she kissed the ground. "This is it she thought, this is finally my beginning." During Tina's entire life, she would hear different ones using the expression, "today is the first day of the rest of my life," now she understood exactly what they meant. "Today is, the first day of the rest of my life, and I am going to live it as if there's no tomorrow. I've spent a lot of time alone, but now, no more lonely days or nights. Tina felt special when she exited the cruise ship with Ernie walking beside her. "I may have entered alone, but I am definitely not leaving alone."

Janice was relatively new in Tina's friends' circle and had no idea of all she had been through, but for some reason she felt that Tina was moving too fast with Ernie. She also felt a little purge of guilt because of the role she played in connecting them. "Suppose something is wrong with him, we know absolutely nothing about his background. Suppose he's a serial killer or worse, a rapist or child molester." With all these thoughts running through her head, it was difficult for Janice to be happy for her friend and it showed up on her face.

"What is it Janice, you seem distracted, is anything wrong?" No Tina, nothing is wrong, why would you ask?" "As I stated, you seem distracted, did you not enjoy yourself on the cruise?" "Of course, I did, I had a blast." "Something is going on with you, is everything alright at home?" "Tina I'm good, the question is, are you okay?" "Do I not look okay? I am ten feet off the ground right now." "Is that because of Ernie?" "Well yeah, who do you think? I've got to thank you again for paving the way for me, everything else was easy." "You don't have to thank me again, but I do wish you would listen to me." "Listen to you about what Janice, you are beginning to worry me, what's going on?" "After I spoke with Ernie something didn't feel right so I called a friend of mine and asked her to do a little digging." "You did what? Digging? Where and for what?" "Digging into Ernie's past." "Okay, and what if anything did you discover?" "It seems that he's a little weird." "Weird, is that a crime? I remember when people thought I was weird, but look at me now,

I am a successful businesswoman, a mother of two wonderful children, and founder of a women's haven, not to mention all the other things I have accomplished. I am not boasting, but being a nerd pays off sometimes." "I didn't say he was a nerd, I' said he is considered weird." "By whom? Janice, you never struck me as someone that would gossip about someone else's character." "You're right, I'm not, but that doesn't change the fact that I'm worried about you." "Well don't, I'm a big girl, I know how to take care myself."

Janice was a little offended as well as annoyed by her friend's attitude. Her only interest was that Tina didn't get caught up in a situation like the women she advocated for. When Janice first met her husband, she knew absolutely nothing about him, so she demanded a resume and a background check. When she first told him that was what she required before going any further with their relationship, he was hesitant, but when he realized that it was his only ticket to her, he gladly complied. "Tina, I am simply telling you what was told to me I have no ulterior motives." "Then mind your own business Janice, as I stated, I am perfectly capable of taking care of myself, and if I need to conduct an investigation on him, I am well qualified to do so; so, if you don't mind, can we just drop it, Ernie is waiting for me." After Tina gave Janice a small piece of her mind, she turned and walked away. "Well, that was downright rude, I hope she doesn't regret not listening to me."

Chapter Twenty-Two

As Tina walked away from Janice in search of her new love, Ernie, she felt bad about the way she handled things with her. Deep down she knew that she should find out more about Ernie's background, especially since Janice seemed to think he was weird. "Usually where there's smoke, there is bound to be a little fire; once the dust settles with Ernie and me, I may ask him about his past, but for now, I am just going to trust that he is the man he's presenting to me."

Nothing or no one could bring Tina down from the mountain she had climbed upon, not even Janice. She was determined not to have another failed relationship. She spotted Ernie and began walking towards where he was standing. As she approached him, he was watching her and thinking how lucky he was to have met such a beautiful, smart, and intelligent lady. He had never questioned her about her age, but he assumed that she was somewhat older because she talked about her children and the fact that they were grown and out of the home. It didn't matter one way or the other to him because either way he was hooked. He took Tina's hand in his and gave her a gentle peck on the cheek. "Hey good looking, I missed you." "Missed me, I haven't gone anywhere, just saying goodbye to my friend." "It seems you have been gone for an hour." Tina blushed and laid her head on his shoulder; "aw, that is so sweet, you missed me."

When Tina finally arrived home, she was exhausted. All she wanted to do was take a hot shower and crawl into bed. She had said goodbye to Ernie at the airport where he had given her a long passionate kiss. Both Tina and Ernie left their vehicles in the airport parking garage, so she didn't need him to drive her home. When she drove up in her yard, she noticed that someone was driving up behind her. "I wonder who this could be at this hour, I really don't feel up to company tonight." She was a little hesitant about getting out of her vehicle because it was late, and she had no idea who it could be. She stayed in the car with the doors locked and the engine running. Someone got out of the other vehicle and began walking towards her. She dug into her purse and took out both her pepper spray and her taser gun. Just as she was about to panic, Ernie walked closer so that she could see that it was him. "What the hell; how did he find me, who told him where I live? I never gave him my address."

"Surprise" came from an excited Ernie. "Surprise is an understatement; how did you know where I live?" "I didn't, I waited until you pulled out of the airport's parking garage and followed you home, I wanted to surprise you." "I may not have told you, but I do not like surprises." "Does that mean you want me to leave?" "It would be rude to ask you to leave after you came all this way, but I was looking forward to a hot shower and falling into bed." "I won't stop you; we can do it together." "Do what together?" "Take a hot shower and fall into bed; so, what do you say, can I stay?" "Sure, why not."

Tina drove her car on into the garage and parked, then turned off the engine and stepped outside. She was feeling both excited and a little frightened at the same time. When they were on the cruise ship, there were lots of other people around, now it was just the two of them. She didn't quite know how she should behave. When she reached the door that led to her kitchen, she slowly placed the key in the lock, a little uncertain as to whether she should go through with letting Ernie inside. Ernie stepped closer to her, put his hand over hers and turned the key in the lock for her. When the door opened, she walked ahead of him, looked back, and said, come in, welcome to my home." Ernie followed close behind her as he entered Tina's kitchen.

"What a beautiful kitchen, do you cook?" "What do you mean do I cook; I have to eat don't I?" "Well yea, I guess you do at that." They both laughed as Tina headed towards the family room. "Ernie." "Yes Tina." "You know that it's rather late and we had a long flight, don't you think it would have been wise for you to go home and get some rest and come back another day?" "That would have been the wise thing to do, but I am not feeling very wise at the moment." "How are you feeling?" "I feel like taking a hot steamy shoulder and crawling into bed." "That is exactly what I've been saying. If you are half as tired as I am, you may need to call it a night and go home." "I'm not ready to go home, I'm hungry. What do you say we go into the kitchen and find something to munch on?"

By now, Tina was beginning to wear thin on her patience. She had no intention of cooking or conjuring up anything for Ernie to eat, she wanted to go to bed. "Didn't you eat on the plane, why are you still hungry?" "I didn't, the stuff they were serving weren't appealing to me." "Well, it was appealing to me, and I had my fill." Ernie, really, laying all jokes aside, it is rather late, and I really would like to go to bed; alone." "Okay, you don't have to give me the whole cow." "The whole cow, what does a cow have to do with you leaving?" "Nothing Tina, just an expression, I will see you later, good night." "Good night, Ernie."

Before Ernie could get to his car, Tina was coming through the front door calling out his name. "What is it honey; did I leave something?" "Yes, you left me, please come back." Ernie turned and started walking towards Tina so fast that he almost tripped. When he reached her, he pulled her into his arms and began kissing her as if he would never stop. When he finally pulled away, Tina's head was reeling. She was so glad that she'd called him back. "Can I stay?" "Sure, you can silly, that's why I called you back." Ernie picked Tina up as if she was a feather and carried her back inside. All her fears and doubts had disappeared. If he was willing to leave when she asked him too without getting upset, or retaliating, she figured he must be on the up-and-up.

Tina and Ernie did take that hot shower, and they fell into bed, but neither fell asleep. Tina wanted to be mysterious, not allowing him the benefit of seeing all of her at once, so she told him to take his shower first and she would follow. "Do you mind if I got my luggage from the car and bring them inside?" "Of course, I won't mind." When Ernie left to retrieve his belongings from his car, Tina looked in the mirror and began talking to herself.

"Are you sure you know what you're doing? Well, you should, it's not like you're a teenager anymore. You are a grown woman so stop behaving like a naive child. This may be your last chance, you had better go for it girl, make him glad he stayed." She was still talking to herself when Ernie walked into the room. "Who're you talking to?" "Myself." "Is that a frequent thing?" "Yep, when you've lived alone as long as I have, you become accustomed to talking to yourself." "Well, I hope you're giving yourself some good advice." "I am, so go take your shower and don't stay in there too long." "Yes mam, I certainly won't.

Ernie had showered and was back in a flash with nothing, but a towel wrapped around him. Tina had spent quality time with him on the ship but had never crossed that line. This was something new, this was the real deal. "That was fast." "You told me to make it quick, so I did; should I join you or wait for you?" "Wait for me, I will be back." "Ok, don't take too long." "I won't, I promise." Tina went into the bathroom with anticipation. It had been quite a while since a gentleman graced her bed with his presence, and tonight she planned to enjoy every moment of it. Everything her mother taught her was going out the window tonight. "This is going to be a night to remember."

As promised, Tina was in and out of the shower within a few minutes. After brushing and flossing her teeth, she rubbed her entire body with body oil, and sprayed a lite body mist all over; then she let her hair down from the ponytail she wore the entire time she was on the cruise. She put some nude lip gloss on her lips to keep them soft and proceeded to walk out of the bathroom wearing an all-black negligee. When Ernie looked up and saw her walking towards him, his heart began pounding in his chest. With every step she took towards him, the pounding became a little harder and a little louder. By the time she reached him, he was beside himself with emotions.

"Whoa baby, you look beautiful. I thought I had taken in all your beauty, but dang! I had no idea you were this fine." Although Tina was now fifty, she looked like she was in her late twenties. Her skin was smooth and wrinkle free, and she had legs like a model. Tina never thought of herself as being beautiful, but at that moment, with him looking at her the way that he was, she felt sexy. She was always charming, but she never knew it, or at the very least never acknowledged it; it was part of her defense. She walked straight to Ernie, who was sitting on the edge of her bed, and stood between his legs. He placed his hands on her thighs and began massaging them. Tina didn't know if she should stay in that position or get into bed, so she just stood there.

After examining Tina's whole lower body from a sitting position, Ernie stood up and pulled her into his arms. She responded by wrapping her arms around his neck and drawing him even closer. Ernie moaned as he buried his face deep into Tina's neck. Tina could feel her feet being lifted from the floor as if she was floating, and then her body being gently placed on the bed. She closed her eyes and waited for the room to stop spinning. Ernie laid her head on the pillow and lowered himself beside her. She opened her eyes to see what his next move would be.

Ernie just lay there beside Tina looking down on her as he slowly ran one hand up and down her body while he rested his head on the other. When she opened her eyes, she looked directly into his; what she saw was thrilling; his eyes were filled with passion and desire; he was savoring the moment, but when Tina opened her big brown eyes, and looked up into his, he could no longer contain himself. In a split second he had removed that little black negligee and threw it to the floor. Tina did not put up any defenses, she was just as eager as he was to discover the rest of Ernie Capers.

Ernie rolled over on his back as he pulled Tina on top of him. "This is not what my momma taught me she thought, this is not it at all." All her thoughts went out of the window except the ones that were whispering sweet words of pleasure to Ernie. She wanted to tell him that she loved him but thought it might be too soon. She didn't want to scare him away, so instead of saying the words, she just kept them in. Tina and Ernie's bodies were entangled like a vine around a pole. You could not tell where one began or the other ended. She did not want to spoil the joy of what she was feeling by allowing her past to interfere as she had done in previous relationships, so she closed her eyes tight to tune out all thoughts accept those of Ernie.

Tina and Ernie made love all night with mini breaks in between. This was so new for Tina; making love was always a chore for her. She loved the other aspects of romance, but until now, she could do without sexual intimacy. "So, this is what I've been missing all these years? I never thought that I could feel this complete about another person." She embedded her head in his chest as he wrapped his arms around her. Around eight o'clock in the morning, they both fell asleep. While she was asleep, she had a wonderful dream about Ernie. She dreamt that they were on their honeymoon in Hawaii. At one point in the dream, the intensity of it woke her up. She turned over to find Ernie missing. She thought perhaps he had gone to the bathroom, but his bags were missing as well.

Tina felt foolish; "how could I have been so gullible? I am too old for this now." She got out of bed and made her way to the bathroom. She had been wanting to go all night but didn't want to pull away from Ernie. As she passed the mirror, she stared at herself and said, you fool, you did it again." "You did what again?" Came a voice from behind her. Tina almost jumped out of her skin. "Ernie, I thought you left." "Why would you think that?" "I woke and didn't see you, and your bags are missing." "Yeah, I got up and took a shower. You were sleeping so soundly and peacefully that I didn't want to disturb you, so I took my bags out to the car. I would never just leave without telling you." "Well would you mine stepping out until I finish in here?" "Sure, I'll be waiting for you in the kitchen."

While Tina was in the bathroom, she showered and dressed for the day. After putting on her underwear, she pulled on a pair of faded jeans with a simple black and white polka dot button down shirt, and a pair of white running shoes. She wanted to look extra nice, so after catching her hair up in a ponytail, she laced her lips with a pale pink lip gloss; she opted not to put on any other type of makeup, or jewelry. When she walked into her bedroom, she noticed that there were some bills folded and placed near her pillow. "I wonder how that got there. Ernie must have dropped it. She picked it up and headed for the kitchen as he had summoned her to do. When she was almost there, she could smell the aroma of coffee and bacon. She smiled as she turned the corner and entered the kitchen. There she found Ernie hard at cooking as if he was a chef at a fast-food restaurant.

"Well look at you, what are you up too?" "I hope you don't mind, I wanted to surprise you with breakfast but then I remembered you don't like surprises; that's why I came back to the bedroom and told you to meet me in the kitchen, I hope you don't mind. "Oh, I don't mind, you can make me breakfast anytime. By the way, I think you dropped this." "No, I didn't drop it, that's yours." "Where did it come from?" "It came from me; I want you to have it." "To do what with?" "Whatever you want, so come on and get your breakfast." Tina was confused, but even more hungry, so she placed the money on the countertop and flopped down on the barstool while waiting to be served.

Ernie outdid himself in Tina's kitchen. He placed in front of her a gourmet omelet, toast, cranberry juice, and coffee. "Thanks Ernie;

the only person that cooks for me other than my housekeeper is my mom, and it has been quite a while since she has. Feels good to be eating a meal in my kitchen that I didn't have to prepare. You really outdid yourself; see, this type of surprise I can handle," she said grinning. "I bet you can." Ernie took his plate and placed it on the bar next to hers, then sat so close to her, that she could feel the heat from his body. Tina leaned in and kissed him on his cheek; "Thanks Ernie, this is nice." "You already thanked me once, that's enough," he said with a smile.

After Tina and Ernie finished breakfast, she told him that because he made breakfast, she would do the dishes, but he wouldn't have it. "No, this is my mess, I'll clean it. I don't want you telling your friends that I came over here and dirty your kitchen and left it that way; I know how you ladies are; my mother is one." Tina laughed at his comment; she appreciated his sense of humor; "it was only through pure serendipity that I met this wonderful man, and I am going to do whatever I need to, to hold on to him, no matter how weird Janice thinks he is."

Chapter Twenty-Three

Tina was on such a natural high that she had forgotten about the money Ernie left in her room earlier. All she could think about was how much she had fallen for him, and how wrong Janice and her investigators were about him. She wondered why her friend would make up such an elaborate lie, "was she jealous of the time she spent with Ernie on the cruise? That must be it, otherwise, it made no sense. But why would she be jealous of me, her life is good, and she seems to be happy with the way things are. Oh well, I am not wasting one more thought on Janice and her bogus accusations."

Tina and Ernie's relationship was in a good place. He came over at least twice every weekday and almost every weekend. He always made her feel special. She had deleted Janice's account of Ernie's personality completely from her mind. She was beginning to think that perhaps there was a future for the two of them. There was one little thing that plagued her mind; each time that she and Ernie made love he would push bills into her hand. If she refused to take it, he would leave it on her nightstand. After asking him several times as to the reason, he would just shrug and say to her, "go buy yourself something nice." To keep from seemingly being ungrateful, Tina would just take the money and put it in her bedside drawer. She knew that something was up, but she didn't want to know what it was; it could ruin everything.

One weekend, Tina and Ernie decided to go out for a change. Most of their dates were at home. They enjoyed spending time alone. "So where are we going Ernie?" "Just be patient, you'll see." "But I want to know, remember I do not like surprises." "This is not a surprise; I just don't want to spoil it by telling you where we're going." Tina decided to just be quiet and wait to see where he was taking her. "Are you upset?" "No, why would I be upset?" "Because you're so quiet, that's not like you." "Everyone knows how to shut up sometime." Ernie looked over at her and smiled, "I love you" he said. Tina responded by just staring at him with her mouth open; he had never told her that he loved her, not even at their most intimate moments. "Did you hear what I said?" "Yes, I heard you," was all she could manage to get out. Ernie just smiled, turned his head away from her, and focused on his driving.

When they finally arrived at their destination, Tina raised her eyes to see where he had taken her, but she did not recognize the building. "Where is this, Ernie? I have never been here before." "I know you haven't, or at least I hope that you haven't." "Why is that?" "Because I want to be the first one to bring you here." Tina's excitement level rose, she believed she was in for a treat, so she refrained from asking any more questions.

Ernie got out of the car, walked around to the passenger side where Tina was sitting, opened the door and held his hand to assist her getting out. Like an obedient child, she caught his hand and pulled herself from the seat. Once out, Ernie pulled her into his arms and kissed her as if it was his last time. Tina felt his passion and responded with her own. When he finally pulled away from her, he took her by the elbow, and began ushering her towards the door. Tina was filled with emotions, passion, and anticipation.

Tina was so anxious to see where Ernie was taking her that it seemed to have taken ten minutes to walk from the parking lot to the entry. When they finally arrived, Ernie stepped in front of Tina and pulled open the door, then stepped back while still holding it open to allow her to enter. When Tina walked inside, she gasped! She turned around and looked at Ernie; "Is this the big mystery? Did you really bring me to a strip club Ernie?" Ernie wasn't sure if Tina was upset or excited, he only knew that he was ecstatic. He looked down at Tina with a wide smile on his face; "so, are you surprise, do you like it?" "Like what Ernie, what the hell is there to like; why in the world would you bring me here of all places?" Tina was so furious with Ernie that she couldn't speak clearly. "Do I strike you as someone who would enjoy coming to a place like this, and why would you want to come? No, don't answer that, just take me home, take me home right now!"

Ernie didn't appear to be bothered by Tina's outrage, he walked over to a vacant table and sat down. Music was playing and Ernie seemed to be enjoying it. He was rocking from side-to-side and bopping his head up and down. Tina had never witnessed this side of him before and didn't know what to make of it. The waitresses were all wearing thongs with a tail and a flower in their hair. On stage were three women dancing and taking off what little clothing they had left. People were rewarding them with bills. Ernie got up from where he was sitting and went closer to where the girls were dancing. It seemed he had forgotten that he had a date. He reached into his pocket and pulled out a roll of bills, then began throwing them on stage where the girls were dancing. The only thing Tina thought of at that moment was Ernie putting money into her hand.

Tina flashed back to the first time she and Ernie had made love, when he left some bills on her bed. When she'd questioned him about it, he just brushed it off as if it wasn't important. But since that time, each time they made love he would push bills into her hand before he left. She got tired of asking the purpose and decided she would just put it somewhere until she decided to give it all back to him. So, each time he gave her money, she would put it in the drawer of her nightstand beside her bed. She didn't understand why he felt a need to give her money after their love making, she certainly was no prostitute, and she was not hard up for cash. She continued to take it just to see how long he would continue doing it. Each time the amount got larger. When it first started, she counted two hundred dollars, but as time went by it had increased to a thousand dollars by the second month into their relationship. Because of the frequency of their times together, she had accumulated quite a stash.

Tina was really feeling Ernie and had reluctantly given him a small portion of her heart, so she intentionally ignored little signs of the weirdness Janice had spoken of. She so desperately wanted this relationship to work. She felt that everyone had some character flaws, and she was not going to get rid of a perfectly good man just because he liked giving her money; but something wasn't adding up, or was it?

Tina wanted to go over to Ernie and demand that he took her home, but something inside of her would not allow her to, so, she just stood there, frozen, in the same spot as when she first entered. She looked at him and saw a whole different person. This was not her Ernie, he was yelling, dancing, and grinding with the dancers like she wasn't in the room. "How disrespectful can one person be to another, what would he think, or how would he feel if I treated him this way?" Tina was trying her best to hold back her tears when suddenly, Ernie turned around as if he remembered that Tina was with him. He looked over in her direction and noticed that she was standing in the exact spot where he left her. He started towards her, but one of the dancers caught his attention and he turned around to accommodate her.

"That's it, I am out of here, he can just go to hell." Tina turned from her frozen position and began walking towards the exit. When she was almost at the door, she turned around and gave one final look in Ernie's direction. He was so engrossed with what he was doing, that he didn't notice. Tina had no idea where she was, but she knew that if she called a cab, they would take her home. After placing her call for a cab, she waited on the side of the building for it to arrive. Fifteen minutes later, the cab rolled up and Tina got inside without a backwards glance. She gave the driver her address and within a few minutes she was safely in her yard. She paid the driver and thanked him, then rolled herself from the backseat and headed towards her front door.

Tina was happy to be home, and thankful that she didn't have to wait a long time outside for a cab. She was unfamiliar with the place Ernie had taken her to and didn't know what the environment was like. She went inside, closed the door, and collapsed on the first chair she saw. She attempted to piece together the night's event. Although she'd shed a few tears before leaving the club, she was not about to waste any more on Ernie. It seemed as if she had been in the dark from the moment she met him, until that very moment, then suddenly, the lights came on. "Janice was right; his ass is weird." As Tina pieced together the puzzle to Ernie Caper, she came to her own conclusion. Ernie felt the need to pretend that she was a prostitute so he could feel comfortable with her. "But why, what could possibly have happened in his life that made him feel the need for strippers and prostitutes? Whatever it was, I am no body's therapist, so I think the best thing for me is to jump ship before I sink."

After Tina had gathered herself and concluded that she was breaking things off with Ernie, she went into her bedroom, opened the drawer where she'd stashed all the bills Ernie had given her over the months, and place them in a large envelop without counting it. On the envelope she wrote, "here's enough to cover several nights at the strip club; enjoy! How am I going to get this to him? I certainly don't want to put it in the mail, and I don't ever want to see him again." She was certain that Ernie would come looking for her eventually and she would give it to him then.

Around midnight, Tina decided to take a shower and get into bed. She had not heard anything from Ernie. "I wonder if he's still at the strip club and if he is, has he realized that I left." After her shower, she returned to her bedroom, turned off the lights and fell into bed. The events of the night were more strenuous than she'd realized, so she fell asleep as soon as her head hit the pillow. When she awoke the next morning, she felt rested and rejuvenated. "I can handle whatever comes my way, this was just a speed bump in comparison to my past experiences." Because she'd taken her shower so late in the night, or early in the morning, she decided to let that do. She dashed some water on her face, brushed her teeth, and headed for the kitchen in her pajamas. It was Sunday and she didn't have to be at work, so she decided that she would stay in and pamper herself for a change.

Tina could not help but think about Ernie and wondered why she hadn't heard from him. It was nearly noon, and he had not checked in to see if she made it home safely or if she was all right. "I believe I owe Janice an apology." Ever since she was stiff with Janice during the beginning of her relationship with Ernie, their friendship had suffered. She didn't want Janice criticizing Ernie which she did each time they spoke, so she disconnected herself from the friendship, and as for Shanell and Marley, she barely saw them. "Some friend I've become; I put some guy before my friends, and just look at what he turned out to be." Tina was too embarrassed to give her friends details about her relationship with Ernie, so that was one more secret she stored in her repertoire. "I will just tell them it didn't work out with Ernie and me because we wanted different things. I wouldn't dare tell them the true story; hell, I don't even know the true story, and if they ever found out that he took me to a strip club and didn't even bother to check on me after I left, what will they think of my judgement?"

Ernie never came to check on Tina. Months passed and she never heard from or about him. She had gone to Janice and apologized for her behavior and for doubting her loyalty and concerns. Janice accepted her apology and Tina asked if she would deliver the envelope to Ernie. "Only if you tell me what's in it." "Oh, no big secret; it's just some money I borrowed from him awhile back she lied. I would give it to him myself, but I really don't want to see him, you understand, don't you?" "Of course, I do, I would be glad to give it to him for you, where can I find him?" "That is one good question, I have no idea." "No problem, I know someone that knows how to find him, I will just ask her where he is." "Whatever way you get it to him is fine by me, as long as he receives it." Janice took the envelope from Tina and put it in her purse. Several days later, she reported that Ernie had received the envelope. "Thanks Janice, I owe you one." "No problem, I was happy to do it, but a strange thing happened." "What happened, what did he do?"

"When I gave him the envelop and told him that it was from you, he said, "from who?" I said from Tina;" He said, "I don't know any Tina, what is it?" "At that moment I didn't respond, I just threw the envelope at him and walked away. Tina, something is wrong with that man, I am so glad you got out of that relationship while you still could. I heard he was weird, but that was beyond weird, that was scary." "He'll be okay, I think he has some unresolved childhood issues." "I think he's crazy, that's what I think." Tina wanted to laugh but she knew that it really wasn't funny, so she just agreed with Janice that he was probably crazy. Despite her caution, she once again got involved with the wrong guy. "What is wrong with me, why can't I be a better judge of character? I thought for sure that Ernie was the one, I'm getting too old now to be someone's fool."

Chapter Twenty-Four

Although things didn't work out between Tina and Ernie, she was not going to let his problems become hers. She had no idea why things happened the way they did with him. "Was it all an act, did he pretended to love me all that time?" She was grateful that she had only opened the door to her heart partially to him, otherwise, she would have been deeply hurt. It only took her a little time to delete him almost completely from her thoughts, and even those brief moments when she did think of him, it would only be to remind herself not to be so eager going forward.

Several years passed and the thoughts of Ernie Capers had completely gone from her mind. Tina had decided to put dating on the back burner and focus on her work. Both of her children were doing well with their lives, and she was expecting her first grandchild. She often wondered if romance had passed her by, and if she was too old now to expect anyone to find her attractive. She had never quite gotten out of the notion that she was unattractive, and unappealing to men. Whenever men would look at her or admire her, she always took it the wrong way. Deep down she used her unattractive ideation as a coping mechanism, so no one would ever attempt to violate her again in any way. If she would have allowed herself to do so, she would have seen what men saw when they looked at her, or what all her friends, and everyone who knew her saw. She was an extremely attractive lady, and at the age of 55, she looked as if she was in her early thirties. But for her to acknowledge that, she would have to go way into her subconscious and drag it out, and she had no intension of doing that. One of the things that made her even more attractive was that she didn't think that she was.

Tina continued her community and charity work and found great satisfaction in doing so. The women's shelter was providing much needed services to women and their children, and she had added on a male wing to accommodate men who experienced domestic violence as well. Tina received many awards and recognitions for being a community leader. At one point in time, she even considered running for mayor of her city, but when she did the research, the amount of time the position required would pull her away from her other commitments. Just like the idea popped into her head, she quickly dismissed it. Her job had become more demanding over the years, and her community involvements were satisfying, as well as necessary. She would let someone else handle the politics of it all.

People began to recognize Tina wherever she went. Her name had become a household word. She was not a vain person, so she did not allow her successes to change who she was. She did, however, took on more and more responsibilities over the years. So much so that she hardly ever thought about romance, and that she had not been in a relationship in years. During a conversation about romance and dating with one of the volunteers at the women's center, Tina made light of the question when asked about her dating by saying, "girl, dating is for the young, as for me, I am over it."

Once those words came from Tina's mouth, there was no turning back, she would stick to what she said come hell or high water. Although Samantha, the younger volunteer, tried her best to convince her that she was still young and had a lot to offer, Tina immediately changed the subject. "Okay Samantha, let's just drop the subject and get back to work." Sam, as she was often referred to, didn't understand Tina's reluctance to talk about love and romance since she was one of the most compassionate and loving human beings she'd ever known. "But Ms. Tina, with all due respect, I do not agree with you when you say that love is for the young only;

everyone wants to give love and receive love, that's human nature." "Well Samantha, maybe I am not human, because my radar tells me that my ship has sailed, docked, and retired." "Well change the oil, tune it up and put it back out to sea, because my instinct tells me that someone will be coming along soon looking for a ride. You've got to be ready Ms. T."

Tina didn't try to argue with Sam, she just walked away mumbling to herself. "If that child doesn't stay out of my face about some darn romance, I am going to stuff her behind in the garbage container." Despite her grumbling, Tina had to laugh, deep down Samantha had struck a nerve. She was feeling a little lonelier lately, but figured it was because she was missing her children. She planned to go visit them, but to do so she would have to take time off from her job and all her other responsibilities. Her children live in two different states. DJ lived in Savannah Georgia and Tiana lived in Charlotte North Carolina. Since she had not taken a vacation in years, now was a good time to do so.

When Tina got home later that night, she sat at her desk in her study, and began checking her calendar for possible vacation dates. "One good thing, I don't have to worry about leaving the children behind anymore, so I can go whenever it's convenient for me." After the children had grown up and no longer needed a nanny, Tina decided to keep Judy on as a housekeeper, so that she would not be unemployed. She allowed her to work part-time at her home and part-time at the shelter. Judy was excited because her salary and benefits did not decrease, in fact, she received several raises over the years, and always got Christmas bonuses.

After searching her calendar for a few minutes, Tina realized that she had not eaten since lunch, and it was now eleven pm. She got up from her chair and strolled to the kitchen. "What am I going to eat? I really don't feel up to cooking anything." She was about to open a can of pork' n beans when her doorbell rang. "I wonder who could be ringing my doorbell at this time of night?" Tina approached the door in record time, she was afraid that something had happened. When she reached the door, she flung it open without asking who was there. Standing on the other side of the door was Ernie Capers.

Tine realized that she had made a mistake by not asking who was on the other side of the door as soon as she flung it open, but it was too late to re-close it. She stood there staring at Ernie as if she had seen a ghost. Ernie just stood there with a crooked smile on his face. "Hi Tina, may I come in?" Tina responded by attempting to slam the door in his face, but he threw up both hands, and began pleading with her. "Please don't close the door Tina, I know that I am the last person on earth you want to see, and especially so late at night." "What do you want Ernie, your money? Well, I sent that to you by a friend, did you not receive it?" "No Tina, I am not looking for any money, and yes, she did give it to me, that is not why I'm here." "You know what Ernie, it really doesn't matter, I don't give a dam why you're here, I do not want to see you, so leave." "Tina please! Just give me one minute and I promise I will go away, and you will never see me again." "I don't see you now, so move so I can close my door, or you will regret it."

Ernie stepped a few paces back from the door as Tina slammed it together. She was furious; "just who the hell does he think I am; does he think he can go away without any explanations, stay away for years, and then come waltzing back whenever he felt the need?" Tina was so furious that she began to cry; she crashed on the closest chair sobbing uncontrollably. This was bound to happen because she had never cried after Ernie disappeared without a trace or an explanation. She had taken all that emotion and put it into her work. She also used it as a tool to help others with their atrocities. Now, here she was, without the ability to rein in her emotions. She was both angry and frustrated with herself for being what she considered weak. "The nerve of that man, how dare he come to my home asking to talk with me as if we were best friends."

Tina could not make head nor tail out of Ernie's visit, but now that the shock was over, she was curious. She looked at the clock and wondered if it was too late to call Janice. She tried reasoning with herself but gave in and picked up her phone and began dialing Janice's number. "Hello Tina, came from the voice on the other end of the phone; is everything alright?" "Hello Janice;" Janice detected that something was wrong by the tone of Tina's voice. "No, nothing is wrong." "Are you sure, because it sounds as if you were crying." "I was, but now I'm fine." "What happened?" "I went temporarily insane." "What do you mean, what did you do?" "Long story; I need to ask you something." "It must be important for you to call me at this hour." You know I would not have called you this time of night if it wasn't important. Would you believe that Ernie showed up at my door a little while ago?" "Are you for real, tonight?" "Yes, and like a fool I opened the door without asking who was on the other side." "You did what? That could have been anyone, please be careful and don't do that again." "I know, but when the doorbell rang so late, I was so afraid that something had happened to one of my family members, that I didn't think."

"So, what do you need to ask me?" "I just wanted to ask if you heard anything concerning Ernie over the past few years or recently?" "I'm not sure what you mean but I had no reason to talk about Ernie to anyone. The only reason I did before was to get some history on him for you. Since you gave me the money to return to him, I have not seen or heard from him since. Why are you asking, you're not considering him again are you?" "Oh, hell no! It's just that he was so adamant that I hear what he had to say that my curiosity is getting the best of me." "Are you saying that he wanted to explain his past behaviors?" "I don't know what he wanted, I never gave him the opportunity to tell me, now I want to know." "Let it go Tina, you will be better off not knowing, and why were you crying?" "Again, it's a long story, one I will tell you someday, but right now I'm going to let you go back to bed." "Okay, you promise?" "Yes, I promise, now good night."

After Tina got off the phone with Janice she started toward her bedroom. Her stomach made a loud growling sound reminding her that she still had not eaten any dinner. She was so wound up that she didn't feel up to the pork' n beans she previously started to eat. She went into the kitchen and poured herself a bowl of dried cereal. After she had finished consuming her cereal, she downed a glass of pineapple juice. "This will have to do for now because I am too exhausted to do anything else tonight."

Tina turned off the lights in the kitchen and headed back towards her bedroom. She could have sworn she heard someone calling her name. "I must be losing my mind, who would be calling my name at midnight?" As she crossed the hallway leading to her bedroom, she heard a loud cry; "Tina, please open the door and talk to me, I need you to listen to what I have to say, and I am not leaving until you do." Tina listened more closely and realized that it was Ernie, he was still outside of her door. She walked over to the door and in a loud voice said, "Ernie, you have two choices. You can either leave on your own or I will help you leave with this thirty-eight, now the choice is yours, which will it be?" "I am not leaving on my own so if you want to shoot me that's okay, at least I will be out of my misery."

Tina knew that she wasn't going to shoot Ernie unless he attempted to break in on her, but she was trying to frighten him into leaving without her having to call the cops. "Ernie, if you don't leave my house right now, I am going to call the police." For a few seconds there was not a sound, then suddenly there was a loud thump on her front door. Tina's frightened level peek as she dialed 911.

"Hello, what is your emergency mam?" "There's someone at my door and will not leave, I think he's trying to break in." "Is it someone you know?" "I believe it's someone I knew years ago, what difference does it make if I know him, can't you send someone out immediately, I am afraid." "One moment mam."

While Tina stood holding the phone waiting for someone to return, Ernie knocked on the door again, then began ringing her doorbell repeatedly. "I've got enough of this; something has got to give." Tina headed for her room to retrieve her gun from the box she kept it in when the receptionist returned to the line. "Mam what is your address?" "It is the street where you will find a dead man if you don't hurry and get someone over here soon." "Okay mam. Just give me your address and someone will be right over." Tina yelled out her address, hung up the phone and pulled out her thirty-eight. She was on her way back to the door when she heard voices. Luckily, a police officer was in the vicinity and took only a few seconds to get to Tina's house.

Tina heard another knock on her door, but this time it was the police officers. She slowly opened it just wide enough to see that Ernie was in cuffs. She felt sorry for him because she felt he had lost his mind. She opened the door wider and stepped onto the porch.

"Hello officer, thanks for getting here so fast." "Can you tell me what happened?" "I would if I knew; he showed up around eleven and asked if he could speak with me about something. I told him I wasn't interested in anything he had to say and thought that he had left. An hour later I heard him screaming my name from outside, asking me to open the door and let him in. I asked him to leave, no, I demanded that he left, but he refused, then began pounding on my door." "So do you know this gentleman?" "To be honest, I really don't; I knew of him, but it has been years since I've seen or heard tell of him." "So, are you telling me that you are not having a lovers quarrel?" "Look at me! Do I look like someone's lover to you? I am frightened out of my mind, get him away from me, but before you do, may I ask him why he came to my house in the first place?"

Ernie was sitting in the police car with his hands cuffed behind his back. Tina walked over to the car and in a strong aggressive voice asked him, "what did you expect to gain by coming to my house this time of night? What is it that you want from me?" "All I wanted was to apologize to you for the way I treated you all those years ago. You see, as a child I was severely abused physically, sexually, and emotionally. I never dealt with the trauma of it and had no idea how to manage my life. Everything that I have done from the time I was eight years old was based on pain. Before now, I have never told another soul, but it has gotten too big to carry. I cannot do it anymore, so before I end it all, I wanted to make peace with you. You were the best thing that ever happened to me in my lifetime, but I didn't know how to accept you. I was afraid, so each time we made love I paid you. In my head, I believed that if I gave you money it would be like just a job, and I wouldn't have to feel any emotion. The thing is though, I fell in love with you, something I hadn't planned on, and something I didn't know how to deal with. I took you to that strip club because I knew that you would be unhappy and walk away from me. I didn't have the strength to walk away from you. When you left you thought that I didn't see you, but I did. I was watching you through the corners of my eyes, and I followed you outside and hid behind a bush in the yard to make sure you were safe until the taxi came and took you home. As soon as you got into the cab, I left the club as well. I went straight home and decided that you were better off without me. I am messed up, and there's no hope for me, so tonight after I apologized to you, I was going to kill myself. When you said that you would do it for me, I decided to push even harder, that way I wouldn't have to do it. I am sorry Tina, sorry for everything. Now that I have told you what I wanted to, I promise to never bother you again, goodbye."

When Ernie had finished explaining to Tina, tears were running down her face. She looked over at the officer, and he too was in tears. "Have you finished talking with him mam?" "Yes, I have, but please take the cuffs off, he needs help, not jail." The officer did as she asked and released the cuffs from Ernie's wrists. He just sat there motionless, as if he was already dead. "Sir, you are free to go, the lady is not pressing charges, but I suggest you go home and leave her alone." "Yes sir, I will." "Officer, you don't understand, I don't want him to go home, he is suicidal." "Where do you want him to go mam?" "I want him to go where he can receive help, he has been ignored and pushed aside too often and for too long, it's time for him to get help. Take him to the hospital for evaluation and I will be there soon." Ernie looked up at Tina and said in a weak childlike voice, "please take care of my car, will you?" Tina just nodded her head as she walked back inside the house. Once inside, she broke down into tears. That could have been her. She could have ended up the same way, but she found comfort in the church and in her work to help others. She had no idea where Ernie's support system was or if he even had one. He never talked about family. Each time she had attempted to ask him about his parents, or whether he had siblings, he quickly changed the subject by kissing her and telling her how much he adored her and that she was his family.

Tina rushed to her bedroom, picked up her purse and headed for the door. Once she was in her car, she said a prayer for Ernie, and for herself that she didn't fall asleep behind the wheels. After her short prayer, she headed for the hospital. When she arrived, she found Ernie sitting in the emergency waiting room with the officer that drove him there. Just as she was walking up to them a nurse came out and called him back to a small examination room. She hesitated for a moment, then caught her breath and followed Ernie, the officer, and the nurse into the room. "Do you mind that I'm here Ernie?" "Yes Tina, I do mind, but I need you, I don't have anyone else." "Where are your parents?" "Both of my parents are deceased, and I do not have any siblings to my knowledge." "What do you mean to your knowledge?" "I was adopted as a baby and I never knew my birth parents, so I don't know if they had any other children." Ernie looked as if he had no fight left in him; he just sat there looking at the floor. "Would you like something to drink Ernie?" "No Tina, I'm fine." "Is there anything I can do for you?" "You are doing it; you are the first and only person that has ever shown any concern for me. Even as a child, I was bullied, and ignored, at school, and often put in isolation or detention for trying to defend myself." "Did your parents ever address you being bullied with the school officials?" "No, and can we please not talk about my parents, they are no longer here and even if they were, they would not care." Tina did not want to bring any more discomfort to Ernie by bringing up his family, so she changed the subject. "Ernie would you be willing to get treatment?" "Treatment for what Tina?" "To help you be able to cope with life. You have been doing it too long on your own." "Life for me ended years ago, I am merely a fragment of a human being. I have no heart, and my soul is hollowed." "That is the reason you need help, to be able to put the pieces of your life back together." "I am fifty-two years old Tina, please, just let it go, just let it go."

Tina sat with Ernie through his entire evaluation without saying a word. When the doctor had completed his assessment, a hospital psychiatrist and a mental health therapist came in and conducted assessments as well. The three of them along with the officer went into a conference room to discuss the outcome. When they returned, they told Ernie that they were going to keep him overnight for observation. Ernie was not pleased, he got up from his chair and headed for the door. The officer stopped him and told him that if he did not comply, he would be cuffed. "Come on Ernie, please let them help you, you are not alone anymore. After listening to Tina's soft pleads, he decided to follow the nurse to the psychiatric ward to be admitted for treatment. Tina was finally able to exhale. She closed her eyes and said a prayer of thanks, then asked God to please be with Ernie.

After Ernie had settled in his hospital room, Tina decided to go home. By now she was feeling the strain of the day. Daylight was peeking through the darkness as a full moon rolled across the half lite sky. She drove up in her driveway at half past six, got out of the car and dragged herself inside. Going to work was out of the question. She would just call her assistant and let her know that she would not be coming in, after all, she was the boss. Tina knew that once her head hit the pillow, she would fall asleep, so she called her office and left a voice message for her assistant. After she had completed her call, she took a long hot shower to wash the residue from the hospital off her body. When she got out of the shower, she applied body oil to her skin, put on her pajamas and crawled into bed. Her first instinct was to turn off her phone, but she thought "what if I turn it off and Ernie needs me, so she turned the volume down low and placed it on the nightstand beside her bed. She laid down on her side and pulled the sheet up to her neck, said a prayer and fell asleep.

Tina always kept her alarm set just in case she overslept, except for weekends when she wanted to sleep in. She intended to turn it off so that she could sleep a little late before calling to check on Ernie, but with all that had occurred, it slipped her mind. When the alarm went off, she jumped out of bed as if something or someone was after her. Within seconds, she came to her senses and realized that it was just her alarm clock going off. She walked over to the bed, pulled back the rumbled bedding and laid her head on the pillow. Although she was still very tired, she could not fall asleep. She kept thinking of the previous night, and all that had taken place. "I figured that Ernie had a messed-up childhood, but I would never have imagined it would be this horrific." Tina allowed her mind to drift back to when Ernie was telling her about the abuse he experienced. "And I thought I had a rough past; mine pales in comparison to his."

After tossing and turning for several minutes, Tina concluded that she was not going to be able to fall asleep anytime soon, too much was on her mind. She threw her long legs out of the bed and sat on the side while her feet dangled beneath her. She looked at her clock beside the bed to see what time it was. "Only nine thirty? I thought I slept longer. Oh well, I might as well get up and go find myself some breakfast, my dinner was pitiful."

Tina was heading towards the kitchen when her mobile began ringing. She turned around to retrieve it from the nightstand where she'd placed it. She picked it up but didn't recognize the number. "Hello." "Hello, Tina?" Came from an unfamiliar voice on the other end. "Yes, this is Tina, may I ask who's calling?" "This is nurse Taylor from Merci Memorial hospital psychiatric ward." "Yes, how may I help you?" "I have you listed as a point of contact for Mr. Ernie Capers, and I am calling concerning payment arrangements." "Payment arrangements, did you speak with Mr. Capers? I do not manage his finances, in fact, I barely know him." "Yes, I spoke with him, and he said that you would be managing all of his paperwork and anything else we needed from him." "Oh, did he now? I will be there as soon as I am dressed and fed." Tina hung up the phone just as Nurse Taylor started to speak again. "Dang! Can't a body have some peace? Every time I attempt to help someone it backfires. He's in the hospital, so whenever I get there, I will be there, right now, I am going to my kitchen and prepare myself a breakfast fit for a queen."

Tina threw her phone on the bed and headed towards the kitchen once again. This time she was able to make it all the way in without being interrupted. She opened the refrigerator door and began pulling things out. When she had finished cooking her breakfast, she placed it on a plate, and decided to eat at her kitchen table, something she seldom did anymore. Most of the time she ate in front of the TV while watching some comedy show. But this morning was special; this morning she had to prepare for the unknown, and to do that, she needed strength and confidence.

She looked down at her sizable portion of bacon, toast, omelet, sausage, grapefruit, juice, and coffee, and smiled. "Now this is what I'm talking about, this is the breakfast fit for a queen." Most mornings, Tina only had a granola bar and a cup of coffee for breakfast. She seldom took time for a full breakfast. She took her time eating, deliberately keeping her thoughts away from anything negative. As she ate, she looked outside the window at all the beauty nature had to offer. She saw a red bird sitting on top of an azalea bush singing its heart out. "Why can't humans be that happy and contented? There's always something going on in our lives that calls for some type of attention. What would I do if I was a bird? Hell, I'd probably have to take care of the little birds, and without appreciation or pay." Tina laughed at herself and continued staring through the windowpanes.

After sitting and looking outside through her window for half an hour, Tina raised herself up from her sitting position and slowly walked towards her bedroom. The last time she left her kitchen, someone was crying out her name. She tilted her head as if she was listening to hear someone calling. "Come on Tina, don't get paranoid." She continued walking until she reached her bedroom. She looked over at the unmade bed and wondered if she should make it or get back in it. After all, Ernie was not her problem or her responsibility. "But who is? If I refuse to help him, who will?" At that moment, Tina was feeling as if she was between a rock and a hard place. On the one hand she knew that she didn't owe Ernie anything, but on the other hand, the person that she was would not allow her to just walk away.

After much debating with herself, Tina decided to make her bed, got dressed, and made for the hospital to check on Ernie. When she arrived at the psychiatric ward, the staff was waiting for her. "Good morning Ms. Tina, we've been trying to reach you." "You have, may I ask why?" "Well, Mr. Capers did not give us your last name, and we need the information to place on his paperwork." "Let's get something straight mam; I am not related to Mr. Capers in any way, he is just someone I happened to have met years ago that showed up on my doorstep last night. Because of whom I am and what I do, I felt obligated to speak up on his behalf. He would have gone to jail for trespassing if I hadn't stepped up, but as for his medical bills, that's all on him; so, no, you don't need my last name."

For a few seconds, you could hear a pin fall; finally, Tina broke the silence by asking, "is it possible for me to see him?" "Yes, mam please do, maybe you can understand what he is trying to tell us." Tina pushed past the staff that were standing looking at her and walked into Ernie's room. When she entered, he was lying on his side looking out of the window. He didn't seem to care that someone had entered his room; he just laid there not moving with his eyes focused on the window. "Good morning, Ernie." When he heard Tina's voice, he slowly turned and looked at her. Tina could see tear stains on his face and her heart felt overwhelmed. "Good morning," he said in a pensive voice. "I was hoping to see you today" "Well here I am, is there anything I can do for you?" "Yes, could you please convince the hospital staff to let me go home, I really don't want to be here." "No one wants to be in a hospital Ernie, but sometimes despite our efforts we need to be." "Hospitals are designed to save people's lives Tina, I don't have a life to save, please set me free and put me out of my misery." With all Tina's experience in dealing with situations at the shelter, she had never encountered such a dilemma. She was no therapist and could find no words for Ernie.

Tina just sat there with her hands folded in her lap looking at the same window Ernie was staring at earlier. "So, what do you say Tina, will you help a friend out?" The word friend was all it took to stir Tina up again. "Friend? When did you and I become friends? Friends look out for each other; friends don't walk out on each other without an explanation; friends don't humiliate each other; friends don't show up in the middle of the night threatening to kill themselves; friends don't try and stiff each other with their hospital bills; so, for as long as you live, do not ever call me friend again, you got it?"

The room became so silent that you could hear the pounding of Tina's heart. Then, Ernie slowly raised up on one elbow, and as he looked at Tina, he began to speak ever so softly. "Yes Tina, I am guilty; guilty of everything you said except one. I have not attempted to stiff you into paying my hospital bills. When I was asked to complete paperwork, I held off because I'd hope you would be able to get me released when you come. I don't need anyone paying my bills. I am a very wealthy man, and besides, I have medical insurance. I do not have anyone to handle my business if I'm unable, except my attorney. Before I showed up at your home, I made out a will leaving all my possessions to you and your charities. Within the contents I also stipulated that should I become hospitalized, you would handle my affairs. So, I wasn't trying to stiff you, I just don't like involving outsiders in my business, do you understand now? If I wanted too, I could buy this hospital."

Tina was silent; "why would he do such a thing; I don't want anything that belongs to him." "I hear what you said Ernie, but my question is why, why me?" "Evidently you didn't hear what I said, and I'm too weak to explain it again. Do you have a pen?" "Yes." "Then write down this name and number please." Tina took a pen from her purse and began writing down information that Ernie gave her. On the list were bank account numbers, the name and address of his attorney, and the password to his safety deposit box. When she'd finished writing, Tina looked down at the list as if she was seeing a ghost. "What's wrong Tina?" "Are you absolutely sure that you don't have anyone else that can handle these things for you?" "I am sure." "What about your attorney?" "While I trust him on some things, I do not trust him with most things. As I stated early, I am a wealthy man, that has been taken advantage of quite often. I know that you will do what is right, I trust you."

"Okay Ernie, I am only going to your safety deposit box because I assume that is where your medical policy is, but beyond that, you will have to manage your own business. You are not out of your mind, just out of control. You have allowed things to pile up on you without dealing with them. Yes, you are older now, but you still have life, which means you still have a chance. I would suggest that you take advantage of this opportunity and get yourself healed. As for you and me, there are no you and me, and as soon as I make sure that you are being taken care of properly, I am out of here. I do accept your apology, but I have not forgotten what you put me through, so whenever you find your place of peace, please, do not come looking for me."

When Tina had finished talking to Ernie, tears were flowing down her face like a river stream. Ernie's heart felt heavy that he had put the one person who cared for him through such turmoil. "I understand Tina, and I know it is a lot to ask after what I've done to you. I promise, if I make it through this, I will always be grateful to you, but I will never bother you again." Tina felt a sense of relief, for some strange reason she believed Ernie when he said he would leave her alone.

The next few weeks were overbearing for Tina. She had contacted the therapist she used at the shelter to do an assessment on Ernie. Upon completion, he determined that he needed to remain hospitalized until he became more stable minded. At first Ernie was reluctant, but after a few sessions with the therapist, he decided to comply with treatment, and began showing signs of improvement. Tina had refrained from visiting Ernie per the therapist's request. She was glad that she didn't have to make that decision on her own.

After several months of treatment, Tina was asked to join Ernie in one of his sessions. At first, she refused to take part, but when the therapist told her that he had a major breakthrough with Ernie and her being there was key to his success, she agreed to go. During the session, Ernie apologized to Tina again for the things that he had done to her, but this time was different. This time he didn't blame anyone except himself. This time there were no tears. This time, he asked for forgiveness.

At the end of the session, Ernie and the therapist thanked Tina for coming in. Ernie knew in his heart that he was seeing Tina for the last time. He was thankful that she cared enough to help him find redemption for his life. Although he had a long way to go, he had made significant progress and was no longer suicidal. Before walking out of the therapist's office, Tina bent over and kissed Ernie on the cheek. "Take care Ernie and have a great life; goodbye." She did not wait for a response. She walked out without a backward glance, putting Ernie Capers behind her forever.

Chapter Twenty-Five

The experience with Ernie made Tina become aware of her own traumatic past. She saw first-hand what could happen to someone when they failed to deal with their situations. For years she buried her emotions in her subconscious and refused to seek professional help. She had convinced herself that she had gotten over all the bad things that happened to her in the past. Now she had to come face-to-face with the reality that her past was very much a part of her present and was preventing her from having a future. Each meaningful relationship that she had, she found a way to sabotage it. But she always managed to place the blame on the men. When she should have placed blame on Ernie, she defended him and even fell out for a time with her friend for telling her about him.

While self-examining her mental status, Tina concluded that she had gotten over the rough spots in her life and was now sailing smoothly. "If I am so together, why am I still alone?" she thought. Tina couldn't help but shed a few tears; here she was now fifty-nine and all alone. She never thought that her life would end up that way.

When she was in her mid-twenties, she had her whole life planned out. She would have the perfect family and the perfect career. As for her career, she was satisfied; she had advanced at an early age and was even thinking of retirement. But her personal life was a whole other story. "Maybe I wasn't meant to be in a relationship; maybe I was created to serve and help others through their hard times."

It had been quite a while since Tina had seen her friends Shanell and Marley. They were still in their dysfunctional relationships and didn't seem to have time for her. "Oh well, I am going to give it one more try, and if Shanell tells me that she is unable to have lunch with me today or anytime soon, I am going to cut her lose forever." She looked at her phone to check for the time before dialing Shanell's mobile phone. "Hello." "Hello Shanell, it's been a long time, how are you?" "Oh, my goodness; girl I was just thinking of you." "You were? I guess great minds think alike." "Yea, I was thinking about the times we shared and the fun we had, I miss those days." "Yeah, I miss them too, so how have you been?" "To be honest Tina, I have been miserable." "Why, what happened?" "You know that I left Nate." "No, you did not! I don't believe you; when did this happened?" "Actually, it has been about one year, I just could not take his abuse any longer." "Good for you girl, good for you. So, what are you up too now that you are a free woman?" "I recently met the most wonderful guy that took my misery away, and for the first time in a long time, I feel loved." "Loved, what do you mean loved, you mean by a man?" "Of course, I mean by a man, why did you say it that way?" "Because at our ages, we don't need to be looking at no man." "Says who?" "Says I, we have grandchildren, what man would want us, better yet, what man do we want?" "Speak for yourself honey, I am in love and I'm loving every moment of it." "Well to each his own."

Tina was so shocked by Shanell's news that she forgot her reason for calling. "So, Tina, what made you call me after all this time?" "I was calling to see if we could have lunch together and try rekindling our friendship, what do you say?" "I say yes, I would like that, have you reached out to Marley as well?" "No, I haven't but I plan too; do you know how she is doing?" "Yes, she is not doing well, she lost her husband a few months ago and it has taken a toll on her mental health." "Why? She should be glad that no good sucker is dead, look at all the hell he put her through." "Tina!" "Well, I'm just saying, she should be crying out of one eye and rejoicing out of the other." Despite her effort not to, Shanell couldn't help but burst into laughter. "There's the Tina I remembered, girl you are one crazy sister."

Since it was around lunch time when Tina called Shanell, she asked if she could meet her at one pm. "Sure, I'll see you at one." When Tina and Shanell met at the restaurant, they were excited to see each other. When they were in reaching distance, they both reached out to embrace the other. "Hello Shanell, it is so good seeing you again." "Same here, I am so sorry that I didn't respond to you when you attempted to reach out, but I was in such a mess that I didn't want you to know just how bad it was." "It's ok, sometimes we have to do what is necessary to keep peace, I'm just glad that you found the strength to free yourself from that toxic situation." "So am I girl, so am I."

Tina and Shanell spent their lunch hour reminiscing about their younger years. "Tina, did you ever find out the name of your mystery man?" "What mystery man are you referring too?" "You know the one you danced the night away with during our clubbing days." "Oh, now that you mention it, I didn't; I have no idea what his name was." "Why don't we go back to the club and see if he's still there." "Shanell, you must be out of your mind, do you know how long that was, and besides, what would I look like going to a club at my age." "I am so sick of you talking about your age. One would think that you are ninety years old. You are still young, active, and attractive, you might be surprised to find that he still goes there." "Yes, I would, he's probably been married for years and have about a dozen grandchildren." "Dang Tina, you went all the way to the grandchildren, you are thinking like an old lady."

When lunch was over and Tina and Shanell parted company, they made a promise to stay in touch and not let so much time pass before they saw each other again. "I tell you what Tina, why don't we have lunch at least once a week." "That sounds great, maybe we should call Marley and invite her as well." "Okay, do you want to call her or should I?" "I will call her, you always made fun of her; you were never as close to her as I was." "That is true, I really liked her though, it's just that she was so darn dingy." "Let it go Shanell, let it go." Both ladies laughed, hugged, and said "goodbye, until the next time."

When Tina returned to her office, she was too wired to do much work. She sat behind her desk and began going over the conversation in her mind she had with Shanell during lunch. Shanell was happier than she had ever seen her, and she looked great. "That new man in her life must be treating her well. Here I am thinking that I am too old for romance. She's a year older than I am and she seemed to have found love. Oh well, if no one wanted me when I was young, I doubt that anyone would give me a second glance now. What am I thinking, I've allowed myself to get all worked up because Shanell's dating? That's Shanell, she and I are different and have different beliefs." As hard as she tried, Tina could not get the thought of meeting someone and falling in love out of her head. "I wonder what it would feel like to have a real man in my life. One that would treasure our relationship and treat me like a queen; I bet that would be nice."

Tina was so distracted that she took the rest of the day off and went home. Once inside, she decided to take a steamy bath. "I feel like pampering myself, I don't need a man to feel good about myself." This was something new for Tina because she always felt common looking, and never did anything special for herself. She was always helping and caring for others, but when it came to her. She almost always neglected herself. She ran the tub almost fill with hot steamy water. As the water was running, she poured a half bottle of lavender bubble bath body wash along with lavender essential oil under the flowing water. She lit several French vanilla scented candles and found some slow jazz music on her iPhone. She poured herself a glass of sparkling cider and sat it on the side of the tub, then she took off her clothes, hung them on the back of the bathroom door, and walked over to the tub. Before getting in, she stuck her toes in to make sure the water wasn't too hot. After she determined that the temperature was just right, she stepped into the tub, and slowly slid herself down to the bottom, causing some of the water to pour over the sides of the tub. She threw her head back and groaned, "now this is what I call living large."

Tina stayed in the bathtub for quite a while before she decided that it was time to get out. "I'd better get myself out of this tub before I shrivel up like a prune." She pulled herself up from the water just as slowly as she had eased herself in. She stepped out on the mat and began gently drying herself with a big fluffy white towel. When she had dried her skin, she picked up a bottle of body oil and began rubbing herself down. Tina thought to herself, "it has been years since my body was touched by a man." She walked over to her full-length mirror and began spinning from left to right looking at her curves. The years had been good to her. Her body was still firm, and her belly was as flat as a pancake. Her breasts were still perkier than the average thirty-year-old. She began to see herself in a new light. She was amazed that she had never really looked at her body before.

Usually when she took a shower or bath, she would dry and lotion herself away from the mirror. She did not want to see what she looked like; she thought that she was unattractive, because that was the way she wanted to appear to men, to prevent anyone from wanting to harm her. In many ways, she was still the nineteen-year girl that got raped. But now it was as if she was seeing herself for the first time. She got a lump in her throat and had to swallow it down. She was amazed by the shape of her body. "Do you mean I had all of this the whole time and never realized it?" Whenever anyone would complement her, she would blush and often felt offended. She believed that they were just patronizing her, but now, here she was with this newfound motivation. What was she going to do with it?

After admiring her body in the mirror for several minutes, Tina slipped into a soft pink silk negligee. She felt feminine and sexy. She walked over to the lazy boy sitting in the corner and sat down. She looked over at her bookstand and decided she would read a book, something she had not taken the time to do in a while. She got up from the chair, walked over to the bookstand, and began looking through her book selections. She had read most of them, but there was one that she'd purchased a few weeks back and had not had the chance to read it. She looked at the attractive cover and began reading the title, My Invisible Lover, by Barbara Williams Brown. Maybe that's what I need, an invisible lover; then I wouldn't have to worry about him cheating, hitting, or lying because I would make him to be whatever I needed at that moment." She laughed at the thought as she walked back to her chair, sat, and began turning the pages of her book.

Because she'd left work early, she had some extra time before making herself dinner. After she had been reading for a couple of hours she placed a bookmark between the pages of her book, laid it on her bed, and headed for the kitchen. By now she was beginning to get a little hungry. Before Judy left for the day, she had prepared dinner for Tina and left it in the refrigerator. All she needed to do was heat it up in the microwave. Tina looked in the refrigerator and pulled out her dinner. "I hope Judy made me something good, I feel like a real meal." When she pulled the covers from the containers, she was excited. Judy had made her roast beef, with carrots and potatoes, one of her favorite dishes. She had also made a green salad, with dinner rolls.

Tina was still in her congenial state of mind as she sat at the table to eat her dinner. She felt a type of serenity that she seldom felt over her lifespan. She sat, slowly eating, and thinking about her current life. She'd made a point of not looking back at her past, because it only caused her grief to do so. She thought of her mom and remembered that she had not spoken to her for the day. She always made a point of calling her mom everyday around the same time, and sometimes she called her several times throughout the day. She picked up her phone from beside her plate and began dialing her mother's number. Mrs. Elena answered the phone with excitement. She was always glad to hear from Tina. "Hey mom, how are you?" "I'm fine, what took you so long to call?" "I'm sorry mom, I had a really busy day and sort of lost track of time, forgive me?" "Okay, I'll forgive you this time, but don't you let that happen again," she said laughingly. "I won't mom, I promise." "It sounds like you're eating, are you?" "Yes mam, I'm eating dinner, I didn't want to wait until after I finished to call since I was already late." Tina and her mom only stayed on the phone for a few minutes before hanging up. "Good night mom." "Good night, Tina Dear, call me tomorrow on time." "Yes mam, I will." When Tina hung up from talking with her mom she was smiling. She felt blessed to still have her mom, healthy and alert.

Tina enjoyed her dinner and got to eat a portion of it while talking on the phone with her mom, it was almost like she was having dinner with her. After she'd finished eating, she washed her dirty dishes, put them away and headed back to her bedroom to retire for the night. The night was still relatively young, and she was not sleepy at all. "I think I will finish this book before I go to bed, I want to see the outcome." Tina picked up her book, sat back on her lazy boy, reclined in a semi-laying position, crossed one leg over the other, and continued reading her novel.

Tina was so engrossed in her book that she didn't realize the time. When she got up to use the bathroom, she looked at the clock sitting on her night table and gasped; it was one A.M. "Oh my goodness, where did the time go?" When she returned from the bathroom, she looked at her book and looked at her bed. She still had a few more chapters to read but she was beginning to feel a little drowsy. She placed the book on the chair and said, "don't you go anywhere, I will finish you tomorrow night." She laughed, turned back the covers and crawled into bed. Minutes after her head hit the pillow, she was out like a light.

Despite going to bed after one AM in the morning, Tina woke up at her usual hour of seven AM. She was excited but didn't know why. "Why am I feeling so hopeful and excited as if something wonderful is about to happen? I hope I'm not getting ready to die." She chuckled as she headed for the shower. She wasn't in the mood for a long shower since she'd taken an exceptionally long bath the night before. She was in and out of the shower within five minutes. After drying and moisturizing her skin, she jumped into her clothes. She always dressed conservatively, but today she was going to change it up a bit. Instead of the usual skirt suit or pantsuit she normally wore, she put on a royal blue, flared shirt dress with shoes to match. She laced her lips with a burgundy lipstick and wore a matching pearl necklace and earrings. When she'd finished getting herself dressed, she went over to the mirror to admire the outcome. "Maybe I should do this every morning, I sort of like how I feel, and my new look. She picked up her purse and the keys to her car and headed outside with her head held high. She felt as if she'd just been told she had won a million dollars.

When she drove up to her office and entered the building, there were several employees in the lobby. At first, they didn't recognize her, but when she said, "good morning," they all stared in amazement before responding. By the time they did respond, she had already crossed the room and was on the elevator headed for the executive floor. Tina never felt superior to any of her employees, not even the janitors. She realized that each person played a role in the success of the company, and she treated them as such. As a result, they had very high regards for her, and would go out of their way to accommodate her needs.

When Tina reached her office, she was still feeling cheerful and optimistic. She sat behind her desk to begin her day. Shortly after she sat and began looking at her schedule for the day, she heard a tap on her door. "Yes, come in." "Good morning Ms. Tina." It was her assistant, Delany, bringing her morning coffee. "Thanks Delany." "Did you have breakfast this morning or did you have your usual granola bar?" "Oh my, I didn't have anything, I was in such a rush to get here that eating breakfast slipped my mind." Delany placed a breakfast ham and cheese croissant on Tina's desk along with her coffee. "I figured that you didn't eat, and even if you had, those granola bars are getting pretty old, you need better breakfasts in the mornings." "Yes Mam, thank you Delany, I will do better I promise." "Oh, by the way, Ms. Tina you look stunning this morning, not that you don't always look stunning, but this morning there's something different about the way you look." "Why thank you Delany, I feel different too." When Delany left her office, Tina could hardly wait to bite into that croissant, she was hungrier than she realized.

Tina was able to get a sizable amount of work completed by the end of her workday. She had cleared her desk of paperwork and attended all her scheduled meetings. As she reclined in her plush office chair, she thought to herself; "it is now time for me to take a much-needed vacation, even if I don't go anywhere special." Tina and Delany had gone over her calendar earlier to make sure she didn't have any pressing commitments coming up within the near future. When they'd completed going over her calendar, she instructed Delany not to schedule anything on her calendar for the next three weeks. "Good for you Ms. Tina, you are one hard working lady, you deserve to have some time for yourself, who knows, maybe you will find Mr. right while you're on vacation." Tina didn't try to defend herself as she normally would, instead she said, "who knows, maybe I will," with a cunning smile on her face.

Chapter Twenty-Six

When the day had ended and Tina finally left her office, she was still feeling quite energetic. She walked into the parking lot where her vehicle was waiting for her. As she drew nearer, it seemed to say, "come on inside, I've been waiting all day for you." Tina pulled open the door, slid in the seat, latched her seatbelt, then started the engine. Before driving off, she turned on the radio, something she rarely did. With music softly playing, she drove out of the parking lot as if she was never going to return.

After about five minutes of driving, Tina remembered that it was Shanell's birthday, so instead of turning towards home, she turned in the opposite direction, and headed downtown towards the gift shop. When she arrived, she sat in her car for several seconds before getting out, trying to decide on what she wanted to give Shanell. This was a milestone for Shanell, she had turned sixty. "What a blessing, she thought to herself, Shanell survived sixty years after all she endured with that no-good husband of hers." She eased herself from behind the wheels of her car and headed inside the gift shop. Once inside, she was just as confused as before. Shanell was never hard to please, but she wanted to give her something spectacular. "I bet she thinks that I have forgotten all about her big day, heck I almost did."

Tina spent so much time looking from one thing to another that a salesclerk came over to assist her. "May I help you mam?" she asked. "Yes, you certainly may," was Tina's reply. The young lady was very pleasant and patient with Tina; she showed her a variety of items before Tina decided on a lavender silk negligee. She remembered that Shanell had told her of some guy she was dating. "I still think that she's too old to be dating but maybe this will help her out, she thought to herself.

Why Shanell wants to be in another relationship after what she went through with her ex is beyond me, but who am I to judge?" Tina had the salesclerk wrap Shanell's gift rather than just putting it in a gift bag. "I want her to know just how much thought I put into selecting this gift." When the gift was all wrapped, Tina paid the cashier and headed out of the store. She was proud of her purchase. "Oh hell, I forgot the card." She turned around and went back inside to purchase a card to go along with her super gift.

After getting the birthday card, once again, she headed for her car. When she was comfortably seated inside, she commanded her phone to call Shanell. "Hello Tina, what's up?" "Not much, I was just on my way home from work and decided to give you a call to see how you're doing." "You're sort of late, aren't you?" "Yes, I was tying up some lose ends before going on a much-needed vacation." Tina didn't let on to Shanell that she remembered her birthday, and Shanell didn't mention it to Tina, she was sure that she had forgotten. "So, what are you doing for the rest of the evening Shanell?" "Nothing much, why are you asking?" I was thinking that I would pick you up and we could go over to Marley's for a bit, she's a little under the weather." "Marley; hell, I don't want to see no Marley today!" "What's wrong with seeing her today? I've put of long enough, I think that we need to go; I will be to your place in about ten minutes, be ready."

Shanell was furious with Tina. "Not only did she forgot my birthday, but I'm supposed to be excited about going to see Marley, I'd rather have my head shaved." Just as Tina hung up from Shanell, she was passing a bake shop; she pulled in and went inside. The baker was decorating a beautiful chocolate cake. "Good evening mam, is that cake spoken for?" "It is now, would you like me to box it for you?" "Yes, I certainly would, this must be my lucky day." When the baker finished decorating the cake, she placed it in a cake box and handed it to Tina. "Thank you so much, you are a life saver." The baker did not ask any questions, just thanked Tina for her purchase as she smiled and took her cash.

Twenty minutes later, Tina rolled up into Shanell's yard where she was sitting underneath a tree. When Tina stopped the car, Shanell stood up and began walking towards Tina with the intension of getting into the car with her. "Your ten minutes sure did take a long time," she said as she pulled the passenger door open. "Where are you going?" "What do you mean where am I going, didn't you say we are going to Marley's?" "Tina could not keep up the facade any longer, she began singing in a very loud voice; happy birthday to you, happy birthday to you, happy birthday my friend, happy birthday to you." Shanell just stood there in shock with her hand covering her mouth. "Oh my God, I thought that you had forgotten." "How could I forget my best friend's birthday, come on over here and give me a hug."

After Shanell got over the shock of Tina's birthday surprise, she walked over and gave her a big hug. "Do you have time to come inside?" "Of course, I do, I have gifts." Tina pulled out the gift bag and the cake and began following Shanell inside her home. "Let me help you with that." "You just get the door; I have everything else." Shanell held the door open as Tina wobbled inside with her arms loaded with goodies. Shanell rushed to the table to direct Tina as to where to place the cake. Although the cake looked delicious, Shanell was more interested in what Tina had in the gift bag.

After safely placing the cake on the table, Tina turned to Shanell and handed her the card and gift. "Happy birthday Shanell, I hope you like it." "Oh, I like it." "How do you know if you like it? You haven't opened it yet." "Because I like everything you've ever given me, you are a great gift giver." Tina laughed as she waited for her friend to open her gift. "Wow! Thank you, Tina, I love it; I am a little surprise though." "Surprise by what?" "The gift choice, I know how you feel about me having a man in my life." "You know Shanell, I thought about it and came to the realization that I can't control everything and everyone. So, if some man makes you happy then I'm happy." "And he does make me happy, but not nearly as happy as I am when I'm making him happy." "Whatever." "So, are we going out to celebrate or what? That cake is enticing, but I don't think it's going to take the place of dinner. What do you say, do we go celebrating Shanell and Tina's style?" "I say let's do it."

Tina and Shanell decided to go to the nightclub where they went dancing as younger ladies. "I don't believe we are actually doing this, what do you think Marley would say if she found out?" "She would probably have a heart attack, so don't tell her Tina." Both ladies began laughing and were still laughing when they walked up to the entrance of the building. "Ok Shanell, turn it down a notch we don't want to attract any attention." "Why not? It's my birthday, I want to be noticed." "By whom?" "By anyone who looks." "Well, if we are noticed it want be because of our youthful appearances." "Speak for yourself, I'm sexy as hell." In spite of her cynicism, Tina had to laugh at her friend's jokes. "Okay sexy momma, you're right, it's your night, enjoy it."

"Tina, do you know what would be funny?" "No, what?" "If your mystery man showed up, you know the one whose name you never got." "Yes, that would be funny." Tina had learned over the years not to follow people up when they appeared stupid, and to her, that was a stupid comment. Although Tina wanted her friend to enjoy her birthday, she felt somewhat out of place. It wasn't that she was uncomfortable being at the club, it was a great establishment where all sorts of classy folk went, but she felt that she might be misunderstood as looking for a hook-up. "So, what's wrong with getting hooked-up, it would certainly be on time; do you realize how long it has been since you've been with a man?" "No Shanell, I have no clue; of course, I know, I live it every day, but I am contented with my life as it is." "No, you're not, you just tell yourself that you are."

After Tina and Shanell had finished eating, Tina was ready to go home. "Can we please stay just a little while longer? I don't know when or if I will ever come back here again." "Why sexy momma, your man won't allow it?" "He wouldn't keep me from coming, but it's not a place where he would be comfortable coming too, and I wouldn't want to come without him, not now." "What is he a monk or something?" "Almost, he's being ordained into the ministry." "So, what happens after that takes place, he dies or something?" "Tina, I swear you're nuts, I'll be a first lady." "Oh, I see, a sexy first lady." Both ladies laughed as they sat and watched the crowd.

After sitting for an hour, Shanell asked Tina if she wanted to leave. "Tina, I don't want to keep you past your bedtime so we can leave whenever you are ready." Tina didn't want to be a party pooper; besides, she was rather enjoying herself. "I'm good, you can stay as long as you like, this is kind of rejuvenating for me since I haven't been out socializing in a while." "Okay girl I hear Ya, just hollow when you're ready." "I will, enjoy your night."

Somewhere in the back of Tina's mind, she was hoping that someone would come over and speak to her, but in reality, she would not acknowledge that she was hopeful. She looked over at Shanell and wished that she could feel as at ease as she did. "After all these years, I still have hang-ups. Why can't I just relax like everyone else?" As she was thinking to herself, a gentleman walked over to her table and introduced himself. "Hello, my name is Zack; I was admiring you from across the room and would hate myself in the morning if I didn't come over and speak to you." "Hello Zack, how are you?" "I'm good, may I ask your name?" "Yes, you may, my name is Tina." "Does Tina have a last name?" "Yes, she does, but she seldom gives it." "Okay, then Tina it is." "Do you mind if I sit?" "Sure, have a seat."

Under normal circumstances Tina would be nervous by now but something told her to play it cool. Tina still looked much younger than her age and often got attention from young guys; this was no exception. She decided to play with it for a while. "So, Tina, are you married?" "No Zack, I'm single, and you?" "I am widowed, my wife passed away two years ago." "I am so sorry, my condolences."

"Thanks, it has been a long hard journey, but I am finally in a place where I can see light at the end of the tunnel." "That's good, I hope things work out for you." Tina no longer wanted to play with this young man, so she tapped Shanell on the shoulder and asked; "are you ready to go?"

"Sure, I was just waiting for you to say the word, but why so sudden?" "I just realized that I have not been home since I left work and I am somewhat exhausted." Zack took the hint and got up from the table. "It was nice meeting you Tina, I hope we meet again soon." "It was nice meeting you too Zack, good night." "Well, he's a cutie pie, why did you let him go?" "Because I don't want anyone that I have to put diapers on." "Gotcha." Tina had no intention of ever seeing Zack again, but the idea that he found her attractive at any age, and especially at her current age was exciting. She felt something come alive inside just thinking about what had just happened.

When Tina arrived home, her emotions were all over the place, by the thought of a younger man finding her attractive. "I think it is time; time for me to do something for myself. I have been helping everyone else while putting my needs and desires on the back burner; things have got to change." At that moment, Tina had no idea what her desires were, but she was darn sure going to find out. Shanell had just celebrated her sixtieth birthday, and she was only a year behind, hell it was time for her to either sing or get of the choir. There had been many times when Tina conflicted with her emotions; on one hand she would declare that she was fine and didn't need a man in her life, she even tried convincing herself that her ship had sailed and that she was too old for love. On the other hand, she would declare that she was going to do something for herself to brighten her life and diminish her loneliness. So, what would be different this time?

One day a few weeks after she'd met Zack while celebrating Shanell's birthday, Tina decided to put her thoughts of doing something for herself into action. Out of the blue, she decided that she would go and join a gym. She was always health conscious and exercised at home frequently in her private gym. She had even hired a personal fitness coach at one point, so joining a public gym was new to her. One of the ladies from work told her that she'd met her husband at a gym.

"Maybe you should give it a try Tina, it couldn't hurt and who knows, maybe you will get lucky as I did when I met Milton." At the time, Tina just smiled and shrugged her shoulders, but after giving it some thought, she said to herself; "Oh well, what the heck, Tandra is right, I have nothing to lose, but I don't want to seem desperate either."

Chapter Twenty-Seven

"Hello Ms. Tina, welcome back, how was your vacation?" "Vacation, did I have a vacation?" Tina asked jokingly. "Don't tell me that you didn't do anything fun on your vacation Ms. Tina." "Okay Delany, I want tell you then." "Come on Ms. T., I know that you had a wonderful time, now do tell." Tina broke into laugher, I'm so sorry to disappoint you Delany, but I spent the time catching up on things at home, and spending time with my mom and friends." "What sort of things you needed to catch up on that you needed three weeks to do it?" "Rest, rest, and more rest." "Okay Ms. Tina, I won't argue with you on that, but I was hoping that you had gone to some resort and met some lucky guy." "Sorry to disappoint, but I am just great; refreshed and ready for combat." Both ladies laughed as Delany started towards the door.

Tina decided to leave work early and head for the gym close by her office building. She heard from several of her colleagues and employees that it was a reputable establishment, and that the staff were very patient and friendly. When she checked out the reviews, she noticed that they had received five stars out of thirty thousand reviews. So, with her mind made up, she closed her office door, locked it, placed the key into her purse, and headed towards the parking lot. "Will you be returning Ms. Tina?" asked a curious Delany. "Not today dear, not today."

When Tina pulled up in the gym's parking lot five minutes later, she began to have doubts as to whether she should go through with it. "Come on Tina, are you going to continue playing tug-of-war with your life, or are you going to do this? Yes, yes, I am. I am tired standing on the sidelines looking at others live their lives while I pretend to live mine. I want a life that consists of more than just having taken care of my children and of everyone else." Tina loved her children and how well they'd turned out, and she loved helping the clients at the shelter, and people in the community and at her job and at church, but if she didn't make some changes soon, she would end up old and alone. That was not something she looked forward to at all.

After some pondering as to her reason for doing this, Tina got out of her car, held her chin up and began walking towards the gym. When she reached the entrance, she pulled open the door and stepped inside. Due to the time of day she chose to go, it was very quiet inside with just a few people scattered about. A tall slender gentleman came walking towards her with a boyish smile on his face. "Hello mam, my name is Kirk, how may I be of service to you on this fine day?" Tina explained to the gentleman that she had a desire to become a member. "Great, come on into my office and we will get you all set up." Tina followed Kirk into his office where he offered her a seat. She politely thanked him as she sat on a stool that was standing in the corner. "Are you comfortable sitting on the stool mam?" "Yes, I am, thank you." At that moment, Tina realized that she had never introduced herself.

"By the way, my name is Tina." "Nice to meet you Tina, is there a last name?" "No, Tina lied, just Tina." Kirk smiled as he recorded Tina's information on the enrollment form. "Okay Tina with no last name, will you be needing a coach?" "No, not at this time, I would just like to have access to the gym for now, I am pretty familiar with most of the equipment.' "You appear to be in good physical shape, have you been working out?" "Yes, I power walk and some other cardio routines, as well as resistance." "Great, then I will just give you the instructions and guidelines along with our policy and regulations. Should you have any questions, I will be glad to answer them for you. Welcome to Girya Fitness Center, where our goal is to help you achieve yours."

Tina thanked Kirk for his assistance, as she shook his hand. "So, are we all set?" "Yes mam, all done, the gym is yours to explore, will you be starting today?" "Tina looked down at her attire and laughed. "Yes, I am, you do have a dressing room, don't you?" "Yes mam, I was just about to give you a guided tour of the facilities." "After you sir."

After Kirk finished showing Tina around the gym, she thanked him again and went to her car to retrieve her sportswear. When she returned, she went into the dressing room and changed. When she walked back into the gym, several guys that were standing together chatting, turned, and looked in her direction. Tina felt a little uncomfortable by the stares, but as she got closer to where they stood, she nodded her head towards them and hurried outside. She carefully placed her work clothing in her car, closed and locked the door, and headed back inside the gym. "I am not going to let a few stares get to me, after all, I'm on a fishing expedition. How can I catch a fish if I'm afraid of the bait?"

When she reentered the gym, the guys had scattered and gone in separate directions. She walked over to the treadmill and pretended that she didn't know how to get it started. A chunky little fellow with an oversized gut, who appeared to be much older than herself, came over and asked if he could assist her. "No thanks but thank you for asking." "Are you sure, I don't mind showing you how it works." Tina didn't want to be rude, so she pushed the button and started the machine. "See, I'm good, thanks." The man mumbled something to himself and walked away.

Tina plugged her earbuds in and pretended to be listening to music. Truth be told, she was listening to hear what those guys that were staring at her, thought of her. She could not make out a thing they were saying so she turned her attention to her workout. After she had been on the treadmill for about thirty minutes, a gentleman that she had not seen when she initially came inside, walked over, and got on the treadmill next to hers. Assuming that she could not hear him with the earbuds plugged in, he didn't speak to her. Tina looked over at him and gave him a shy seductive smile. He responded with a nod of his head, and a half smile. She looked at his ring finger, and there it was, a big shiny wedding band. "Oh well, she thought, this one's out." Tina stayed on the treadmill another couple of minutes after the gentleman got on next to her. "I think I will call it a day, at least I have broken the ice, next time maybe I won't feel so intimidated and out of place." With a towel draped around her neck, she headed towards the exit. Just as she was about to push the door open, she heard someone calling out to her. She turned around to see Kirk running towards her. When he reached her, he apologized for yelling her name out so loud. "What is it, is something wrong?" "No, I neglected to tell you that this is bring a friend week, and since your membership starts on a Monday, you may bring a friend along until midnight next Monday as a thank you for choosing our fitness center." "Thanks Kirk, it was certainly a pleasure meeting you." "Believe me, the pleasure is all mine." Kirk was aware of the age differences between him and Tina when he requested her birthdate to be included in her membership application, but that didn't stop him from admiring her. "She's one hot lady, some guy sure is a lucky man." "Was that all?" "Yes mam, that's it, have a wonderful evening." "Tina smiled at Kirk and exited the building, leaving him standing there drooling.

When Tina arrived home from the gym, it was much earlier than she usually got home from work. Judy had left for the day and the house felt empty and quiet, yet peaceful. She decided to take a hot shower before doing anything else. She went into the bathroom, stripped off all her clothing and hopped into the shower. After a long hot shower, she climbed out and put on a pair of silk pajamas. Although she wanted to take a short nap before dinner, she was to wound up to do so. She was proud of herself for taking the initiative to finally do something for herself. She looked at herself in the mirror, and as usual, saw a plain-looking face staring back at her. "Maybe if I start wearing makeup I would look better." Except for an accessional lip gloss, Tina had never worn make-up. She seldom went to the beauty salon to have her hair and nails done, she had convinced herself that it was a waste of time and money, and that she could do all those things for herself. While still looking at herself in the mirror, Tina began twirling around and looking at her body from different angles. She turned her attention to her face, but she still did not see the ravishing beauty that was staring back at her.

"Oh well, she thought, not much is going to change this face, but I will give it a try." She looked at her dressing table but there was nothing to see except several shades of lip gloss, some perfumes, and lotions. She glanced down at her watch to check the time. "If I hurry, I can make it to the mall and back before dark" She grabbed her purse and headed for the door. Tina always loved big cars, and the Lincoln parked in her yard reflected that. She slid inside and started the engine. The neighbor across the street was raking her yard and pretending not to see Tina as she backed out of her driveway. Tina could see her peeping under her glasses, trying to figure out why she'd come home so early and where she was now going. "Keep guessing old lady, keep guessing." Tina was accustomed to her nosy neighbor spying on her; actually, she thought it was adorable.

Chapter Twenty-Eight

When Tina arrived at the mall, she jumped out of the car as if something or someone was chasing after her. She headed towards the entrance on a mission. Once inside, she went straight to Delta Beauty and began looking around, but didn't have a clue as to what she needed. She was beginning to feel helpless when a beauty consultant walked up to her and asked if she could be of assistance. Tina felt a sense of relief. "Yes, you certainly may; I am trying to determine what makeup I need." "What are you currently wearing?" "Lip gloss." "Are you saying that you are not wearing any other makeup?" "Exactly; I have never worn anything on my skin except various face creams and lotions, am I hopeless?" "No, you are gorgeous, I could have sworn that you were wearing foundation, your skin is flawless. "Thanks for the ego boost, so can you help me?" "Sure, once you tell me what look you are going for, I will be glad to assist you." "What look? I just want to look different, you know, pretty." "You are pretty without the makeup, but I understand what you're saying, you want to enhance your beauty."

Tina smiled at the consultant and asked, what is your name?" "Oh, I'm sorry, we got to talking and I forgot to introduce myself, I am Tina." "Nice meeting you Tina, my name is Tina as well." "Swell, Tina said laughingly, perhaps same names mean same ideas." After chatting with Tina for a while, the beauty consultant took Tina over to the middle of the store and introduced her to the make-up artist. Luckily, the artist had some free time in between appointments and was able to help Tina. She had Tina sit while she gave her a step-by-step lesson on applying makeup. Tina was intrigued, the artist was knowledgeable and friendly, and was very patient with her. When Tina left the store, she had a professional makeover, a supply of makeup, as well as a lesson on makeup that she didn't know existed.

Tina went home with all the supplies and knowledge she needed to do her own full-face makeup. She had a bag stuffed with goodies; inside her bag she had, primer, foundation, cream, concealer, blush, highlighter, bronzer, setting spray, mascara, eyeliner, eyelashes, and of course, lip gloss. She could hardly wait to go inside and take another look at her purchase. Tina was so excited that she had forgotten to eat, but when her stomach began to rumble, she put down her bags and headed for the kitchen.

After dinner, Tina went into the bathroom to take a shower. She did not want to wash the makeup off her face. For the first time in her life, she felt pretty. She looked in the mirror at her well-made-up face and began to cry. "It has taken me all these years to really look at myself, and I am not too bad looking." Instead of taking a shower, Tina decided that she would not shower since she had done so when she came home from the gym. "I am going to bed with my make up on and when I get up in the morning if it's still there, I am going to wear it to work and shock everyone. Now that I've gone to the gym, got a makeover, and bought a ton of makeup, what's next?" Tina wanted to change her lifestyle and was making small efforts to do so, but she just wasn't sure what to do. After pondering around different ideas in her head, she gave up and went to bed.

When Tina woke up the next morning, she got out of bed and went straight to the bathroom and looked in the mirror. She wanted to see if her makeup had stayed on. There it was, just like it was when she went to bed, everything was still intact. "This might seem crazy, but I'm not washing my face. I will carefully brush my teeth without interfering with my makeup, and sponge bath my other body parts." She was determined to let her colleagues see the new and improved Tina. After her sponge bath, she pinned her hair back, so that she could reveal her entire face without distractions. She wanted them to get the full effect. Normally Tina dressed conservatively, but today she was going to wear something she purchased from Macy's while she was at the mall. Something that she would never have dreamt of wearing before. She looked inside her closet and pulled out the beautiful royal blue crew neck midi dress with a contrasting three quarter sleeve jacket. She hung a white diamond pendant necklace around her neck, and diamond stud earrings in her ears. She almost always wore low to flat heels to work, but today, she stepped into a pair of three inches' black pumps with ankle straps. She was now ready for the day.

When Tina arrived at her office an hour later, she was experiencing all sorts of emotions. For some strange reason, she felt young again, as if the years had not passed. At the same time, she felt a little foolish for feeling the way she had. Her main emotion was that of excitement and anticipation; she wanted to see the reaction of her co-workers when they saw the changes in her appearance. She eased herself from the seat of her car, straightened her dress, took a deep breath in, exhaled, and headed towards the door. When she reached the door, she slowly pulled it open to draw attention to herself. Once the attention was caught, she threw her head up and began walking towards the elevator to her office. "Good morning, everyone." Tina did not wait for a response before saying, "it's a beautiful morning, isn't it?" She was walking with a confidence that she'd never experience, and this time it was not the act of a clown.

When she'd reached the elevator's door she turned around and looked at the two gentlemen colleagues standing with their mouths slightly opened. "What's wrong fellows, cat got your tongues?" She smiled, gave them a wink, and stepped inside the elevator. Once inside her office, she placed her purse on her desk, and picked up her phone to page her assistant. "Hello Delany, would you mind bringing me a cup of cappuccino please." "Of course, Ms. Tina, I will be right there." Delany had not seen Tina when she arrived and had no idea of the shock she would receive when she entered her boss's office.

"Yes, Tina responded to the tap on her office door, come on in Delany." Delany pushed the door open, and walked inside; "good morning Ms. Tina; OMG, what happened to you? "You look amazing. I have never, ever, seen you with makeup." "Good morning to you too, Delany, thanks for the cappuccino and the compliment; I thought that I would try something different, do you like it?" "I love it Ms. Tina, you look like a completely different person. Don't get me wrong, you are always beautiful but today you are stunning." "Thank you, Delany, do you think that I look good enough to catch a fellow?" "Oh Ms. Tina, you definitely do." Tina laughed and explained to Delany that she just wanted to feel the experience of wearing makeup. "I see you gals always wearing it, so I decided, why not; no special reasons." "Okay Ms. Tina, if you say so," as she winked and left the office.

When Delany closed the door behind her, Tina burst into laughter. "Oh, my goodness, do I look that presumptuous?" She opened her laptop and began strolling through her calendar to check her upcoming appointments. Most of her meetings were scheduled with people she'd done business with within the past, or colleagues from work, but there was one name listed that she did not recognize. She picked up the phone and dialed Delany. "Hello Ms. Tina, what can I do for you?" "There's an upcoming meeting with a Mr. Godfrey, do I know him?" "I don't believe that you do, he called while you were on vacation and scheduled an appointment to meet with you." "Oh, I see; do you know what it's about?" "No, I don't, he did not give me any information, just that he wanted to meet with you to discuss business." "Ok, check your agenda to see if you will be available at that time, I don't think I want to meet with him alone; for some reason I am getting a weird vibe." "Ok Ms. Tina, will do."

The meeting with Mr. Godfrey was scheduled for later in the week, but Tina just could not seem to shake the feeling that she was having. She'd met with tycoons from all over, and never had this type of anxiety before or after a meeting. "I will be glad when this meeting comes and ends, it's doing a number on my emotions." Tina decided to complete her own little background check on this guy, so she began a google search. She saw a lot of Antonio Godfreys but couldn't make head nor tail as to who this guy was, or why she felt so compelled to check him out. She picked up the phone and called Delany. "Yes Ms. Tina." "Delany, do you have any other information on this Mr. Godfrey that you haven't given me? I would like to know a little about him before meeting with him on Thursday." "No mam, he only gave his name, but he did leave a phone number in case we needed to cancel or reschedule." "Let me have that number, I think I will give him a courtesy call." "Okay Ms. Tina, I will look it up and text it to you if that's ok." "Sure, do that." Within seconds after Delany hung up from speaking with Tina, her phone began ringing. "Hello, Media Electronics, this is Delany, how may I direct your call?" "Hello Delany, this is Antonio Godfrey, is it possible that I may speak with Mrs. Tina Bradshaw?" "Hold sir, I will check." While Antonio held the line, Delany paged Tina and informed her that he was on the line. "Would you like to speak with him?" "Yes, I would, put him through please, thank you."

Hello Mrs. Bradshaw, how are you on this fine day?" "Hello, Mr. Godfrey, is it?" "Yes, Antonio Godfrey." "How may I help you Mr. Godfrey?" "I am calling to verify an appointment I have scheduled with you on this coming Thursday." "Yes, what about it?" Antonio was caught a little off guard by Tina's seemingly lack of interest. Obviously, he didn't know the savvy business tycoon, by the name, Tina Bradshaw. Antonio cleared his throat before speaking again." I am aware that you were on vacation when I made the appointment, so, I was just calling to see whether you may have any questions before our meeting." "As a matter of fact, I do; can you tell me a little about yourself and what this meeting is in reference too."

"Of course, you know my name; I am founder and CEO of Media Marks, and I have a proposal that I would like to present to you but would prefer to wait until our meeting before going into details. Will that do for now?" "I guess it will have too, I will see you on Thursday unless there was something else you needed to say." "No, that's it, looking forward to seeing you again."

After Tina hung up the phone, she realized that Mr. Godfrey said he was looking forward to seeing her again. "What does he mean, looking forward to seeing me again, when has he ever met me?" Now she had something else haunting her. Who was this man, and why did he want to do business with her company? "Now that I have a business associated with his name, I may be able to locate him on google search." With her mind focused on getting some type of information on this man, Tina began searching the internet to see what she would come up with. When she put his name along with the business name in the search box, bam! There he was, picture and all. Mr. Antonio Godfrey, big as life, businessman of the year, five years in a row, and one heck of a looker. Tina went on to read his bio and was amazed by each sentence.

Tina just sat there staring at the photo of Mr. Godfrey trying to figure out if she'd ever met him and if so, where? Nothing came to mind, so she decided to dig further. She just had to know as much about this man as possible before her meeting with him. Or was there another reason she wanted to know? It had been quite a while since Tina had come face-to-face with such a distinguished-looking gentleman. Although many of her colleagues were men, and most of them were sharp, they had nothing on Antonio. And besides, those guys all worked for her, and she saw them every day. Most of them were married with children and some grandchildren. She never really saw them as men, just colleagues.

As Tina stared at the face in the photo staring back at her with a devilish smile, it seemed to come to life. "Oh my god, its him, it's the gentleman from the club. After all these years, I finally know his name, but why now, what does he want from me?" Tina closed her eyes and began reminiscing about the times she danced with the nameless stranger at the club and the way he'd made her feel. "I don't know if I can do this, maybe I will have him meet with Hanson, and they can fill me in later. Tina hadn't thought about the mystery man for years, she'd put him out of her mind. Now here he was stirring up old emotions that she didn't know what to do with. No one at work knew her story about the mystery man from the club, she never told anyone. Shanell and Marley were the only ones that knew, and she was sure that they had forgotten him just as she had.

After staring at Antonio's picture for over ten minutes, Tina pulled herself back into reality. "I have got to get some air, and I've got to talk with someone about this. Shanell of course, was the lucky choice. She picked up her phone and dialed Shanell's number. "Hello Tina, what gives?" "Hello Shanell, what do you mean?" "I mean what's going on, you don't normally call me from work unless you need to talk." "Are you free for lunch?" "I can make myself free, where too?" "Can you meet me at Sonny's Wings and Burgers?" "Dang Tina, you know that I'm vegan, why can't we go somewhere else?" "Because I feel like some wings, and they have the best in town, besides, they have vegan food, you can get a salad or something, come on girl, what do you say?" "I say, I will see you in twenty minutes, besides, I'm dying to hear what you have to tell me." "Thanks, Shanell, I knew that I could count on you?"

When Shanell hung up from speaking with Tina, her curiosity peeked. "I wonder what's going on with Tina. It will be nice if she tells me that she finally met someone, it has been a long time that she's been alone, I sincerely pray that things are changing for her. Oh, well, let me stop jumping to conclusions, I guess I will find out soon enough." Shanell was in the middle of something when Tina called, but she gladly put it aside to assist her friend. It would take her fifteen minutes to drive to Sonny's, and five of them had already gone. "I guess I will have to do a little speeding to get there on time, I don't want to be late for this." Shanell rushed out of her office and into the parking lot to her car. She hopped in behind the wheels and sped out of the parking lot into traffic. As soon as she entered the freeway, a state trooper got behind her. "No, not today, please not today." Shanell turned on her emergency flashes and sped on down the freeway. The trooper stayed behind her but did not pull her over. When she reached her exit, she looked in her rear-view mirror and low and behold, the trooper was right on her tail. "Dang! It Looks like I may be getting a speeding ticket."

Shanell pulled over to Sonny's and stopped her vehicle. The trooper pulled up beside her and rolled down his window. "What's the emergency mam?" Shanell's first instinct was to lie, but she looked the officer straight in the eyes and said, "I'm hungry?" The officer couldn't help but laugh. "Would you like to come in and have lunch with my friend and me? There she is pulling up now." The officer opened the door to his vehicle and got out. "Why not, why the hell not?" He began walking towards Shanell as an, astonished Tina looked on. She had often warned Shanell about her fast driving and now she was going to get arrested. She was somewhat hesitant to walk over to where her friend was standing so she just stood watching Shanell as she conversed with the officer.

"Come on Tina, those wings ain't goanna wait all day." Tina slowly walked towards Shanell and the officer. "Hello, how are you doing?" "We're doing well, this is officer Williams, he will be having lunch with us, apparently, he loves wings too. Officer Williams, this is my friend Tina." "Hello Tina, please to meet you." "Same here sir." Tina was wondering, what did Shanell do, why would she invite someone else knowing that she needed to talk with her. "I hope she's not playing matchmaker again, cause if she is, I'm going to kill her."

Tina, Shanell, and Officer Williams shared a wonderful lunch. He shared the incident about Shanell's speeding and her excuse for doing so. "That's my Shanell, always has an answer for everything, that is why we are having lunch together today, to get some answers for myself." "See, said Shanell, looking over at the officer, I told you that I had an emergency." "Yes, you did, but you said it was because you were hungry. It has been nice sharing lunch with you ladies, but I must get back to work, but before I do, let me give you a little piece of advice Shanell; do not speed, I will not be as lenient the next time." "Okay officer, thanks for everything, and thanks for keeping too lonely ladies' company." Officer Williams nodded his head towards the ladies and walked out of the restaurant.

"Well doggone Shanell, what was that all about?" "That was about saving my behind from getting a ticket." "How in the devil did you get him to have lunch instead of serving you with a speeding ticket?" "I think that I caught him off guard, besides, he was hungry." "Well, whatever the reason, I'm glad you didn't get a ticket." "Yea, you, and me both, but I wouldn't have been speeding if I wasn't trying not to be late for our meeting. So, tell me, what is so important that I had to rush here." "I never said you had to rush, you put the time on it. I just said lunch, and you said twenty minutes." "Yea, but the way I figured, you had something juicy to tell me and I didn't want to wait to find out what it is." "Nothing juicy, just want to run something by you." "Okay, let's have it."

Tina took a deep breath before speaking. Girl, "Is it that bad?" "No, it's not bad, at least I don't think so." "Well spill, this suspense is killing me." "Shanell, do you remember many years ago during our diva days, when I danced with the same guy several times at the club without ever knowing his name?" "Yes, I remember, but why are you bringing him up now, you don't think he would still be coming to the club do you?" "Oh, hell no, he's probably settled down with a cozy little family." "It wouldn't be cozy and little now, heck he probably has grandchildren." "Could you stop with the humor and listen to me." "Ok, Tina, I'm sorry, what happened, did he die?" Tina couldn't help but to laugh; only you Shanell, only you; no, he didn't die." "Well, how would you know, you never got his name remember."

By now Tina was feeling a little put out by Shanell's warped sense of humor, she was finally feeling some of what Marley felt when she was around Shanell. "Please, will you just listen for a minute? You are making me think twice about telling you anything." "I'm sorry Tina but you look so serious, I'm almost afraid to hear what you have to tell me." "It's nothing bad Shanell, actually, it's quite interesting." "Well in that case, go ahead, what's up with the mystery guy from your distant past?" Despite her annoyance with her friend, Tina couldn't help but to laugh at her comment.

"When I returned from my vacation and checked my calendar, I had a meeting scheduled with a man by the name of Antonio Godfrey. I was a little concerned as to who he was, but when I attempted to check him out, there were so many people with the same name, and I had no other information. Just when my assistant was preparing to call him for additional information, he called and asked to speak with me. When I asked him the reason for the meeting, he identified himself as being CEO of this media company.

When the call ended, he said he was looking forward to seeing me again. After we hung up, it dawned on me that I didn't know him, so why would he make such a comment; so, I looked up the name of his company." "Oh yea, what did you find?" "I found him, my mystery man." "What makes you think that he is the same person, it has been years since you danced with him, and even then, it was only a few times." "I would know that face anywhere. Remember, I was remarkably close to it." So, what does this mean Tina?" "I don't know, that's why I'm talking with you, to get some advice." "Well, I'm sorry but my advice well has run dry." "Girl, you're no help. To be honest with you though, I just wanted to share that with you, I don't need any advice, it's just a business meeting." Tina felt better after sharing her news with her friend, but she was still curious as to the reason this man chose to seek out her company.

After her long lunch with Officer Williams and her friend Shanell, Tina headed back to her office. When she'd settled in her chair behind her desk, she turned her laptop on and took another look at Antonio. "There must be more to his story than what's printed here." She began scrolling up and down trying to find something more. All the information on Antonio Godfrey was limited, no mention of family. "Well, this is strange, you would think that a major player like him would have a more extensive bio." Tina finally gave up on her search and decided to get some work done. After all, she would be seeing him in a couple of days.

Finally, the workday ended for Tina, and she was ready to go home, but instead of going home, she headed for the gym. She needed to get her mind off Antonio, and what better way to do it than to break a sweat. When she arrived at the gym, she took her sport shorts, sneakers, and crop top, and headed for the dressing room. She looked around but didn't recognize any of the faces in the place including the trainers. "Good, she thought, there want be anyone asking if I need assistance." After She'd gotten into her gym clothing, she placed her business attire in her locker, and made for the treadmill. When she was about to step on it, a rugged looking fellow came up beside her and stopped. "May I help you?" she asked. "Oh, I'm sorry, I didn't mean to stare but you are the finest thing I've seen in here in a long time." "First of all, I am not a thing, and second, if you don't mind, I would like to get on with what I came here to do." "And what is that, if you don't mind my asking." Tina refused to answer him and hopped onto the treadmill and started walking at a fast pace. "Wow, I'm impressed." "Believe me, it is not my intention to impress you." "I'm sorry mam, I didn't mean to offend you, but you are a beautiful lady; I will just be on my way, have a great evening."

Though Tina was flattered she was also annoyed by the way the man approached her. When he turned his back, she tried to catch a glimpse of his full body. "Not bad," she thought, "but I don't like his attitude." Come on Tina girl, get a grip, wasn't the purpose of joining the gym in the first place was to attract men? How are you going to do that if you keep pushing them all away?" She took a deep breath, got down from her treadmill and walked over to where the man who'd approached her earlier was working out.

"Hello sir." "Yes" "I just wanted to apologize for my behavior earlier." "Apology accepted but can you explain why you are so defensive; all I did was give you a complement." "It wasn't the complement that offended me, but the choice of words." "Do you mean that I called you a fine thing?" "Yes, those are the words." "Sorry, but where I come from, most women like to be called a fine thing." "Well, where I came from I don't. Listen, I just wanted to apologize, you have no way of knowing that I have a son around your age." "What does age have to do with it?" Tina found herself blushing before she said, "maybe I'm just behind the times." Her moment in the gym seemed to have been spoiled, so she went to the dressing room to gather her clothes. On her way out, several other gentlemen were looking at her as well. "This is not going to work; I think they may be on to me." Tina picked up her pace and headed outside of the building and to her vehicle. When she reached her car, she slowly turned and looked behind her to see if anyone was still looking at her; she had become paranoid. When she saw that no one was paying any more attention to her, she opened the door to her vehicle and climbed in behind the wheels. "Well, there goes nothing."

Tina knew that if she was to have a chance at a personal life, she would have to loosen up. "This uptight attitude is getting me nowhere." With all her life's accomplishments, she was still self-conscious when it came to socializing outside of her safety zone. She could facilitate meetings with a room full of people looking at her and hanging on to her every word; she could present at seminars with thousands of onlookers; she could stand before judges and present evidence of domestic violence for her clients; and she ran a multi-billion-dollar conglomerate, with hundreds of subordinates, but she felt uncomfortable with one-on-one conversations with the opposite sex, especially if it became personal. She never gave much thought over the years as to why relating to men was so difficult for her, but she never realized until now that it was. She had held on to the idea that all men were alike, and that none had good intensions.

Most of the men that Tina aligned herself with, except for her employees and colleagues, were abusive in some form. From the time she was eight years old when her male family member assaulted her, until her marriage to an abusive husband, she had low opinion of men. All her friends were in abusive relationships, and she was the founder and owner of a haven for abused women. Even when she attempted to date in the past, she encountered some type of abuse, whether verbal or emotional, so no wonder she was so stiff when it came to men.

Tina realized that she had not dealt with her past in the healthiest ways, but she felt she had her life under control despite her past. Often when assisting her clients at the shelter, she recommended and referred them to seek counseling. She had even contracted a therapist that specialized in domestic violence and addictions to work with her clients, so she knew full well the benefits of therapy. Tina felt that if she was to seek counseling, she would be forced to disclose the family member that assaulted her as a child, and she did not want that to happen. She'd convinced herself over the years that they were both young and that he didn't understand what he was doing. It was easier that way since she idolized him.

As she drove herself home from the gym, tears began to flow from Tina's eyes. She was beginning to think that maybe she wasn't as together as she'd led herself to believe. She remembered once when she was married to Derrick, how he shouted out that she was crazy and needed help. She remembered how she'd laughed in his face and told him to go suck lemons. "Now that I'm thinking about it, maybe I do need help, it's never too late to find a peace of mind." As quickly as the thought of therapy entered Tina's mind, she dismissed it just a fast. "Hell, I went through all these years without pouring my guts into some therapist's ears, I may as well spend the rest of my years trying to live, I don't think that I've done half bad." Tina shrugged her shoulders as if to shake off whatever was bothering her and continued home at high speed.

When Tina arrived home, she got out of her car and went inside. She gently closed the door behind her as if someone else was entering with her. Tina began looking around the room as if this was her first time being there. She looked at the beautifully decorated rooms with everything in their places. She looked at the pictures and artwork on the walls, and her designer drapes, hung by an interior designer. For the first time in years, she really saw her home. It looked like a museum, not a home. She walked into her bedroom where once again, everything was in order. Suddenly she felt the need for a little dysfunction and disorganization.

Without changing clothes, Tina turned and walked back outside; she was going to a place where the house was messy, and nothing was in order. What better place than her friend Marley's house. Marley had her three grandchildren, and they were as wild as field Deer's. She stepped back into her vehicle and headed west to her friend's house. "I sure hope she's home; I would hate going all the way there to find out she's not at home." She didn't want to let Marley know she was coming because she would straighten up before she got there. She wanted everything to be just as she imagined it; messy.

Tina arrived at Marley's house in a record fifteen minutes; it usually took her almost thirty minutes to drive from her home to Marley's, especially in the evening traffic. Before getting out of the car, she just sat there for a few minutes drinking in the peaceful scene. There were no fancy porch chairs, or perfectly trimmed scrubs in the yard; just a porch swing that was swinging back and forth by the force of the wind. Tina began smiling as she let herself out of her car. She walked up on the porch and rang the doorbell.

When Marley asked, "who is it?" Tina decided to prank her as she had done so often in the past. "It's me, the neighbor," Tina lied. Before she could gather back her composure, Marley swung open the door with a big grin on her face. "Hi neighbor, want you please come in." "How did you know it was me?" "Come on Tina, did you really think you could fool me that easily?" "Yes, I use to do so, and quite often if I remember correctly." Both ladies burst into laughter; "come on in girl before I give you a piece of my mind." "I hope you give me a good piece because I didn't have any dinner." "What brought you over on an empty stomach unannounced?" "I got to thinking about you and the kids and thought it would be a good breakout to come by. I didn't want you going to any trouble for me, so I didn't let you know beforehand." "That is perfectly alright as long as you don't mind the mess these children have made." "It really is fine, that is part of the reason I chose not to call, I needed some noise and disorganization, and chaos." "Well, you got it."

Marley's grandchildren finally calmed down by dinner time, and sat mannerly at the table, eating their meals. "Tina, would you care to join us for dinner, I have more than enough." Tina's first instinct was to say no. She didn't eat at most people's houses, but this would be an exception. "Sure, if you think there's enough." Yes, there is plenty enough, so get a plate and dig in." Tina didn't need to be told twice, she picked up a plate and helped herself to a large portion. She was glad that she decided to stay for dinner, the food was delicious, and the children were on their best dining behaviors. "I could get use to this Marley, eating meals with family, it has been quite a while since I've had dinner with my children as a family." "Shouldn't they be coming home soon, they always come for your birthday." Yes, normally they would, but this year my birthday falls on a Monday, so I've asked them not to come." "Do you really want to be alone on your birthday?" "No, not really, but it's only one day, and I will be going to see them soon.

When dinner was over, Tina helped Marley clean up before sitting in the family room and watching a movie with the children. When the movie ended over an hour later, Tina yarned and stood up. "I had better be getting home, I have a busy day at work tomorrow. Thanks so much for letting me crash you and the kids evening." "Oh no, thank you, it is not often I get adult company and especially such famous ones." Tina never thought of herself as being famous with all her accomplishments and achievements, to her she was just Tina

Bradshaw. "Well thank you, we are going to have to do this again and soon." "Tina, I'm sorry we didn't get much alone time, seems like you have something on your mind." "Not really, just life and the ups and downs of it, but I'm fine." "Okay, if you say so, but you know if you ever need a listening ear, I am here for you." "Thanks Marley, I will definitely keep that in mind." Tina hugged the children and her friend and left, waving, and throwing goodbye kisses as she made her way to her vehicle.

When Tina had sat comfortably behind the steering wheel of her car, she lowered her head and took several deep breaths. She was feeling much better leaving Marley's than she did when she arrived. "It's just something about being around kids, make you forget all about your troubles, at least for a while." She lifted her head and started the engine. Before driving off, she checked to see if Marley and the children were still watching her through the glass door. Thankfully, they had gone back inside. She let out one more deep breath then headed towards home.

Chapter Twenty-Nine

Today was the day that Tina would meet face-to-face with her past mystery man. She spent most of the night tossing and turning trying to figure out in her head, his purpose for wanting to do business with her company. "After all these years, why am I so nervous to meet this man, after all, we have met before, I just didn't know his name." After thinking back, Tina became a little angry. She distinctively remembered asking him his name on one occasion, and he flat out refused to tell her. "Just who did he think he was, some god?"

The next morning, Tina took a little longer getting ready for work than usual; she wanted him to see just what he'd let slip through his fingers all those years ago. "I wouldn't want him now if he was served on a golden platter, that time for me has passed." Despite her I don't care attitude, Tina was beside herself with curiosity, and anticipation. After carefully applying the new makeup she'd purchased a while back, she finally got herself fitted into a sleek purple dress, with matching earrings and black shoes. She left her neck bare but slipped a diamond bracelet around her wrist. To get a more professional look, she put on a black silk blazer. Now, she was ready for the day; ready to meet Mr. "I never told you, my name."

Tina often got to work early, but today she was super early. When she arrived, there was no one else on the premises, just as she wanted it. She went inside and turned on the lights, then decided to make her own coffee instead of waiting for Delany. When the coffee had finished brewing, Tina poured herself a cup and headed towards her office. She was so worked up that she forgot to add sugar and cream. Once inside her office, she turned the lights on, sat her coffee cup on her desk and opened the blinds allowing the sunlight to shine through. She picked up her cup and took a sip. Tina could not stand black coffee so you can imagine what she did next. As soon as the bitter coffee touched her tongue, she blew it out of her mouth. "Dang! Is this how the rest of my day is going to be, because if it is, I may as well go home now."

As the morning progressed, Tina became so involved with a project she was completing that she had forgotten all about her meeting with Antonio Godfrey. With her shoes kicked off and her feet relaxing, she picked up the ringing phone. "Yes Delany, how may I help you?" "Mr. Godfrey is here for his meeting with you." "Okay, give me a minute and send him in." "Yes mam, will do." Mr. Godfrey was a little put out with Delany for telling him he had to wait for a few minutes. He was not accustomed to waiting for anyone, he was on time, and he expected Tina to be too. "What do you mean have a seat, she'll be with me in a few, I have an eleven o'clock appointment, it is eleven o'clock and I'm here, I shouldn't have to wait." "I'm sorry Mr. Godfrey, Ms. Bradshaw will see you in a few minutes, it won't be long." "Well, I certainly hope not, my time is valuable, I don't have any to waste."

While Antonio was debating back and forth with Delany, Tina was busy composing herself. When Delany figured enough time had passed, she walked over to where Mr. Godfrey sat, and said, "Ms. Bradshaw will see you now sir." "Thank you," responded a somewhat disgruntled Antonio, as he followed Delany to Tina's office. Once at the door, instead of knocking as she normally would, she pushed the door open, and said, "Ms. Bradshaw, Mr. Godfrey." Tina was expecting them since she'd told her assistant to give her a few minutes before showing him in.

"Hello Ms. Bradshaw, good to see you again after all these years." "Hello Mr. Godfrey, finally got to know your name, how are you?" "Doing well thank you; you are still as beautiful as I remembered." "Thank you, I am surprised you remembered me, it has been quite a while." "Yes, it has, but some things, and some people you just don't forget, have you forgotten about me?" "What would have been the purpose of remembering?" "Oh, I don't know, just something to hold on too during times of loneliness." "So why did you want to meet with me?" Tina asked, deliberately changing the subject. Antonio scratched the side of his face as if something had bitten him, then said in a more professional tone, "I have a business proposition that I would like to run by you," he stated, as he avoided looking directly into Tina's eyes. "Sure, please have a seat and let me hear what you have to say."

Tina made her way behind her desk and sat as she motioned for Antonio to sit across from her. When he bent over to take a sitting position, Tina kept her eyes fixed on his face. There was something about him that she'd never noticed before. She realized that he was a relatively tall and attractive man, but she did not remember him being unusually tall, or so incredibly good looking. Something inside of her made her legs go weak, and when she attempted to speak, her words would not come out. "Is everything alright Ms.

Bradshaw, you seem a little distracted." "Yes, of course, I'm fine; I just lost my balance a little when I sat, she lied."

When Tina and Antonio were both comfortably seated, he began explaining his proposition to her. He wanted to merge a portion of his company with hers and come on board as co-CEO. "Are you kidding me, why would I accept such an offer?" "Before you turn me down, have your attorney look over my proposal, discuss it with your board members, and then get back to me. You will find that it is a hell of a good business move." "First of all, Mr. Godfrey, I am giving serious consideration to retiring, therefore, I'm just not sure that I want to take on such a tremendous amount of additional responsibility at this stage of my life." "That is one of the reasons I would come on as co-CEO, that way all of the extra work would not land on your shoulders." "Ok, I hear what you're saying, but what I don't get, is why." "What is it you don't get Tina, Ms. Bradshaw? And I just told you the reason." "Why my company? There are lots of other companies out there, why the interest in merging with mine?" "Because I've done my research; this is not just a spur of the moment decision, I have been discussing the idea with my team for over a year, and we finally decided to pitch the idea to you. I don't expect you to make any decision today, or even in the next few days, but I do hope that you will seriously consider it and get back to me within the next few weeks if possible. So, what do you think, will you at least do that?" It was now Tina's turn to scratch; she reached behind her head and began scratching her neck without realizing it. She looked at Antonio with some apprehension, but finally agreed to at least give it some thought.

"Okay, Mr. Godfrey, I will give your proposition serious consideration and will do my best to get back to you as soon as possible. After I've made my decision, I will have my assistant call and set up a follow-up meeting to discuss the results." Thank you, Ms. Bradshaw, that's all I'm asking, just give it a chance." He rose from his seat and extended his hand towards Tina. She stood as well and returned the handshake. "Thank you for thinking of my company, I will get back with you soon." You are quite welcomed Ms. Bradshaw, I look forward to our next meeting, and hopefully we won't be so formal." Tina ignored his last comment, pulled her hand free from his, and returned to her seat as a way of dismissing him. Antonio caught the hint and walked towards the door. Just as he placed his hand on the doorknob, he turned around and looked back at Tina. "Yes, was there something else?" "No, there isn't," then turned and walked out of her office. "Huh, I wonder what that was about?"

Over the next few days, Antonio Godfrey kept creeping into Tina's thoughts. She couldn't figure out for the life of her why he specifically contacted her. "I don't know what's on his mind, but that ship has sailed and docked. There ain't no going backwards for me, especially not that far back." She smiled to herself and decided to ride it out. After she had gone over the entire proposal, she asked Delany to set up a meeting with her board members to discuss Mr. Godfrey's proposition and hear their opinions on his request. This was a decision she did not want to make on her own.

"Okay Ms. Bradshaw, meeting is all set, the earliest date on your calendar was Next week Thursday. Everyone is free and has agreed to attend, is that good for you?" "Yes Delany, that's perfect timing, it gives me a chance to do some more research before meeting with the others. Of course, I don't know how well Mr. Godfrey will accept the extended date, he seems a bit impatient." "Yes, he does, doesn't he, I picked up on that when I told him that you would see him in a few, he didn't like that at all." "Well, he can take it or leave it the choice is his. Please see what next available time I have after the staff meeting and set something up with him." I will get right on it." Tina was grateful to have such an efficient assistant as Delany and often told her so.

During the meeting, Tina was able to answer all the questions that was presented to her by the board members except one; "why our company?" "That is the million-dollar question, one that I've asked Mr. Godfrey, so I will share with you what he said to me. According to Mr. Godfrey, after conducting his own research into our company, he deduced that our company would be the best fit for him and his company's goals. My question to you though is this; how do you feel about his proposal to assist me as co-CEO?" "Well Ms. Bradshaw, you have never steered us wrong in the past, so as far as I'm concerned, whatever decision you make, I will support one hundred percent." Thanks for the vote of confidence Hanson, but I really would like for everyone to be on board with the final decision." "I think we're all in sync with allowing you to make the final call, right guys?"

Everyone agreed that they were fine with whatever decisions Tina made. "I am just appreciative that you thought enough of us to include us when you have every right to make this decision solely on your own. Shows what a great person and leader you are, thanks Ms. Bradshaw." When Hanson had finished speaking, Tina was in tears, she really did admire her staff, and was overjoyed by the amount of respect they had shown her over the years. "Okay then, after I've made a final decision, I will send you guys a copy, and a memorandum of this meeting. Thanks for coming and brainstorming with me; meeting's adjourned, have a good remainder of your day."

After everyone had left the conference room, Tina leaned back in her chair at the head of the table and smiled. She felt so accomplished yet so unaccomplished. She still had the responsibility of making the decision and did not want to take a biased approach. She deliberately did not tell the other board members about her personal encounters with Antonio because she didn't want to be judged. Now she was back to square one; she had to find a way to separate her past emotions for this gentleman and establish a professional relationship the way she would with any other client. But could she, do it? On one hand, she didn't want to appear too lenient, but on the other, she didn't want to be overly hard core. "Okay Tina, you can do this, he's just another business quest, you've done this hundreds of times."

Chapter Thirty

Three days had passed since Tina met with the board concerning the merger with Antonio Godfrey, but she was still indecisive about what she should do. Her attorney had looked the proposal over to see if there were any loopholes, but there were none to be found. The thing that bothered her the most was his suggestion of coming on board as co-CEO. That did not appeal to her at all. "Maybe, just maybe, I will need to meet or at least speak with Mr. Godfrey once more before accepting or dismissing," which she was leaning more towards.

Tina picked up the phone and dialed her assistant. "Yes Ms. Bradshaw." "Delany, would you please see if you can set up a conference call with Mr. Godfrey." "Sure, when would you like me to set it up?" "Now, if he's available." "Yes mam, I will get right on it." As quick as she could put her phone down, it began bussing. She picked it up again assuming that it would be Mr. Godfrey. "Yes, hello, this is Tina Bradshaw." "Hello Ms. Bradshaw, I have Mr. Godfrey on line two." "Thank you, Delany, I have it from here."

"Good afternoon Mr. Godfrey, this is Tina Bradshaw, thanks for taking the time to speak with me." "Hello Ms. Bradshaw, I'm never too busy to speak with you. Am I to assume that you've reached a decision?" "If you did you would be making the wrong assumption. As a matter of fact, I have not; I need a little more input on your role, and why it would be necessary for you to co-CEO with me before I make my decision." "I just think that it would be a good business move." "Yes, you've made that abundantly clear before, but you're only merging a portion of your company, is it the least profitable portion?" There was silence for a few seconds, then Godfrey began to speak again as he cleared his throat. At that moment, Tina's decision became clear to her, but she would hear him out.

"Well, yes, that particular area of the company is not as profitable or as popular, but with your company's backing and my helping to steer it, it will supersede both of our expectations." Godfrey was a savvy businessman, and he knew that he was not dealing with an average businessperson. He felt caught in deceit and attempted to justify his proposition. Tina just listened as he buried himself deeper and deeper into the hold he'd dug. When he had finished trying to convince Tina that accepting his proposal was the way to go, he asked her, "so what do you think Ms. Bradshaw, do we have a deal?" If only he could have seen the look on her face. "This is what I think Mr. Godfrey; I will have my assistant call and set up an appointment with you and we will discuss the outcome as previously planned, is that good for you?" "Yes, I will be waiting to hear from you, thank you." "Thank you, Mr. Godfrey, have a good afternoon," as she slowly placed the phone on its receiver.

"Just who does he think he's dealing with, some rookie? I have been in this business long enough to know a skunk when I smell one." Tina was somewhat disappointed, because on some level she was curious to know more about the mysterious Mr. Antonio Godfrey. "I guess I will never know, because I don't think I will be taking any walks down his avenue any time soon." "Delany, please set up a meeting with Mr. Godfrey, but no rush." "Will this be a staff or private meeting?" "Private, just Mr. Godfrey and myself." "You have space on your calendar for after lunch on tomorrow, would you like for me to see if he's available then?" "What part of no rush did you not understood?" "Ok, I'm sorry, I will recheck your calendar." "No, I'm the one sorry Delany, I didn't mean to take my frustration out on you, but anytime next week or the week after will be fine." Delany felt better that Tina had apologized, she was not accustomed to her snapping at her that way and wondered what caused it.

Delany scheduled the meeting between Tina and Antonio one week from the date of their phone conversation. Antonio was shocked when he received the call because he believed that he had blown his chances. "I should have known that a class act like Tina Bradshaw wouldn't just ignore a situation. Of course, she did let me off all those years ago by not finding out my name. Maybe she just wasn't interested enough to care." Contrary to Tina's lack of knowledge about Antonio's past, he knew practically everything there was to know about hers. He had kept up with her over the years and was impressed with her story. This meeting was promising to be quite interesting. After thanking Delany for the information in a very pleasant tone, he politely said good-bye and hung up the phone. Delany remembered his last visit to the office and shrugged her shoulders. "Must have gotten up on the right side of the bed this morning," she said out loud to herself.

The day of the big meeting between Tina and Antonio had arrived. Tina awoke that morning with a headache. "Of all days to have a headache, why today?" She slowly dragged herself out of bed and walked over to the bathroom mirror. She looked into her eyes and saw that she had dark circles as well as bags underneath them. "Oh well, who cares, after all, my trying to impress a man day is not today." After much deliberating about what to wear, she decided to dress in black, so she pulled on a black silk skirt with matching jacket. Underneath, she put on a black laced sleeveless shirt with ruffles at the neckline. She accessorized it with black pearls, and a black bracelet around her wrist. Then with black pantyhose, she stepped into a pair of black pumps. After all that was accomplished, she laced her lips with a light gold lipstick and highlighted it with clear lip gloss. To feel extra feminine, she sprayed her favorite juicy couture perfume on her neck and wrist. When she had finished dressing for the day, she looked in the mirror at her result and burst into laughter. "Well dang! It looks as if I'm going to attend a funeral." She thought maybe she had gone a little overboard with the black, but since she was running a little behind schedule, she wouldn't have time to change. She picked up her purse and keys and headed for the door without stopping to get breakfast. "Oh well, this meeting may turn out to be a funeral after all."

Tina was determined that she would cut Antonio's plan off at the knees, and that this meeting was just a formality. When she arrived at her office building, the parking lot was empty. A slow jazz was playing on the radio which put her in a mellow mood. She felt a sense of peace that she had not felt since speaking with Antonio a few weeks earlier. Today would bring an end to something that never began, but always hung in the balance of her mind. She opened the door to her Audi Q7 and slowly threw one leg out while the other one followed. Once out of the vehicle, she stood as if in attention, then straightened her skirt before walking towards the building. Since she was the first one to arrive, she unlocked the door, opened it and stepped inside. Once inside, she closed the door behind her, disarmed the alarm, then headed for her office to get a jumpstart on her day.

On a normal day, Delany would have a steamy cup of cappuccino waiting for her on her desk, but today was far from a normal day. Today she would let someone know what it feels like to underestimate her intelligence. Today, she would once and for all, bury the ghost of the mystery man of her younger days. She was excited about her meeting with Antonio; the thought of it made her adrenaline rise to a new level of high. Instead of getting her own morning drink, she decided to wait on Delany, after all, some things just needed to remain constant. When she'd been sitting behind her desk for about ten minutes, she heard the alarm, warning that someone was entering. She checked the monitor and saw that it was Delany, right on time as always.

"Good morning boss, you're early this morning." "Good morning, Delany, yes I am, wanted to get a head start on my meeting with Mr. Godfrey this morning." "Great, I prepared the conference room before leaving on yesterday." "That's great, and I do appreciate it, but if you don't mind, please set everything up in my office. This meeting should only take about forty-five minutes, and I would like to not be disturbed for the duration of it." "Yes mam, so you won't be needing me to sit in with you?" "No, not for this meeting, I think that I will be alright." Delany was careful to set up Tina's office on time, remembering the dissonance she experienced with Mr. Godfrey before, because of a few minutes' delay in his appointment with Tina. When everything was in order, Delany brought in a fresh pot of coffee along with Tina's cappuccino and placed it on her desk. "Will there be anything else mam?" "No thanks Delany, everything's fine; thank you." Delany smiled at Tina as she left her office; call if you need me, I will be just on the other side of the door." "I will."

Delany had just made it back to her desk when the door to her office opened. She looked up and saw a well-dressed Antonio Godfrey standing just inside her office. "Good morning, I hope I'm not too early." "Good morning Mr. Godfrey, Ms. Bradshaw is expecting you, I will let her know that you're here, please have a seat." "Thank you" as he humbly sat and waited. "Yes Delany." "Mr. Godfrey is here for your meeting." "Thanks, send him in, better yet, bring him in." Delany stood up and addressed Mr. Godfrey; "Ms. Bradshaw will see you now sir; please, right this way. She led Antonio to Tina's office and tapped on the door before opening it. Before Tina had a chance to respond, Delany pushed the door open and said, "Ms. Bradshaw, Mr. Godfrey; then backed her way out.

Tina stood as Mr. Godfrey entered. "Good morning, please have a seat" as she pointed towards the chair opposite where she sat. "Good morning, thank you," as he planted his behind down on the plush chair. "May I offer you a cup of coffee?" "Yes please, I would love a cup." "How would you like it?" "Black thank you, no sugar." "Yuck." "Pardon me." I said yuck; what's the point of drinking coffee if you're not going to put anything it?" "I could ask you the same thing; what's the point of messing up a good cup of coffee with cream and sugar?" Tina laughed; you got me on that one, but I drink coffee for the taste, not the effect." "Yes, to each his own, or in this case, her own." Tina handed Antonio his coffee and positioned herself back in her chair opposite him.

"So, Ms. Bradshaw, I take it you've reached a decision." "Yes Mr. Godfrey, this time your take is on point; I have reached a decision, but before I tell you what it is, let me brief you a little on trying to pull a fast one on me. Tina really didn't have to say any more at this point, because Antonio knew what her answer was going to be. "Ms. Bradshaw, before you give me your answer, or your briefing, may I please say something?" "Of course, you may, what is it?" Tina was intrigued to see what other rabbit Antonio planned to pull out of his hat.

Before speaking, Antonio took a long deep breath just as he'd done the last time they'd spoken, only this time it was in person. Tina saw the worried look on his face as he attempted to speak. "What is it Mr. Godfrey, are you going to remind me again of what a fool I would be to let this opportunity slip through my fingers?" "No Tina, you're no one's fool. As I told you before, I have kept up with you over the years, and I know firsthand what a shrewd business powerhouse you are. I wouldn't dare try and pull anything that's not above board on you." "Okay, then please enlighten me, because from where I'm standing, you are trying to pull a fast one on me." "May I ask you a question?" "Sure, what is it?" "Did you at any point based your decision on our past?" "What past Mr.

Godfrey, we don't share a past. Are you referring to those few times we danced at the club a hundred years ago?" "I guess when you put it that way, it would seem foolish." "As you said earlier, I am a professional businesswoman who would never allow something as trivial as not knowing someone's name from years ago, that would have no merit even if I did, determine a business decision. So, Mr. Godfrey, whatever decisions I've made is based solely on your presentation, do you understand?" "Yes, I do, I guess that was a stupid question." "Yes, it was, what I don't understand is why would you ask it in the first place."

Once again Antonio found himself in an uncomfortable position with Tina. "I do have a reason, Tina; may I call you Tina?" "I would prefer that we remain professional, but frankly, whatever you call me is irreverent." "Okay, I will need to go back in time and come out again for you to fully understand where I'm coming from, may I do that?" "I don't know if we have enough time for us or you to go back too far, I only allocated forty-five minutes for this meeting, and we've lost ten of them already." "This is important to me, so if you could find it in your heart to extend our meeting a little longer, I would really appreciate it." "Okay Mr. Godfrey, I will tell you what I'll do, since our meeting is bracing lunch, I will extend it, but I'm going to need to eat because I haven't had any breakfast. I will have my assistant order out and if you like we can work through lunch." "Great! That will work out just fine. I promise I will be as brief as possible."

"Now that we have the extra time, maybe you should step on back in time so you can be out by lunch." "Ok, where do I start?" Remember when we were younger and found comfort in each other's arms on the dance floors?" "If that's the way you want to remember it." "Come on Tina, I'm not the only one that felt something, and I don't believe for one minute that you've forgotten." "Dancing with a nameless stranger years ago is not something that I think about or remember. Sure, I can think back and remember the details when you bring it up, but prior to now, I had no reason to bring it up or think about it, so yes, I have forgotten about it, why haven't you?" "Because it was you that inspired me to become the man that I am today. Because of you, I am someone I can be proud of; because of you, I feel worthy; all because of you." Tina started to open her mouth to speak, but Antonio shushed her. "Please, let me get this out while I have the opportunity, this may be my last chance."

Tina sat quietly listening to Antonio as he poured his soul out to her. "Look at me, I am six feet five. When I was seventeen, I was six feet four, that's when you knew me." Tina couldn't contain herself any longer; "I didn't know you when you were seventeen, what are you talking about?" The reason you didn't know me or saw me around the community was because I didn't live in or near your neighborhood. I lived in Dover." "Dover?" "Yes, Dover Delaware. I lived there with my grandparents, but every summer since I was twelve, they would send me to South Carolina to spend time with my uncle, the one that owned the club where we met. I was not old enough to go to the club, but when I turned sixteen, because of my physique, and height, I could pass as older." "So, what are you saying?" I am saying that the man you danced with was not a man at all but a seventeen-year-old boy who was passing himself off as a man." Tina was stunned and in disbelief. "Do you realize how old I was at the time?" "I knew that you were a woman, but you looked so young for your age. I thought that perhaps you were nineteen or twenty, but I overheard you and your friends talking about not being a spring chicken. I took it upon myself to do a little digging and found out that you were thirty. I knew that if I told you, I would never get to see you again, so I wouldn't give you my name for fear you would discover my secret. I had fallen so hard for you that I became lovesick. At the end of summer, I didn't want to return home, so my grandparents asked my uncle if I could stay indefinitely. Every chance I got I came to the club looking for you and hoping that I didn't blow my cover. Just to hold you in my arms and make your day a little brighter just for a little while meant the world to me. When I finally turned eighteen, I decided that I was going to tell you my name and age, but then this article came out about your successes, and I knew that I would have nothing to offer you. I had just finished high school and had no intension of going to college, so I was not, and felt that I would never be worthy of you." Normally Tina would have been asking questions and making all sorts of comments by now, but instead, she just sat there as if she was frozen.

Antonio was speaking at a rapid speed because he knew that when Tina did speak, it wouldn't be pretty. The last time I saw you I was nineteen. It had been a long time since I'd seen you and had no idea that you would be at the club on that night. When you and your friends came in, I saw you looking around, and then some guy approached you. I wanted to tell him that you belonged to me, but that would have been foolish so I walked up from behind you and in my deepest voice, asked if we could dance. Once again you made my night. You placed your hand in mine, and we walked out onto the dance floor not saying a word. That was the night when I decided that I was going to make something out of myself. That was the night when I said to myself, one day, I will be worthy, and one day I am going to make her mine. So, I went to college, graduated at the top of my class, and moved to South Carolina."

As Antonio continued, Tina sat in disbelief. All the while thinking to herself, "do you mean to say I carried a torch for a teenager?" She felt betrayed, but mostly she felt dirty. "How could she not have known that he was so young?" Well, for one, she always saw him in dim settings, and as he stated, he looked much older than he said he was. "I guess you're wondering what happened all those years in between, and why I'm just now confessing." "When Tina was finally able to speak, she said, "not really, but I'm sure you're going to tell me." "Yes, I am, I'm no longer holding back. I may still not be worthy of you, but I am not going to allow those fears to control my actions any longer." It was weird to hear someone say that they didn't feel worthy of her, because that was the way Tina felt her entire life. Maybe if she didn't have such a low opinion of her own self-worth, she would have noticed she was dancing in the arms of a teenager. At that moment, a small tear dropped from Tina's eye. "Don't cry Tina, please, this is not to make you feel bad, but to help you understand where I am coming from today. The reason it is so important to me to be a part of your company."

Tina wiped the teardrop from her eye, as Antonio continued his story. "So why now? "My life has taken many turns and twists. When I graduated from college and moved to South Carolina, it was to pursuit a career, but as many young men do, I started chasing behind young girls to get out of my system what I had never experienced. You see, all through high school and college I was somewhat of a hermit. I never dated, so when I graduated college, I was teased by my friends because I was still a virgin. They told me that no woman would want a man without experience, so I decided that if I wanted to come to a lady such as yourself, I had to come straight. That meant to me that I needed to get some experience, so I did. In fact, I got so much experience that I ended up getting a young lady pregnant. Because of the way I was brought up without my mom and dad, I couldn't see myself doing that to a child of mine, so I made the decision to get married and be a good father to my son. About three years ago, my wife was killed in an automobile accident. I felt guilty that I was free. Free from a loveless marriage, so I decided to become a hermit once again. For two years I spent all my time working and building my company. That is when I added the new division and began brainstorming about merging it with yours. Personally, I never thought that merging would bring me closer to you, I had given up on that idea, but I had hope that I could work with a legend such as yourself. Strange thing though, when I laid eyes on you again after all those years, you looked the same, and the memory of how you felt in my arms came rushing back. So, you see, if you deny my proposition, I will understand, but just know that I have no ulterior motives." "What makes you think that I am going to deny your proposal?" "Just a feeling I have."

"So, Antonio, to be clear, why is it so important that you tell me all this now? What bearing does it have on a business decision? I don't see the relevancy." "You implied earlier that I was trying to pull a shady deal on you, so I wanted you to understand that the way I feel about you, I could never do anything to undermine you." "But you have, you allowed me to believe all these years that you were a mature adult." "In all actuality Tina, I was. What other seventeen-year-old do you think could have made you felt the way that I did?" Tina didn't answer, but her mind traveled back to those nights and how she felt. She blushed at the thought of falling for a kid. "So, tell me Antonio, when are you stepping back into current time?"

"Before I do, I would like to apologize for my deceptive behaviors and ask for your forgiveness." "There's nothing to forgive for either of us, that was a long time ago, and water under the bridge." "But I need to hear you say that you forgive me." "Okay, I forgive you, so can we put this behind us and move forward?" "Are you saying what I think you are?" "I don't know; it depends on what you think I'm saying." "Are you saying that we can move ahead with the merger?" "No, that is not at all what I'm saying." "Well excuse my French, but what the hell are you saying?" "What I'm saying is that before your confession, I was prepared to turn your offer down, what I'm saying now is that I am willing to listen to further explanations as to your reason for wanting to come on board as co-CEO." "I can see why that would concern you, but I assure you that my coming on board as co-CEO would help the transition run smoother, and you wouldn't have to pay anyone else to cover the position." Okay Mr. Godfrey, I am feeling a little hungry here, can we discuss this further during lunch?" "Sounds good."

Antonio Godfrey was very suave, so as they were leaving Tina's office together, several of the female employees turned to gaze at them. Neither Tina nor Antonio noticed because they were deep into conversation as they walked through the lobby. "I was sure that you said we were eating in, I even heard you ask your assistance to have lunch delivered, what changed?" "You're right, that was my original plan, but a woman can change her mind, can't she?" "Sure, she can, I have no complaints, actually I'm flattered." "Well don't flatter yourself, this has nothing to do with you and everything to do with me needing a change of scene. You have laid quite a bit on my plate, and I need to be able to digest it all." "I will take it where I can get it, so where are we going?" "Not far, there's a deli just down the street in walking distance."

Tina and Antonio walked the short distance to the restaurant chatting as if they were old friends. She even laughed at some of his corny jokes. It felt good to be in the company of the opposite sex even if it was business. For some reason she felt comfortable with him. All the old anxiety she'd been feeling concerning him the last few weeks seemed to have vanished. She felt somewhat the way she did when she danced with him years back minus the intimacy. It seemed that she had crossed a milestone with him. After all the years of not knowing his name or his story, she was now able to close that chapter of her life without questions or self-doubts. There were times when she felt that Antonio didn't tell her his name because he didn't want to be associated with her. Those thoughts went along with the low opinion she had of herself. When it came to business, Tina was confident, competent, and assertive, but she never mastered the art of self-confidence in her personal life, though she put up a good front.

When Tina and Antonio reached the Deli, he stepped in front of her and reached for the door. Tina felt special, she was used to just pushing or pulling the door open herself, no matter whom she was with. As Antonio stepped to the side still holding the door, Tina gracefully entered. Antonio came in behind her; "So, madam, where would you like to sit?" "I would like to sit somewhere in the back if there's any available tables." "So, are you ashamed to be seen with me?" "Why would you make that assumption?" "It's not an assumption it's a question in the form of a joke." Tina felt a little foolish as she replied. "I would have to be out of my mind not to want to be seen with you, have you looked in the mirror lately?" "I can say the same about you; you are one beautiful lady. After all these years, you are still turning heads." Tina couldn't hide the redness on her face as she began to blush. "Yes, but in what direction?" "You know I never would have imagined that you would have a sense of humor, you always seemed so serious minded." "Sense of humor, what make you think that I am humorous?" "Even though you are trying to be Ms. professional CEO, the authentic you pops out from time to time." Tina didn't feel up to debating her personality, so she just smiled and said, I think our table is ready."

Although Tina's plan was to have a quick lunch outside of the office, she found herself enjoying Antonio's company. They barely mentioned mergers or positions. They were so tuned into each other that they both hung on to every word that was uttered. "So, Tina, tell me, why have you been single all these years?" "I've spent most of my time focusing on my career, and when I did allow myself to take a break and meet someone, it turned out to be the wrong someone, so finally, I gave up and just resolved to being single and alone. It's better than being in a dysfunctional relationship." "You should not be afraid to step out there and give it a try." "I have tried Antonio; I even joined a gym in hopes of attracting someone." "So, did it work?" "No, unfortunately it didn't I just ended up feeling foolish." "I am not going to sit here and accept that no one approached you at the gym; I would put my bet on you not responding, am I right?" Tina laughed and asked, "can we change the subject, this is becoming boring."

When Tina and Antonio had finished with their lunches, she looked across at him and asked, "Antonio, would you believe what time it is, and we have not accomplished a thing." "Yes, we have, we have gotten to know each other a litter better and that is important if we are to be working together." "I suppose you're right, but it's time I get back to the office." "So, am I to return to your office with you?" "Yes Antonio, I mean Mr. Godfrey, you should return to my office so that we may conclude our meeting." Just as they'd walked out of the office and down the street to the café,' they began their journey back to the office, side by side, chatting and laughing as if they were old friends.

When Tina and Antonio returned, they attracted the same curious stares as they did when they were leaving. "It seems that some of your colleagues are somewhat curious." "About what?" "About the man that has taken up so much of your time today." "Curiosity never hurt anyone." "I suppose you're right." Tina was accustomed to her colleagues and employees trying to keep tabs on her, so this was nothing that mattered to her. As Tina pushed open the door to her office, Antonio followed. "Please, Mr. Godfrey, have a seat." "So, are we back to being formal now?" "I hadn't realized that we stopped." Tina walked around her desk and sat opposite

Antonio. "Is this formal enough for you?" Antonio couldn't help but smile at Tina's comment. "Okay Ms. Bradshaw, you've made your point." "Great, then shall we get back to work?"

"So, Mr. Godfrey, this is what I'm proposing; I will accept your proposal on a contingency." "Care to elaborate?" "Of course, if you had waited until I finished my statement. What I am proposing is that we give it a one-year trial; if at the end of the year my company shows significant profit and potential from the merger, and there are no signs of a hostile or any other type of takeovers, all contingencies will cease, and the merger would be fully effective immediately. What do you say, can you live with that?" "This is not exactly the direction I was hoping for, but I will take it where I can get it. Sounds like a plan, how soon will you draw up the contract?" "I will get right on it, and should have it ready for your review by the middle of next week, is that soon enough for you?" "Yes, indeed it is, I will be waiting to hear from you, and thanks for giving me this opportunity I promise you won't regret it." "I sure as hell hope not, but we shall see."

Chapter Thirty- One

After her meeting ended with Antonio, Tina felt drained. It was an exhausting day both professionally and emotionally. "Dang! My life seems like a mystery drama. I bet I would make a fortune if I turned it into a movie." She allowed her mind to travel back and forth from her younger life to her present life. She took a deep breath and exhaled. "What now? After all these years, I find out that someone admired and looked up to me." The clients at the shelter respected and looked up to Tina, and there were her employees and colleagues that sang her praises every opportunity that presented themselves, but that was different. Having a man tell her that she was his motivation from a personal perspective, felt refreshing, even if it was a hundred years ago.

At the end of her workday, Tina decided not to go straight home, but instead, headed towards her friend Shanell's home; she just had to tell someone about her conversation with Antonio, and who better than her best friend. On the drive to Shanell's, she played the day's event over and over in her mind, rewinding and replaying like a cassette. "Why does it even matter," she thought, it was such a long time ago and I was oblivious to his age. I never would have danced that intimately with a seventeen-year-old, much less fantasized about him, had I known." "Oh well, shaking her shoulders as if she had suddenly become chilly, it certainly was an experience."

Tina was so involved in her reminiscing about Antonio, that she didn't realize she had reached Shanell's home, she had driven the distance by habit. As she drove up into her friend's yard, she noticed a familiar head popping out of the front door. "My, my, what brought you over this time of evening on a workday?" Tina climbed out of her vehicle laughing; "what do you mean, aren't I allowed to come to your house anytime I like without reservations?" "Of course, you are girl, come on inside, but really though, as glad as I am to see you, I know you well enough to know that something is up." "You know me well alright, and something is definitely up." "Well, have a seat and tell me all about it." Tina dropped down on the nearest chair. "Girl, you would not believe what I just learned." "Well stop stalling and tell me." "Hold your cookies girl, let me catch my breath." Shanell was not known for her patience, so she poked Tina and said in an excited voice, woman tell me what's going on, I want to know now; I don't want to wait until you catch your breath, it may not be as interesting then." Both ladies burst into laughter at Shanell's lack of patience. "Ok, here it goes."

Tina began telling Shanell all the things that Antonio had told her earlier. "You mean to tell me, that big, tall hulk of handsome was only seventeen years old? Girl, I was always sort of jealous of you, but seventeen?" "Come on now, I didn't tell you so you could make fun of me, I just wanted to share with you because you lived through it with me." "I'm sorry, but that is the last thing I thought you were going to tell me, why don't you write a book about it." "There's too much on my plate as it is, I don't have time to write no book!" Then let me write It." "Okay, so how many pages will your book consist of, one or two?" "What do you mean?" "I mean what other information will you be putting into your book, because I sure as hell won't be giving you anymore." "Come on Tina, don't treat me this way." "Sorry, but my personal life is mine, and I do not want it exploited in a book, even if you change the names. Write your own story, lord knows you have some to tell." "Very funny Tina, very funny."

After Tina had finished shooting down Shanell's idea of writing a book about her and Antonio, she decided that it was time for her to go home. She gave her friend a big hug and thanked her for listening. She knew that all the shenanigans about writing a book were just Shanell making fun out of an otherwise unfunny situation. She smiled a warm affectionate smile as she thought of her friend and all the years, they were friends. From the time they were born into the world, their mothers who were best friends had them together. They laid in the nursery together, played in the same playpen, baptized together, went to school together, participated in each other's weddings, and always lived short distances apart. Yep, Shanell was always her best friend, and always had her back; her ride-or-die. Just as she was pulling into her driveway, she gave one last smile and said out loud, what in the world would I have done without my good friend Shanell?"

When Tina brought her car to a stop, she climbed out, locked the doors, and headed for the front door. She turned the lock, went inside as she did every day, and hung her keys on the key holder on the wall. For some reason, something felt different, she felt lonely; extremely lonely. She folded her lips together and proceeded to her bedroom. Once inside, she threw her purse on a chair in the far corner of the room and started towards the bathroom. When she entered, she walked over to the mirror to examine her appearance.

She stood staring at her reflection, turning her head from side to side to expose any wrinkle she may have had. Tina still looked quite young for her age; that she accepted. When she'd finished examining her facial features, she undressed and took a long warm shower. She wanted to wash away the stress of the day.

Once out of the shower, Tina carefully dried her delicate skin, and rubbed oil over her body. She let her hair down and brushed it out, then caught it back up into a ponytail. She felt much better, so she headed straight for the kitchen without a stitch of clothes on. As she approached the kitchen humming a familiar song, she felt young again. Her body was still firm, and shapely. Those trips to the gym had aided in her physical condition. She walked over to the refrigerator and took out the container that Judy had left with her dinner inside and placed it in the microwave. While it was heating, she poured herself a cold glass of lemonade. When the timer went off on the microwave, she pulled the container out, placed the contents on a plate, and made her way to the table, naked and barefooted. She felt blessed on so many levels, but she was still alone. "Well, one good thing about living alone, I can eat naked at my dining table, or do anything else I choose without having to worry about anyone seeing me."

Tina finished her dinner in silence, no music, no TV, just the sound of her chewing. When she'd finished eating, she placed her dishes in the sink, and went back to her bedroom. She crawled into bed and turned on her television. As she was shifting through the channels searching for something interesting to watch, her phone began to ring. She picked it up and looked at the caller identification but did not recognize the number. "She quickly answered it thinking it may be someone in need of help.

"Hello." "Hello Ms. Bradshaw, this is Antonio Godfrey, how are you tonight?" "I am fine, but why are you calling me at home, is everything ok?" "Yes, everything is more than ok, everything's great!" "Then what can I do for you?" "That is the million-dollar question. There's a lot you can do for me, but for now I will settle for your going to dinner with me to celebrate our victory." "It's not a victory yet remember; we have a year ahead of us." "I realize that, but we made a major step today, I think it's worth celebrating, don't you?" Every instinct in Tina's body told her to say no, but she replied, "yes we did, so maybe a celebratory dinner is appropriate." "Great, where and when, I will let you decide." "Let me?" "Sorry, poor choice of words; would you do the honor of deciding where we will have dinner?" "Sure, I'll get back with you on tomorrow, at the moment, I am in the middle of something." "What, watching TV?" As hard as Tina tried to hold it in, she burst out laughing; "how did you know?" "I heard the sound in the background." "Yes, well I'm having some me time, I will call you tomorrow." "Okay, goodnight." "Good night."

After Tina hung up the phone from Antonio, she lost interest in what she was watching on tv, somehow, it just didn't seem to measure up to the conversation she had just shared with him. She found herself smiling at the thought of sharing yet another meal with Antonio. "Come on girl, didn't that man told you that he is considerably younger that you are, so why are you even going there? Well, it doesn't hurt a girl to fantasize." During Tina's lifetime, she had often found comfort in having mini conversations with herself, and even fantasizing about what her life could be like. Somehow, it served as therapy. So now, here she was again, dreaming about the once nameless man. Tina imagined herself as his wife, and what it would be like. All the things she wanted to experience in a relationship had passed her by. She wanted to share grandchildren with her husband as they sat on the porch swing and watched them play in the yard. She wanted to lay in bed and watch old movies while being playful and fooling around, but all of that was just a fantasy now, because none of it would ever happen; it was too late for her. The thought of her never experiencing the fulfillment of her dreams made her a little sad, but not to the degree of shedding tears. Instead, she smiled at the thought of her grandchildren and wondered when she would get to see them again. Her birthday was coming up, and even though she'd told her children not to make a fuss, she was hoping that they would.

Tina was so engrossed in her thoughts that she didn't realize the time. The show she'd been watching had ended and so did several others. "Oh gosh, it's almost two in the morning and I'm no way near sleepy. What is going on with me?" She wondered what Antonio would think if she gave him a call, especially this late, or early morning. She picked up her phone and looked at the number he'd called her on earlier, then slowly reached out her finger and pushed the dial button. After just one ring, Antonio answered, which startled her.

"Hello Tina, is everything okay?" "Yes, everything's fine. I am so sorry I dialed you this time of morning, but I was putting my phone on the charger and must have somehow dialed you accidentally" she lied. "Oh, that's okay, I was awake anyway." "Why so early?" "Oh, I didn't get up early, I just haven't gone to bed yet." "Oh, why not, is everything ok with you?" "Yes, better now that you've accidentally called me." "How pray tell did my calling made you better?" "It just did, so let's leave it at that." Tina didn't want to leave it at that, she wanted to pry. "Since my phone decided that it wanted to call you, are you awake, or are you just up?" Believe it or not, I am, wide awake." "Do you feel up to talking?" "With you? I can't think of anything else I'd rather be doing." Tina blushed. So, if you don't mind, I would like to ask you a personal question." "Does it matter whether I mind, I get the feeling you are going to ask anyways, so, go ahead, ask away."

After carefully arranging her words, Tina asked Antonio, "are you dating anyone?" "No, I'm not, why do you ask?" "Just curious." "Is that the only reason you want to know?" "What other reasons could there possibly be?" "I don't know, but now I'm curious." "I just asked because after spending time with you at lunch, I came to believe that you are a nice person, and you certainly are easy on the eyes. With that being said, I just wondered why some lady hasn't snapped you up." "Maybe I'm waiting for the right one to come along and snap me." "Well don't wait too long, our clock is ticking you know." "What clock are you referring to, I hope it's not the biological ones." Both Tina and Antonio began laughing at his silly comment. When they settled down from their burst of laughter, Tina said, "Antonio, on that note I think I'm going to call it a night." "Call it what you may, but its morning." "Yeah, you're right, but I'm going to bed now." "Okay Tina, but this conversation is far from over, just keep in mind that you owe me." "Just what do I owe you?" "I will tell you when I decide to collect." "Ok Antonio, I look forward to collection day, but in the meantime, goodnight again." Good night, Tina, sleep well, I know I will."

Antonio may have slept well but Tina spent the rest of the night tossing and turning. She couldn't figure out why she was so disturbed and restless. Her mind drifted back to the years when she was a young woman smitten by a young handsome man that wooed her on the dance floor and had refused to give his name. Part of the excitement was the mystery. Now here she was again years later, still shivering at the thought of what might have been. As she laid there reminiscing in the dark, she closed her eyes and fell asleep.

Chapter Thirty-Two

When the clock alarmed at six A.M., Tina pushed it off and turned over on her pillow. "This is one of those days when it's good being the boss, I'm staying home today." After fifteen minutes had passed, she rolled over and jumped out of bed. She'd forgotten about an early meeting she had that would not be good for her to miss or reschedule, so she dragged herself to the bathroom and took a cool shower to take away her drowsy feelings. "I am definitely taking a few days off for my birthday, I need something exciting to happen in my life, not just fantasies."

Prior to having lunch with Antonio and rehashing her past, Tina had accepted that romance had passed her by, and she was not going to chase after it. So, what changed? Antonio did; Tina was curious on so many levels when it came to him. She wondered about the real reason for him not remarrying after his wife died, and why he'd remained single all these years. Could it have been that he really had fallen for her, or was that just another ploy to get her to agree to his business proposition? Either way, it shouldn't matter since she was planning on retiring from work as soon as she could, then she wouldn't have to see Antonio ever again. The thought of not ever seeing him disturbed her a little despite her determination. "Why on earth am I still having these thoughts, am I going through some type of mid-life crisis or something?"

Tina finished getting herself dressed for work in a fog. She was so wrapped up in her thoughts of Antonio that she didn't pay much attention to the outfit she'd chosen to wear. When she'd finished putting on her shoes, she went to the kitchen to grab some breakfast. "This is going to be a long day; I don't want to face it on an empty stomach." Although she felt hungry, she didn't want to take the time to make breakfast, so she settled for cold cereal and coffee. On her way out, she reached and grabbed a banana from the fruit bowl sitting on a nearby table.

When Tina reached her car in the garage, she was humming a tune that she'd made up in her head. She was feeling happy and filled with anticipations. The sun seemed brighter than usual as she headed towards her office. Everything seemed different for some reason. Tina made it to her office parking lot and realized that she was the only person there. She looked at her watch to check the time. "My goodness, no wonder I'm the only one in the parking lot, I'm almost an hour early." Tina decided to use the extra alone time to catch up on some fantasizing, so she got out of her car and headed for her office. As she approached, the night guard came from around the corner. "Good morning Ms. Bradshaw, you're mighty early this morning." For a second, Tina was startled; after regaining her composure, she replied, "good morning, Joseph, how are you this bright morning?" Joseph was always happy to see Tina, he had carried a torch for her for as long as he could remember, but she never had a clue. "I am great Ms. Bradshaw; my day is always better after seeing your lovely face." Tina smiled at Joseph and continued walking towards her building as if in a hurry. "Thanks Joseph, you say the kindness things."

When Tina entered the building, she was a little out of breath; speed walking and talking at the same time had tired her out. "Maybe it's time for me to hit the gym again she thought, my stamina is slimming down." Although Tina had the perfect gym at home, she had gotten a little lazy of late, and put her exercising on hold. "Now may be a good time for me to get back to my exercise routine, after all, there are still things I would like to accomplish without feeling tired and worn out."

When she reached her office, she stepped inside and turned on the lights. Her office was always more than just an office to her, it was somewhat of a sanctuary. A place of serenity and peace;' a place where she could meditate and brew ideas, her own oasis away from home. Unlike a lot of offices, Tina had her space designed to fit her personality. Aside from the normal desk, chairs, and technical equipment, she had a formal living and dining room included, with a fireplace and waterfalls. Very few got to see behind the French doors that hid her office's comfort zone.

She placed her purse on her desk and proceeded to open the closed French doors that led to the other dimension of her office. She took off her shoes and carefully planted her bottom on her beautiful Newdale sofa. Her intention was to sit and fantasize for a few minutes before beginning her workday. With barefeet, she threw her head back in a relaxed position. Before she could get her first fantasy to brewing, Tina had fallen fast asleep. During her sleep she began dreaming that she was working on a proposal that was long overdue. She completed it and had Delany call and scheduled a meeting with the staff so that she could present it.

Tina was startled out of her sleep by a knock on her door. "Ms. Tina, are you alright?" It was Delany. Tina jumped to her feet as if she'd been caught doing something illegal or immoral. "Oh, my goodness, yes, I'm fine, what time is it?" "It's nine o'clock;

normally I wouldn't have disturbed you, but you have a meeting in half an hour, and I needed to update you on the status. When you didn't answer your door, I came in because I saw your car in the parking lot and felt something may have been wrong. Are you ok?" "Yes, I'm fine, just had a late night, and didn't get much sleep last night. I didn't mean to fall asleep, just wanted to rest my mind for a while." "Ok, as long as you're fine that's all that matters." "Thanks Delany, have a seat and tell me what you've got." Delany sat on the chair opposite Tina as she looked around the beautiful room. "This is simply gorgeous Tina; I marvel every time I look into this room." "Thanks Delany, now tell me what you've got, we don't have much time, thanks to me." Delany gave Tina an affectionate smile, as she prepared to brief her for her meeting.

Once the meeting between Delany and Tina ended, it was time for her meeting with her staff. After Delany left Tina's office to go to the conference room, she looked back to see if Tina was following. There was no Tina in sight, so Delany proceeded to the conference room alone, hoping that Tina would show up shortly. The conference room filled with staff in a few seconds after Delany's arrival, but still no Tina. Delany was beyond concerned; "what on earth is going on with Tina, this is not her usual behavior."

Just as Delany attempted to exit the room to go check on Tina, the door opened, and the CEO entered with a smiling face.

"Good morning, everyone. I would say that I am sorry that I'm late, but quite frankly it would be a lie." Everyone looked at her in shock, what happened to their boss and who was this impersonator?" Tina felt great; she'd reach a place in her life where she felt empowered; There was nothing holding her back from being her best self. For some odd reason, she didn't feel the need to explain or apologize for being late. She was always on time, no one ever expected an apology for her timeliness so why bother explaining why she was late? It was her business and it felt good.

While everyone was waiting for an explanation from Tina, she sat at the head of the table and began her meeting. She discussed the merger with Antonio's company and the one-year probationary period. She explained that Mr. Godfrey would be coming along to oversee the transaction. "Delany, I will need you to ensure that a proper office is prepared for Mr. Godfrey before his arrival, along with an assigned parking space. This meeting is just to bring you all up to speed, not a question answer session. If you have any questions, please address them with Delany and she will answer them for you, otherwise, this meeting is adjourned; thanks for coming."

Everyone was still confused by Tina's sudden change of attitude. Some were intrigued, while others were furious. "How dare she come into the meeting late and said she wasn't sorry about it," said one staff member. "I thought it was a bold move," stated another. "Well go Ms. Bradshaw," stated yet another. Tina could hear the mumbling and whispering behind her back, but for once in her life, the talking didn't faze her, she didn't give a fat rooster's ass what they said or thought. Tina walked past the remaining staff in the conference room at a fast pace and headed for her office. "Let them think what they may, she thought, I really don't give a dam."

When Tina arrived back at her office, she sat and took off her shoes. "What a wonderful day, she thought; what a wonderful day." Just as she was about to pick up her phone, there was a tap on her door. "Yes, come in." "Ms. Bradshaw, said Delany, Mr. Godfrey is wanting to know if you will have time to meet with him on today, he doesn't have an appointment." "What time is he wanting to meet?" "Now?" "What do you mean now, is he waiting outside?" "Yes mam." "Then by all means, send him in."

Tina was trying to get her feet back into her shoes when Antonio pushed the door open and walked in. "Good morning Ms. Bradshaw, sorry to bother you without an appointment, but I was in the neighborhood and wanted to speak with you." "Good morning Mr. Godfrey, but was there something wrong with your phone?" "No there wasn't, but I figured if I called first, you would have made me schedule an appointment for later and I wanted to see you today." "Why the urgency, could it not have waited?" "Perhaps it could have, but that would have meant a few more days of torture." "What would have tortured you?" "May I sit please?" "Sure, I'm sorry, please, have a seat."

Antonio looked around to determine the perfect place to sit. He wanted to sit so that he could look straight into Tina's eyes. When he'd found the perfect spot, he sat, pulling his jacket tail from beneath him. "Thank you, this is better." "So, now are you ready to tell me what has been torturing you that has to do with me?" Antonio took a deep breath as he began to explain. "Tina, may I call you "Tina?" "For now, yes you may, but don't make it a habit while we are at work; what is it?" "Ever since our last meeting, I have not been able to stop thinking about you. Now this may not be the proper place to discuss this, but I wanted to clear the air." "Why do you think the air needs to be cleared, what's going on?"

As Antonio sat there rubbing his two hands together, Tina became annoyed. "Does he think that I'm expecting something from him, is that why he's sweating like a faucet?" Antonio could see the confusion and annoyance on Tina's face. "Oh, no, I'm sorry, I don't mean to upset you, it's just that I don't know how to approach the subject." "What subject are you referring too?" "The subject of you and I." "There are no you and I, what are you talking about. Please get to the point before I jump to conclusions. "You're right Tina, there's no you and I, and that is part of what's bothering me." "What is the other part?" Antonio laughed as if what Tina asked was funny, but in all actuality, he was scared out of his wits. "The other part is that there may never be a you and I." "And just where down the road did you come up with the idea that you and I were a possibility?" "Thirty years ago." Tina was quiet, she had no idea how to respond, so she just sat there staring at him as he continued.

"Tina, I realize that in a few weeks, we will be seeing each other daily in a professional capacity, but the thought of being that close to you and yet that far away is horrifying. So, what I'm proposing is that we establish a friendship that's conducive to a work relationship, which could possibly lead into a personal relationship." Tina continued sitting in silence while Antonio tried explaining what he meant by all the mumble jumble that he'd just dispelled. "So, what do you think?" "What do I think about what Antonio?" "Weren't you listening?" "Yes, I was but I didn't hear anything, what is it you're trying to say?" Antonio became frustrated that Tina was pretending not to get it. Just as Tina was silent during his presentation, he was now in silent mode. "So, are you just going to sit there wasting my time, or is there something specific you are trying to tell me? You need to come on out with it and stop beating around the bushes." Antonio believed that he had overcome his insecurities around Tina, but here they were in full bloom.

Antonio sat frozen in his seat as he stared into Tina's curious eyes. "Antonio, are you alright?" "No, no I'm not." "What is it, is there anything I can do for you?" "Yes, there is, you can cut a man some slack." "What on earth are you referring to too, what slack do I need to cut? You're not making any sense, but you want some type of response from me." "What do you mean I'm not making any sense, I am trying to explain to you my feelings, but as always, when I'm around you I feel foolish and insecure." "There's no need for you to feel insecure around me, especially if we are going to be working so closely together, and as for feeling foolish, it's you that's causing yourself to look foolish; out with it already."

Despite his nervousness, Antonio had to laugh. "I agree with you Tina, so I am going to stop beating bushes as you stated and just lay it all on the table." "Well, it's about doggone time." "I guess what I'm asking or hoping if it's at all possible for the two of us to become friends before we begin working together." "Friendships take a while to develop, we begin working together next week, so I think that may be impossible, besides, I have about all the friends I can handle." "So, what are you saying, you don't want to be friends with me?" "No Antonio, that, is not what I'm saying, but what is the rush?" "The rush is that I spent my entire life hoping and praying that one day I would be in your life, not just professionally but personally. What I want Tina is a relationship with you and I figured becoming friends would be a great starting place." "Well, you thought wrong, I am not looking for romance at this stage of my life." "What do you mean this stage of your life, woman you are still in your prime." "Prime or no, even if I was to become romantically involved with someone, it certainly wouldn't be someone young enough to be my son." "Ouch! You certainly are not old enough to be my mother, what, about twelve years?" "That is eleven too many." "Come on Tina, you have got to be kidding, you wouldn't let a small thing such as and age difference deprive you of a beautiful experience, would you?" "No, but what make you think that being in a relationship with you would be beautiful?" "I know with all my heart that I could make that smile on your face even wider if you would only give me a chance."

All the insecurities that Antonio had at the beginning of their conversation seemed to have vanished. He was boldly stating his desires and anticipating a positive response. What he didn't know was that Tina carried her own set of insecurities. Her low self-esteem had not completely vanished. Although she was flattered by all the attention Antonio was giving her, she was also wondering what he saw in her. Why would he pass on all the beautiful women in the world for a chance with her? "So, does silence give consent?" Antonio asked. "You are quite the comedian, aren't you?" Tina responded. "Since you became silent, I assumed that you were leaning towards giving me a chance." "Sorry if I disappoint you but your assumption is wrong. I am just wondering what your motives are." "My motives, after I poured my soul out to you, are you saying that you still don't trust me?" "I am sorry Antonio; trust is not something I give easily. It has been my experience that trusting someone often leads to disappointment."

With sad eyes, Antonio looked at Tina not knowing how to come back from her statement of trust. He wondered who had broken her heart but refrained from asking. After rubbing his chin for a few seconds, he looked at Tina and stated with a passionate voice, "I am so sorry that life has thrown you such curve balls, but if you would allow me to, I will help you to restore your trust, at least within me." "That's very thoughtful of you, Tina said with a smile, but the universe has stolen all the trust or desire to trust that I ever had. It's not you, it's everyone. Don't feel sorry for me though, this is how I function, and has been for years." "Okay, so will you at least think about what I proposed earlier?" "There's nothing to think about Antonio, I really need to get back to work, we have wasted enough time for today."

After Tina's dismissal of Antonio, he stood and walked towards the closed door. "You asked me not to feel sorry for you, but it's all I can do not to cry; as many years as we've lived, you're still living in the past. I do feel sorry for you; sorry that someone or some ones have caused you to become cynical and closed minded. These are the years that we should be living our best lives, and you chose to close the door on yours. Well, I won't bother you anymore, from now on, it is strictly business, I certainly wouldn't want to waste any more of your precious time." After he'd finished speaking, he opened the door and exited without giving Tina a chance to respond.

"What was that?" Tina felt weak as she walked over to the door where Antonio had just gone through, and closed it shut. She didn't know exactly how to feel. On one hand she felt anger, but on the other, she felt hurt. Antonio had ruined her day and that was not sitting well with her. She wondered if they would still have their celebratory dinner or was that too personal for him. "Why is he so angry? What have I done to him? He's the one that has kept secrets all these years. Who does he think he is? Better yet, who the hell does he think I am?" All Tina's emotions turned to anger, she no longer felt hurt. "I'll be dammed if I will allow that lying camouflage of a man to cause me grief, I've had enough of that to last a lifetime." Tina walked back to her desk, sat, and began rummaging through documents on her desk. After about thirty seconds of work, she sat staring at the walls with her cheek resting in her hand. She was in such a daze that she didn't hear the knock at her door.

"Hello, may I come in?" Came from a familiar voice. At the sound of the voice, Tina snapped back into the moment. She looked towards the door and saw Antonio walking towards her. "What is it now Mr. Godfrey, haven't you said enough?" "No, I haven't, not at all; what I mean is, I was totally out of line and out of character. I apologize from the deepest part of my heart; will you forgive me?" "There's nothing to forgive, all is forgotten," Tina lied. Antonio did not buy that Tina was not affected by his outburst or that she had forgotten, so he asked her again; "Tina, please forgive me for the things I said, I was only trying to ruffle your feathers the way you ruffled mine." Tina didn't ask for an explanation; she didn't need one. She was beginning to get the picture. Antonio was really interested in pursuing a relationship with her, and that just wasn't going to happen.

"Listen Antonio, I am flattered that you want to explore a friendship or relationship with me, but if I am to be completely honest with you, the friendship I can do, the relationship is of the table." Antonio was shocked that Tina was aware of his desires for her. "Okay Tina, I will take it where I can get it,' if friendship is all you want, I will be the best friend you've ever had. So, how about our dinner to celebrate our business milestone, have you decided on a time and place?" "No, I haven't, I've been busy, but if you're still interested in going, I will make reservations and let you know by the end of the evening." Sounds great, I will be listening to hear from you. In the meantime, I won't insert myself any further into your day, good day Tina." "Good day Antonio."

Tina felt better that Antonio had returned to apologize. Even though she'd convinced herself that his outburst didn't have any effect on her, deep down she knew that she was lying. Instead of the blank stare she had before, she was now sitting upright behind her desk with a smile on her face. She felt light, as if a heavy burden had lifted from her heart. She picked up the phone and began dialing her favorite restaurant, Blane's Bar and Grill. When she'd confirmed their reservations, she called Delany and asked her to call Mr. Godfrey and give him the place and time of their dinner meeting. She didn't want Delany to know that the dinner was personal because she didn't want her reading anything into it. "Sure Ms. Tina, I will contact him right away.

When Delany contacted Antonio to give him the information, he wondered why Tina had not called herself. Was she still angry with him? He almost picked up the phone to call her and asked but decided that he would play by her rules. He would just show up at the restaurant and pretend that it didn't bother him that she had involved a third party. "Women, I'm having the hardest time figuring them out. Just when you think you've made some progress, it's back to square one. My grandmother certainly didn't prepare me for this." Antonio was determined to win Tina's heart, and he didn't plan to take forever to doing it. He only had to convince her of his love for her, and that age was not a factor, it was just a number abbreviating your life experiences. But how would he convince her of that when his first encounter with her was when he was a teenager and she a young woman. It didn't matter to him then and it didn't matter now, but Tina on the other hand was hung up about it.

Three days after Antonio's intense conversation with Tina concerning where they stood with each other, when Tina had made it abundantly clear that she was not interested in a romantic relationship with him or anyone else, he received a call. When he looked at his phone to identify the caller his heart skipped a beat; it was Tina. He didn't want to seem desperate, so he allowed the phone to ring out. When it stopped ringing, he pushed the redial button to return her call, but it went straight to voicemail. "Dang! I hope I didn't mess up, Tina's no fool." He was about to dial her again when the message alert sounded. "Let me see what she had to say before I call her back." Antonio carefully listened to the message Tina left for him. "Hello Antonio, I haven't heard from you since Delany called with the details of our dinner reservations. Since the reservations are for this evening, I'm assuming that you are unavailable. Please do me the courtesy of letting me know so that I may cancel the reservations, thanks." Antonio was intrigued by her message and decided to wait a few minutes before returning her call. "Let her sweat the way she's making me sweat."

After a few minutes had passed, Antonio picked up his phone, looked at Tina's name then placed the phone back in his pocket. Another five minutes and still no response from Antonio. "What is going on with this man, he pretended that he wanted to have a celebratory dinner in owner of merging our companies, and now he seems to be avoiding me. I don't have time for these childish games." Tina picked up her phone with force, but before she could push the dial icon, her phone began to ring, it was Antonio. She answered with an attitude; "yes, hello." "Hello Tina, how are you?" "Didn't you get the message I left you?" "No, I didn't," Antonio lied, he didn't want her to think that he had ignored her call. "What was the message?" "Are you planning on meeting me at the restaurant this evening for dinner?" "No, I don't;" before he could explain Tina flew off the handle. "Well, you could have told me, I shouldn't have to call you to find out." "I was planning on calling you in a few to find out your address and what time you wanted me to pick you up." He was laying it on thick. "So no, I wasn't planning to meet you there; do you have a problem with me picking you up?"

Antonio's comment caught Tina off guard. Her first instinct was to say that she would meet him at the restaurant, but something wouldn't let those words form on her lips, instead she said, "I will text you, my address." Antonio smiled; he felt as if he had made some small progress with Tina. If she could see his face through the phone, she would see one happy man. "Okay, I will pick you up at six thirty." "Don't be late, our reservations are at seven." "Yes mam, I will be there."

When Tina hung up from talking with Antonio, she had the same strange feeling she always got after speaking with him. "What is it," she thought. Am I intimidated by this man? I thought that I had gotten past these feelings of inadequacies and intimidations." Antonio was experiencing similar emotions after hanging up from Tina. He felt hopeful and somewhat anxious. After all, this was the woman of his dreams for many years, the one that slipped through his fingers; the one he intended to capture, and this time, hold on too. Just the thought of looking into her eyes and touching her beautiful face, made him dizzy. "Snap out of it boy, get yourself together; don't mess this up before you get it started." Antonio couldn't help himself; he had a grin so wide that his cheek stood out like a clown. He could hardly believe that Tina accepted his invitation to pick her up so easily. For the first time since he reconnected with her, he felt that he might have a chance. Although he was hopeful, he didn't want to scare her off; he would take things slow.

Tina had chosen a restaurant where she had performed on open mic night many years before. For some reason it just seemed appropriate for their celebration. She remembered how as a young lady her friend Shanell had coerced her into performing one of her poems, and the thrill she felt as she performed. Though it was a long while back, she still remembered the ambience of the night. As she placed her phone on her desk, she smiled at the memory of her younger self and some of the crazy things she and her friends did. Shanell had a way of pulling her out of her shell when no one else could. "I wonder if Shanell would like to go with us to dinner tonight. I think I will give her a call and invite her." Little did she know that inviting Shanell to go along would put a damper on Antonio's plans for the night.

"Hello Shanell." "Well, hello lady, what gives?" "I was wondering if you would like to come along with Antonio and I to celebrate bringing our companies together." "That sounds like a celebration that the two of you should have, you don't need a third wheel." "You wouldn't be a third wheel, you're my best friend, who better to celebrate with." "Tina, don't tell me that after all these years you are still naïve." "Naïve? What are you talking about; I invite you to dinner and you criticize me for it." "No Tina, it's not meant as a criticism, it's just that after all these years you still don't get when a man is interested in you." "Shanell, this has nothing to do with love interest and everything to do with business." "If you say so, but the answer to your question is no! You will not use me as an escape goat." "I don't need an escape goat, I just thought that you might enjoy the evening with a friend, sorry for the assumption." Shanell felt bad that she had upset her friend, so she tried to amend it. "I'm sorry Tina, I was just messing with you, the truth is, I already have plans for tonight, if you'd asked me earlier, I could have arranged it, but it is too short notice for me to wiggle out of my commitment now." "It's okay, I knew it was a long shot when I asked, but I thought I would give it a try anyway."

When Tina ended her call with Shanell, she thought of what her friend had said during their conversation. "Why would she call me naive just because I wanted her to go with me." Her mind drifted further into the conversation where she said that Antonio wanted to be alone with her. Tina was not naïve nor stupid; she knew exactly what she was doing. She did not want to be alone with Antonio for fair of him bringing up personal feelings. "If he tries to get personal, I will just have to divert his attention in a different direction, I'm not up to no flirting tonight."

When Tina arrived home after work, she was exhausted. Mostly from her thoughts throughout the day. She could not get her mind of Antonio. She was beginning to regret ever agreeing to having dinner with him. "Why didn't I just leave well enough alone, and to top it off, I'm allowing him to pick me up. Maybe I should just give him a call and have him meet me there." She looked at her phone where she had laid it on the side table but changed her mind again. I Guess I will just go ahead and get this over with, after all, it's just one evening."

Chapter Thirty-Three

After much debating back and forth with herself about her dinner date with Antonio, Tina decided that if she wasn't to be late, she needed to shower and get dressed. She looked at the time and hissed. Although she'd left work an hour early, she was still short on time. It was now five o'clock and she hadn't even begun to get ready. She walked into her bedroom and began stripping off her work clothes. When she had taken off the last piece, she walked into the bathroom to take a quick shower. With the water steamy hot, Tina stepped in and began lathering her body with a lavender body wash. The water was so relaxing that she began humming as she twisted around underneath the running water. After ten minutes in the shower, she got out and began drying herself with a heated towel. She walked over to the mirror and looked herself up and down. "Not bad for a seasoned woman." Tina's body still looked firm and shapely, and she was proud that her skin was smooth without wrinkles or cellulite. She was always conscious of her appearance and made sure that she stayed in shape and used lots of moisturizers and sunscreens. She was also big on taking herbal supplements. Tina had also stopped eating red meat and chicken years ago, which contributed to her youthful appearance.

"What in the world should I wear this evening. I don't want to look flashy, but I don't want to appear drabby either." After rumbling through her closet, she decided on a royal blue sleeveless V-neck dressy casual top with black tailored trousers. She accessorized it with a silver and onyx pendant and matching earrings. Because her arms were bare, she added a royal and black tigers eye bracelet. After dressing, she covered herself with her bathrobe and carefully applied her makeup. When she had finished her makeup, she removed the rubber band that was holding her hair in place and let her hair fall around her shoulders. She removed the robe and stepped away from the mirror to get a full view of her finished look. "Wow! I look fantastic if I do say so myself."

Tina was still admiring herself in the mirror when she heard the doorbell ringing. She looked at her watch and realized that it was six twenty-five. She stepped into her three -inch royal blue slippers and made her way to the front door. Pretending not to know who was on the other side of the door, she asked; "who is it?" "It is I madam; Antonio." When Tina pulled the door open to let Antonio in, he just stood there. "Hello Antonio, please come inside." "Wow! I was expecting you to be beautiful because you always are, but you are simply breathtaking. Do you know how beautiful you are?" "Thanks for the complement, and yes, I have a pretty good idea as to how I look." "Well, you've earned the rights to be conceited."

Tina didn't try to explain to Antonio what she meant by knowing how she looked. She was never one to feel beautiful, but tonight she would accept her compliment and leave it at that. "You look rather dashing yourself, are we going to dinner or the prom?" Antonio laughed, as he turned from side-to-side so that she could view his whole attire. He was wearing a dark gray designer suit with a black shirt and gray tie. "Are you ready mam?" "Yes, just let me get my purse." Tina walked back into her bedroom with her legs trembling, to retrieve her purse. When she returned, she said with a cracked voice, shall we go." Antonio pulled open the door and caught Tina by the elbow. She wanted to pull away but didn't want to seem childish, so instead she allowed him to guard her towards the car. He opened the passenger's door to his Audi A8 and held it until she climbed inside. "Thanks" "You're most welcomed." Once seated, he gently closed the door and walked around to seat himself.

For the first five minutes, Tina, and Antonio rode in silence. It was Antonio that finally broke the silence. "So, have you been looking forward to this evening?" "I really haven't had time to give it much thought until today, Tina lied; I have been extremely busy." "I understand, but it was all I could think of for the last several days." Tina wanted to respond but she didn't know what to say, so she said nothing. Antonio looked over at her and decided to change the subject. "Are you looking forward to getting started on the merging of our companies in a few days?" "Yes, that I am looking for to, I want to see how well things will take off; are you?" "Yeah, I'm looking forward to it as well, it has been a dream of mine, that's coming true."

When the conversation concerning the merger ended, Tina and Antonio seemed to have been at a loss for words. They both became silent again. Tina was thinking to herself how the night would go, and Antonio was thinking how the night might end. Both were in their own world now. A few minutes later, they arrived at the restaurant. Once out of the car, Antonio handed his keys to the parking valet, and began escorting Tina inside the restaurant. They approached the hostess as she greeted them and checked for their reservation. "Follow me," she said, as she proceeded to direct them to their table. After thanking the hostess, Antonio pulled out the chair for Tina to sit, and then carefully assisted her as she slid her legs underneath the table. "Thank you." Tina felt like a princess, or maybe a queen. Of all the men she had dated, none were as attentive as Antonio, he was quite the gentleman. She remembered his gentleness and charismatic moves on the dance floor when he was just a teenager. She blushed at the thought of leaning her head on his broad shoulders and getting lost in the moment. "Well, that was then, and this is now." "A penny for your thoughts." "Oh, my thoughts are worth far more than a mere penny." Antonio smiled, and said, I hope at least one of them is about me." "Why on earth would I be thinking of you?" "Maybe because I'm sitting right in front of you." "Right, so why would I need to think of you if you're sitting right here." "No reason Tina, no reason at all." Antonio was beginning to feel a little annoyed by Tina's attitude.

After placing their orders, Antonio tried to strike up another conversation with Tina. This time he was being careful not to cross any lines. "So, tell me Tina, are you still friends with the two ladies that came to the club with you?" "Yes, as a matter of fact I am. I invited one of them to join us tonight, but she had made other plans." "Why did you feel the need to invite a third party? This is our celebratory evening." "I just thought that it would be nice for her to celebrate with us since she's my best friend." "Well, forgive me if

I'm not sorry she wasn't able to come, I wanted to spend this time alone with you." "Well, you've got your wish, we're alone."

Tell me Tina, and please don't become offended and leave me sitting here alone, but what is it that you are afraid off?" "What are you referring too, I'm not afraid of anything." "I'm referring to the two of us. Each time I get a little personal with you, you become defensive. We promised to be friends, and friends get personal sometimes." "Frighten is not a word I would use to describe my defensiveness; remember I told you that I do not trust anyone, that hasn't changed." "Yes, I remember you telling me that, but you never told me what caused your distrust to such extent." "No, and I never will." "But we are friends, and friends share stuff, maybe I can help in some way." "We are not friends yet; we are working on becoming friends. Even my friends that have been in my life since childhood have no idea the things I've encountered in my life, so I'm not about to share them with a stranger." "Is that how you see me, as a stranger?" "Not a total stranger, but not someone that I feel comfortable sharing my story with." "Have you ever considered speaking with a therapist?" "Yes, I thought about it, but that is as far as it has gotten, in my thoughts." "Are you afraid to speak with a therapist?" "No, I just don't see the need." "You must have seen the need at some point, or you wouldn't have contemplated seeing one." "Could we please change the subject; you're stirring up a pot that I've taken off the stove." "Okay Tina, we will not speak of it for now, but I am not letting this go, we have to figure this out if we are ever going to be friends," "Then goodbye friendship, because this conversation is over, forever."

Antonio respected Tina's request to change the subject, but his mine began working overtime trying to figure out why she was so distrustful of others. "What happened to her, what happened to this beautiful woman that I'm madly in love with?" He looked over at Tina who seemed to have been in deep thoughts; "honey, may I have this dance?" Tina snapped back into the moment and realized that the band was playing a rather slow song. She had not danced with Antonio in years and didn't know if she wanted to do so now. "Can we sit this one out?" "We have been sitting them out, this is the last song of the night." "Okay, Tina said reluctantly, I guess I can manage one dance."

Antonio walked around to Tina's side of the table and helped her to her feet; he tucked her arm in his and walked on to the dance floor. Once on the floor, he slowly turned Tina around to face him as he gently pulled her into his arms. He knew that once he had her

343

that close to him, it would be difficult for her to resist him. Tina responded as he had hoped. She leaned her head against his shoulder and closed her eyes as she moved to the beat of the music. In the beginning, Antonio had his arms around her shoulder, but by the middle of the song, he had slipped one arm around her waist whilst the other continued to rest on her shoulder. He closed his eyes and tuned out everyone else in the room. It was just Tina and him, just like in the old days. As the song began to come to an end, Tina tilted her head upward to look into Antonio's face as he was looking down at hers. Their eyes met and locked, and their lips found each other's. Antonio lightly brushed his lips against hers; when she didn't pull away, he kissed her as if she was a delicate rose. Tina returned the kiss with pleasure.

The band had ended the song, but the music was still playing in Tina's and Antonio's heads as they rocked from side to side. Tina came to her senses and pulled herself away from Antonio's chest. "Thanks, he whispered, that was nice." "Yes, it was she responded, as they headed back to their table; it has been quite a while since I've been out dancing." "Exactly how long has it been?" "Don't go spoiling the evening with unimportant details." "There's nothing that can spoil the magic of this evening, I've had a wonderful time, hope we can do it again soon." "That would be nice, I must admit that I have been closed of lately." Well, if you will allow me to, I will see to it that you get out more often. Not just get out but have fun doing so." "Fun, what is that?" "It looks like what we shared tonight; just letting down our defenses and enjoying the moment." "I can live with that."

During the drive to Tina's, the two of them chatted like old friends. Antonio was more relaxed than he had been in years, and Tina had managed to let her guard down, and let go of her insecurities, at least for the night. "So, tell me Tina, why did you choose that particular restaurant?" "Mainly because of my history with it. It is where I did my first stand-up presentation." "Oh really, I think that I remember that." "You remember no such thing, that was a long time ago and you were not there."

After what seemed like only a few minutes, Antonio was pulling into Tina's driveway. He stopped, got out and went around to the passenger side to help Tina. He held his hand towards her, and she caught his fingers and guided herself from the seat. Once out of the car, she held her head up and looked into his eyes with a smile of gratitude. "Thanks' Antonio, you have been a true gentleman this evening." "You're welcome, you bring out the best in me." Antonio was wondering if Tina was experiencing the same type of emotions that he was. As for him, he was floating somewhere in the clouds. He continued walking with Tina to her front door holding on to her elbow, as he guided her along. Tina felt girly as she strolled along beside him.

When they'd reached the door, Tina reached into her purse and took out her keys. When she began to unlock the door, Antonio took them from her hand, and said, "allow me." Tina never said a word, as she let go of the key. He placed the key into the lock and opened the door, then handed them back to Tina and took a step away from the door. He was hoping that she would invite him inside, but he was not going to be the one suggesting it.

"Thanks Antonio, and thanks for picking me up, this has turned out to be quite an evening." "It was my pleasure. I am so glad that you had such an enjoyable time, I would have been disappointed otherwise." With a smile on her face, Tina stepped inside the house, turned around to face Antonio then said, "good night, I will see you at the office bright and early Monday morning." Despite the disappointment of not being invited inside, he returned the smile and said, "good night, Tina, sleep well." Tina closed the door while Antonio stood on the other side waiting to see if she would change her mind and ask him in. When he heard the click of the lock, he realized that wasn't going to happen. Although the evening didn't end the way that Antonio had imagined, he was still hopeful that he would get through to her before long. Getting through to her meant that he would win her heart. He slowly walked away from the door towards his vehicle, humming a song he'd listened too earlier at the restaurant.

Chapter Thirty-Four

The evening with Antonio had ended rather early so Tina decided that she would watch a movie on the TV. It was Friday night, and she wouldn't have to get up so early in the morning. She went into her family room and turned on the television. As she was searching for something to watch, her mobile phone began ringing. She picked it up thinking that it would be Antonio, but instead it was her friend Shanell. "Hello girl, have you made it home yet?" "Yes, I have, as a matter of fact, I just walked in a few minutes ago." "So, tell me how did your date with Mr. young and handsome go?" "His name is Antonio, and the evening went well, I had a lovely time." "So, now aren't you glad that I didn't tag along." "Why would I be glad that you didn't go?" Isn't it obvious? So that you could have some alone time with your date."

"First of all, Shanell, it was not a date, it was dinner; and second, if I did not want you to go, I would not have invited you to do so." "Hao, there's no need in chopping my head off, I just thought that there was more to it than just dinner!" "Whatever gave you that idea was wrong. Even if I were looking for someone, it most definitely, would not be Antonio." "Why not, what's wrong with him?" "Nothing is wrong with him, but he's twelve years my junior." "So?" "So, we are not discussing this anymore, good night, Shanell." "Okay, be like that, good night."

After Tina's conversation with Shanell ended, she was no longer in the mood for a movie. She placed the phone on the nightstand and began undressing. She took off her makeup and brushed her teeth' then put on her nightie and crawled into bed with a book in her hand. Just when she'd gotten comfortable on her pillow and turned the first page of her book, her phone began ringing again. She picked it up and answered, this time it was Antonio. "Hello Antonio, is everything alright?" "Yes, everything's fine, I just wanted to hear your voice before I passed out for the night." "Oh, my goodness, are you that exhausted?" "Actually, I'm feeling quite youthful, just thought I would turn in early since there's nothing else to do."

"Antonio." "Yes." "I hope that I didn't give you the wrong impression tonight." "The wrong impression about what Tina?" "Are you going to make me spell it out?" "Yes, I want to hear you say the words, what am I being misled about?" "Okay; so, I guess I have no choice but to spell it out. I am referring to earlier at the restaurant when we were dancing, and I got caught up in the moment." "Was that all it was?" "You didn't think it was anything more, did you?" "Of course not, Antonio lied, we both got caught up." "Good, because I wouldn't want you to think that I was flirting." "No! I would never think that, not you!" "What does that supposed to mean?" "Nothing Tina, nothing at all; sorry I disturbed you, pleasant dreams." Before Tina could respond, Antonio hung up.

Tina wanted to feel some type of way by Antonio's abruptness, but instead she shrugged her shoulders and looked at her phone; "good night and pleasant dreams to you too;" Then placed it back on the nightstand. She was somewhat hyped by her conversation with Antonio, so reading was a done deal for the night. She placed the book on the nightstand beside the phone, turned over on her pillow, and fell asleep within minutes.

When Tina woke the next morning, she was in a cheerful mood. She decided that after breakfast, she would work in her flower garden. She wobbled down to the kitchen still in her nightie, and slippers. After a hardy breakfast that consisted of a large omelet, toast, and coffee, she returned to her bedroom to put on her gardening clothes. She had brushed her teeth before breakfast but decided to take her shower after she'd finished working in her garden. She pulled a wide rim sun hat on top of her head and headed outside. It had been years since Tina worked in her garden. She had a groundskeeper that kept up the flower garden and the rest of the yard. She looked around trying to find something to do in it but gave up when she realized there was nothing for her to do. "Oh well, since the garden doesn't seem to need me, I will just sit and enjoy the beauty of it, and the morning breeze." She sat in the swing chair underneath a tree near the garden where the fragrances of the flowers were relaxing. She closed her eyes to soak it all in when she heard footsteps. She opened her eyes to see where the sounds were coming from just as Antonio was approaching her from around the corner of her house.

"Good morning, Tina, don't you look refreshing sitting there. What with the big hat, are you working?" Tina was glad to see him, she seldom had company, especially on a Saturday morning, and never in her garden. Antonio walked over to the swing where Tina sat and stood in front of her. "So, are you gardening this morning?" "That was the idea, until I realized there was nothing left for me to do; would you like to sit?" Antonio was shocked that she didn't question him for showing up unannounced. Then came the question;

"what brought you to my garden so early in the morning?" He looked affectionately at Tina as he explained his motives. "I woke up with you on my mind and felt this strong urge to see you. I figured that if I called to asked if I could come over, you would find all sorts of excuses as to why it wouldn't be a good idea, so I just got into my car, and here I am.?" Tina just looked at him and smiled, then asked; would you like some coffee?"

Coffee? Antonio was shocked out of his mind. "Sure Tina, I would love some coffee." "Well come on inside and I will make you some." "Okay, but could we just sit out here for a while, it feels so surreal." "Of course, we can, it has been some time since I felt this relaxed in the early morning. Sometimes we get so caught up in the corporate world that we miss these small but significant things." Antonio could hardly believe that he was sitting underneath a tree with the woman he'd loved for most of his life, smelling flowers and having a conversation. He didn't want to spoil the moment by going inside for coffee. "Could we skip the coffee and just enjoy each other's company?" "Yes, but you are the one that said you wanted coffee." "I was just being polite, truth be told, I don't really like coffee." "You don't like coffee? I though you liked it black." Tina and Antonio laughed as they rocked back and forth on the swing.

"Antonio;" "Yes;" "Why did you hang up so abruptly last night, did I say something to offend you?" "So, you want to revisit last night do Ya?" "Not really, just wanted to know. I am an extremely sensitive being and would hate to think that I hurt your feelings." "I'm a big boy Tina, my feelings don't hurt that easily." "Then why did you hang up?" "Because it was late and I didn't want to upset you, so I thought it was best that we called it a night, but I'm here now, doesn't that make up for my behavior on last night?" "I guess so." "Friends?" "Friends."

Tina and Antonio spent the entire morning sitting on the swing and talking outside her garden. Finally, Tina stood up and said, "this has been great, but I am getting hungry." "Does that mean I have to leave?" "Why would you want to stay, don't you have anything better to do than sit underneath a tree talking with me?" "What could be better than this?" "You could be spending time with a beautiful young lady and having fun." "But I am spending time with a beautiful young lady, and I am having quite a bit of fun." "Antonio, you know what I mean, stop pretending that you don't." "Yes, and you know what I mean, so stop pretending as if you don't know." "Well, let me just lay my cards on the table. Just in case I didn't make myself clear before, I am not seeking a relationship with you or anyone else, but if I were, it would not be with you." "Ouch! That cut deep. You've made yourself perfectly clear but let me be just as clear. I am not giving up just because you are not comfortable with who you are and have trust issues." Tina was becoming furious; "we decided that we would become friends, that's the reason I shared dinner with you on last night, and that is the reason I allowed you to remain here this morning, but beyond that you can forget it." "And just why is that Tina, can you honestly give me one good reason why we can't pursuit a relationship based on our friendship?" "Sure, I can; for number one, we've only been friends for five minutes, need I say anymore?" "You said "number one" are there other numbers, if so, you need to put them all out on the table now and stop giving them to me in small increments." "For the one hundredth time, I am not interested in building a relationship with you, I don't have to give you any other reasons." "And for the ninety-ninth time, I do want an intimate relationship with you, and I can give you one hundred reasons."

Tina was becoming increasingly perturb with Antonio's persistent attitude. "Why can't we be friends and leave it at that?" "I will tell you why; because you have never been loved the way that you should have been, and I am here with all this love, waiting to bestow upon you. Before you throw your hands up again, hear me out. Neither you nor I are getting any younger, and time refuses to stand still just for the two of us. I have wasted too much time looking for love where it didn't exist, and I get the feeling that you have too. Now, you don't have to tell me what happened in your life to cause you to be so bitter towards men, but I want to be the one that erases it from your mind and your soul, all you need to do is let me in." Tina was speechless as she sat trying to absorb everything that Antonio had just said to her. She was experiencing all sorts of emotions. She didn't know if she should applaud him, cry, or curse. So, she sat there, just glaring in his direction. "So, now would be a good time to speak girl."

When Tina was finally able to compose herself, she carefully chose her words. She began speaking in a very soft voice. "I hear you Antonio, you are absolutely on target, we are not getting any younger, especially me. As a matter of fact, I have a birthday coming up in a few days to remind me just how old I am. While I am flattered that you find me attractive, and in need of being loved, I decline your offer of a relationship, for the last time. There will be no more discussion of it, so please, let it go!" "Tina, I was told that if something is worth having, it is worth fighting for, so I am not giving up. For now, I will let it go, but just know that my feelings cannot be compartmentalized." After he had responded to Tina's final words on the subject, he caught her hands in his, kissed her on the cheek, and said, "thanks for a lovely morning, Tina, I can't think of any other place I would rather have been." Once again, before Tina could respond, he was off and around the corner halfway to his vehicle. Once there, he turned and looked at her, then smiled and blew her a kiss. As furious as she was with him, she had to return the smile. He winked at her as if to say," I'll be back," then got inside his vehicle and drove away.

Tina was still standing in the spot where Antonio left her smiling, as she watched him pull out of her driveway and headed down the street. "I don't know what I am going to have to do to convince him that I'm not interested in him in any way other than business, and possibly friendship. If he doesn't let this go, friendship will be out of the question, and I will only deal with him at work when I absolutely need too." Tina turned around and headed back to her garden. She sat down to rethink the morning but found herself disengaged from her previous feelings. She got up from the swing chair and headed for the house. She walked into the kitchen and took off her sun hat and placed it on the kitchen table. For some reason she wasn't feeling herself. Maybe it was the heat from the sun, or maybe the heat that Antonio was projecting. Either way, she needed to talk with a friend, one with a level head.

After going over and over her conversation with Antonio about a relationship between them that was not going to happen, Tina decided to call her friend Marley. Marley had grown over the years much more than Shanell had. While Shanell was still lots of fun to be around, she was also a little off the chains when it came to being serious. She acted with her heart and seldom allowed her head to interfere. Marley on the other hand was mostly all head, with a little heart. Tina picked up her mobile phone and began calling Marley. After just a couple of rings, Marley was on the other end of the phone. "Hello Tina, I was just thinking about you." Really, what on earth about?" "I was thinking that you have a birthday just around the corner and was wondering what you had planned." "I haven't planned anything; I just want to spend a quiet evening at home listening to music and watching some of my old favorite tv shows." "Well, that sounds boring, maybe you should go out and shake a leg." "Shake a leg? That sounds funny coming from you." "Maybe, I've loosened up in my older years." Both Tina and Marley laughed at her joke before Tina remembered why she had called Marley in the first place.

"Marley, on a more serious note, I would like to talk with you about something." "What is it Tina, is something wrong?" "No, not really, I just find myself in a situation where I'm having some difficulties trying to put things into perspective. I know that you are the one person I can rely on to be objective and sensible, so I need some advice." "Listen, why don't I come over to your place, I don't have anything else on my agenda for the day." "Would you? That would be great, I will make us some lunch." Okay, I will see you in half an hour."

Tina's mood perked back up as she prepared lunch for her friend Marley. "Boy if Shanell ever finds out that I'm seeking advice from Marley and not her, she will be devastated. Shanell always clanged on tight to Tina because they were friends since infancy. No matter whom Tina befriended, she always felt that she was the closest and dearest, and seldom wanted to share. "I will just ask Marley not to mention it to Shanell, and I will tell her when it's all worked out." Tina was still talking out loud to herself when Marley rang the doorbell. She pulled off her apron and hurried to the door. "Hello girl, as she embraced her friend; that was fast." "After we hung up, I just grabbed my purse and keys and headed to you. It's not often that you ask my opinion on anything, so I am excited to know what it could be." "Sit down and I will fill you in on all the glory details.

Marley was so proud of her friend's successes and often told her so. "Tina, each time I'm in your presence I feel blessed. You have done so well for yourself. I just wish that after all these years you would have found someone to share it with." "Thanks Marley, I appreciate your complements and concerns, but the concerns are not necessary, I am quite contented with my life as it is and see no need to make any changes in it." "Okay, I'll stop pushing. So, tell me, what is so important that you need my advice?" "It's not advice I need, just a listening ear." "Okay, so what's going on, you're not pregnant, are you?" Both ladies fell out laughing at Marley's question. "No Marley I'm not pregnant, that is so funny coming from you."

While Tina had finished preparing their lunches, Marley waited patiently for her to share whatever it was she wanted to share. Finally, after she'd placed everything on the table, she sat opposite Marley and sighed. "Marley, you remember the story I told you about finding out who the mystery guy is from years back." "Yeah, you said something about you and him possibly working together?" "Yes, I also told you that he was just a teenager during that time." "Yes, so what's the problem now, is he suiting you for child abuse?" Once again Tina was surprised by Marley's humor and burst out laughing to prove it. Marley, for Pete's sake be serious. if I wanted jokes, I would've called Shanell." "Alright, I'm serious, what's going on Tina?" That sounded like the Marley Tina knew and loved.

"Not only will I be working with Mr. handsome and available, but he seems to believe he can win me over." "Win you over, in what way?" "According to him, he has loved me his entire adult life and wants to have a romantic relationship with me." "Oh, I see, so, how do you feel about that?" "That is where the problem comes in. I don't want a relationship with him, and I've been very clear and upfront about it, but he won't leave it alone." "Is he stocking you? You wouldn't want a repeat of that other nut you dated." "No, he's quite the gentleman, and not the stocking type. But just as adamant as I am about not getting involved with him, he's just that adamant that he does want to be in a relationship with me. I have tried everything, even throwing up the age differences but he will not bulge. What should I do?" "You should give it a chance before you shoot it down. This maybe your last opportunity for love." "But

Marley, I'm not looking for love, as you stated earlier, I have a birthday coming up in a few days and I will be turning sixty years old." "So, what does that mean, are you dying when you turn sixty?" Tina was confused, where did her judicious friend go and who replaced her with this dictatorial being? "No, I certainly hope I don't die when I turn sixty because I'm planning to retire soon after and really begin living." "And are you telling me that there's no place where you can fit love in?" "I'm telling you that I have all the love I need within my life. I have my family, my children, and grandchildren, and of course the love of my dear friends." "I hear you, but you don't hear yourself. You are excluding certain parts of your life because you feel you're too old. Girl, my life right now at sixty-one is better than ever, and I don't mean with no well-meaning females either, if you know what I mean."

Tina was beginning to think that maybe she'd called the wrong friend. "Okay Tina, from what I'm gathering, you've managed to find the perfect man, or better yet, the perfect man found you, but for some reason, oh yea, you're too old, you are just going to let him slip through your fingers?" "Marley, you don't get it. I have passed that stage of my life. Maybe if I had dated all along things would be different, but life from that perspective has passed me by, it's too late for me." Marley stood looking at her friend who was now in tears and wondered what she could say to get through to her. When Marley had returned to school some years back, she pursued a master's degree in counseling, and later became a licensed counselor. Tina knew that Marley had returned to school, but with her own busy schedule, she never bothered asking what she was studying. If she had any idea that Marley was a therapist, she would never have invited her into her situation. If she hadn't sought counseling years ago, she certainly wouldn't be interested in any now, and especially from a friend.

"For goodness' sake Tina, listen to yourself. You're never too old to love and be loved. Now whether you want to share those feelings with Antonio, that's entirely up to you, but you need to share them with someone while you are still vibrant and active and have so much to offer. Look at you; you are turning sixty, but if you don't tell anyone they will never know by the way you look and carry yourself. You don't look a day over thirty-five, and you're more active than any thirty-five years old I know. Age has nothing to do with love." After Marley had finished putting in her two cents, she asked Tina if she had overstepped. "Of course not, I just wasn't expecting that from you. You were always more like me, thinking with our heads." "Yes, but I've learned over the years that sometimes you have to get your heart involved as well."

What started out as a bright sunny day had now turned into a dreary cloudy looking day. Tina was beginning to feel as gloomy as the weather. "Thanks for the lunch, Tina, I'd better be getting on home before the weather gets worse." "Sure, any time, don't let it be so long next time." "I won't. I hope that I've been some help to you on some level." "You have been, more so than you realize. I'm still not interested in pursuing a relationship with Antonio, but I will keep an open mind to other possibilities." "That's my girl, that's what I'm talking about, and while your mind is open, ask it what is the real reason you want give Antonio a shot." "Girl, go on home, you have no idea what you're talking about." "No, but you do."

Marley left Tina's house confident that she had gotten through to her on some level. She loved her friend and only wanted her to be happy, but as hard as she tried convincing her, she didn't believe that she was. Tina stood watching as her friend exited her driveway. She was so glad that she thought to call her. When she'd seen the last end of Marley's car going down the street, she turned and walked back inside the house. "Well, it's back to square one;" but was it, had Marley open a can of worms that she had closed for years? While she was pondering her conversation with Marley through her mind, her phone began ringing; she looked down at it and saw Antonio's name showing. She walked away and left it ringing on the table. "I can't deal with him right now, why is he being so persistent? I have told him repeatedly, but he won't stop pressuring me." As she continued playing the day out through her mind, her phone rang again; she had the same response. After about ten times of ignoring his call, she finally picked up the phone and with a harsh voice asked, what is it you want from me Antonio? I have told you how I feel, anything else is harassment." "Harassment! Is that how you really feel? I'm sorry, I promise I will never call you again, from this moment on, it'd business only, goodbye Tina, sorry to have bothered you."

Now Tina was really feeling bad. "Maybe I shouldn't have used the term harassment, but he wouldn't let it go. Oh well, maybe now he gets it. I'm sorry it had to come to this, but he left me no other choice if I'm to have peace where he's concern." Tina continued trying to find ways to justify what she'd said to Antonio earlier. Despite feeling that she had done the right thing, she felt a stabbing pain in her heart. She'd convinced herself that she didn't want to be in a relationship with him, but she loved the attention, now that was gone. "Nice going Tina, you messed up again, no wonder you are alone, what man would want someone who's as skeptical and critical as you are?" She laid on her bed and began to cry, something she had not done in a long while. As she laid there sobbing uncontrollably, she thought of all the things that brought her to this point. The more she reminisced about her past, the harder she wept. After what seemed like hours of crying and feeling sorry for herself, Tina sat up on the side of the bed and just stared in one direction. Her mind seemed to have gone blank; she had no thoughts and no more tears to shed. "That's it, I'm done; see, this is the reason I shut men out of my life, all they ever do is causes heartache. I am going to call Antonio and apologize for referring to him as being a stocker, and them I never want to see him again outside of the office." She picked up her phone and dialed his number.

Just because she felt the need to call Antonio didn't mean that he wanted to speak with her. He looked down at his phone as the call was coming through and turned his head in the opposite direction. "Just who the hell does she think she is? I poured my heart and soul out to her and all she has to offer me are sarcasm and insults. It has taken me all these years to build the confidence I needed to confront her about my feelings, and in an instant, she has kicked me right back down into that old spot of self-doubt. I wish that I had never contacted her, then I wouldn't have known how it felt to be kicked in the gut." Tina didn't give up, she felt that Antonio was avoiding her, with good reason, but she was going to apologize to him one way or the other or die trying. She continued calling his phone with the hope that he would get tired, ignoring it and answer her. Antonio became so annoyed by Tina's persistence that he picked up his phone and threw it into the garbage can, then got his keys and headed outside to his car.

Once on the open road, Antonio felt a little calmer than when he left home. He was riding along listening to the radio when an old song came on that he and Tina once danced to. His first instinct was to turn the radio off, but instead, he turned the volume up. It seemed that every strand of hair on his body stood in attention. "Why! Why! Why! Why can't I get this woman out of my heart" I have tried everything I could think off. I married another woman, dated dozens of women, but nothing worked, so what now, must I die from a broken heart?"

Tina continued dialing Antonio's number, but still no response. Finally, she decided to leave him a voice message. "Hello Antonio. I wanted to say this in person, but since you refuse to answer your phone, and I certainly understand your reason, I will just leave my apologies. I am so sorry for calling you or implying that you were stocking or harassing me. I realize that those were harsh words, but I just didn't know any other way to get through to you. There are things about me and my life that you don't know, and I don't care to explain. Yes, I'm bitter, but with good cause. You are not to blame for my atrocious life, and I should not have taken it out on you. However, I still maintain that the difference in our ages is a major factor for me. If you were ten years older, our conversation would sound a lot different. We cannot majestically make you older, or me younger, so that's that. Again, I'm sorry for the way I handled things, hope it doesn't interfere with our work relationship, good-bye." After she had finished recording her message, she felt better. "it's not my fault he wouldn't pick up his phone; if he had, he could have responded. This way, I have no idea if he accepted my apology or not."

When Antonio returned from his drive, he walked inside and picked his phone up out of the trash. He cleaned it off and placed it on the coffee table, then sat on the sofa and stretched his legs out as far as they would reach. Thirty seconds after he sat down, he'd fallen asleep. As he slept, he had the most pleasant dream. Tina had finally come to her senses and realized that the difference in their ages no longer mattered. She was ready to give them a chance. The ringing of his mobile phone woke him up. He jumped from the table still in dream mode and answered the phone. It was his friend Denzel. After speaking with his friend, he hung up and decided to see if Tina had left any messages.

After listening to Tina's message, Antonio was shaken up. The apology had no effect on him, but the fact that she had lived such a painful life was heartbreaking. His heart began pounding and all he wanted to do was take her in his arms and comfort her. He wanted to tell her that it was alright, that he would make all her pain go away. "How do I do that; how do I make her pain disappear if she won't let me in?" He listened to her message over and over just to make sure he didn't miss anything. "There she goes with the age thing again. Now that I know what's standing in our way, I am going to figure out how to remove them. I will send her a text saying that I accept her apology. I don't want her feeling bad or missing any sleep because of me, but I am going to back off for a while."

When Tina saw that Antonio had sent her a text message, she was anxious to read it. "Hello Tina, I received your message and accept your apology. Thanks for clearing that up for me; no, our work relationship will not be affected, and I will respect your wishes for me to leave you alone." After reading Antonio's message, Tina exhaled, and placed her phone on the table. "Well, that's that, I am going to take a long steamy shower and wash this long day off of me."

Chapter Thirty-Five

The weekend ended and it was time for Tina to return to work. Today was the beginning of her and Antonio's working together as co-CEOs. She was a little nervous, but not nearly as nervous as he. She decided to go into the office early so that she would have time to relax a little before starting her day. When she drove up in the parking lot, she noticed a black Porsche in Antonio's parking space. Antonio had received his official packet which included codes, keys, and designated parking space. "Dang! It seems like Antonio had the same idea as me." She slowly got out of her car and began walking towards the office building. When she'd reached the door and reached out to put in the security code, the door flung open. "Oh, I'm sorry Tina, did I frighten you? I forgot something in my car and was going to get it." "No, you didn't frighten me, Tina lied, I heard you coming." "Good, I wouldn't want to do anything to spoil our first day working together." Tina just smiled and continued walking towards her office. She went inside, turned on the lights, closed the door behind her, then walked over and sat behind her desk. A few minutes after she'd sat, there was a knock on her door.

"Come in Antonio." "Are you psychic, how did you know it was me?" "I didn't see any other cars in the parking lot when I arrived, nor did I see anyone else come in since." Antonio chuckled as he handed Tina a steaming hot cup of coffee. "I like to start my day off with a cup of tea, so I thought I would bring you a cup of sweet white coffee, hope you don't mind." "Of course, I don't mind, and thank you for thanking of me." He wanted to tell her that he thought of her every wakening moment but decided not to; instead, he said it's just something I do, no thanks necessary," as he left Tina's office with a smile on his face.

The first workday with her new colleague had gone well and Tina was able to relax. Antonio had adjusted to his position with the company in record time. He was right, she didn't have to do any extensive training, he knew exactly what he was doing. He fell into place and captured the hearts of the other staff members. She was beginning to believe that the merger was not such a bad idea; now if they could just manage to keep their personal feelings out of it, things would be great. Tina was so busy with her staff and meetings that she had no time to reflect on her morning with Antonio. It was now lunch time, and she was feeling famished. She left home without eating breakfast so that she would be the first to arrive at the office. Antonio had similar ideas and put a curb in her plan. She didn't mind though, after all he had brought her coffee, and didn't mention anything beyond business.

Tina picked up her purse and made towards the door. When she pulled it open, Antonio was standing on the other side with his fist in the air. His unexpected presence startled her for a second. "Hey, what are you doing standing at my door?" "I was just about to knock when you opened it." "Was there something you needed to see me about?" "No, not really, I was going out for lunch and wanted to see if you wanted me to bring you something back." "Thanks, that's kind of you, but I am on my way out to lunch now." "In that case, if you don't mind, may I tag along, I don't know where the best restaurants are in this neck of the woods." "Sure, let's go." "Am I driving?" "No, you may ride with me, we're just going a little way down the road."

When Tina and Antonio entered the parking lot there were several staff members looking in their direction. "Do people always stare you down when you leave your office?" "No, only when I leave with a good-looking man." "Oh, so I'm good looking?" "Do you need confirmation?" "From you, yes." Tina smiled as she crawled into the driver seat of her vehicle and got behind the wheels. "Are you a good driver?" "You are about to find out, fasten your seatbelt." Antonio humbly fastened his belt as he was instructed without saying a word.

When they reached the restaurant, Antonio jumped out and walked around to the driver's side to assist Tina. "Always the gentleman she thought; why couldn't he have been a few years older, just five or six years older, maybe then I would consider giving him a chance." "So, what's on your mind?" "Huh?" "You seem to be in deep thought, something at work?" "Oh no, I was just wondering if the restaurant is crowded, this is the lunch rush hour." "One way to find out is to go inside; are you ready?" "Sure, let's go; I am hoping that the crowd is slim because I have a busy afternoon all the way through to this evening." "Yes, one of those meetings happens to be with me." "Yes, it is, well you're the last on the list for the day."

When Tina and Antonio entered the restaurant, just as Tina had hoped, there were only a few people scattered around. "Do you come here often?" "Yes, a couple of times a week, it's one of my favorite dining spots." Antonio kept trying to make small talk during lunch. He was a little confused as to where Tina's head was. He understood her issues concerning their age differences, but beyond that he questioned whether she would have been interested in him. He wanted to ask, but he promised that they would only discuss business, and quite frankly he was getting sick and tired of being rejected by her. It didn't feel good at all. "So, Tina, how's the two friends that use to come with you to the club, Shanell and Marley, right?" "They are fine, just spoke with both of them a few days ago." Tina was comfortable with the small talk, but Antonio was bored as hell, he hoped that he'd never ask Tina to have lunch with her. If he wasn't riding with her, he would have just left, rude or not.

"Are you alright Antonio? You seem a little distracted." "I have never been better, just thinking about work," he lied. "Well, we can go and get back to it if you're finished with your lunch." "I am more than finished, let's go." "I think we need to take care of our tab before leaving." "Sure, no worries, I've got it." "You only need to take care of yours, I'll handle mine." "Whatever you say." Antonio did not put up any fights about the bill, he paid his as she'd asked. Normally, he would have gone around and pulled Tina's chair out for her, but instead, he walked out ahead of her without a word. Tina was so self-absorbed that she hadn't noticed. She got up from her chair and began following him. She didn't catch up to him until she reached the car. "What were you running from?" Antonio didn't answer, he waited until she unlocked the car then slid in and laid back on the head rest. "Are you okay?" "Why wouldn't I be, I just had lunch with the great Tina Bradshaw." "Are you being sarcastic, because if you are, there really isn't any reason to be." "No Ms. Bradshaw, it is not my intension to be sarcastic at all, just a little anxious to get back to the office and prepare for my meeting."

The drive back to the office was quiet. Neither Tina nor Antonio could find anything to say to each other. Tina turned on the radio and began singing along. Antonio kept his head thrown back and pretended to be asleep. Once the short trip back to the office was over and Tina had pulled up in the parking lot, Antonio opened the door and got out. "Thanks for lunch Tina, see you at four." Before Tina could respond, he was almost at the entry door. "Why on earth does he do that? Make some remarks and walk away without waiting for a response." She gathered her purse and followed suit.

Antonio was angry and didn't know why or with whom. All he knew was that he was in a lousy mood. "Hello Mr. Godfrey" one of the female administrators said as she batted her eyes at him. "Hello," he mumbled back as he hurried to his office. Once inside, he sat behind his desk and took several deep breaths. "How do I handle this? I cannot go on pretending as if Tina is just another colleague, she is so much more than that to me." He sat there with his head in his hands hoping that she would walk through the door. When she didn't show up, he turned his attention back to work.

Antonio was deep into completing an action plan when a knock at the door interrupted him. "Yes, who is it?" It's me Mr. Godfrey, Amelia, your newly appointed assistant." He had forgotten that Tina appointed Amelia to work with him as his assistant. "Come in, please." Amelia came in and stood, waiting for Antonio to invite her to sit. "Yes, how may I help you?" "I'm not here for you to help me; I am here to assist you with your meeting this evening with Ms. Bradshaw." "Why so early, do we need to go over something before she gets here." "Our meeting begins at four; it is five minutes until it starts; I don't think we will have any time to go over anything before she gets here. May I sit please?" Antonio looked at his watch and gasped. "I didn't realize that the time had gone by so fast; I'm sorry, yes, please, have a seat" as he pointed towards the chair adjacent to his. "Thank you."

Amelia sat with her legs cross showing all her legs and a small portion of her upper thigh. She had on a red low-cut blouse that exposed her full chest. She leaned slightly forward and bent over to further expose her chest in an attempt to catch Antonio's attention, but his only reaction was annoyance. "Before Ms. Bradshaw arrives, let me explain my dress code to you." "Oh, you don't have to do that, we already have a dress code." "Yes, but you will be working directly with me, and I have my own guidelines." Before Amelia could get out another word, Tina was knocking on the door. "Yes Ms. Bradshaw, come in, please have a seat." He pointed to the chair directly in front of him. "Thanks, Mr. Godfrey," as she took her seat.

During the entire meeting with Antonio, Tina was aware that Amelia was flirting with him. She didn't mind from a personal standpoint, but from a professional perspective, she was somewhat irritated by her blatant behavior. As the meeting continued, Amelia was more cavalier with her flirtatious behavior despite Tina's disapproval looks. "So, Ms. Bradshaw, what do you think of the idea?" "Sounds great." "Do you have any further recommendations before closing?" "Yes, if you don't mind, I would like to look everything over without distractions, if that's ok with you." "You're the boss, I have no objections, but I thought I presented a pretty good proposal, if I do say so myself, what was the distraction?" "I apologize but there's a lot going on in my head that I don't care to discuss, so if you are done, I think I will go on back to my office. I will get back with you first thing in the morning, will you be free for a brief meeting?" "Of course, I will, what time would you like to meet?" "My calendar is clear for tomorrow so whenever you're free just pop in." Amelia looked down at her watch and said, looking directly into Antonio's eyes, "I'm sorry, but I want be able to do an impromptu meeting on tomorrow, I have other commitments." "That's' ok, you weren't invited, this meeting will just be between Mr. Godfrey and myself, you won't need to be present; as matter of fact, you may leave now."

Antonio couldn't help but notice the hostility in Tina's voice when she dismissed Amelia. He waited until she had cleared the room before asking, "was that your distraction?" "Yes, it was, I am not in the habit of having someone flirting while I attempt to conduct business." "I can assure you that it was not because of my encouragement. Just before you came into the office, I requested a meeting between the two of us to discuss a dress code. She blatantly told me that you already have a dress code in place." "Yes, I do, but she seldom follows it, and until now there was no need to call her out on it, however, if you feel the need to enforce it, by all means do so, we don't want any trouble." "Yes mam, I will get right on it; thanks for your support."

"About the proposal, are you still needing to look them over?" "Yes, why wouldn't I, nothing has changed." "You mean you still don't have a clue as to the contents of that proposal." "That's exactly what I mean; I'm sorry but Amelia was just a little over the top." Antonio was a little intrigued by Tina's behavior, he felt that one of her concerns was a little jealousy, at least he hoped it was. He wasn't about to suggest that to Tina though, the wedge between them was wide enough as it was. "Ok, Mr. Godfrey, I will take these home with me tonight and go over them and will see you in the morning." "Looking forward to it, enjoy the rest of your evening."

As Tina was leaving the office, she thought, "this just might work." The tension of working closely with Antonio was drifting away and she was looking forward to their business relationship as well as their friendship. Antonio on the other hand was battling demons. He wanted nothing more than to take Tina into his arms and make passionate love to her, but he knew that it was wishful thinking. He watched her from the back as she exited his office and his heart flipped in his chest. "If only I could convince her to love me, or convince myself to let her go, maybe this lump in my heart would go away."

Early the next morning Antonio was knocking on Tina's door. She looked at her clock before she said, "yes, come in." When Antonio walked in, she looked surprised. "Just where are you going so early in the morning?" "Have you forgotten?" "Forgotten what?" "Our meeting." "No, I haven't forgotten, but why so early, I haven't even had coffee yet." "There's a solution for that." He held up two cups of steamy hot liquid, coffee for her and tea for himself. "Just as you like it, white, sweet, and hot." He handed Tina the coffee then sat and made himself comfortable. So, did you get a chance to go over the proposal from yesterday's meeting?" "Yes, I did, and I must say I am impressed; I'm glad that I decided to take a second look." "You mean a first look because you were not feeling it at all yesterday. Tell me, did Amelia's behavior disturb you that much?" "It wasn't so much the behavior as the timing of it. We were in a meeting pertaining to work, and she chose to flaunt herself at you. She could have done that after hours or in the lobby." "Are you saying that you don't mind her flirting with me as long as it's not on company time?" "Exactly." "Okay, just want to be sure." "What does that mean?" "Nothing to concern yourself with; so, tell me, are we implementing the proposal as it is or are there revisions?" "We are accepting it as is, no revisions necessary." "Then thanks for meeting with me this morning, I will get right on it. Antonio got up from his seat, walked towards the door, looked back at Tina, and said, enjoy your coffee and have a pleasant rest of the day." He opened the door and was out in a flash. Tina sat staring at the door with her mouth open. She missed the chance to respond once again.

Chapter Thirty-Six

Everything was going well for Tina at work and at home, but she was beginning to feel somewhat restless. Her birthday was fast approaching, and she was dreading it. She thought of the conversation she shared with her children telling them not to do anything special for her birthday. As much as she would love to have seen them and spend time with them on her birthday, she didn't want them coming so far for just one day, especially since her birthday fell on a Monday. She'd decided that she would pamper herself by going to the spa and getting the works. "Yes, that is exactly what I will do." Tina decided to keep the date of her birthday from Antonio and her other friends. She was sure that Shanell and Marley would have forgotten, or at least she hoped that they had. She decided to leave work early on the Friday before her birthday and would take Monday off to celebrate. When she got home, she felt more exhausted than usual, so she went into the bathroom and took a long calming bath with chamomile and lavender.

After her bath, Tina felt exuberated. She was also feeling a little excited though she didn't understand why. "Maybe I will call the children and see what they're up to. She started to pick up the phone, but her better judgement told her that if she did, they would know that she was feeling lonely, so she picked up a magazine instead. Just as she began turning the pages, her phone alerted her that she had a message. She looked down and saw that it was from Shanell. "Whose birthday is around the corner, what are we doing to celebrate?" Despite her disappointment, she had to laugh; "why did I think Shanell would forget my birthday, heck she probably remembers the hour and the minute." She picked up her phone and began typing a response. "Hello Shanell, girl, I am spending this one alone; just me, myself, and I, glad you remembered though." "The hell you are, I have it all planned. Marley and I are picking you up and taking you out on the town, girl this is a huge milestone; you only get to be sixty once."

Tina knew that there was no need in arguing with Shanell once her mind was set on something. "Okay, where are we going?" "Just leave it up to me." "I will, but please no nightclub, those days are over for me." "Are you saying you don't want to dance sixty in?" "I am saying no nightclub; do you hear me?" "Yes Tina, I hear you loud and clear, and I promise not to take you to a nightclub." "Well, where are you guys taking me, I sure would like to know so I can dress appropriately." "You always dress nice, so whatever you chose to wear will be appropriate." "Suppose I wear my garden hat and cowgirl boots." "If that makes you happy, then wear them." Tina stopped texting and dialed Shanell's number. Both ladies were laughing uncontrollably. "Shanell, you have got to be the craziest person I have ever known; shouldn't Marley be in on this conversation?" "We've spoken already, and we are in sink; your birthday will be memorable I promise." Okay Shanell, I will see you ladies on Monday." "Monday? We are taking you out tomorrow night." "Come on Shanell, that's not fear; you are telling me this now?" "Do you have something better to do tomorrow night?" "No, but you know I don't like celebrating before my actual birthdate." "Oh, for once Tina, jump out of the box, do something different. Its, only two days early." "I was planning on getting a Petti and Manie." "You have all day tomorrow to get those, I will pick you up around eight." "Okay Shanell, I will put my happiness in yours and Marley's hands for one evening." "Okay, see you on tomorrow night."

Although Tina had convinced herself that she wanted to be alone for her birthday, it was nice not having to do so. She was smiling to herself and thinking what great friends she had. She may not have had a husband or even a great lover over the years, but she had some incredibly good friends; friends that often put her needs ahead of their own. She was so touched by their loyalty that she began to cry. Once again, her phone began to ring, she looked down to see if it was Shanell calling back, but instead it was Antonio. "Hello Tina, are you alright?" "Yes, why wouldn't I be?" "You left the office early without my permission, or me knowing, wanted to check to make sure everything was alright." "Since when do I need your permission, and yes, I'm fine." "Well, aren't you going to thank me for caring?" "Thanks Antonio, I appreciate your concern, but you don't need to worry about me." "But I do worry about you, more than you will probably ever know." "I wish you wouldn't, I'm fine and have every intension of staying that way."

Tina woke up on Saturday morning excited. She had no clue what Shanell and Marley had in store for her but whatever it was, she was ready for it. She knew that her children wouldn't be calling before Monday because they were aware of her superstitions. As much as she wanted too, she was not going to give in and call them. By ten A.M., Tina was at the nail salon. When she'd finished getting her nails done, she headed for the mall. She wanted to get herself a new outfit. I don't know where Shanell and Marley are taking me, but I am going to dress to impress." She didn't go to the hair salon because she'd just had her hair done a few days earlier.

When Tina got home from the nail salon and shopping mall it was after three pm. She was hungry, but not tired. She didn't want to overeat because she was sure she would end up at some fancy restaurant." She made herself a small garden salad and had a glass of lemonade. "That should hold me until I get my porter house steak." She laughed to herself, then went into the bathroom and began setting her hair. After she had finished setting her hair, she took a warm shower. She didn't want the steam to mess with her hairdo. When she'd finished her shower, she carefully oiled her body with a new fragrance oil she'd picked up while shopping. It smelled like a combination of lavender and honeysuckle, but not too heavy on either. After rubbing the oil over her body, she put on her bathrobe and went into her bedroom to check the time. She still had three hours before the girls were to pick her up. "Hum, what shall I do with all this time?"

After pondering around the house for a while, Tina decided to watch a movie on tv to speed up the time. Every movie she found was a romance one; something she was not in the mood for watching, so she left the room without turning off the TV and went outside to her garden. The flowers were blooming and had the air scented with various fragrances. Her mind wandered back to the day when Antonio came and sat with her on the swing underneath the tree. She smiled when she thought of his confession of love for her. If only he was older or she was younger, maybe things would be different, but as it stood, nothing was going to change her mind. She knew that Antonio was a good man and a good catch for some woman, but that woman would never be her. Thinking of him made her think of what she'd missed over the years. How she had poured herself into her work and gave up on her personal life. "Well, it's too late now, and I cannot rewind the clock." After a few minutes of reminiscing, she went back inside the house, she didn't want to get all sweaty again.

Finally, it was seven o'clock; Tina rushed into the bathroom still in her bathrobe and splashed some cool water on her face. Then she proceeded to apply her makeup. She could hardly wait to put on that dashing outfit she'd bought earlier. When she completed her makeup, she took the curlers from her hair. She looked at the bed where she had laid out her attire for the evening earlier and did a little happy dance.

When Tina was searching for her perfect outfit, she felt like royalty, so she decided to wear royal blue. She picked up her royal blue jumpsuit and held it up to get a better view. She was never a flashy dresser even as a young woman, but she was always stylish. Tonight, was a little different; she was going to be bold, making the statement that you can be an older woman and still be sexy.

After admiring her attire, Tina stepped into her royal blue, deep V-neck belted jumpsuit with chiffon overlay that hung from the shoulder. She chose to wear a small diamond pendant in sterling silver with a sterling silver Rolo chain necklace, which dropped in her chest. Her earrings were small diamond studs that matched her necklace. When she had finished dressing herself, she picked up her comb and began styling her hair. Her first thought was to pull it back into a ball, but since that was the way, she mostly wore it to work, she decided to let it down. She brushed it out and let it hang around her shoulders. No one would ever imagine that she was celebrating her sixtieth birthday had they not known; she didn't look a day over forty. Tina stepped into her silver shoes, then picked up her silver purse, just in time. The doorbell was ringing; the girls had arrived.

When Tina opened the door to let Shanell and Marley in, they were blown away. They had no idea that Tina would dress this way.

In fact, they had gone shopping for her and bought an outfit just in case she was improperly dressed for the occasion. "Hello ladies, please come in, may I get you something to drink before we leave?" "No, you may not, I don't want no diet Pepsi." Come on Shanell, she has regular Pepsi too." Both Shanell and Marley burst into laughter, but Tina didn't feel the humor.

Wow Tina! You look amazing, doesn't she Marley?" "She certainly does. Tina, I have seen you looking great before but tonight there's something different, as if you are making some type of statement girl." "I am Marley, just because we grow older doesn't mean we have to give up on our appearances." "All I can say is that you're stating it well, put me to shame girl! "Thanks for the compliments, but the two of you are making statements of your own, you look great!" "So, are you ladies telling me where we're going?" "Come on girl and get in the car, trust me, you will have a great time." "Okay, Shanell, I'm in your hands."

When Tina walked outside, a limo was waiting with the driver standing beside it. She gasped! "Wow! What is all this, a limo, and a driver?" "Nothing but the best for our girl; this will be a night that you will never forget, one that is going to change the trajectory of your life forever." "Now you really have me curious; what on earth have you planned for me?" Neither Shanell nor Marley answered Tina's questions, they just smiled and climbed into the limo.

The limo ride seemed to have been taking forever. After about fifteen minutes of riding, Tina could no longer hold her piece. "Come on girls, we have been riding for an hour, where are we going?" "Tina, we've only been riding for fifteen minutes. We have tickets for a play, but Marley forgot them at home, so we must make a detour to pick them up." "Won't that make us late?" "No, the play doesn't start until nine, we have plenty of time." A play, Tina was excited at the idea of seeing a play, it had been a while since she'd seen one. "What play are we seeing?" "Stop being so inquisitive, you will see when you get there." "Okay, I will not ask another question until we get there." "Good."

When the limo pulled into Marley's yard, nothing seemed out of character. Tina peaked out the limo's window to watch her as she entered her house. Little did she know that they had reached their destination. Marley and Shanell had hired a valid driver to transport all the cars to the church parking lot down the street. "What in the world is taking Marley so long Shanell?" It's getting late." "You know Marley, she probably lost the doggone tickets." "Well why don't you go and see." "Alright, but you had better come too, if she lost them, we will all need to help her look for them." You're right, wait up, I'm coming."

"Why are you taking your purse Shanell?" "Have you forgotten; I never leave my purse anywhere." "Well wait, let me get mine as well, you have me paranoid." Tina was playing right into Shanell's plans, as she ran back to retrieve her purse. "Why is it so dark, she could at least have turned on the porch lights." "She wasn't expecting us to come looking for her, besides, weren't you supposed to stop asking questions?" When they reached the door, Shanell raised her hand to ring the doorbell. "We don't need to ring no bells; she knows that we're out here." "Yes Tina, but this is not our home so I will ring the bell." "Go ahead, push the dam thing, I'm getting sick of you already." Shanell laughed as she pushed, which was the signal that they had arrived.

When Marley opened the door, Tina stepped inside before she was invited. "Why is it so dark in here Marley?" Because I wasn't planning to stay." "Did you find the tickets?" "Yes, I have them right here." "Well, let's go." When Tina turned to leave, the lights came on and the crowd yelled, Surprise! She slowly turned around to face her audience. Both of her children were there along with her mother, and all her siblings. She looked around for her grandchildren, but there were no children to be seen. Suddenly, it hit home, this is where the celebration was. "Say something Tina," said Shanell. She was in shock, no one had ever been able to surprise her. When she was finally able to speak, she said "I'm going to kill you two, didn't I tell you that I wanted to spend my birthday alone?" "Yes, but did you really?" "No, I didn't I am so glad that you did this for me, come here. Tina wrapped her arms around her two friends' necks and squeezed them both tight. Then she went over to her children and the rest of the clan with teary eyes. She had never felt more special or more like royalty than she did at that moment.

After the greetings, Tina could see the layout of her party. The decorations were beautiful. There was even a dance floor with a DJ. Everyone was wearing similar attire to hers. "This is amazing ladies, I'm just speechless." "Okay Ms. Tina, Marley and I have a request." "What's that?" Since we surprised you, you were not able to make your proper entrance, so we would like for you to do that now." "Okay, I think I can manage that." Everyone was seated around the room as the lights dimmed. The DJ began playing soft music as Shanell acknowledged the honoree. "Ladies and gentlemen, I present to you the birthday girl, Tina Bradshaw." Tina threw her head back as she sauntered through the crowd. Everyone was cheering and applauding. When she reached the end of the walk, there was a familiar looking figure standing there. "May I have this dance?" Without saying a word, she placed her hand in his and they headed for the dance floor.

The DJ was playing the song that was playing the night Tina danced with the mystery man for the first time. She laid her head on his broad shoulders and closed her eyes. "You look so beautiful, like a goddess." Thank you, but how did you know about my birthday, and who invited you to my party?" "Shanell on both accounts; she contacted me and told me that she and Marley were planning this surprise party for you and wanted to know if I would be available. I said, hell yes, count me in. I would not have missed it for any reason. Are you glad to see me?" "I am always glad to see my friends, so of course I am." "Still playing hard to get I see." "Whose playing? Antonio let's not spoil the night; I'm having such a wonderful time." "Is that what I'm doing? Well, we certainly can't have that." Antonio walked off the dance floor leaving Tina standing there alone.

Although he'd walked away from Tina, his arms felt empty. He wanted to run back to her and try confessing his love for her one more time, but he felt defeated. For the first time, he really felt that this was it. He took one more glance in her direction as he walked out the door. "Where are you going Antonio?" "Shanell, I'm leaving, it was a mistake for me to show up here." "Don't tell me that you're giving up." "Sometimes, it come to a point where that is the only option." "Do you love her?" "With all my heart." "Then make her feel it; make her feel like she's the only woman in the room." "She is." "Then show her, take her in your arms and don't say a word; let your emotions speak for you."

Tina was standing in a corner talking with her daughter. "Mom, what is going on with you and that guy over there?" "What guy?" "The one that's staring at you?" "Oh, he's a guy from work, probably feel a little out of place." "So why don't you go and make him feel welcome, after all it is your party." "Maybe later, right now I just want to talk with my beautiful daughter." "Well, your beautiful daughter and handsome son, along with your gorgeous mom are leaving." "Leaving, why?" "We promised grandma that we would take her home early so that she can get ready for church tomorrow. The children are at your house with the nanny, so DJ and I are going to take her then go on to your house where we will be spending the night." "Oh, well I will come on home so I can spend some time with you guys." "Mom, it's your party, you can't leave, besides,

Aunt Shanell rented a hotel suite for you, so we will see you on Monday." Tina was feeling a little overwhelmed and on the verge of tears. "Go ahead mom, enjoy yourself, you're only sixty once." Tina felt that she had the most understanding children in the world. She kissed both her children and her mother as they left the party.

After Tina's children and mom left, Tina was a little more relaxed. She walked over to Antonio and stood beside him. He was looking in a different direction and didn't see her approaching. When he turned around, she was standing close beside him. "I am sorry Antonio, I didn't mean to hurt your feelings, but tonight is just so full of surprises." "Apology accepted, so may I have this dance?" "Are you sure you can handle it?" "Yes baby, I can handle it."

When Antonio took Tina's hand and pulled her on to the dance floor, this time a fast song was playing. Tina threw her head back laughing as she danced to the beat of the music. Antonio was drinking in all her beauty and became intoxicated by it. "Are you alright?" He was unable to hear her over the loud music, so he pulled her into him and leaned his ear to her mouth. "What did you say?" "I asked if you were alright?" "Why wouldn't I be?" "I don't know; you look a little pale." "You just think that you've whipped me on this dance floor." "I may not have whipped you, but I'm certainly whipped, shall we sit?" As they started towards the sitting area, the DJ began playing a love song. Antonio caught Tina by the hand and slowly turned her to face him. She responded by walking into his arms.

The music seemed endless, and with Tina's mom and children gone, she felt that she could let her hair down. She didn't know how a sixty-year-old was supposed to feel, but she certainly didn't feel any different than when she celebrated her twenty-first birthday, at least not in her mind. She wanted the night to last forever because she knew that come tomorrow, things would go back to the way they were. As she laid her head on Antonio's shoulder, she closed her eyes and pretended that he belonged to her. If only she knew that he did. He belonged to her in so many ways; he was captured by her beauty and a prisoner for her love. He realized that he needed to be free but didn't have the strength to break the chain. At that moment, he felt a sense of joy and contentment that he'd never experienced. Even when he was a young man and held Tina in his arms on the dance floor, he had reservations about his worthiness of her, but tonight; tonight, there was this thing inside of his head telling him that he was where he belonged. All the years of hard work ensuring that he could measure up to Tina had paid off. He stood tall and felt empowered. He was not going to allow her to shoot him down anymore. He was going to be the man that he prepared himself to be. With Tina's head still embedded on his shoulder, he pulled her closer to him as if he was trying to pull her inside of him. Tina responded by tightening her grip around his waist.

This was it, Antonio had won, or at least he felt he had; now came the test of the night. The song ended and Tina and Antonio went over to the bar to get drinks. "Wow! That was some long song." "Yes, it was, are you bragging or complaining?" "Neither Antonio, I was just making small talk." "You don't have to do that; we have plenty to talk about." "Here we go again, dance one slow dance with a man and he thinks you have fallen for him." "Tina was disturbed by the moments she shared with Antonio, but she was determined to remain hard core. "What on earth do we have to talk about tonight that we haven't already talked about?" "Not much different, only tonight you will hear me." Tina was a little intrigued by his authoritative attitude. "Oh, really now; I was under the impression that I always listened to you just haven't always agreed with you." "You disagreed because you never really heard me, because if you had we wouldn't be having this conversation now." "Tina was waiting for Antonio to walk away as he usually did when she disagreed with him, but this time he moved closer to her. So close in fact, that she could feel the heat from his breath. When his cheek was inches away from hers, he whispered; "tonight is going to be different, I will talk, and you will listen." All she could say was, "okay, sure" in a squeaky voice."

As Antonio stood looking down on Tina, she saw something different; something she had never seen before. He was not an eighteen-year-old boy, but a fully grown matured man. A man who had built an empire to impress her, or so he said. A man, that for months wanted to love her for the person she was, a man that she had pushed away more times that she cared to remember. "Okay, so when does all this conversation take place?" She asked Antonio as she looked into his eyes. Antonio pretended not to be shocked by her response and replied; when I escort you to your suite tonight." "What suite are you referring too?" Didn't Tiana tell you?" "Tell me what?" Tina was becoming a little rattled by now. "What do you mean Tiana didn't tell me, what does my daughter have to do with you escorting me to some suite?" "Not just some suite, your place of relaxation for the night, just you and yourself." "Shanell told me about reservation at some hotel, but I thought she and Marley would be there with me; I don't want to be in no hotel room alone, I might as well be at home if I'm going to be stuck in a room all alone."

"Wait up now you're going too fast; first-of all, the getaway is my gift to you. Your friends told me that you were planning to spend your birthday in solitaire, so I thought, if she wants to be alone, why not do it in style, with room service and the whole works, so, happy birthday." "So, what's second of all?" "What?" "You said "first-of all" but you only said one thing, so, what's second?" "Uh-huh, you've got jokes." "Seriously though Antonio, that, is so sweet of you to do; you're turning out to be a really good friend." Antonio smiled to himself and thought within his mind, "yeah right, friends." If she wanted to keep telling herself that they were just friends he would just let her, but after tonight, the friendship card would be traded in for a romantic one. "So what time are you taking me to this evening of paradise?" "Are you saying that you're ready now?" "As ready as I'll ever be." Tina was feeling increasingly relaxed with Antonio and felt that they had finally reached a mutual place of friendship.

Shanell and Marley were busy entertaining the birthday guests while Tina spent most of her time either dancing with or talking with Antonio. "Tina, let me speak with Marley and Shanell, then we will be on our way." I need to speak with them as well so how about let me go first." "Whatever you desire my dear, it's your birthday. "Tina walked over to her two friends with a big grin covering her face. When she got close enough to them, she stretched out her arms to include both. They closed in the gape and the three of them just stood there in a loving friendship circle, for minutes.

"Thank you, ladies, for a great birthday, I didn't think anything could top my last birthday celebration, but I think it's a tie." "Tina, you know there's nothing that Marley and I wouldn't do for you, so are you really happy?" "Of course, I am, why do you ask?" "Well, I did invite Antonio without your knowledge or permission." "Yeah, you planned a whole party without my knowledge, what is one more little detail?" "I know right; so, are you enjoying him?" "Yes, I am, he's becoming a great friend." "Is that all he is to you?" "Shanell please don't ruin a great night by going there, I told you both that anything other than friendship with him was out of the question, so for the last time, please, would you just let it go!" "Okay Tina, both Me and Shanell will let it go if you answer one question for us." "What's that Marley?" "Is that the way you dance with all your male friends?"

Tina was only a little annoyed with her friends, but she had to admit to herself, she had been a little frisky with Antonio on the dance floor, but it was harmless. "Antonio didn't seem to be bothered by the way I danced with him." "Oh, come on Tina, you know that man is crazy in love with you, and if you were to be honest with yourself, you would admit that you have a thing for him as well. Now, I am not trying to ruin your perfect night, but don't you think it's time to give the age thing a rest?" "I am going to pretend that this conversation never took place, and I'm going back to the beginning. You girls did a super job of putting this together and catching me with my guards down, I never had a clue. I am so thankful for your love and commitment to me over the years that we've been friends. A person could not ask for better friends, and now if you guys will excuse me, I'm going to begin my one-night staycation." She embraced her friends again, and planted a kiss on both their cheeks, then off she went to find Antonio.

Chapter Thirty-Seven

When Tina left Shanell and Marley to go look for Antonio, she found him standing in a corner with a beautiful young woman looking up in his face. Compared to his six feet five inches, she looked like a little child looking up to her father. When she walked over to where they stood talking, she said "Antonio, are you ready to take me to my hotel?" The young woman blushed and started to walk away. "Don't leave on my account, Antonio and I are just friends." The woman's face relaxed from its tensed position while Antonio's entire demeanor changed by Tina's confession of friendship between them. He looked at Tina and said, "give me a few minutes and I'll be glad to drive you, what are friends for."

Tina walked away a little sulky, she'd asked for that, but it was humiliating for him to dismiss her that way in the presence of someone else, especially another female. After fifteen minutes had passed, Antonio came over to where Tina was sitting and asked her if she was ready to be chauffeured to the hotel. "So, now I'm being chauffeured, earlier you were escorting me." "Well things change."

"Is it because of that beautiful woman you were talking with?" "What does it matter to you whom I talk with, you've made yourself quite clear." "No need to get an attitude, I just asked?" "Okay, let's go friend." Antonio began walking towards the door not checking to see if Tina was coming behind him. When he got to the door, he stood and held it open until she caught up.

Wow! You didn't have to leave me; my legs aren't as long as yours." "That's ok, you caught up." "What's wrong Antonio, is it something I said?" "No, Tina, nothing is wrong, don't spoil all the wonderful time you had tonight with your family and friends. "Nothing can spoil this night for me, I will remember and treasure it for the rest of my life." "What was your favorite part of the night?" "Just the fact that I wasn't alone mainly, but the whole evening is memorabilia, as I said, I will cherish it forever."

"What hotel are we going to Antonio?" "Not we." "Well, you are taking me there so it's us until it isn't." "You're right; can't you wait and be surprised again?" "I don't normally like surprises, but I'm going to try and contain myself, in the meantime, can we talk about something else." "Sure, what would you like to talk about, work?" "No, not work, not tonight." "What else is there, unless you want to talk about how wonderful it felt to be dancing together again." "That was nice. Tonight's the first time I danced since we danced at the restaurant during our business celebration." "Why is that?" "Well for one, I gave up that part of my life." "And two?" "Okay, wise guy, you got me back." "But seriously Tina, it seems like you've given up on living and is just existing, why?" "It may seem that way to you, but believe me, I am contented with my lifestyle." "If you say so." "And I do, by the way, you still haven't told me what my daughter has to do with your gift of a hotel treat." "She was supposed to tell you about the suite and that it was a gift from me." "Why her?" "Because I was afraid you would not accept it if I told you upfront, so I asked her to do the dirty work." "It's ok, no harm done."

The hotel was only a fifteen minutes' drive from Marley's house, but it seemed like hours to Antonio. He was excited yet frightened. He wanted so badly to spend the night with Tina. It didn't matter if he slept on the bathroom floor, as long as he was in the same room as her. "We are here." "Oh, my goodness Antonio, you have really outdone yourself. I have never been to the Unitus Hotel, but I've always wondered what it looks like on the inside." Well tonight you will get the opportunity to find out." "Yes, thanks to you. I never had a reason to stay here because it is so close to home." "I hope that you enjoy it and all the amenities." "Thanks, I'm sure that I will."

When Tina and Antonio entered the lobby of the Unitus Hotel, he did not stop by the registers desk, but headed straight for the elevator. "Hey, don't we need to sign in?" "Everything has been taken cared of Tina, all you need to do is relax." "Sounds easy enough." "Did you see those ladies at the desk staring at you?" "No, I didn't notice, why did you?" "I thought they were looking at you because you didn't register." "And how would they know if I registered or not?" "I don't know, I just saw them looking as all." "I don't get it; what with all the questions about who I talk with or who looks at me, what's it to you?" "You don't have to be so mean about it, I was just making conversation." "Why do you feel the need to make small talk, what's wrong, are you having second thoughts about staying here tonight?" "No, I just didn't want you to feel uncomfortable." Antonio started to say something really mean but thought better of it and instead, kissed her on the cheek; "I love you too boo." Tina was caught off guard by the kiss and didn't have time for a comeback.

Tina and Antonio got on the elevator and was headed towards her suite when she suddenly had an epiphany; Oh My god, I didn't pack a bag. I was so excited about the idea of a night of pampering, that I forgot all about my personal belongings." Don't panic, it will be all right." They got off the elevator in search of the room number. "Are we on the top floor?" Yes, we are, at the very top of the tower." "Wow! I am going to milk this, maybe I should stay two nights." "You are, remember your daughter said she will see you on Monday?" "I thought she said on Sunday." "That's because that was what you wanted to hear at the time." "Okay Dr. Godfrey." When they reached their suite, Antonio put in the code and opened the door. "Step inside your weekend oasis mam." Tina walked into the room in aw; the suite was like a dream, with flowers in every corner of the room. "here's your keys, this is where I say goodnight and leave you to yourself." Tina took the keys from Antonio's hand while looking at every inch of the room. "Aren't you going to make sure I get settled in?" "Do you want me too?" "Of course, I do silly, why wouldn't I, after all it is your gift to me." "Yes, it is, but what does that have to do with me settling you in?" "Nothing, but I thought as a friend, you might want too."

Tina was feeling a little nervous for some reason and didn't want Antonio to leave her alone. "Can't you at least stay for a little while until my nerves are calmed?" "Why are you nervous, what's going on in that pretty head of yours?" "I'm thinking maybe because I haven't eaten since early today. I assumed that Shanell and Marley were taking me out to dinner, so I was saving my stomach." "There were plenty of food at the party, why didn't you eat there?" "I guess I got caught up in everything, and in the excitement of it all, I forgot to eat anything." "Well, we can't have you going to bed on an empty stomach, now, can we?" He looked at the time and realized that the hotel's restaurant would soon be closing. I don't think we will be utilizing room services tonight, but if you're hungry, I will go out and get you something to eat." "I can go with you, let me get my feet back into my shoes." "No, you stay and relax, I'll be back in a few."

Antonio reached his hand toward Tina before leaving. "Oh, let me get my purse." "Your purse, did you put the keys in your purse?" "No, I was going to get some cash to pay for my meal." "Woman please, hand me the key so that I don't bother you to open the door when I return." "What would you like to eat?" "Surprise me." "Okay, but don't start complaining when I bring back something you don't like or want, you know how you ladies are." "What do you mean, how us ladies are?" "You are always indecisive about what you want to eat, and then when someone brings you something you find all sorts of fault with it." "I promise to eat whatever you bring tonight without complaining; besides, I am too hungry to complain." Antonio smiled as he took the key from Tina's hand and walked out of the room.

After Antonio left to go for food, Tina decided to check out the rest of the suite. She went into the luxury bathroom and discovered that there was a jacuzzi sitting in the middle of the room. The towels were a pretty lime green color and were soft as cotton. There were candles and bath oils of various fragrances; there were even matching his and her bathrobes. She looked at the vanity and saw a beautiful pink cosmetic case filled with everything she needed for the night sitting on top. Inside were body washes, feminine wash, toothpastes, soaps, lotions, shampoo and conditioners, floss, mouth wash hairbrushes and combs. What was amazing is that they were all the brands she used. Upon further investigation of her Suite, she discovered a beautiful pink nightgown with a matching robe hanging in the closet, and fluffy pink bedroom shoes. Next to the robe were slacks, blouses, a dress, and a pair of lady's jeans. "Wow" she thought, someone really went all out for me, this is amazing." She turned and saw a small overnight bag sitting on a corner table. When she opened it and looked inside, it contained beautiful soft panties and matching bras in her size. Everything she needed for the next two days was there. So, that's why Antonio told her that it would be all right; he knew that all these things were here for her.

Tina really wanted to get in that jacuzzi, but she didn't know how long it would be before Antonio returned, and she wouldn't want him to catch her inside. She walked over to the television and touched its flat screen rubbing her hand across it. "Do I want to watch TV tonight of just sit quietly and soak it all in?" While she was trying to decide how she would spend her evening, she heard the door to her suite opening; Antonio had returned and was coming inside. "Hey, that was fast, I thought you would have been gone for at least an hour or so." "This is what happens when you have connections, you don't have to wait long." "Great, now let me see what you have, and I promise, I am going to enjoy it."

When Antonio took the food he brought Tina from the bag, he had two of everything. "Oh good, you're eating with me!" "I didn't plan to; I was going to take mine with me." "You may as well stay and eat while it's hot, it doesn't taste the same once you reheat it." "Are you sure you don't mind. I wouldn't want to intrude on your evening." "No, I don't mine, I would love the company."

Antonio wanted to be hopeful, but he didn't want to make assumptions and set himself up for more heartbreak. "I would love to stay and have dinner with you, it will be fun." Antonio placed the food on the already set and decorated table that Tina had overlooked. On the center of the table were fresh cut carnations of various colors in a crystal vase. Beautiful China sitting in elegant charger plates, sterling silver flatware and cutlery, cloth napkins, and crystal wine glasses completed the decorum. "I am impressed, you guys thought of everything, or was it all you?" "I am guilty; it was all me." "I noticed the table is set for two, how did you know I would invite you to stay?" "I didn't, I was just hoping."

"This is delicious Antonio, thanks for getting it for me." "Sure, I couldn't let my best friend starve." Antonio had pre-ordered the meal because he figured Tina would get hungry after the party. He'd decided to order for two just in case. Their meals consisted of filet mignon with duchess potatoes and roasted broccolini, a light garden salad, croissant rolls drizzled in butter and honey, and green tea.

Tina and Antonio ate their meals in silence. For some strange reason, neither could find anything to talk about. What Antonio wanted to talk about would probably not sit well with Tina, and Tina was careful not to say anything to offend Antonio. Both wanted to be in each other's company, and neither wanted to say or do anything that would end the evening prematurely. When Tina had eaten her fill, she pushed her plate aside with a grin. "I can't believe I ate the whole thing." "You did say that you were hungry; I'm just glad that you approved of the meal choice." "Oh, I approved, you can tell by looking at my empty plate." "Yeah, I think we were both a little famished tonight, I cleaned my plate as well." "The question now is, are you ready for me to leave? I don't want to wear my welcome out." "If you're tired and ready to leave I certainly understand." "That is not what I asked you; do you want me to leave now that we've finished eating?" "No, can you stay a little while longer? I am still wound up and would love the company." "Okay, I will stay on one condition." "What's that?" "If you agree to talk to me." "Ok, is there something specific you want to talk about, because I've been talking all evening." "Yes. There is, don't worry about putting those things away, housekeeping will be here shortly to get them." "You thought of everything, haven't you?" "Yes Tina, where you're concern, I leave no stone unturned." Tina smiled at Antonio but chose not to respond.

After housekeeping had cleared all the dining supplies away, Tina and Antonio sat to have that talk that Tina promised him.

"Okay, what is it you wanted to discuss?" "Not discuss; talk; I want to talk with you; I want to understand you; I want to get to know you and find out what makes Tina Bradshaw tick." "Well, that could take a while, what is it you want to know?" "Everything; I want to know everything about you." "Why Antonio, why do you need to know so much about me?" "You seem so unauthentic to me, and I would just like to understand why." "What are you saying that I am a fake?" "Not in the real sense, but you always seem to either have your guard up or your fangs out." "I don't think that I like where this conversation is headed, perhaps you should go." "See, that is exactly what I mean. What you say and do are seldom what you mean, why is that?" "You don't know me at all so stop trying to put a label on my character." "That is not what I'm doing, and no, I don't know you, but I would love to. I would love to know your favorite everything without asking anyone. Tonight, I was on the mark, but I had to get input from your daughter and friends. Let me in Tina, be real with me." "I have been real with you, but that's not good enough for you, I can't even begin to imagine what it is you think I'm holding back or keeping from you. My life is my life, and I don't need to share it with anyone else. You and I are building a friendship that I hope will last for a long time, but beyond that, I don't think I owe you any explanations." "You are right, you don't owe me anything, but as a friend, I know that something unresolved in your life is affecting your happiness. I just want to help; I want you to be happy. These first sixty years of your life have not been lived to the fullest, I want the next sixty years to be different, but if you don't let me or someone in, it won't get any better." "What is it that you think I'm keeping from the world; and why does the world need to know?" "Not the world Tina, just me." "Then why do you need to know?"

"I'm tired Antonio, maybe you should go home, and get some rest as well." "Did I tell you that I was tired, why are you trying to get rid of me now?" "I am not trying to get rid of you, I said that I am tired and would like to go to bed." "Okay, then go to bed, but I will be right here when you wake up." Tina became outraged by Antonio's boldness. She picked up the hotel phone and began dialing. "What are you doing, who are you calling Tina?" "I am calling a cab to take me home, you can have this suite and everything in it, I no longer want to stay." "What has gotten into you, I thought that you and I were making progress. I accepted your request to just be friends and when I try to fulfill that role, you become upset. It is difficult to know what I'm getting with you from one moment to the next." "Then leave me the hell alone, and you won't have to worry about getting anything." "That I will not do; now you can call a taxi and go home, or you can run me home, but that won't change a thing, you will still be unhappy, and don't tell me that you're not, because I know better. I am going to be the kind of friend that you need, not the kind that you want. You have been calling all the shots for too long, let someone else have a chance at it for a while."

Tina was shocked by Antonio assertiveness; usually by now he would have stormed out and left her hanging, but this time he was in her face. "What do I have to lose, you don't want to love me anyway, so I might as well speak my mind." "Speak it with someone else, I have nothing more to say." "Put the phone down Tina, if you are that adamant about me leaving, I will go, you won't need to call a cab." Tina hung the phone up and sunk down on a nearby chair. She didn't burst into tears, but she wanted to do so. This man was pushing all her buttons, and she'd had enough. She refused to allow any man to control her or tell her what she should or should not be doing. "Tina, are you crying?" "No Antonio, no man will ever make me cry again." "Good, because all I want to do is make you smile."

Chapter Thirty-Eight

Tina's birthday weekend celebration had come to an end, and things were back to normal; everything except Antonio and Tina's relationship. He had given in to her threats of calling a cab to take her home and left the hotel leaving her alone. As much as he wanted to stay and spend that time with her, he could see that his presence was causing her discomfort. He didn't understand what was going on with her, but his leaving didn't mean he was giving up, quite the contrary, he was more determined than ever to win her heart.

When Tina's staycation was over, she packed her bags with the things Antonio had bought for her and called a cab to take her home. Antonio had offered to come back for her on Monday, but she told him that she would get home on her own. She arrived home early Monday morning so that she could visit with her children before they left to go back to their homes. The grandchildren were still asleep when she arrived, but Tiana was up making breakfast and DJ was sitting at the bar looking on as he visited with his sister.

"Well good morning birthday girl, I trust you had a wonderful weekend; and why are you here so early?" asked DJ. "Good morning, I had a marvelous weekend, Tina lied, but I wanted to come and spend some time with you guys. I am hungry, is my name in that pot?" "Yes, mother dear, said Tiana, your name is in the pot, but tell me about your weekend." "What can I say, it was the perfect getaway, and I enjoyed every minute of it." "I won't ask you to go into details, but I am so happy that you got to spend some time away from home with someone you care about." "Tina wanted to ask her what she meant, but she was too tired to follow her up. After Antonio left her at the hotel, she was unable to fall asleep, and spent the entire night tossing and turning until morning. She spent Sunday taking advantage of the hotel's amenities. Later that night she had a repeat of the following night, she could not get Antonio out of her head which kept her wide awake the entire night.

"Mom, you look a little tired, did you not get much rest over the weekend?" "Oh, I got some, just not enough, but I will make up for it tonight." "Good, would you like an omelet?" "Sure." "Okay, all this small talk about omelets and names in the pot, I want to know exactly what happened with you and that Antonio guy last night." "My goodness DJ where is that coming from? Nothing happened between us; he took me to the hotel, and I spent the weekend alone." "What sense did that make, to go to a hotel to be alone; I don't get it." "It wasn't just to go to a hotel DJ, but mom needed some time with herself. When she's home she is always going to the shelter, or someone is constantly calling her. This was just a little get-away for her to relax." "And did you mom?" "Did I what son?" Did you relax? You seem rather tense to me, that's why I wanted to know what happened with Mr. I'll take care of everything." Tina burst into laughter as she affectionately rubbed her son on the top of his head. "Always the protector son; thanks for looking out for mom, but I am fine, just a little tire from so much excitement." "Mom, were you really surprise or were you just pretending to be?" "For the first time in my life, Shanell and Marley were able to surprise me, they really out done themselves, I've got to call them later on tonight and thank them again."

Mom, tell me, were you so excited to be going to a hotel alone that you forgot your gifts at Marley's?" "I didn't forget them son, I asked Marley to keep them for me, I didn't want to take them with me to the hotel." "Well, I didn't leave my gift at Marley's." "You didn't. Where is it? I want to open it." "Okay, go ahead and open it, it's right outside the door." "Outside the door, I didn't see any gift when I came in earlier, what is it?" "You said you wanted to open it so here; you will need these to get it open." Tina stood looking at DJ with her mouth open as he handed her keys to a brand-new Porsche Cayenne and in her favorite color of royal blue.

Tina stood looking at her son with teary eyes and anticipation. She didn't remember seeing any strange vehicles in the front of the house when she came up, so she wondered what it looked like. "You must have brought it out after I came inside, because the only vehicle I saw were the rental car the two of you drove here." "Does it matter though when I put it out there, just go and check it out." "What color is it?" "Mom, go outside and see for yourself, why are you stalling?" When she walked outside, she got another big surprise, "Oh my goodness DJ, I can't believe that you bought me a Porsche, and a blue one at that." "Not just me, it's from Tiana, and the grandchildren as well, we wanted you to have something special to mark this milestone in your life; we love you ma." Tina opened the door to her new car and sat inside; while she was basting in her excitement, the three grandchildren came outside and got inside with her. At that moment, she forgot that she had ever had any problems in her life. She felt so full of love. After she had spent some time marveling over her new vehicle, she heard her stomach growled which reminded her that she had not eaten breakfast. "Tiana, is my omelet cold?" "No mom, I was waiting until after you opened your gift to make it, I will have it ready for you in a few."

When Tina sat at the table to eat her breakfast, she had the biggest smile on her face. "What are you smiling about mom?" "Just thinking about the days when I gave birth to you and your brother, how blessed I felt, and that feeling is still so prevalent with me today. God has blessed me with the best two children in the world." "Why, because we gave you a car?" "Not so much that you gave me a car, but that you thought enough of me to give me such an elaborate and lavish gift. I love it, but it doesn't compare to how much I love you guys." "Thanks mom, we love you too."

"So, mom, asked Tiana, what's next?" "What do you mean?" "Today is your actual birthdate, what are you going to do to celebrate and with whom." "I am celebrating right now, here with you guys, it doesn't get any better than this." "Yes, but we will be leaving shortly after breakfast." "So soon? I thought you would be here for most of the day." "I'm sorry mom but our flight is at twelve pm, plus we must return the rental car. We came specifically for your birthday celebration, but we will come back in a couple of months to spend a week with you, how does that sound?" "Sounds marvelous, I will be looking forward to it, but in the meantime, when did you guys have time to purchase a car?" "Here we go with the questions again; I ordered your car several weeks ago and had it designed especially for you, then I had it shipped here to the dealership, now does that satisfy your curiosity?" "Yes, it does, and thanks again for coming and for everything." "You don't need to thank us mom, but you're welcomed."

Tiana, DJ, and the children left shortly after breakfast and headed for the airport. Tina watched as they pulled out of her driveway. She kept waving and throwing kisses until they were no longer in sight. As happy as she was, she felt a little saddened by their departure. "Wow, this has been some weekend!" With everything that was going on with her children, she had completely forgotten about Antonio, but with the house so quiet again, he came racing back to the front of her thoughts. She wondered what he was doing at work. She picked up her phone to call him but changed her mind and placed the phone on the table. She had enjoyed talking with Antonio until he started to dig into her past and personal life. She felt that he had attacked her character. "Just where does he come of, calling me fake, the nerve of him." She remembered why she was upset with him and was glad that she'd decided not to make the call.

There was still most of the day left for Tina to finish celebrating her birthday. Since it was Monday, she knew that her friends would probably be at work, so she wondered what she could do alone and not be bored. After a few minutes of brainstorming, she thought; "I should sleep the day away since I barely got any the last two nights; only problem with that is I'm too wound up to fall asleep. I know what I'll do, I am going to make me a special birthday dinner for one, and later watch old movies. Who knows, I might just call out on Tuesday and get some much-needed rest.

Tina was wearing the skinny jeans that Antonio bought her and left in the closet. She was also wearing the lacy pink V-neck blouse that he bought. She went into her closet and pulled out a pair of pink running shoes and put them on her feet. She pulled her hair into a ponytail and caught it with a rubber band. She was ready for whatever came next, but was she?

Chapter Thirty-Nine

Tina was on her way to the kitchen to begin making her birthday dinner, when she heard a knock on the door. "Who could that be?" She went to the door half expecting it to be Shanell or Marley or both, but when she pulled the door open, Antonio was standing on the other side of it, carrying a large box. "Hello Antonio, this is a surprise, I thought you were at the office." "I was, but I left; I wanted to come by and deliver your gifts from Saturday night. Marley gave them to me yesterday because she figured you would want to look at them. She's at work and won't get home until late tonight." "You didn't have to go to all that trouble, but thanks, I am anxious to read my cards and look at my gifts as well." "May I come in?" "Sure, I'm sorry please come in," she pulled the door open wider so that Antonio and his packages could maneuver through it.

Antonio stepped inside the house and laid the box on a nearby table. "That looks heavy." "It's not." So, good morning, how are you feeling this morning after a weekend of rest and fun?" I did have lots of fun, but unfortunately, not much rest." "Why is that, wasn't that the purpose of the staycation?" "Yes, but I was too excited to sleep,

I will make it up tonight." "Sorry to disappoint you but you won't be getting much rest tonight either." "And just why not?" "First, let me say happy birthday. May I have a hug?" Tina was a little reluctant to hug Antonio. She wondered what his motives were and wanted to ask him so, but instead, she walked over to where he was standing with his arms stretched out towards her and wrapped her arms around his waist. He closed his arms around her and held her close for a few seconds without saying a word. Tina was the first to pull away. "So, was that good enough?" "Yes baby, that's good enough for now." Tina didn't ask him what he meant by "for now," she just smiled and walked away from him.

"So, Tina, what do you have planned for today?" "Since I've already had a party, I thought I would make myself a special dinner and spend a quiet evening alone with myself." "Is that what you really want to do?" "Yes, it's what I want." "Okay, then I will go ahead and cancel what I had planned for you." "What is it, what did you plan?" "I thought that the two of us could go on a picnic at this special place." "I am not one for the great outdoors. I don't do picnics because I don't like eating outside." "Why not? Picnics are fun." "It's just not something I like to do. Too many gnats and bugs flying around, and not to mention mosquitos." "There are no insects flying around in the air where I want to take you, but it's clean and peaceful." "I could go for peace." "Ok, then is it a date?" "I wouldn't quite call it a date, but why not, might be interesting." "At the very least I hope that you find a little peace." "I am fine Antonio, really, I am. Just like everyone else, I have a past, but that's behind me." "Okay Tina, whatever you say. I respect and care for you too much to keep upsetting you, so I promise I will try my best not to do that again." "Now, that's music to my ears; what time is the picnic, and what do I need to wear?"

"What you're wearing is fine; well maybe you want to change your shoes and blouse for something less dressy, you wouldn't want to get them dirty, and the time for the picnic is right after you finish reading your cards and opening your gifts. Mind if I watch?" "Oh yea, my presents, bring them over here and let's take a look." Antonio did as Tina asked and took the box holding her cards and gifts to her. "Please sit them there on the coffee table, thanks." Tina sat on the sofa and Antonio sat on a side chair in front of her. "I see you love opening gifts." "Yes, it's one of my favorite things to do." "I will keep that in mind." Tina didn't respond to Antonio's comment but proceeded to opening her gifts. Since there were only a few wrapped gifts, she started with those first.

The first gift she opened was from her friend Marley. "Oh, my goodness, I wasn't expecting Marley to give me a gift after throwing me a birthday party; this is so sweet and so like her." "What is it?" "It's a smart watch; I almost feel guilty opening my gifts without them." "Well, why don't you save the gifts for later when you are with your friends." "That is a great idea, I see you're good for more than just dancing." Tina regretted saying it the minute it came out of her mouth, but too late, she could not put it back. "So, you thought dancing was all I'm good at? Tina, you broke my heart." They both laughed while Tina continued opening and reading her cards. "Wow! By the time I finish opening all these cards, I will be a millionaire." "Girl, you're already a millionaire, you just don't realize it." "I won't ask where that came from." "If you've finish with opening your gifts, may we please go now, I would like to catch some daylight." "Give me a minute, let me change my shirt and shoes." "Yes mam, but please don't take too long." "I won't, it'll only take a minute."

Curiosity was getting the best of Tina; she wondered where Antonio was taking her; she never liked being blindsided. After changing her shirt and shoes, she came back to where Antonio was waiting for her. "Well, that didn't take long; I thought for sure I would be able to read all my messages and emails before you got back." "Goes to show you that you don't know me at all; I'm a woman of my word. If I say give me a minute, then a minute it is." "I am beginning to realize that." "So where are you taking me Antonio?" "Be patient woman, you will see once we get there." "Why can't you tell me?" "I want to surprise you." "Another surprise? I don't know if I can handle any more surprises." "I promise; you will handle this one just fine." Tina never really liked surprises, but she sucked it in and said, "okay, I will take you at your word." "Good girl, now come on let's go." "It has been quite a while since anyone called me a girl."

Antonio led the way outside with an excited Tina following closely behind. He walked around to the passenger side of his Dodge Ram 3500 and opened the door. Wow! Said Tina, as she slid into the passenger seat; we're riding in a truck, now I am intrigued." Antonio just smiled at her, as he closed the truck door, then walked around to the driver's side and slid into his seat. He latched his seatbelt and started the engine. Before pulling off, he looked over at Tina without saying a word. "Why are you staring at me?" "Not staring, just admiring; don't you know that you are the most beautiful woman that I have ever laid my eyes on?" "Well, you must not have laid your eyes on many." "Why do you say that?" "All those beautiful women in the world and many of which are much younger than I am." "Yes, there are many, but in my eyes, you hold the metal." "I'm not going to argue with you." "Good, because you would lose."

When Antonio had finished complimenting Tina, he shifted the gear into driving position, and drove out of her driveway. They were silent as the truck roared down the freeway; both in their private thoughts. After about fifteen minutes, Tina could no longer keep silent. "Well dang Antonio, how much longer?" "Just a few more minutes." Just as Tina was about to open her mouth to ask another question, Antonio exited off the main road down a rock road. Although she was fascinated by the beautiful scenery, she kept her thoughts to herself. She was so engaged in admiring the landscaping that she didn't realize Antonio had stopped the truck.

"Okay, we are here." Tina turned around and saw the most alluring log cabin she had ever seen. It had the shape of a large doghouse. Surrounding the entire house were various types of flowers and shrubs, and a screen in porch with ceiling fans that wrapped around the front and sides of the cabin. Just behind the house was a beautiful lake with crystal clear water. "So, what do you think, do you think this is appropriate for celebrating the rest of your special day?" "Yes, it is, this is the most beautiful cabin that I have ever seen, does it belong to you?" "Yes, it does." "You never cease to amaze me, are we having our picnic in the cabin?" "No, we're not, but we are going inside." "So, what's the purpose of going inside, if we're eating outside?" "We are not spending the entire evening eating, are we? Can you just have a little faith in me?"

Antonio opened the door to the cabin and stepped back to allow Tina to enter. "Wow!" She said as she looked in every nook and cranny. "Beautiful isn't she." "She, you gave the cabin a gender?" "Yes, I call her Serenity." "That is an unusual name for a building." "Serenity is more than just a building, she's a haven, a place of peace and relaxation, and is also therapeutic. I hope it will serve all those purposes for you today, and when you leave, you will be lighter. I hope that you will just allow yourself to relax for once and not be so uptight." "I know how to relax." "How, by swinging underneath a tree with a sun hat on your head looking at a garden that someone else reaped the pleasure of working?" "Until you've tried it, don't knock it."

"Are you hungry Tina?" "Go ahead, change the subject; no, I'm not hungry yet, I had breakfast with my children remember." "Well since you're not hungry, let's go for a walk, I would love to sure you that special place I told you about." "So, this is not it?" "This is only part of it." "Okay, if the other part is half as gorgeous as this part, I can't wait to see it." "I promise; you will not be disappointed." "I don't see how I could be, given all that I have seen already."

Antonio was feeling more optimistic about him and Tina than ever before. Each time he'd try to dismiss the idea of being with her, a little flicker of light would flash before his eyes. She was being extremely nice to him and didn't seem to have her fangs out. As she was climbing down the steps, he reached up and caught her hand. When she reached the bottom step, she did not pull her hand free from his. Seemed like every strand of hair on his body stood up. They began walking together, hand-in-hand, down a narrow path towards the lake. "This is so nice Antonio, the air is so clean and cool, and there are no bugs flying around." Antonio didn't want to break the spell, so he responded by tightening his grip on her hand.

When they had gone about a hundred feet down the side of the lake, Tina looked up at Antonio and asked him how much further before they got to his special place. "It's just around those trees, so close your eyes." "How am I supposed to walk with my eyes close?" "I will be your eyes for a few minutes, just lean on me." Tina did as

Antonio asked and closed her eyes. Antonio encircled her waist with his arms as he guided her around the trees and bushes. Tina tried to stay in friend mode as she placed her arms around his waist. "Okay Antonio, don't let me fall." "I would die before I let that happen, so keep walking."

After a few minutes of walking with her eyes closed, Antonio stopped. "Okay baby, you can open your eyes now." When she opened her eyes, she got the surprise of a lifetime. There was a beautiful waterfall with the water trickling down perfectly shaped rocks. Beside the fall was a flat bed of sand, and a beautiful maple tree covering it with shade. Tina noticed a large trunk-shaped box and walked over to examine its contents. "What's all this?" "That my dear is our picnic." "When did you put this out here, do you think that it's still edible?" "Of course, it is, it wasn't out here that long, I had someone put it there just before we got here."

Antonio opened the box and pulled out a picnic tablecloth and spread it down on the ground. After he had neatly laid the tablecloth, he began taking food from the thermal box. Tina stood there watching as he pulled one thing after the other out. He knew that Tina did not drink alcohol, so he had a bottle of non-alcoholic champagne, cheese, crackers, and wings. He also had the perfect little birthday cake. When he'd finished putting out the food, plates, napkins, and silverware, he turned on his cell phone and began streaming some of his favorite songs. He looked at Tina standing there watching him and said to her, "come on down babe, let's get this party started." Tina was very active and had no problem getting down on the cloth beside Antonio. So. "What do you think?" "I think that you are amazing and that you are going to make one lady the luckiest woman on the planet." "Now I'm confused." "What are you confused about, that was a compliment." "I don't need a compliment, just your undivided attention." "Okay, you have it, what's up?"

Antonio didn't respond to Tina's question, but instead began putting cheese and crackers on a plate and handed it to her. "Are you trying to tell me to shut up and eat; where are my wings?" Despite trying his best not too, Antonio burst into laughter. "Woman, you are by far the most difficult and challenging person I have ever met. No, please don't stop talking, I love listening to you, but just don't push me towards anyone, I'm satisfied just where I am." By now Tina knew not to push his buttons too hard, so she smiled as she sat up and leaned back on a large rock behind her. The idea of romance between the two of them was nowhere in her thoughts. She was just enjoying the comfortable and relaxing atmosphere. "Antonio." "Yes baby." "Do you think we could take a dip in the lake after we finish our lunch?" "We could, but where is your bathing suit?" "I get your point, so, what are we doing after we leave here, or is this it?" "Is this not enough for you Tina?" "It is quite enough, but I heard you say that we were coming back to the house, what will we be doing there?" "Anything your heart desires." "Okay, hope you don't have to eat those words.

When Tina and Antonio had finished eating and cleaning up their picnic, he caught her by the hand and said in a deep sexy voice; come on baby, let me take you to part two of your birthday celebration." Tina looked up at his tall masculine frame and for the first time during their time together, she felt a strong attraction for him. She thought to herself, "I could get used to this, then without thinking she placed her arms around his waist. Antonio responded by placing his arms around her shoulders. Holding each other closely, they walked in silence back to the cabin. When they arrived, with his left arm still resting around her shoulder, he took his right hand and unlocked the door. He pulled the key from the lock, placed it in his pocket, then pushed open the door. He didn't want to let Tina go because he didn't know if she would ever let him get that close to her again. When she attempted to release her arm from around his waist, he pulled her around facing him and looked affectionately into her eyes. He wanted so badly to kiss her but didn't want to offend or antagonize her. She slowly dropped her arm from around his waist and asked, "so, are we going in or what?" Antonio opened his mouth to answer her, but nothing came out. He was still staring into her eyes trying his best to control the emotions that were trying to control him. "Antonio! Are we going inside?" As he slowly gathered himself, he directed his eyes towards the entrance and said, "sure, come on inside and let's talk."

Chapter Forty

Talking was the last thing Tina wanted to do with Antonio. She didn't want him asking about her past or suggesting that she needed to see some shrink, but if they didn't talk, what else was there to do? Tina walked into the cabin and just as she'd done when they'd first arrived, began looking at the beautiful interior of the cabin. "Antonio, I have to say it again, this is the most beautiful cabin I have ever seen." "You've only seen this room, let me give you the grand tour." "Great, but can you show me the bathroom first?" "Sure, right this way madam." When Tina returned from the bathroom, Antonio resumed his tour of the rest of the cabin. Near the entry to the family room, was a large eat-in kitchen that lead to a formal dining room. "Antonio, this is amazing." He pushed open another door to expose a beautifully decorated bedroom. "Wow! Can it get any better?" "I don't know, you tell me," as he led her down a short hallway. At the end of the hall was a stairway that led to a loft. She climbed the few steps and spotted the most spectacular media /game room. As she looked around, she gasped with her hand covering her mouth. "This is where we will be spending the rest of the evening, is that alright with you?" "Yes, it is more than alright." "There is one more room." "Where, I thought we covered the entire cabin." "Almost, when you went straight to climb the stairs, there was a room to your left." "Okay, take me to it your majesty." "Follow me."

As Antonio led the way to the last room in the cabin, Tina followed closely behind in anticipation. What more could he have to show her that it would be more beautiful than what she had already seen. When he reached the door, he pushed it open and stood back to allow her to enter. Once again, Tina's mouth flung open as wide as they could. "Oh Antonio, this is lovely." The door opened to a huge second bedroom, the master. Inside was a king size bed with a headboard the shape of the cabin with a nickel-plated ceiling fan above the bed. The heavy drapes matched the beautiful gray coverlet on the bed. Two nightstands and dresser matched. The beautiful fireplace also shared the designed. There was a round table with two chairs sitting in the far end of the room, and a recliner near the bed. Another corner held a desk made of logs, with an office chair matching the chairs sitting at the table. When she turned to check out the other side of the room, she noticed a sitting area with a built-in fireplace and a plush rug lying on the floor in front of it.

She also saw the most unique sofa. In front of the sofa was a log coffee table with several books and magazines neatly stacked on top. There was also a refrigerated cooler stocked with various beverages. When Tina had finished salivating over the room's decorum, she turned and looked at Antonio with admiration. "You are such an amazing guy, please don't lose yourself on the wrong person." "I have no intension of doing that, but would you explain what you mean." "I mean, it would be easy for someone to take advantage of your kind heart and your accomplishments, just don't let that happen." "Would you ever do that to me Tina?" "Of course not, I wouldn't think of doing that to you or anyone else." "I know, and that is exactly why you are the only woman I have ever brought here. This is my special place, my serenity, and I wanted to share it with someone who's special to me." "Thanks Antonio, I'm so touched." "Are you touched enough to give me a little hug?" "Sure, why not, what harm can it cause?" Tina walked over to Antonio and wrapped her arms around him and squeezed him just a little. She may not have intended for there to be any harm, but man, did she ever cause some.

As Tina laid her head against Antonio's chest and gave him what she considered a friendly hug, he was clenching his teeth. His heart began beating faster and he had to hold back the tears that were forming in his eyes. All the memories of past times holding Tina and dancing with her came pouring into his mind. He slowly responded to her gesture by pecking her on the cheek. He would not allow himself to hug her back, because he was afraid that he wouldn't be able to contain himself. Tina pulled away and asked, "what's next?" Antonio was so choked up that he just walked away and beckoned for her to follow. She humbly followed behind him as he led her back to the media/game room. "I want to watch a movie, are you gamed?" "I am, where do I sit?" "Right here beside me."

Previously, Antonio had arranged the seating so that the reclining loveseat would be placed directly in front of the seventy-five-inch TV. He was hoping that Tina didn't catch on to the fact that he'd purposely placed the chair there so that he could sit close to her. He had chosen a romance movie to calm her defenses. "What are we watching Antonio?" "Do you have a preference?" "No, not really, I will leave the choice in your capable hands." Antonio picked up the remote and turned on the set. He searched until he found the movie he wanted and clicked on it, then went over and sat beside her. She did not take her eyes off the TV, that hug had left her a little weak in the knees, but she had no intension of revealing that to Antonio.

While the movie played on the TV set, a whole other movie was playing in Antonio's heart. He got up from the chair and turned off the lights. Tina looked over at him but didn't say a word. About halfway through the movie, Antonio exhaled. "Is everything ok?" "No, everything is not ok, are you enjoying the movie?" "It's okay, why do you ask?" "Because if it's just ok, then you're not really enjoying it. We can turn it off and do something else if you'd like." "Are you sure you wouldn't mine?" "No, I don't mind." "Good, because I am not much of a TV fan. I didn't want to insult your feelings after you went to all this trouble, but I would rather be fishing in that lake." Antonio burst into laughter. "Spoken like a true lady, let's go fishing."

After gathering the fishing gears, Antonio said to Tina, "what exactly are we using as bait?" "We can put some of those left-over chicken wings on the hooks." "You don't plan to catch any fish, do you?" "I guess that wasn't a thought-out idea," Tina said laughingly. "No, it wasn't. Tina, I think it's time." "Time for what Antonio?" "Time to clear the elephant in the room." "I wasn't aware that there was one." "Yes, you are, we both feel it's presents." "So how do you suggest we get rid of him?" "Remember when I told you earlier that we would talk when we returned to the cabin?" "Yes, I remember, but I was hoping that you had forgotten." "Why is that?" "Because I don't find any pleasure in digging up old bones." "But if the bones are keeping you from having a life, or a future, then why not dig it the hell up?" "Just what makes you think that I don't have a life?" "Maybe my words are too specific, but I can see that you are holding something back." Then you must have tunnel vision because you are way off base."

After the conversation with Antonio, Tina was ready to call it a day and go home. However, Antonio was trying to figure out the best approach to get Tina to let down her wall and share her story with him. "Antonio, can we please go home, I'm feeling a little tired from the weekend." "Sure, we can, but will you sit with me for just a little while, I have something I want to share with you." Antonio reached his hand towards Tina the way he did years back at the club when he would ask her to dance. Tina placed her hand in his and he led her to the sofa.

When they were seated, Tina looked over at Antonio and saw that he had a worried expression on his face. "What is it that you feel the need to share with me?" He reached over and took both of her hands in his. Before saying a word, he pulled them to his lips and gently kissed them. Tina was speechless as she looked into his teary eyes. Before she could ask what was bothering him, he began to speak. "Tina, my sweet Tina. I know that we promised to be friends, and I know that the only reason you are here with me today is because of that friendship, but baby, I am dying inside. I can no longer function as your friend, so if friends are all we can be, I am going to have to cancel." "Cancel what, our friendship?" "Please, allow me to finish."

"Years ago, when I was him and you were her, and we danced to the beats of our hearts, I felt this strong pull towards you, but even then, I felt the wall that you had so carefully built to protect yourself. I wanted to tell you that it was ok, and that I would protect you from whatever unpleasant things life had thrown at you, but I was in no position to make promises. When I returned years later and I held you in my arms as we danced, I could still feel that wall, so I knew that you had not removed it. Now, I don't know what caused you to build it, and I promise, if you don't want to tell me, I will never ask again; but if you would allow me to, I would like to take it down, piece by piece. All you've got to do, is open the door a little, just enough for me to see inside." "Antonio, I haven't a clue what you're talking about."

Determined to get through to her Antonio decided to take another route. "Ok Tina, I have spilled my feelings to you on more than one occasion, and your only response was that I am too young for you. What would be the ideal age for you to become involved with someone?" "There is no such thing as an ideal age." "Exactly, so what's keeping you from loving me?" "I have already explained that to you and quite frankly I'm tired going back and forth with it." "Yes, you have, but in all fairness, if it was the other way around, and I was twelve years older than you, how would you feel about being in a relationship with me?" "It wouldn't matter Antonio, because I am just not interested." "In me or in in anyone?" "In anyone." "There you have it; it's not me, it's you, and that is the reason I want to help you. You don't have to see a therapist, just talk to me, tell me who hurt my baby and how; let me comfort you."

Tina was tempted to fall into Antonio's arms and tell him everything that happened to her from childhood through adulthood, but her mom had raised her to be a lady, and for that reason she had to carry herself as such. Ladies held their heads up high, no matter what life threw at them, and when ladies love, they "loved like ladies. "Instead of giving in to her emotions, she turned a different corner. She jumped up from beside Antonio and yelled at him. "Just who do you think you are interfering in my life. I didn't ask you to help me with anything. I don't need or want your help, so please just leave me alone." Her outburst only confirmed what Antonio suspected. He allowed her to get it all out before speaking again. "Are you done now?" "Yes, I am, so please be the gentleman that you are and take me home."

Antonio walked over to where Tina ran off too and caught her by the shoulders. When she attempted to pull away, he drew her into him. In that instant, the night of her rape came rushing back to her memory. She shook her head as if trying to shake it out of her mind and yelled at him to "let her go." Her screams landed on deaf ears; he continued holding on to her with a firm grip. She began punching him with both fists. He just stood there holding her as she pounded back and forth on his chest. When she was exhausted, she fell into Antonio's chest with tears running down her face. "Please Antonio, don't rape me, I couldn't live through that again; please just take me home." Antonio reluctantly released his hold on her as he walked her over to the sofa. "Sit down Tina. Do you honestly believe that I would do anything to harm you?" Tina was still crying and looked up into Antonio's face with tears streaming down her face.

"Antonio, I just want to go home, will you please take me?" "Tina, you know I will take you home, but right now, we need to come to terms with this unfinished business in your life. I won't ask who raped you, but we need to talk about it, believe me, it helps." "How would you know how I feel?" "I know, because as a boy, I was raped as well." Tina sat upright in the chair from her slouched position and looked into Antonio's brown eyes and asked, "you were what; by whom?" "When I was the age of ten and by a high school student." "How?" "This is not about me, it's about you." "But you brought it up." "Okay, if it will help you to release some of the pain you've been holding inside all these years, I will tell you. My mom was a high school teacher, and often she would bring one of her female students to spend the night. On several occasions, after my mom had gone to bed, one of the girls would come into my bedroom and assault me. The very first time it happened, she stuffed something in my mouth and told me I had better not take it out. When I told her that I was telling my mom, she threatened me. She said that she had friends in high places, and she would have me, and my mom killed. I believed her so I kept it to myself. My grades

443

began to suffer, and I developed behavior problems. That is the reason I spent so much time with my grandparents during the summer months; to distance me from trouble. My mom started me seeing a counselor to address my behavior issues, but I never told the therapist. I think he figured it out because of the direction the therapy took, which helped me tremendously. When I was in my second year of college, it began to haunt me again, so I contacted my old therapist, and told him everything, It was then that I was able to get the help I needed to be able to cope with what had happened to me. So, if it seems that I was trying to pull something out of you, it is because I know the symptoms all too well. I didn't want to come straight out and ask you, and I didn't want you to feel alienated by my constant probing, but I know that you need help." "It is too late for help; besides, I don't want you or anyone else to feel sorry for me. So, what happened with the girl that violated you?" "When I found out that she was working with young children, I had my therapist report it to law enforcement." "Were they able to do anything after so long?" "Yes, she was arrested and taken to jail. After her arrest, several young boys, and a couple older ones came forward and accused her of rape and molestation. I wish that I was strong enough to have reported her before she had the opportunity to hurt anyone else, but I was afraid. I blamed myself for so long, but now I realize it was not my responsibility or my fault, but hers."

"Tina, can you tell me what happened to you?" "No, Antonio, I can't." "Why not?" "Because I would have to relive it all over again and I can't do that." "You already are. Every time a man gets close to you, you live it. The only way you will ever be able to go a day without thinking about it, or not have it affect you in some way, is to meet it head-on. Can you do that with me?" "Why is it so important that I share my life's story with you?" "You know the answer to that, but your past won't let you accept it." "For the last time Antonio, I do not want an intimate relationship with you or anyone else, and if I did it wouldn't be with a man young enough to be my son." "Ouch! You are only twelve years older than I, remember." "Yes, how can I forget you keep reminding me." Okay Tina, I will leave you alone if you do one thing for me." "What is it? Let me hurry up and get it done so that you will leave me alone." "Just sit with me for ten minutes and let me show you something, will you?" "Sure, I can do that."

Before agreeing to sit with Antonio, Tina didn't think to ask him what he was planning to show her. She shifted her body in a more comfortable position before asking, "what is it you want to show me?" Antonio hustled closer towards her and placed his hand on her knee. Her first response was to slap his hand away from her but instead she looked at it as if it was a snake. With one hand on her knee, he took the other one and placed it around her shoulder. Her eyes were still stained from her tears as he bent over and gently kissed them. "What are you trying to prove Antonio?" Shush! You promised me ten minutes." He kissed one eye and then the other; he trailed his lips to her cheek, then her ear, and down to her neck. She closed her eyes as he slowly tilted her head and brushed her lips with his. She wanted to pull away but could not find the strength to do so. Just as she opened her mouth to speak, his lips closed on hers. She touched his face as she pulled him closer. He whispered, "I love you" into her ears. She wanted to say those words back to him, but they would not form in her mouth. His lips moved away from hers, and once again found the hollow of her neck. Tina was lost; lost in a world she had never been in before; a world of majestical feelings and emotions. She gasped and called out his name. "Antonio!"

When Antonio's ten minutes were up, he pulled away from Tina, stood up and reached for her hand. "I promised to take you home, let's go." "Has ten minutes passed?" "Yes, I ran over by a minute." Tina caught Antonio's extended hand and pulled herself up. "Do we have to go right now? I would like to talk." "Whatever you want baby, I am always here, and you will always be at the top of my list. "I think that I trust you enough to share some of my life's story with you." "Just some of them?" "Yes, a lady never tells all."

Antonio sat back down on the sofa and pulled Tina down beside him. "I am all ears, no judgement, no pity, just love and understanding." "Thank you, Antonio, this means a lot to me. Before I began my cathartic session with you, I want to thank you for not giving up on me, even when I said hurtful things to you. Most men would have bounced long ago, but for some reason you chose to stick around. That is what I call a great friend."

Tina was still uncomfortable about sharing her experiences with Antonio, but him telling her his story made it a little easier. She began by telling him about the molestation during her childhood by her family member and her best friend's brother. "Can you tell me which family member?" "No Antonio, that is the one thing I cannot tell you." "Then I will assume that is was a brother or someone closer to you?" "Can we just skip that part?" "Sure, we can." Tina began to shuffle in her seat as she began telling him of the rape when she was nineteen. The more she talked, the more she wanted to tell him. He sat listening, trying his best not to show any expressions.

He could see the pain in Tina's face as she shared her story with him. He wanted so badly to pull her into his arms and comfort her, but he knew that it was not the right time. When Tina had reached the end of her story, she was weeping uncontrollably, and tears were flowing down her face. Antonio couldn't take it any longer; he pulled her into his arms and wept with her. Tina latched on to him as if her life depended upon it. Together they found comfort and held on to each other until the tears had all dried up.

The room was so quiet that you could hear the falling of a feather. Tina slowly pulled herself away from Antonio's arms and sat upright on the chair. "Thanks Antonio, as I said earlier, most men would have walked away from me a long time ago. Thanks for not giving up on me even though I had given up on myself." "You don't need to thank me, when you care about someone, and I do care for you deeply, you will have the patience to see them through their hard times." "What if I had never told you, would you have gotten tired of trying?" "No, I wouldn't have gotten tired trying, but at some point, I would have to respect your decision and let it go." "Does that mean you would have given up on our friendship?" "No, it means that I would let it go, not let you go." "So, what now? I just spilled my guts to you about my entire life, what do you do now?"

"I am going to continue doing what I've always done." "What's that, harass me?" "No silly, love you. I am going to continue loving you, and I promise that when you get over this age hang-up of yours you will be able to see just how much I really do love you."

After listening to Antonio's confession of his love over and over for her, Tina felt it was only fair that she explained to him one last time why she was no longer interested in pursuing a romantic relationship with him. "Still sitting, she looked at Antonio and gave him a great big smile. "I see someone is feeling better." "Yes, I am, and I owe it in part to your persistence. Do you know that I have never shared my stories with anyone before now, not even my closest friends?" "So, you've been keeping all this bottled up inside of you your entire life, I can see why you appeared so bitter." "Do I really seem bitter to you?" "Most of the time you do, but not to everyone, just me." "I'm so sorry Antonio, I promise to do better in the future." "Are you saying that it's possible for us to share a future together?" "Sorry, no, that's not what I'm saying at all. Give me a few minutes and let me see if I can make you understand." "Okay, I'm all ears."

"Antonio, you are a great guy, probably the greatest guy that I have ever met, but our timing is off. You are going to make some lucky lady incredibly happy, but I am not that lady. As a young girl, my mother taught me to behave in a certain way in everything that I do. I've been taught grace, self-respect, and respect for others. I was also taught that there's a difference between just being a woman and being a lady. She taught me to be a lady, so I know very little about being a woman. She instilled in me that ladies stay in their places and behaves as such." "So, tell me something Tina. What the hell does being a lady have to do with your loving me, and our age difference? Haven't you heard that age is just a number" Age marks the time spent on earth, it does not dictate who we choose to love. You are not a minor or a teenager, I have not crossed any age barriers, so you can drop the age shit and speak to me as an adult. I don't care if it's the lady talking or the woman, just be honest with yourself. Your mother did an excellent job of raising you, now it is time you pull yourself from the age of nineteen and walk on over to the adult side of life. If you are unable to do that, then maybe you should take my suggestion and see a shrink."

When Antonio had finished responding to Tina's explanations, he got up from the chair and reached his hand out to her. "Come on, if you are so hell bent on going home, let's get the hell out of here, I cannot stand much more of this agony. You keep dangling a dash of hope at me and just when I go to bite, you pull it away. How long has it been since a man made you feel special, because it's obvious you don't see yourself as being special. All this talk about being a lady is just a scab to cover up your insecurities. If I sound harsh, I don't mean too, but I am tired as hell tiptoeing around your feelings when it's clear you don't give a dam about mine. Come on, let's get the hell out of here."

Normally, Tina would have stiffened up at Antonio's blatant statements about her character, but she decided that she was going to give as good as she got. "You don't want me to help put things back into place before we leave?" "You don't need to worry about that, someone will take care of it, so let's go." "What is your hurry, I thought it was my birthday celebration, so I get to say when we leave. Besides, I'm not ready yet." "Woman, I mean, lady, you are the one who's been crying for the last hour for me to take you home." "Well, from this point on, I call the shot. I am hungry, those little crackers and wings have long gone, I want something to eat that has substance, can you do that?" Antonio was shocked by Tina's change of attitude; he wondered what was really going on with her. Instead of asking, he just decided to play along. "Yes mam, I will have you something to eat in a few." Tina walked over to the window and looked out. "I didn't see any restaurants when we were coming in here, so where will the food be coming from?" "Don't worry, I have my sources."

While Tina was still looking through the window, Antonio got on his cell and made a call. "Okay, all set, food will be here in a jiffy." Tina didn't ask again where the food was coming from, she just smiled at him and walked towards the door. "Where are you going Tina?" "Outside to catch some air and clear my head." Antonio didn't know what to expect when she returned, but he was hopeful that it would work in his favor." After about five minutes, Tina returned inside. She walked straight up to Antonio without hesitation and put her arms around his neck. She pulled him towards her and placed her lips on his. Antonio became blinded by emotions that he had stored and controlled for so long as he encircled her waist with his arms. As he returned her passionate kisses, tears began flowing from his eyes. This is what he had been praying for, and now it felt unreal.

Neither Tina nor Antonio heard the knock at the door when the caterer arrived with their dinner. After several more attempts, he pushed the door open to find the two of them locked in each other's arms. He cleared his throat as he placed the trays on the table to catch their attention. Both Tina and Antonio jumped apart as if someone had caught them with their hands in the cookie jar. "Hello sir, I knocked several times, but no one answered. I figured you had gone for a walk, so I pushed the door open and came inside, I hope you don't mind. "Sorry about that, no, it's ok. Do you mind setting everything up?" Tina and I will take a walk by the lake until you've finished."

While the caterer was setting up their dinner, Tina and Antonio headed for the lake holding hands. When they reached the lakefront, Tina sat on the bench overlooking the water, Antonio sat beside her and turned her face towards his so he could see into her eyes. Without saying a word, he kissed her as he continued holding her face in his hands. "I love you Tina, so very much, please don't break my heart again." Tina responded by returning the kiss. She didn't know how she felt, so she said nothing.

After sitting on the bench for about ten minutes, the caterer approached them. "The table is all set, and everything is ready, I will see you later?" "Thanks Eddie, I appreciate you." "Come on baby, let's go and see what they've prepared for us." "Are you saying you don't know." "I left it in their hands, just told them that you are special to me." "Really, I'm curious to know what they made for your special friend."

Tina and Antonio left the lake immediately after the caterer told them that their dinner was ready. When they reached the entrance to the cabin, Tina realized that no one was there. "Are they not serving us?" "Did you not hear him say that he would see us later? That means that we are on our own, but don't worry, I will serve my lady." The afternoon had drifted into evening, and Tina's stomach was reminding her that it had been a while since she had eaten. She went into the bathroom to freshen up while Antonio went in a different direction. When she returned, candles were burning on the table and soft music was playing in the background. She walked over to the table and Antonio pulled out the chair for her to sit.

After Tina was comfortably seated, Antonio sat across from her. "This is nice Antonio, just what I need to end the day." She lifted her food cover to discover the most scrumptious looking grilled salmon with lemon pasta covered with lemon and white wine sauce, butter and garlic green beans, balsamic roasted baby carrots, with a fresh garden salad and buttered yeast rolls. "Wow! I'm impressed." "Thanks Tina, nothing but the best for you on your sixtieth birthday."

After Antonio and Tina's birthday celebratory meals, they retired to the family room; each carrying a drink of choice. Antonio red wine, and Tina, red sparkling cider. They sat on the chair beside each other. Antonio didn't want to say or do anything to interfere with the progress he'd made with Tina. He took a sip of his wine all the while looking into Tina's eyes. "So, what now Tina?" "What do you mean?" "You declared that for the rest of the trip you're calling the shots, so what do we do next?" "I think we should head home; tomorrow is a workday; I only took off today." "Just in case you have forgotten, you're the boss, you can take another day if you so desired." "You are absolutely right, I am a little tired, can we stay here tonight?" "Sure, we can, you may have the owner's suite." "Thanks Antonio, you're awesome; I am going to take a shower before going to bed."

After Tina and Antonio finished their conversation, she started towards the bedroom then turned and looked at Antonio. "What is it babe?" "I am not prepared for a sleep over; we didn't bring any sleeping clothes or hygiene accessories." "I think you will find everything you need in the closet and bathroom." When Tina entered the bedroom, she walked straight to the closet. Hanging inside was the most beautiful night gown and bathrobe set. A pair of matching slippers were also visible. She took the gown and robe from the hangers and carried them to the bed where she carefully laid them. She kicked off her sneakers and replaced them with the slippers then headed for the bathroom. There she found a caboodle filled with various hygiene products. Everything she needed was inside. Sitting on the side of the bathtub were various essential oil fragrances, and scented candles. As she was admiring everything, she heard a soft knock at the door. "Is everything alright Tina?" "Yes Antonio, everything is fine, thank you so much." Instead of responding, he turned around and went to his own room to prepare for the night.

Tina decided that a long warm bath would be the perfect ending to a perfect day. She ran the tub half filled with warm water and poured in some lavender oil and vanilla bubble bath lotion. She lit one of the candles that was sitting on the side of the tub, then took off her clothes. After carefully hanging her clothes on the back of the bathroom door, she walked over to the tub and lowered herself in. The warm water wrapped around her body as if it was embracing her. She closed her eyes and soaked in the moment. With her eyes still closed, she heard what sounded like footsteps. She would not allow herself to believe that Antonio would dare come in and invade her privacy. Suddenly, she felt a warm hand touch her cheek. She opened her eyes and there he was, bending over her, touching her face.

"Antonio, what are you doing?" "No more than you allow." "I didn't allow you to invade my privacy." "You could have locked the door. Besides, don't you need your back rubbed, I mean scrubbed?" "Now that you're here, that would be nice, but don't get any ideas." "I won't get any, I already have a few of them." "Well then, just keep them to yourself." "It would be better if I shared them with you." "In your dreams." "Then let me dream."

Antonio picked up the bath loofah and began slowly and gently rubbing it across Tina's back. "That feels good." "What about this?" whilst kissing her neck. "Tina opened her mouth to speak but nothing came out. She just stayed in her position allowing Antonio to scrub her back, neck, and chest. She opened her eyes and looked deep into his. "Antonio." As his lips closed in on hers. "Do you need me to help you from the tub?" "No, I can manage, I just need you to go." Antonio got up from the side of the bathtub, and slowly walked out of the bathroom. "Woah! That was a close call; Tina girl, get yourself together."

After pulling herself from the tub, Tina walked over to the vanity and looked at herself in the mirror. Something seemed different to her. She felt less heavy, like she'd dumped a load of weight from her mind. Antonio had been so patient with her; he deserved a little more compassion and consideration than she had given him in the past. After all, he had feelings too. Tina continued looking at herself in the mirror trying to see what she thought Antonio saw in her. Looking back at her was a beautiful lady who had spent most of her life hiding in her own shadow.

With her oiled and moisturized body covered in a beautiful silk night gown, she slid her feet back into the plush bedroom slippers and started making her way back to the bedroom without putting on the robe. She was hoping that Antonio wouldn't be in her bedroom when she arrived, because she didn't know if she had enough strength left to resist his charm. When she pushed the door open to the bedroom, she saw Antonio leaning on the side of the bed propped up on one arm. "I thought you went back to your room." "I did, but I came back." "Why?" "I have some unfinished business to attend to." "What might that be?" "Come on over here and I will show you."

Tina hesitated before walking over to the bed where Antonio was sitting. "Exactly what is it you want to show me?" "I want to show you how much I love you, but first, I need to know that you are alright." "Just how do you plan to accomplish that?" "Come lay down beside me, I promise to be a gentleman; and by the way, did I tell you that you look like an angel?" "Thanks, I appreciate the compliment."

Tina crossed the large room and went to the bed where Antonio was now lying on. When she'd reached the bed, he reached out and caught her hand. As she got closer to him, he slid over making room for her. With hesitation, she crawled in bed beside him. "What am I doing" she thought to herself. Once on the bed, Antonio stretched out his arms so that when she laid on the pillow, she would be resting in them. Just as he'd hoped, she laid in his outstretched arms, and he gently folded her into them.

Tina, I realize that you have been through a lot in your life, and although you had a breakthrough today, I don't want to push you too hard too soon. I am perfectly happy with the progress we made today. I can rest easy tonight knowing that you will be here tomorrow. My question is, are you still holding on to the concept that I am too young for you?" "It's not a concept Antonio, it's my belief and My philosophy, those things just don't vanish. I told you," "Yeah, I know, you're a lady." "I think you're missing the point." "Maybe I am, but can you put aside your philosophical ideologies for tonight and just enjoy being here in my arms. I promise I will just lay here with you and if you tell me to leave, I will leave, ok."

It felt good lying there in Antonio's arms, it had been such a long time since she'd been with any man. Antonio's breathing had calmed, and he was talking about everything and nothing. His voice sounded like a soft melody to Tina as she drifted into a peaceful sleep. As she slept, she began dreaming about Antonio. He looked down at her sleeping body and smiled. "Dang! Am I that boring?" Just as he was about to close his eyes, Tina turned to face him. She threw one leg across his and snuggled closer to him. Despite his efforts to resist, he responded by holding her closer. He realized that she was asleep, but at that moment, he was beside himself with longings, as her body pressed against his. Tina's dream became more intense as she pressed against the hardness of Antonio's body; She kissed his lips and made a groaning sound. Antonio murmured as his body responded to her touch. Eventually, Antonio fell asleep with Tina wrapped in his arms.

The next morning, Tina awoke before Antonio. When she realized that her leg was entangled in his, and she was lying in his arms with her body pressed against his, she tried to ease herself away from him before he awoke. He opened his eyes and looked at her. "I'm so sorry Antonio, I must have been dreaming, I didn't mean to get all over you." "I'm not complaining, are you alright?" Yes, I'm fine." "Then let me show you how I feel about you. You will not have to dream about it." "Are you saying let us have a one-night stand?" "Call it whatever you want to, let us just give it a try.

Antonio was leaning on one elbow looking down at Tina, trying to convince her to put away any thoughts of distrust or age differences. She did not hear a word he was saying because she was fighting the temptation to pull him on top of her and give him the kiss of his life. "Did you hear what I said?" Tina answered by reaching up and pulling him down on top of her. His lips found hers and they were lost in each other for a moment. Antonio raised his head and looked into her eyes, "Are you okay Tina?" "Never better, just love me!" And love her he did..................